PRAISE FOR F. PAUL WILSON'S BOOKS

"F. Paul Wilson is a hot writer, and his hottest, and my favorite creation, is Repairman Jack. No one does this kind of weird meets crime better that Wilson. Gripping, fascinating,

have, *Crisscross* is another great adventure into inner-city weirdness."
Emporia

"

ALSO BY F. PAUL WILSON

Repairman Jack Novels
The Tomb
Legacies
Conspiracies
All the Rage
Hosts
The Haunted Air
Gateways
Infernal
Harbingers*

The Adversary Cycle
The Keep
The Tomb
The Touch
Reborn
Reprisal
Nightworld

Other Novels

Healer	*Mirage* (with Matthew J.
Wheels Within Wheels	Costello)
An Enemy of the State	*Nightkill* (with Steven
Black Wind	Spruill)
Dydeetown World	*Masque* (with Matthew J.
The Tery	Costello)
Sibs	*The Christmas Thingy*
The Select	*Sims*
Implant	*The Fifth Harmonic*
Deep as the Marrow	*Midnight Mass*

Short Fiction
Soft and Others
The Barrens and Others

Editor
Freak Show
Diagnosis: Terminal

*forthcoming

F. PAUL WILSON

CRISSCROSS

A Repairman Jack Novel

TOR®

A TOM DOHERTY ASSOCIATES BOOK
NEW YORK

This is a work of fiction. All the characters and events portrayed in this book are either products of the author's imagination or are used fictitiously.

CRISSCROSS: A REPAIRMAN JACK NOVEL

Edited by David G. Hartwell

A Tor Book
Published by Tom Doherty Associates, LLC
175 Fifth Avenue
New York, NY 10010

www.tor.com

Tor® is a registered trademark of Tom Doherty Associates, LLC.

ISBN 0-765-34606-0
EAN 978-0-765-34606-3

First edition: October 2004
First mass market edition: June 2006

Printed in the United States of America

0 9 8 7 6 5 4 3 2 1

For my mother
(even though certain sections will appall her)

ACKNOWLEDGMENTS

Thanks to the usual crew for their editorial help on the manuscript: my wife, Mary; my editor, David Hartwell; his assistant, Moshe Feder; Coates Bateman; Elizabeth Monteleone; Steven Spruill; Blake Dollens; and my agent, Albert Zuckerman.

Special thanks to my gunnies: NY Joe (Joe Schmidt), Angel (Janada Oakley), and Ken Valentine, for their invaluable assistance. As usual, I did a little improvising along the way, so any errors in the weaponry department are mine.

SUNDAY

1

This little jaunt was a departure from Jack's SOP of meeting prospective customers in a place of his choosing, but he didn't expect any problems this go-round. Beekman Place was hardly a Manhattan trouble zone.

The day was so nice he'd decided to walk. No big deal. Only a couple of miles from his apartment, but a big jump in rental price. A cab ride would deprive him of this beautiful day.

Autumn was strengthening its grip on the city: cooler temperatures, gustier winds . . . sweater weather. Jack's was a cranberry V-neck, worn over a blue-and-white plaid shirt and tan slacks. The preppy look. Never out of place in Midtown. Medium-length brown hair, medium-brown eyes, medium height, medium build. Nothing special about him. Just the way he liked it. Practically invisible.

The summer haze had fled south, leaving the midday sky a piercing blue; red and yellow leaves whirligigged from branches, and all the Duane Reades sported ghosts and goblins and spiderwebs in their windows. The official Halloween countdown had dwindled to less than twelve hours.

Just last night Vicky had put on her Wicked Witch of the West costume—green skin, warty nose, the whole deal—and modeled it for Jack. She fairly vibrated with anticipation. Nine years old going on forty, she loved dressing up, and *loved* candy. Halloween was the one day of the year—well, maybe Christmas too—that Gia let her daughter's sweet tooth call the shots. Come November 1 it would be back to reality: Boca Burgers, kasha and beans, and one—just one—piece of candy for dessert.

And for me, Jack thought, one Whopper with cheese to go, please.

He'd come down Central Park West, past a large, cheering rally of some sort on one of the park greens, walked east over to First Avenue, then turned downtown. The Trump World Tower was looming large in his vision when he hung a left onto East Fifty-first. A block later he stepped onto Beekman Place. It ran between Fifty-first and Forty-ninth. Right. A whole two blocks long.

Felt like he'd stepped from a wrestling match into a library. The bare-bones bustle of First Avenue was gone, replaced by party-colored trees lining quiet pavements. He'd Googled the area before coming over. Interesting history. Nathan Hale had been held prisoner in one of these mansions before his execution. Billy Rose used to live here, so had Irving Berlin, although his old place now housed the Luxembourg mission to the UN.

Jack walked past canopied front entrances attended by liveried doormen until he came to the brick and granite front of 37 Beekman Place. He nodded to the Hispanic-looking doorman in the gray uniform with black piping.

"Can I help you, sir?" His English carried only a hint of a Spanish accent. The nameplate over his left breast read *Esteban*.

"I'm here to see Mrs. Roselli. She's expecting me."

Esteban led the way into an echoey lobby: white marble floor, white marble walls, white marble ceiling. He lifted the receiver attached to an intercom in the left lobby wall. "And who shall I say is calling?"

"Jack."

"May I have your last name, sir?"

"Just Jack. Like I said, she's expecting me."

He looked dubious but pressed two numbers on the pad. "Ms. Roselli? There is a 'Jack' here to see you."

Esteban listened a few seconds, then hung up. "Apartment one-A, sir." He pointed to a hallway leading off the lobby. "First door on your right." He stared at Jack. "Are you related?"

"No. We've never met. Why do you ask?"

"Just curious. I've been working here two years and you're the first company she's had. You'll like her. Nice lady. The best."

Glad to hear it, Jack thought. Nice ladies were always easier to work for than the not so nice. Later this afternoon he'd be meeting another nice lady customer.

But so far Maria Roselli was a mystery. She'd e-mailed him from his Web site, leaving a phone number, saying it was important. When Jack had called her back she was evasive about who had referred her, saying over and over how she was so worried about her son and how she needed Jack's help.

She was the second customer in two days who'd refused to say who'd referred her. Jack liked to know how his customers managed to find him. His services weren't exactly the kind he could advertise in the *Times*' classified section. He'd made some enemies along the way, so he tended to be wary of customers who popped up with no identifiable references.

But Beekman Place . . . the class of people who had a beef with him didn't live in seven-figure East Side co-ops.

So he'd agreed to meet Maria Roselli without knowing who'd referred her. He'd also agreed to meet at her place. She'd said she was physically handicapped and it would put a burden on her to meet him elsewhere.

Hadn't liked that either, but something in her voice . . .

Anyway, here he was. He knocked on 1A and a dog started barking.

A woman's voice on the other side said, "Hush up, Benno. It's all right."

Oh, hell, Jack thought. Another woman with a dog.

Maybe he should turn and go.

The voice rose in volume. "Come in. It's open."

He took a breath and reached for the knob. Might as well see what was up. He hadn't committed to anything. Nothing said he couldn't walk away if he didn't like the setup.

2

An angular, dark-haired woman, maybe mid- to late-fifties, sat on the thin cushion of a straight-backed chair. Both gnarled hands rested on the silver handle of a wooden walking stick. Dark eyes and a long nose with a slightly bulbous tip were set in a smooth, round, puffy face that didn't go with her wizened body.

Close at her side sat a Rottweiler the size and consistency of a fireplug. He barked once, then settled into fixing Jack with a relentless basilisk stare.

"You're not quite what one would expect," the woman said as Jack closed the door behind him.

The collar of her white turtleneck hung loose around her wrinkled neck. She wore gold-beige slacks and brown shoes. Jack didn't know much about fashion, but her clothes, though simple and straightforward, shouted *money*.

So did the apartment. The decor revealed that she or her husband suffered from a severe case of sinophilia—the front room was festooned with oriental screens, statues, carved stone heads, stone rubbings, temple paintings, inlaid tables of teak and ebony, all immaculate and spit shined.

. . . not quite what one would expect . . .

Jack heard that a lot. People with problems called a guy named Repairman Jack and expected to see a Bo Dietl clone. Sorry.

"And what would one expect?"

"I'm not sure. You look quite . . . ordinary."

"Thank you." He put a lot of effort into ordinariness. Ordinary was invisible. "You are Maria Roselli, I take it?"

She nodded. "I'd offer you lunch but the maid's not well and didn't show up today. Please have a seat."

"Not yet."

He walked to the Cinerama picture window. The East River ran below, Queens lay beyond. He needed to know something about this lady before he got involved with her, but wasn't sure how to broach the subject. He looked down and saw a park with a dog run.

"Nice little park."

"Peter Detmold Park. Benno loves it down there."

Jack turned and looked at her frail frame. "You walk him often?"

She frowned and shook her head. "No. Esteban takes him out before and after his shift. They're fond of each other."

"I'm sure." Might as well get down to it: "Do you know an older woman named Anya?"

Maria Roselli's brow furrowed. "I don't think I do. What's her last name?"

"Mundy."

She shook her head. "No, I do not know anyone by that name."

"Truth?"

"Of course. Why do you ask?"

"Nothing."

But it wasn't nothing. Over the past four or five months three women with dogs had passed through his life—a Russian lady, a younger Indian woman, and a Long Island yenta. Each had known more about Jack's life and situation in the cosmos than they should have. He couldn't help wondering if he might now be dealing with a fourth.

But New York does have a huge population of women

with dogs. They couldn't all be mysterious witchy types with preternatural knowledge. A woman with a dog could be just a woman with a dog.

"One more question: Where did you get my name and number?"

"From someone who would prefer not to be identified."

"I need to know this before we go any further."

She looked away. "I need your help. Can we make a deal? I'll tell you when you find my son?"

Oh, jeez. A missing person job. That wasn't Jack's thing.

"Mrs. Roselli, I—"

"Maria. Please."

"Okay. Maria. Missing people are better found by the police. You need access to computers, databases, networks, all stuff that I don't have, so—"

"I don't want the police involved. At least not yet. I have a good idea where he is, but I can't contact him. If he's fine, and he very well may be, I don't want to cause him any embarrassment."

No cops . . . a good start. Jack dropped into the chair she had offered. He'd give a little listen.

"Okay, Maria. Where do you think he is?"

"First, can I offer you a drink?"

"That's okay."

"Tea?"

He realized he was not yet properly caffeinated.

"Well, I wouldn't mind some coffee if you've got it."

"I've got green tea and that's what you'll have. It's much better for you than coffee. Loaded with antioxidants."

The only times Jack drank green tea was in Chinese restaurants, but what the hell? Be wild.

"Okay. Tea it is."

"Good. You can make me some too while you're at it." She pointed to his left. "The kettle's in the kitchen."

Jack had an urge to tell her what she could do with her kettle, but another look at those gnarled, twisted fingers changed his mind.

"Sure. Why not?"

As he moved toward the kitchen, she struggled to her feet and hobbled after him on her cane. Benno followed her.

"Let me tell you about Johnny first."

"Johnny? How old is Johnny?"

"Thirty-three. He's a good boy. Really, I know all mothers say that, but Johnny really is, despite his privileged life. I made my money the old-fashioned way." She gave him a tight smile. "I inherited it. Before his death, Johnny's father created a generous trust fund for him, contingent on Johnny's graduation from college. When he did graduate—*cum laude,* I'll have you know—he became an instant millionaire."

Swell, Jack thought. Find a thirty-something trust fund brat. Only one way this could go from here: downhill. He felt like heading for the door, but he'd already promised her a cup of tea. So he'd let her ramble.

"But he didn't squander it. He had a flair for business so he joined a brokerage house—Merrill Lynch, Paine Webber, Morgan Stanley, one of those multiname firms. I don't pay much attention to such things. Doesn't matter anyway. What is important is that he was an astounding success. He handled my money along with his and by the end of the nineties he had increased my net worth to an amount that I can only describe as obscene." Another tight little smile. "Well, almost obscene. God only knows what Johnny himself was worth."

Even better, Jack thought sourly. She wants me to find a Gordon Gekko wannabe.

The kitchen was small but equipped with a glass-door Sub Zero refridge and a Dacor range. She pointed to a corner cabinet. "The tea is on the first shelf."

Jack found a box with *Green Tea* in red letters; those were the only English words, the rest was Chinese. As he pulled it out he noticed a dozen or so pill bottles lined against the wall on the counter. Maria must have followed his gaze.

She raised one of her twisted hands. "Rheumatoid arthritis. No fun. The medicines that don't make me sick give me this moon face."

Close up now Jack could see a lacework of red splotches across her nose and cheeks. He felt a twinge of guilt about his annoyance at having to make her tea. Maria's hands didn't look useful for much. Good thing she had money.

"What do you do for food when the maid's not around?"

"What anybody does: I have it delivered."

As he filled the kettle Jack said, "Back to your son: I'd think that if someone that high powered disappeared there'd be a ton of people looking for him. Especially his clients."

"He didn't disappear. He quit. Despite all the money he was making, he became disillusioned. He told me he was sick of being lied to—by the companies, even by the research teams in his own brokerage. He didn't feel he could trust anyone in the business."

So maybe Johnny wasn't a Gekko. Sounded like he had something resembling a conscience.

"This is pre-Enron, I take it."

She nodded. "After hearing about all the double-dealing from Johnny, the Enron scandal came as no surprise to me."

Jack found two gold-rimmed china cups—with the emphasis on *China*—and dropped a tea bag in each.

"So he quit and did what?"

"I think he . . . I believe 'snapped' is the term. He gave a lot of his money to charities, worked in soup kitchens, became a Buddhist for a while, but he couldn't seem to find whatever it was he was looking for. Then he joined the Dormentalists and everything changed."

The Dormentalists . . . everyone had heard of them. Couldn't read a paper or ride a subway without seeing their ads. Every so often some movie star or singer or famous scientist would announce his or her membership in the Dormentalist Church. And the exploits and pro-

nouncements of its flamboyant founder Cooper Blascoe
had been gossip-column fodder for years. But Jack hadn't
heard much from him for a while.

"You think they've done something to your son?"

Every so often the papers would report sinister goings-
on in the cult—mind control and extortion seemed to be
two favorites—but nothing ever seemed to come of the
accusations.

"I don't know. I don't want to believe that anyone has
done *anything* to Johnny, especially not the Dormentalists."

"Why? What's so special about them?"

"Because being a Dormentalist transformed him. I'd
never seen him so happy, so content with life or himself."

The kettle whistled as the water started to boil. Jack
filled the cups.

"I've heard that some cults can do that."

"I quickly learned not to call it a cult in front of Johnny.
It made him very upset. He went on and on about it being a
church, not a cult, saying that even the United States government had recognized it as a church. I still thought it was
a cult, but I didn't care. If Johnny was happy, so was I."

"Was? I take that to mean things changed."

"Not things—Johnny changed. He used to stay in
touch. He'd call me two or three times a week to see how
I was doing and to give me a sales pitch on Dormentalism. He was always trying to get me to join. I must have
told him a thousand times that I wasn't the least bit interested, but he kept after me until he . . ." Her lips tightened
as moisture gathered in her eyes. "Until he stopped."

"Just like that? Three calls one week and nothing the
next?"

"No. They tapered off as he started to change."

"Change how?"

"Over the past few months he's grown increasingly remote and strange. He started insisting that I call him
'Oroont.' Can you imagine? He's been Johnny Roselli all
his life and now he'll answer only to Oroont. Two weeks

ago he didn't call at all, so last Sunday I began calling him. I've left at least a dozen messages but he doesn't call back. I have a key to Johnny's apartment, so on Wednesday I sent Esteban to have a look—you know, in case Johnny was sick or, God forbid, dead. But he found it empty—no furniture, nothing. He'd moved out and hadn't even told me. I know it's got something to do with the Dormentalists."

"How do you know he didn't just quit them and head for California or Mexico or Machu Picchu?"

Maria shook her head. "He was too involved, too much of a true believer." She nodded to the teacups. "They've steeped enough. Bring them into the living room, if you would."

With a cup and saucer in each hand, Jack followed Benno who was following Maria. As she settled into her straight-backed chair, Jack set the cups on the intricately inlaid top of a bow-legged oriental coffee table.

"He's still there," she said.

"Where?"

"At their New York temple—on Lexington Avenue. I know it, I can feel it." One of her gnarled hands wriggled into a pocket and came up with a photo. She handed it to him. "Here. That's him."

Jack saw a slim, very intense-looking dark-haired man. The dark eyes and slightly bulbous nose were identical to Maria's. He looked to be about Jack's age.

"I was only nineteen when I gave birth to him. Perhaps we were too close as he was growing up. Perhaps I coddled him too much. But after George died he was all I had. We were inseparable until he went away to college. That nearly broke my heart. But I knew he'd have to leave the nest and find his own life. I just never thought I'd lose him to some crackpot *cult!*" She all but spat the last word.

"So, no wife and kids, I gather."

She shook her head. "No. He always said he was holding out for the right woman. I guess he never found her."

Or maybe he was just a tad too close to Momma?

Maria stared at him over the rim of her teacup. "But I want *him* found, Mr. . . . I never did get your last name."

"Just Jack'll do fine." He sighed. How to tell her? "I don't know, Maria. It seems like you could get more bang for your buck with someone else."

"Who? Tell me. You can't, can you. All you have to do is work your way into that Dormentalist temple and find Johnny. How hard can it be? It's one building."

"Yeah, but it's a worldwide organization. He might not be there. He could have been assigned to the Zambia chapter or whatever."

"No. He's in New York, I tell you."

Jack sipped his bitter green tea and wondered how she could be so sure.

"Why don't we start with calling the New York temple and asking if he's still there?"

"I've already tried that. They tell me they release no information about church members—wouldn't even confirm or deny that Johnny was a member. I need someone to go inside and find him." She leveled her dark eyes at Jack. "I will pay you twenty-five thousand dollars in advance to do that."

Jack blinked. Twenty-five large . . .

"That . . . that's a lot more than I usually charge, Maria. You don't have to—"

"The money means nothing. It's a week's interest from my treasury notes. I'll double it, triple it—"

Jack held up a hand. "No-no. That's okay."

"You'll have expenses, and perhaps you can use whatever is left over to offset the fee for someone who can't afford you. I don't care about the money, just *find . . . my . . . son!*"

She underscored the last three words by rapping the tip of her cane against the floor. Benno, who'd been stretched out next to her, jumped up from his nap and looked around, ready to attack.

"Okay." Jack responded to her pained expression, to the need calling through her eyes. "Let's say I do work my way into this temple, and let's just say I find your son. What then?"

"Tell him to call his mother. And then tell me you've found him and how he is."

"And that's it? That's all?"

She nodded. "That is all. I simply want to know if he's alive and well. If he doesn't want to call me, it will break my heart, but at least I will be able to sleep at night."

Jack finished his tea in a gulp. "Well, that's a relief."

"Why? What else did you think I'd want you to do?"

"Abduct him for deprogramming."

She chewed her upper lip. "And what if I did?"

"No deal. If he's not being held against his will, I won't yank him out. I believe in everyone's inalienable right to be stupid."

"What if he is being coerced?"

"Then I'll do what I can to yank him. If I can't, I'll do my damnedest to provide you with enough probable cause to get officialdom involved."

"Fair enough." She extended her right hand. "Then we have a deal?"

Jack gently gripped her twisted fingers. "We do."

"Excellent. Look in the top drawer of that bureau over there. You will find an envelope and a newspaper article. Take both. They're yours."

Jack did as she asked. He opened the white legal-size envelope and thumbed through the bills—all Grover Clevelands.

"What if I can't deliver?"

"Either way, keep the money. I know you'll try your best."

He looked at the sheets of newspaper. A multipage, two-week-old article on Dormentalism from *The Light* by someone named Jamie Grant.

The Light . . . of all the papers in New York, why'd it have to be *The Light*? He'd had a bad experience with one of the paper's reporters a few months ago. Memories

from June flooded back and swirled around him . . . his
sister, Kate . . . and that kid reporter . . . what was his
name? Sandy Palmer. Right. The kid had given him a few
gut-clenching moments.

"Make sure you read that," Maria said. "It will serve as
a good primer on Dormentalism."

Jack checked out the title: "Dormentalism or Dementedism?" He smiled. Whoever Jamie Grant was, Jack liked
him already.

He tucked the envelope into a front hip pocket but held
on to the article.

"I'll get to work on this right away."

"Wonderful." Her smile faded. "You won't fail me,
will you?"

"Not if I can help it. All I can guarantee is that I'll give
it my best shot."

Maria Roselli sighed. "I suppose that's all one can ask
for. What will be your first step?"

Jack held up the newspaper. "First I'm going to have to
learn about this Dormentalism stuff. Then I guess I'll become a convert."

Back on the street, Jack was tempted to make a quick run
to Gia's—she lived less than ten blocks uptown from
Maria Roselli's—but his visit had taken longer than expected and he was running late for a meeting with another
customer.

In the old days, long before he was born, a person
could have hopped the El on Second Avenue. Or Third.
Today he settled for a crosstown bus at Forty-ninth Street.

He'd take the 27 over to the West Side and catch a subway up to Julio's.

He dipped his Metrocard and found a seat on the half-full bus. As he unfolded the Dormentalism article he glanced up and noticed one of the ads above the opposite seats. He looked closer. Damned if it wasn't for the Dormentalist Church. He stood for a closer look.

DORMENTALISM!

Another better *You* slumbers within! **The Dormentalist Church** will help you awaken that sleeping part of you. Reestablish contact with your hidden self now! DON'T DELAY! Momentous change is coming! You don't want to be left out! PREPARE YOURSELF! Join the millions of Seekers like Yourself. Find the nearest **Dormentalist Temple** and discover the Other You ... before it's too late!

A toll-free number and a Midtown address on Lexington Avenue ran along the bottom. Jack jotted them down on the margin of the article.

"You'll stay away from that lot if you know what's good for you," said a creaky voice behind him.

Jack turned and saw a chubby, hunched old woman staring up at him from a nearby seat.

"Sorry?"

"You heard me. How can they call themselves a church when they never mention God? They're doing the devil's work, and you'll endanger your immortal soul if you even go near them."

Jack instinctively looked around for a dog of some kind, but didn't see one. She wasn't carrying anything big enough to hide one.

"Do you have a dog?" he said.

She blinked up at him. "A dog? What sort of question is that to ask? I'm talking about your immortal soul and—"

"Do ... you ... have ... a ... dog?"

"No. I have a cat, not that it's any business of yours."

A sharp reply leaped to his lips but he swallowed it. Just some Paleolithic busybody. He glanced back at the ad. The last line bothered him.

Other You . . .

He'd got to the point where the word *other* triggered all sorts of alarms. And now this old lady warning him against the Dormentalists. But the strange women who'd been popping in and out of his life lately never appeared alone. They always had a dog along.

Jack dropped back into his seat. Second-guessing every little thing that happened was a sure shortcut to the booby hatch.

"Just trying to give you a friendly warning," the old lady said in a low voice.

Jack looked back and noticed she was pouting.

"I'm sure you were," he told her. "Consider me warned."

He turned to the article from *The Light*. "Dormentalism or Dementedism?" delved into the early days of the cult—sorry, church. Founded by Cooper Blascoe as a hippie commune in California during the sixties, it mushroomed into a globe-spanning organization with branches in just about every country in the world. The Church—apparently they liked an uppercase *C*—had been run by a guy named Luther Brady, who Grant called a "propheteer," since Blascoe had put himself into suspended animation in Tahiti a couple of years ago.

Whoa. Suspended animation? Jack hadn't heard about that. No wonder Blascoe hadn't been in the news. Suspended animation does not exactly make you the life of the party.

The reporter, Jamie Grant, contrasted the early Dormentalist commune, which seemed little more than an excuse to have orgies, to the upright, uptight corporate entity it had become. The Dormentalists' cash flow was top secret—apparently it was easier to ferret eyes-only

documents out of NSA than the Dormentalist Church—
but Grant estimated that it was well into nine-figure
country.

The question was, what was it doing with all the
money?

Except for a few high-profile locations in places like
Manhattan and L.A., the Church was run on a tight budget. Luther Brady's doing, Grant said—he had a business
degree. Grant reported that the High Council, based here
in New York, had been buying plots of land all over the
place, not only in this country but around the world,
spending whatever it took to secure them. To what end
was anyone's guess.

In the next installment, Grant promised in-depth pro-
files of the inanimate Cooper Blascoe and on Dormentalism's Grand Poo-bah, Luther Brady. And perhaps the
reason behind the ongoing land acquisitions.

Jack refolded the article and stared out the window as
the bus crossed Fifth Avenue. He watched a young,
orange-haired Asian woman in black talking on a cell
phone as she waited for the walk signal. A guy next to her
was talking into two phones at once—on a Sunday? The
pair of antennae gave him an insectoid look. On a week-
day in Midtown there were so many antennae on the
street it looked like an ant farm.

Nobody wanted to be disconnected anymore. Everyone was on call twenty-four hours a day for anyone with
their number. Jack recoiled at the prospect. He had a prepaid cell phone but he left it off unless he was expecting a
call. He often went days without turning it on. He loved
being disconnected.

Back to the article: As much as he liked its sardonic,
in-your-face style, he felt vaguely dissatisfied with what it
didn't say. It concentrated on the structure and finances of
the Dormentalist Church without going into its beliefs.

But then, according to the tagline, this was only part
one. Maybe those would be covered later.

4

Jack got out at Broadway. Before heading for the subway he picked up the latest copy of *The Light,* which turned out to be last week's issue. It came out every Wednesday. He thumbed through it but found no follow-up article. He did find the paper's phone number, though.

He pulled out his cell and dialed the number. The automated system picked up and put him through a voice tree—*"If you don't know your party's extension"* blah-blah-blah—that required him to punch in the first three letters of Grant's name. He did as instructed and was rewarded with a ring.

Not that he expected Grant to be in on a Sunday, but figured he'd break the ice with a voice mail to set him up for some talk tomorrow. But someone picked up on the third ring.

"Grant," said a gravely woman's voice.

"Is this Jamie Grant, the reporter?" The article's tone had given him the impression that Grant was male.

"One and the same. Who's this?" She sounded as if she'd been expecting someone else.

"Someone who just read your Dormentalism article."

"Oh?" A sudden wariness drenched that single syllable.

"Yes, and I'd like to talk to you about it sometime."

"Forget it," she said, her voice harsh now. "You think I'm an idiot?"

A loud clatter broke the connection. Jack stared at his phone.

What did I say?

5

Jack was late and Maggie was already waiting at Julio's when he arrived.

During his uptown ride on the 9 train he'd got to thinking about how he'd go about earning the money Maria had given him. Since he didn't know a single Dormentalist—at least no one who admitted it—he'd have to be his own mole. Infiltrating the lower echelons would probably be easy, but wouldn't get him access to membership records. He needed an advance placement course, or maybe become someone they'd usher into the inner circle.

And that had given him an idea.

So he'd made an unscheduled stop at Ernie's ID and described what he needed. Ernie wasn't so sure he could deliver.

"I dunno, man. This ain't my usual thing. Gonna hafta do a lotta research on this. Gonna take time. Gonna cost me."

Jack had said he'd cover all his expenses and make the extra effort more than worth his while. Ernie had liked that.

As Jack entered the bar, Julio pointed out Maggie—no last name, which was fine with Jack—sitting at a rear table, talking to Patsy. Well, more like listening. Patsy was a semi-regular at Julio's and a Patsy conversation usually consisted of him talking and the other party trying fruitlessly to get a word in. Jack could see Maggie nodding and looking uncomfortable in the rear dimness.

Jack ambled over and laid a hand on Patsy's shoulder.

"This guy bothering you, lady?"

Patsy jumped, then smiled when he saw Jack. "Hey, Jacko, how's it goin'? I been keepin' her company while she's waitin' for you."

He had a round face and a comb-over that started behind his ear. He wore double-knit slacks and watched the world through aviator glasses day and night, indoors and out. Wouldn't surprise Jack if he wore them to bed.

"That's great, Patsy. What a guy. But now we've got some private talk, so if you don't mind . . ."

"Sure, sure." As he began backing away he pointed to Maggie. "I'll be at the bar. Think on what I said about dinner."

Maggie shook her head. "Really, I can't. I have to be—"

"Just think about it, that's all I'm askin'."

Oh, and somehow along the way Patsy had got the idea that he was quite the ladies' man.

"I wish we didn't have to meet in a bar," Maggie said as Patsy sauntered away and Jack pulled up a chair.

With a minimum of effort she could have looked okay. Fortyish with a pale face, so pale that if she told Jack she'd never been out in the sun, he'd believe her. Not a speck of makeup, thin lips, a nice nose, hazel eyes. She'd tucked her gray-streaked blond hair under a light blue knit hat that looked like flapperwear from the Roaring Twenties. As for her body, she appeared slim, but a bulky sweater and shapeless blue slacks smothered whatever moved beneath. Beat-up Reeboks completed the picture. She sat stiff and straight, as if her vertebrae had been switched for a steel rod. Her whole look seemed calculated to deflect male attention.

If that was the case, it hadn't worked with Patsy. But then, Patsy was game for anyone without a Y chromosome.

"You don't like Julio's?" Jack said.

"I don't like bars—I don't go to them and I don't think they're a good thing. Too many wives and children go hungry because of paychecks wasted in places like this, too many are beaten when the drinker comes home drunk."

Jack nodded. "Can't argue with you on that, but I don't think it happens much with these folk."

"What makes them so special?"

"Most of them are single or divorced. They work hard but don't have too many people to spend on but themselves. When they go home there's no one to beat. Or love."

"What's wrong with giving their drink money to charity?"

Jack shook his head. This lady was no fun with a capital NO.

"Because they'd rather spend it hanging out with friends."

"I can think of lots of ways to be with friends besides drinking."

Jack looked around at the bright afternoon sun angling through the front windows past the bare branches of the dead ficus and the desiccated hanging plants, so long deceased they'd become mummified. "Another Brick in the Wall" wafted from the jukebox, its metronomic beat augmented by Lou's hammering at the GopherBash in the corner.

What's not to like?

She'd been just as uptight yesterday at their first meeting. He found it hard to believe that this priss was being blackmailed. What had she ever done that would let someone get a hook into her?

Her hands were clasped together on the table before her in an interlocking deathgrip. Jack reached over and gave them a gentle pat.

"I'm not the enemy here, Maggie."

Her shoulders slumped as she closed her eyes and leaned back. Tears rimmed her lids when she looked at him again.

"I know. I'm sorry. It's just . . . it's just that I'm not a bad person. I've been good, I've lived a clean life, I've sacrificed for others, done good works, given to charity. Criminals, mobsters, drug dealers, they commit crimes every day and go about their lives unscathed. Me, I make one little mistake, just one, and my whole world is threatened."

If she was telling the truth, and Jack believed she was, he was sorry for her. He couldn't help responding to the hurt, fright, and vulnerability seeping through her facade.

"That's because you've got something to protect—a job, a family, a reputation, your dignity. They don't."

Maggie had been under a blackmailer's thumb since August. All she would say about the hook was that someone had photos of her that she'd rather not be made public. He'd been squeezing her and she was just about tapped out. She wouldn't say what was in the photos. She admitted that she was in them, but that was it. Fine with Jack. If he found the blackmailer and the photos, he'd know. If not, none of his business.

"And another difference between you and the sleazeballs is they'll hunt down a blackmailer and rip his lungs out. You won't, and this oxygen waster knows it. That's where I come in."

Her eyes widened. "I don't want anyone's lungs ripped out!"

Jack laughed. "Figure of speech. Probably better than this guy deserves, and it would be way too messy."

She stared at him a moment, an uneasy light in her eyes, then glanced around. Though no one was in earshot, she lowered her voice.

"The person who gave me your name warned that you played 'rough.' I'm against violence. I just want those pictures back."

"I'm not a hitman," he told her, "but this guy's not going to just hand over those pictures, even if I say pretty please. I'll try to get it done without him knowing who I'm working for, but a little rough and tumble may be unavoidable."

She grimaced. "Just as long as no lungs are ripped out."

Jack laughed. "Forget lungs, I want to know who told you I played rough. What's his name?"

A hint of a smile curved her thin lips. "Who said it was a he?"

She wasn't going to come across. All right, he'd wait. And watch. Customers without references earned extra scrutiny.

"Okay. First things first: Did you bring the first half of my fee?"

She looked away. "I don't have it all. I had very little money in the first place, and so much of that is gone, used up paying this . . . beast." It seemed to take an effort to call her blackmailer a name. Who was this lady? "I was wondering . . . could I pay you in installments?"

Jack leaned back and stared at her. His impulse was to say, Forget it. He didn't do this for fun. Too often a fix-it involved putting his skin on the line; might be different if he had a replacement, but this skin was his one and only. So he liked a good portion of his fee up front. Installments meant a continuing relationship, excuses for being late, and on and on. He didn't want to be a bank, and he didn't want a long-term customer relationship. He wanted to get in, get out, and say good-bye.

And besides, dealing with a blackmailer could get ugly.

But the twenty-five large nesting in his pocket brought back the previous owner's words . . .

Use whatever is left over to offset the fee for someone who can't afford you . . .

Maybe a lady who said she did good works and gave to charity deserved a little herself.

Still, he couldn't bring himself to agree right away.

"Well, like I told you yesterday, this could be a tough job, with no guarantees. Getting your photos isn't enough. I have to get the negatives as well. But if he used a digital camera, there won't be any. Digital photos will exist on a hard drive somewhere, and most likely on a backup disk somewhere else. Finding all that will take time. But that's Stage Two. Stage One is finding out *who* is blackmailing you."

She shook her head. "I just can't imagine . . ."

"Got to be someone who knows you. Once we identify him, we'll need to steal all copies of whatever it is he's holding over you without him knowing you were behind it."

"How can you do that?"

"The ideal scenario is to make it look like an accident—say, a fire. But that's not always feasible. If you're not his only victim—I know of one guy who's made a career out of blackmail—it makes things a little easier."

"How?"

"I can liberate more than just your stuff."

"I don't understand."

"If he's got multiple victims and just your stuff winds up missing, he'll know it was you. If I wipe out everything I find, he'll have a number of suspects. But even with your stuff gone, he'll keep trying to squeeze you."

"But how—?"

"He'll assume you'll think he still has the photos. That's why we have to pave a way out for you."

"You sound like you've done this before."

He nodded. The blackmail industry kept his phone ringing. Most victims couldn't go to the cops because that meant revealing the very thing they were paying the leech to keep under wraps. They imagined a trial, their secret trumpeted in the papers, or at the very least making the public record. A certain percentage, pushed to the point where they couldn't or wouldn't take it anymore, decided to seek a solution outside the system. That was where Jack came in.

"Many times. Maybe even for your unnamed source."

"Oh, no. He'd never—" Her hand flew to her mouth.

Gotcha, Jack thought, but didn't make an issue of it. He'd narrowed down her source to a little less than half the population. At least it was a start.

"As for the installments . . . we'll work something out."

She smiled, this time revealing even white teeth.

"Thank you. I'll see you get your money, every penny of it." She dug into her black no-name pocketbook. "I *was* able to bring the hundred dollars you asked for."

She handed him a hundred-dollar bill and two folded sheets of paper.

Jack slipped the bill under his sweater and into the breast pocket of his shirt. The blackmailer had demanded a thousand as his next payment. He was going to get only a fraction of that. And Jack was going to send it.

He had a reason for doing it himself. But more important, the payment would allow him to track down the blackmailer. He'd done this before: Send the money in a padded envelope with a dime-size transponder hidden in the lining, then follow the transponder.

He unfolded the first sheet of paper—Maggie's perfect Palmer-method handwritten note saying she didn't have any more to send at the moment. Good. Just what he'd told her to write. The second was the address. The money was supposed to go to "Occupant." A street address and a number followed—plainly a mail drop. Jack did a double take at the street—Tremont Avenue in the Bronx . . . Box 224.

"Son of a bitch!"

"I beg your pardon?"

"I know that address and I know who's blackmailing you."

"Who?"

"A walking, talking virus."

"But what's his name?"

Jack could see his round, sweaty-jowled face with eyes and mouth crowded close to the center of his face, held there by the gravitational field of his big, pushed-up nose. Richie Cordova, a fat, no good, rotten, useless glob of protoplasm. Not two months ago Jack had ruined most of Cordova's stash of blackmail goodies. Obviously he'd missed Maggie's photos.

"Nobody you'd know. He's the guy I mentioned before, who's made a career out of blackmail."

Maggie looked frightened. "But how did he get those pictures of me and . . . ?"

And who? Jack wondered. Male or female?

He had a pretty good idea of how it had gone down. Cordova's legit grind was private investigations. Someone hired him for a job that had put him in Maggie's orbit. The shitbum spotted something hinky, took a few pictures, and now was using them to supplement his income.

"Bad luck. The wrong guy in the wrong place at the wrong time."

She leaned forward. "I want his name."

"Better you don't know. It can't do you any good. Might even buy you some trouble." He looked at her. "I mean it."

"Yes, but—"

"You believe in the soul, I assume?"

"Of course."

"This guy's is a petri dish."

She slumped again. "This is terrible."

"Not really. Granted you've got a better chance of goof-ups if you're on the string to an amateur than a pro, but I've already dealt with this particular pro. I know where he lives and where he works. I'll get your photos back."

She brightened. "You will?"

"Well, maybe I shouldn't guarantee anything, but we've gone from Stage One to Stage Two in a matter of minutes. That's a record. We still have to send him that money though."

"Why? I thought that was to trace him. If you already know who he is—"

"There's a reason we're shorting him. I want to rattle his cage, make him get in touch with you. When he calls, you've got to cry poverty—"

She barked a bitter little laugh. "It won't be an act, I can tell you that."

"Be convincing. What that does is set the stage for your sending him no more money when and if I retrieve your

photos. You simply haven't got it. Remember, he's got a
lot invested in his blackmail assets. We don't want him
connecting you to losing them. No telling what he'll do."

Instead of looking concerned, Maggie smiled as if a
terrible burden had been lifted.

"This is going to work, isn't it," she said.

"Let's not get ahead of ourselves."

"No, it is. I can feel it. God turned away from me for a
while—not without good reason—but now I see His
hand again in my life. He led me to you, to someone who
has already dealt with my tormentor. That can't be just a
coincidence."

Coincidence . . .

Jack felt his shoulders tighten. He hated coincidences.

6

Jack watched Maggie leave, nimbly sliding past Patsy as
she gave him the brush.

Months ago a lady—a Russian lady with a big white
dog—had told him there'd be no more coincidences in
his life. He'd seen no hard evidence yet that she'd been
right, but certain incidents that he might otherwise consider happenstance seemed to form a pattern when he
looked for one. True, you could always find connections
if you looked hard enough and stretched the imagination.
That was how conspiracy theories were born.

But Maggie had it right: Her picking him to help her
with Cordova seemed like a hell of a coincidence. On the
other hand, Cordova did a lot of blackmailing. It wasn't
impossible that two of his victims—Emil Jankowski in
September and Maggie here at the tail end of October—

would call on Jack. Not too much competition in the fix-
it field.

Still . . .

He popped out of his seat and headed for the door,
waving to Julio as he passed the bar.

Out on the street he peered up and down the sidewalk
until he spotted Maggie's blue knit hat bouncing away to
his right. He took off after her, keeping his distance. He
hoped she'd snag a cab but no, she bounded down the
steps of a subway entrance.

Damn. Following her on a Sunday wouldn't be easy.
No crowds to hide in. With a mental shrug he headed
down. The worst that could happen was she'd spot him
and he'd have to ad lib an explanation.

He hung back on the stairs till he saw her head for the
downtown side. When she hopped on an A train he slipped
into the following car and positioned himself where he
could watch her through the glass. She pulled a book from
her bag but didn't open it. She stared at the floor, looking
lost, as if the worries of the world were all hers.

She rode that way down to West Fourth where she
switched to the F. Along the way she didn't look around
much, too lost in her thoughts to notice anyone following.

She stepped off at Delancey and Jack followed her up
to the streets of the Lower East Side. The buildings here
were former tenements that maxed out at five stories.
Canopied oriental and kosher food stores sat cheek by
jowl along the stained gray sidewalk.

He gave her a block lead but grew a little uneasy as he
started to recognize his surroundings. He'd come down
here just last August to confront a priest who had hired him
but managed to pull one over on him. What was his name?
Father Ed. Right. Father Edward Halloran. His church had
been around here somewhere, St. Somebody-or—

He stopped dead as he followed Maggie around a corner. There, across the street, looming over the surround-
ing tenements, sat the hulking, Gothic, granite-block

mass of the Church of St. Joseph. The old building wasn't
in any better shape than the last time he'd seen it. The
large rose window centered over the double doors was
caked with grime, as were its twin crocketed spires, but
the latter boasted the added decoration of white stripes à
la city squab.

The doors stood open and people, mostly older with an
immigrant look, were wandering inside.

Jack had been in the rectory to St. Joe's immediate left,
but not the building to the right where Maggie was hurrying up the front steps, passing a sign that read *Convent of
the Blessed Virgin*.

A nun? Maggie was a nun?

Well, it sort of fit with her uptight personality. But he
guessed she wasn't *too* uptight, otherwise Cordova would
have nothing to hold over her. And since she was connected with St. Joe's, Jack had a pretty good idea who had
referred her: Father Ed.

Okay. One mystery solved. But another remained.
Why blackmail a nun? Seemed like a waste of effort.
Nuns didn't have any money—unless Maggie came
from a wealthy family.

Jack glanced at his watch. Five to four. He'd promised to
take Gia and Vicky out to dinner, but that wasn't till seven.
Maybe he'd invest an hour or so here and see if he could
learn any more. Maybe Maggie wasn't a nun. Maybe she
merely worked at the convent . . . but he doubted that.

He spotted an all-purpose convenience store/take
out/coffee shop catercorner from the church. Maybe he
could watch from there.

He crossed over and bought a cup of stale coffee in the
traditional blue-and-white container from the Korean
proprietor. No sooner had he stepped to the window and
taken his first bitter sip when Maggie reappeared. She'd
changed into a gray skirt and jacket over a white blouse.
Her hair was tucked under a black wimple with a white
band. She hurried down the convent steps, up the church
steps, and disappeared inside.

Well, that settled the is-she-or-isn't-she question. But Jack wanted a little more info. He stepped outside and crossed back to the church, dribbling his coffee onto the pavement as he went. On the far side he tossed the empty cup into a trash basket, then climbed St. Joe's front steps.

To the right, white vinyl letters snapped into a black message board that listed the Mass schedule. Sunday had one every ninety minutes till noon, then one last chance at four.

To the left, a worn black-on-white sign heralded the Church of St. Joseph's Renovation Fund and sported a thermometer to track the progress of contributions. One-hundred-thousand-dollar increments were listed to the left of the graduated column up to the goal of $600,000; the red area that marked the level of contributions hadn't even filled the bulb. Not surprising, considering the chill economic climate and the low-income level of the parish.

Jack edged through the entrance and stood in the vestibule. The nave stretched ahead through a second set of doors. A sparse crowd for the four o'clock Mass, so he had no trouble spotting Maggie. She sat behind a well-dressed man. Occasionally she'd lean forward and whisper something. He'd nod and she'd lean back.

The priest on the altar was not Father Ed; he displayed about the same level of interest in what he was doing as his parishioners, which was not much. Jack tuned him out, trying to get a fix on the relationship between Maggie—if that was her name—and her man friend. He'd thought at first that they might be having an affair, but he sensed a distance between them.

About halfway through the Mass the man rose and sidled to the aisle, then headed back toward Jack. He looked to be about fifty, with a good haircut and features that might be described as distinguished looking except for the haunted look in his eyes and the circles beneath them. He gave Jack a friendly nod and a reflexive smile as he passed. Jack nodded back.

Jack counted to five, then stepped to the front doors. He watched the man stand on the corner, looking for a cab. It took a couple of minutes but he snagged one and it headed uptown.

Jack leaned against the rusty iron railing by the building-fund sign and waited. Soon the parishioners began to filter out. He spotted Maggie among them, head down, lost in thought.

"Sister?" he called softly. "Can I have a word with you?"

She looked up and her initial look of confusion vanished in wide-eyed shock.

"You! How did you—?"

Jack motioned her closer. "Where can we talk?"

She glanced around at the final parishioners straggling from within and heading down the steps.

"In a moment this will be as good a place as any."

"You're kidding."

"No. I can't be seen strolling around with a man, and certainly not sitting in a *bar* with him."

Jack noted the emphasis on "bar."

He lowered his voice. "What's your real name, sister?"

"Margaret Mary O'Hara." She flashed a tiny smile. "The kids at the parish school used to call me 'Sister M&M.' They still do, but now they spell it differently."

Jack returned her smile. "Sister Eminem. That's cool. Better than Sister Margaret. That'd make you sound ninety years old."

"Around the convent I'm known as Sister Maggie, but lately I *have* felt ninety years old."

Movement caught Jack's eye. He spotted a white-albed altar boy at the front doors, kicking up the hooks that held them open.

"Hi, Sister," he said as he spotted her.

"Hello, Jorge," she said with a genuine smile, wider than Jack had ever seen from her. "You did a good job today. See you in school tomorrow."

He nodded and smiled. "See ya."

When the doors had closed she turned back to Jack.

"Obviously you followed me. Why?"

"Too many unanswered questions. But at least now I know who referred you. Does Father Ed know you're being blackmailed?"

She shook her head. "No. He just knows I need help and can't go to the police. I went to him for advice and he suggested you. Did . . . did he hire you for something?"

"You'll have to ask him. My memory's very unreliable."

The answer seemed to please her. "That's good to know."

"Are you and that man I saw you with in the photos together?"

"I'd really rather not say."

"Fair enough." Jack looked around. They were alone on the steps, alone on the deserted street. A man and a nun standing a good two feet apart. No one could infer anything improper from that. "How bad can the photos be?"

She looked at her feet. "He sent me copies. Very bad. Nothing left to the imagination."

"Well then let me ask, How much can they hurt you? I'm assuming you were with a guy, but even if you weren't, I mean, they made some openly gay guy a bishop, so what could—?"

"Good gravy, Jack. Those were Episcopalians. This is the Catholic Church."

Good gravy?

"You're kidding, right? After what Catholic priests have been up to?"

"*Some* Catholic priests. None that I've ever known. But this is different. *Nuns* are different. My order would banish me. I'd be out on the street with no home, no savings, and no job."

"Seems pretty cold."

"I love my order, Jack. But more than that, I love serving God and I love teaching these children. I'm a good teacher. It's not false pride when I say I can and do make a difference. But even if I was allowed to stay in the convent, I couldn't be allowed to teach." She took a deep, shuddering breath. "Those pictures threaten everything I hold dear in my life."

Jack watched her and wondered how so many facets of her life had combined to ruin it. If she'd been Margaret Mary O'Hara, single public school teacher, she could thumb her nose at Cordova. *Yeah? So?* But she was Sister Maggie and that was a whole other ball game.

"Okay, answer me this: How much money do you have?"

"We take a vow of poverty but are allowed to put a little away for special circumstances. Whatever I had is all but gone now, paid to that . . . that . . ."

"Yeah, I know. Any family money you can tap into?"

Her mouth twisted. "My father's long dead, my mother died over the summer, penniless. Every last cent she had was eaten up by the nursing home."

"Sorry to hear that. But I'm confused. Having seen the way this creep operates, I can't understand him going after someone with a vow of poverty. He tends to like deeper wells."

Sister Maggie looked away. After a few heartbeats she sighed and pointed to the sign behind Jack.

"He wants me to steal from the renovation fund. I'm one of the overseers."

"Really." This was an interesting twist. "How could he know that?"

Another look away. "It has to do with the photos. I can't say any more."

"All right then, why not simply quit that position?"

"He said if I don't pay, or if I quit working with the fund, he'll make the photos public and ruin me *and* the fund. The fund's having such a tough time as it is, a scandal will sink it."

"Whatever they show, you can say they're fake. You wouldn't believe how they can manipulate photos these days. Seeing used to be believing. Not anymore."

"First off," she said, "that would be lying. Secondly, I have been working closely of late with the other person in the photos. What they show would not seem so preposterous to anyone who knew us."

"So what you're saying is even if they were fakes, very good fakes, they'd still mess up your life and the building fund."

She nodded, started to say something, but couldn't get the words past her trembling lips.

Jack felt his jaw clench as he watched tears of helplessness rim her eyes. Sister Maggie seemed like good people. The thought of that slimy, belly-crawling son of a bitch turning the screws on her, and probably enjoying every minute . . .

Finally she found her voice. "He stole something from me . . . a very private moment . . ."

"And you want it back."

She looked up at him. "No. I want it erased." She pointed to her heart. "From here"—then touched her forehead—"and from here. But that can't happen while those pictures are out there."

"Don't worry about it. I'll take care of it."

She looked into his eyes and didn't seem to like what she saw there.

"But without violence. Please. I can't be a party to violence."

Jack only nodded. No promises. If an opportunity to put the hurt on the slob presented itself, he might not be able to resist.

He'd have dinner with his ladies tonight, then he was going to pay a visit to fat Richie Cordova.

7

After a quick shower and a change of clothes, Jack stuck Sister Maggie's hundred-dollar bill into a padded envelope, addressed it to Cordova, and dropped it in a mailbox. Just in time to make the late pickup.

Then he stopped in at the Isher Sports Shop on the way to Gia's. The front doorbell jangled as he pushed through. Jack wound his way toward the rear of the store through the tilting, ready-to-topple shelves overcrowded with basketballs, snowboards, baseball bats, even boxing gloves. He found Abe, proprietor and sole employee, out of his usual spot behind the rear counter and over by the rack of hockey sticks. He was talking to a young woman and a boy who looked maybe ten.

"All right," Abe was saying to the boy in a testy tone. "Stand up straight already. Right. Unstoop those shoulders. No jaded slouch till you're at least twelve—it's a law. There. Now you should look straight ahead while I measure the stick."

Abe with a sporting goods customer—usually a theater-of-the-absurd playlet. Jack stood back and watched the show.

Abe stood five-two or -three and was a little over sixty with a malnourished scalp and an overfed waistline. He wore his customary half-sleeve white shirt and black pants, each a sampling menu of whatever he'd eaten during the course of the day. This being the end of the day, the menu was extensive.

He grabbed a handful of hockey sticks and stood them one at a time in front of the kid. The end of the handle of the first came up to the level of the kid's eyes.

"Nope. Too long. Just the right length it should be, otherwise you'll look like a *kalyekeh* out there on the ice."

The kid looked at his mom who shrugged. Neither had the faintest idea what Abe was rambling about. Jack was right with them.

The second stick reached the kid's chin.

"Too short. A good match this would be if you were in your skates, but in shoes, no."

The end of the third stick stopped right under the kid's nose.

"Perfect! And it's made of graphite. Such tensile strength. With this you can beat your opponents senseless and never have to worry about breaking it."

The kid's eyes widened. "Really?"

The mother repeated the word but with narrowed eyes and a different tone.

Abe shrugged. "What can I say? It's no longer a sport, hockey. You're equipping your *kaddishel* to join a tumel on ice. Why put the little fellow in harm's way?"

The mother's lips tightened into a line. "Can we just pay for this and go?"

"I should stop you from paying?" he said, heading for the scarred counter where the cash register sat. "Of course you can pay."

Her credit card was scanned, approved, a slip was signed, and she was on her way. If her expression hinted that she'd never be back, her comment left no doubt.

"Get out while you can," she muttered to Jack as she passed. "This guy is a loon."

"Really?" Jack said.

Abe had settled himself onto his stool and assumed his customary hands-on-thighs posture as Jack reached the counter. Parabellum, his blue parakeet and constant companion, sat in his cage to the right pecking at something that looked like a birdseed popsicle.

"Another highwater mark in Abe Grossman customer relations," Jack said, grinning. "You ever consider advertising yourself as a consultant?"

"Feh," Abe said with a dismissive gesture. "Hockey."

"At least you actually sold something related to a sport."

The street-level sports shop would have folded long ago if not for Abe's real business, locked away in the cellar. He didn't need sports-minded customers, so he did what he could to discourage them.

"Not such a sport. Do you know they're making hockey sticks out of Kevlar now? They're expecting to maybe add handguns to the brawls?"

"Wouldn't know," Jack said. "Never watch. Just stopped by to let you know I won't be needing that transponder I ordered."

"Nu?" Abe's eyebrows lifted toward the memory of his hairline. "So you're maybe not such a customer relations maven yourself?"

"No, she's still onboard. It's just that I've already dealt with the guy who's squeezing her. He's the one the last transponder led me to."

"Cor-bon or something, right?"

"Close. Cordova. Some coincidence, huh?" He waited for Abe's reaction.

"Coincidence . . ." His eyes narrowed. "You told me no more coincidences for you."

Jack hid his discomfort. "Yeah, I know, but coincidences do happen in real life, right?"

Abe shrugged. "Now and then."

"Watch: I'll probably find out he's a closet Dormentalist."

"Dormentalist? He's a rat, maybe, but is he meshugge?"

Jack told him about Maria Roselli and her missing Johnny, then asked, "You know anything about Dormentalism?"

"Some. Like a magnet it attracts the *farblondzhet* in the head. That's why the Dormentalists joined the Scientologists in the war against Prozac back in the eighties.

Anything that relieves depression and allows a clearer view of life and the world is a threat to them. Shrinks the pool of potential members."

"I need to do a little studying up. What's the best place to start, you think? The Web?"

"Too much tsuris separating fact from opinion there. Go to the source."

He slid off the stool and stepped into the little office behind the counter area. Jack had been in there a few times. It made the rest of the store look neat and spare and orderly. He heard mutters and clatters and thuds and Yiddish curses before Abe reemerged.

"Here," he said as he slapped a slim hardcover on the counter. "What you need is *The Book of Hokano*, the Torah of Dormentalism. More than you'll ever wish or need to know. But this isn't it. Instead, it's a mystery novel, starring a recurring hero named David Daine, supposedly written by Dormentalism's founder, Cooper Blascoe."

Jack picked it up. The dust jacket cover graphic was a black-and-white melange of disjointed pieces with the title *Sundered Lives* in blazing red.

"Never heard of it."

Abe's eyebrows rose again in search of the Lost City of Hair. "You should have. It was number one on the *Times'* bestseller list. I bought it out of curiosity." He rolled his eyes. "Oy, such a waste of good money and paper. How such a piece of turgid drek could be a bestseller, let alone make number one, makes me dizzy in the head. He wrote six of them, all number ones. Makes one wonder about the public's reading tastes."

"Whodunnit?"

"I have no idea. Couldn't finish it. Tried once to read *The Book of Hokano* and couldn't finish that either. Incoherent mumbo jumbo." He pointed to the book in Jack's hand. "My gift to you."

"A bad novel. Gee, thanks. You think I should buy *The Book of Hokano* then?"

"If you do it should be used already. Don't give those gonifs another royalty. And set aside a long time. A thousand or so pages it runs."

Jack winced. "Do they have Cliff Notes for it?"

"You might find something like that online. All sorts of nuts online."

"Still, millions of people seem to believe in it."

"Feh! Millions, shmillions. That's what *they* say. It's a fraction of that, I'll bet."

"Well, it's soon going to be a fraction plus one. I'm a-goin' to church."

"You mean you're joining a cult."

"They call themselves a church. The government agrees."

Abe snorted. "Church smurch. We should listen to the government? Dormentalists give up control to their leaders; all decisions are made for them—how to think, what to believe, where to live, how to dress, what *country* even! With no responsibility there's no guilt, no outcome anxiety, so they feel a mindless sort of peace. That's a cult, and a cult is a cult no matter what the government says. If the Department of Agriculture called a bagel an apple, would that make it an apple? No. It would still be a bagel."

"But what do they believe?"

"Get yourself *The Book of Hokano* and read, bubbie, read. And trust me, with that in front of you, insomnia will be no worry."

"Yeah, well, I'll sleep even better if you find me a way to become a citizen again."

Impending fatherhood was doing a number on Jack's lifestyle, making him look for a way to return to aboveground life without attracting too much official attention. It wouldn't have been easy pre-9/11, but now . . . sheesh. If he couldn't provide a damn good explanation of his whereabouts for the last fifteen years, and why he wasn't on the Social Security roles or in the IRS data banks as ever filing a 1040, he'd be put under the Homeland Security microscope. He doubted his past could withstand that kind of scrutiny, and he didn't want to spend the rest of his life under observation.

Had to find another way. And the best idea seemed to be a new identity . . . become someone with a past.

"Any more from your guy in Europe?"

Abe had contacts all over the world. Someone in Eastern Europe had said he might be able to work out something—for a price, of course.

Abe shook his head. "Nothing definite. He's still working on it. Trust me, when I know, you'll know."

"Can't wait forever, Abe. The baby's due mid-March."

"I'll try to hurry him. I'm doing my best. You should know that."

Jack sighed. "Yeah. I do."

But the waiting, the dependence on a faceless contact, the frustration of not being able to fix this on his own . . . it ate at him.

He held up the book. "Got a bag?"

"What? Afraid people will think you're a Dormentalist?"

"You got it."

8

"Slow down, Vicky," Gia said. "Chew your food."

Vicky loved mussels in white wine and garlic sauce. She ate them with a gusto that warmed Jack's heart, scooping out the meat with her little fork, dipping it in the milky sauce, then popping it into her mouth. She ate quickly, methodically, and as she worked her way through the bowl she arranged her empty shells on the discard plate in her own fashion: inserting the latest into the previous, hinge first, creating a tight daisy chain of glistening black shells.

Her hair, braided into a French twist, was almost as dark as the shells; she had her mother's blue eyes and perfect skin, and had been nine years old for a whole two weeks now.

Every Sunday since his return from Florida, Jack had made a point of taking Gia and Vicky out for what he liked to think of as a family dinner. Tonight had been Vicky's turn to decide where they ate and, true to form, she chose Amalia's in Little Italy.

The tiny restaurant had occupied the same spot on Hester Street off Mulberry since shortly after the discovery of fire. It had gained the status of a Little Italy institution without becoming a tourist trap. The main reason for that was Mama Amalia, who decided who got seated and who didn't. No matter if a stranger had been waiting for an hour on a busy night, if she knew you from the neighborhood or as a regular, you got the next available table. Countless tourists had left in a huff.

Like Mama Amalia could care. She'd been running her place this way all her adult life. She wasn't about to change.

Mama had a thing for Vicky. The two had hit it off from the start and Mama always gave Vicky the royal treatment, including the traditional two-cheek air kiss she'd taught her, a big hug, and an extra cannoli for the trip home. The fact that her mother's last name was Di-Lauro didn't hurt.

The seating was family style, at long tables covered with red- and white-checkered cloths. With the crowd light tonight, Gia, Vicky, and Jack wound up with a table to themselves. Jack worked on his calamari fritti and a second Moretti while Gia picked at her sliced tomatoes and mozzarella. She and Vicky were splitting a bottle of Limonata. Normally Gia would have been sipping a glass of Pinot Grigio, but she'd sworn off alcohol as soon as she discovered she was pregnant.

"Not hungry?" Jack said, noticing that she'd only half finished her appetizer.

Gia had let her blond hair grow out a little but it was still short by most standards. She wore black slacks and a loose blue sweater. But even in a tight top he doubted anyone would know she was pregnant. Despite nearing the end of her fourth month, Gia was barely showing.

She shrugged. "Not particularly."

"Anything wrong?"

She hugged her arms against herself as she glanced at Vicky who was still absorbed in her mussels. "I just don't feel right."

Now that she'd said that, Jack noticed that she did look a little pale.

"A virus?"

"Maybe. I feel kind of crampy."

Jack felt a stab of pain in his own stomach.

"What kind of cramps?" He lowered his voice. "It's not the baby, is it?"

She shook her head. "No. Just . . . cramps. Only now and then, few and far between. Don't worry."

"Don't worry about what?" Vicky said, looking up from her mussel shell rosette.

"Mommy's not feeling so hot," Gia told her. "Remember how your stomach was upset last week? I think I may have it now."

Vicky had to think a moment, then said. "Oh, yeah. That was gross, but not too bad. You'll be okay if you drink Gatorade, Mom. Just like me."

She went back to arranging her shells.

A virus . . . Jack hoped that was all it was.

Gia grabbed his hand. "I see that look. Don't *worry,* okay? I just had my monthly checkup and Dr. Eagleton says everything's going fine."

"Hey, if she can't tell whether it's a boy or a girl yet, how do we know she—?"

Gia held up her hand in a traffic-cop move. "Don't go there. She delivered Vicky and she's been my gynecologist ever since. As far as I'm concerned she's the best OB on the planet."

"Okay, okay. It's just I worry, you know? I'm new to this whole thing."

She smiled. "I know. But by the time March rolls around, you'll be a pro."

Jack hoped so.

He poked at his calamari rings. He wasn't so hungry anymore.

Jack returned to his apartment after dropping off Vicky and Gia—who was feeling better—at their Sutton Square townhouse. He'd been carrying his .380 AMT Backup at the restaurant but wanted something a little more impressive along when he visited Cordova's place—just in case he got backed into a corner.

He wound through the Victorian oak furniture of his cluttered front room—Gia had once called it "claustrophobic," but she seemed used to it these days—and headed for the old fold-out secretary against the far wall. He occupied the third floor of a West Eighties brownstone that was much too small for all the neat stuff he'd accumulated over the years. He didn't know what he was going to do with it once he and Gia were married. It was a given that he'd move to Sutton Square, but what would happen to all this?

He'd worry about it when the time came.

He angled the secretary out from the wall and reached for the notch in the lower rear panel. His hand stopped just inches away. The hidden space behind the drawers held his weapons cache—and, since Florida, something else. That something else tended to make him a little queasy.

He pushed his hand forward and removed the panel. Hung on self-adhering hooks or jumbled on the floor of the space lay his collection of saps, knives, bullets, pistols. The latest addition was a souvenir from his Florida trip, a huge Ruger SuperRedhawk revolver chambered for .454 Casulls that would stop an elephant. Not many elephants around here, and the Ruger's nine-and-a-half-inch barrel made it impractical as a city carry, but he couldn't let it go.

Another thing in the hidden compartment he couldn't let go—or rather, wouldn't let go of him—was a flap of skin running maybe ten inches wide and twelve long. Another leftover from that same trip, it was all that remained of a strange old woman named Anya. Yeah, a woman with a dog, a heroic little chihuahua named Oyv.

He'd tried to rid himself of this grisly reminder of the horrors that had gone down in Florida, but it refused to go. He'd buried it once in Florida and twice again during the two months since he'd returned, but it wouldn't stay. By the time he got home it was already here, waiting for him. As little as a year ago he would have been shocked, repulsed, horrified, and questioning his sanity. Now . . . he simply went with it. He'd come to the gut-wrenching realization that he was no longer in control of his life. Sometimes he wondered if he'd ever been.

After the third try he'd given up on burying the skin. Anya had been much more than she'd let on. Her strange powers hadn't prevented her death, but apparently they stretched beyond the grave. For some reason she wanted him to have this piece of her and was giving him no choice about it. That being the case, he'd go with the flow, certain that sooner or later he'd find out why.

He unfolded the rectangle of skin, supple and fresh as new leather, showing not a trace of decomposition, and stared again at the bewildering pattern of pocked scars crisscrossed with the lines of fine, razor-thin cuts. It meant something, he was sure. But what?

Quarter folding it, he put it away and picked up his Glock 19. He checked the magazine—9mm Magsafe Defenders alternating with copper-jacketed Remingtons—then slammed it home and chambered a round. He changed into darker clothes and traded his loafers for black Thorogrip steel-toed boots. He already had the AMT strapped to his ankle. He slipped the Glock into a nylon small-of-the-back holster and was good to go.

10

Jack stood on Cordova's front porch and pulled on a pair of latex gloves. Last time he'd been here, the house had had no security system. But the owner had had a gun, and he'd taken a shot at Jack as he'd escaped across a neighboring roof. After Jack's break-in, chances were good Cordova had sprung for a home alarm.

He looked around the neighborhood. Nobody out and about. Sunday night and people were either asleep or watching the 11 o'clock news before heading for bed.

Williamsbridge sits in the upper Bronx—so far up that the subway lines run out of track and trestle just a couple of stops above it. Mostly a grid of old, post-war middle-class homes and row houses, the area has seen better days, but lots worse too. Crime here, they say, is on the wane, but Jack spotted a couple of guys dealing under the El as he drove along White Plains Road.

He'd cruised the main drag before hitting the house because he knew from the last time that Cordova liked to hang at a bar called Hurley's between 223rd and 224th.

He'd double-parked, popped in for a look around, spotted fatso stuffed into a booth at the rear, and left. He parked half a block down from Cordova's place. He'd brought the car because his plan was to rock the blackmailer's boat by stealing his files and his computer hard drive.

Cordova's house was older than his neighbors'. Clapboard siding with a front porch spanning the width of the house. Two windows to the left of the front door, two above the porch roof, and one more looking out of the attic.

Jack checked the porch windows. Alarm systems installed during construction could be hidden, but the retrofitted ones were easy to spot. He reached into the large duffel bag he'd brought along and pulled out a flashlight with duct tape across the upper half of the lens. He aimed it through one of the front windows across the parlor to another in the left wall of the room. No sign of magnetic contact switches. He angled the beam along the upper walls to the two corners within sight—no area sensors near the ceiling. At least none he could see.

Okay. He'd risk it.

He pulled out his latest toy, a pick gun. They came in electric and manual, to be sold to locksmiths only. Sure. Abe had let him try both last month. Jack had found he preferred the manual over the electric. He liked to fine-tune the tension bar, loved to feel the pins clicking into line.

He went to work. He hadn't had any trouble last time, even with his old pick set, so now—

Hell, it was the same lock. That set Jack on edge. Not a good sign. If Cordova wasn't going to spring for an alarm system, the least he could do was change the locks.

Unless . . .

The pins lined up quickly. Jack twisted the cylinder with the tension bar and heard the bolt slide back. He stepped inside with his duffel, holding his breath against the chance that he'd missed something. The first thing he did was search for a keypad. If anywhere it would be right next to the door. The wall was bare. Good sign.

He made a quick check of the room, especially along the wall-ceiling crease but found no sensors. He was struck—as he'd been the first time he'd been here—by how neat and clean everything was. For a fat slob, Cordova maintained a trim ship.

Jack waited, ready to duck back outside, but no alarm sounded. Could be a silent model, but he doubted it.

Okay, no time to waste. Last time he was here Cordova had surprised him by coming home early. Jack wanted to be gone ASAP.

Flashlight in hand he ran up to the third floor. He stopped on the threshold of the converted attic space where Cordova kept his computer and his files, the heart of his blackmail operation.

"Shit!"

The filing cabinet was gone, the computer desk stood empty. He checked the closet. Last time he'd been here it was a miniature darkroom. Still was, but no file cabinets.

This explained the lack of security. He'd moved his operation. And the most logical site for relocation was his office at the other end of the park.

Time to go for a ride.

11

The gold letters on the window heralded the second-floor tenant.

CORDOVA SECURITY CONSULTANTS
LTD.

Jack shook his head. *Ltd.* Who did he think he was going to impress with that? Especially when his *Ltd.*

was situated over a Tremont Avenue oriental deli with signs in English and Korean sharing space in its windows.

The inset door to the second floor lay to the left, sandwiched between the deli and a neighboring bakery. He walked past it twice, close enough to determine that it was secured with a standard pin and tumbler lock, and an old one to boot. He also noticed a little video lens pointed down at the two steps that led up to the door.

He hurried back to the car and pulled his camo boonie hat from the duffel, then returned to Tremont—officially East Tremont Avenue, but hardly anybody used the *East*—or the *Avenue*, for that matter.

Still a fair number of people on the sidewalks, even at this hour; mostly black and Hispanic. He waited till he had a decent window between strollers, then stepped up to the door, pick gun in hand. He kept his head down, letting the brim of the hat hide his face from the camera. Probability was ninety-nine percent that it was used to check on who wanted to be buzzed in and not connected to a recorder, but why take chances? He set to work on the lock. Took a whole five seconds to open it, and then he was in.

Atop the stairway he found a short hall. Two offices up here, Cordova's facing the street, the second toward the rear. He stepped up to the first door, an old wooden model that had been slathered with countless coats of paint over the years. An opaque pane of pebbled glass took up a good portion of the upper half. When Jack spotted the foil strip running around its perimeter, he knew where Cordova had stashed his dirt: right here.

Why pay for a security system at home when his office was alarmed?

But if this system was as antiquated as it appeared, Cordova was going to pay.

Oh, how he was going to pay.

But Jack needed to lay a little groundwork first. He'd tackle that tomorrow.

12

Back in his apartment, Jack thought about calling Gia to see how she was feeling, but figured she'd be asleep by now. He'd planned to watch a letterbox version of *Bad Day at Black Rock* in all its widescreen glory on his big TV—John Sturges and William Mellor knew how to stretch CinemaScope to the breaking point—but that would have to wait. *The Book of Hokano* was calling.

So Jack settled into his big recliner and opened the copy he'd picked up at Barnes & Noble. The two-inch spine was intimidating, but he opened it and began to read.

Abe hadn't been kidding: Dormentalism was a mishmash of half a dozen different religions, but the original parts were way over the top. And dull. *The Book of Hokano* made a civics textbook read like *The Godfather*.

He flipped through until he came to the appendices. Appendix A was called *The Pillars of Dormentalism*—a rip-off of the Pillars of Islam, maybe?

Looked like there were more than five. A lot more. Oh, goody.

He began to read . . .

First . . . there was the Presence and only the Presence.

The Presence created the World, and it was good.

The Presence created Man and Woman and made them sentient by endowing each with a xelton, a Fragment of Its Eternal Self.

In the beginning Man and Woman were immortal—neither the flesh of the body nor the xelton within sickened or aged.

But Man and Woman rebelled against the Presence by believing they were the true Lords of Creation. This so displeased the Presence that It sundered Creation, dividing it in half. The Presence erected the Wall of Worlds to separate this, the Home world, from its twin, the Hokano world.

These two parallel hemi-creations are mirrors of each other. Therefore each object in the Home world, living or inanimate, material or immaterial, has an exact counterpart in the Hokano world—separate but intimately linked.

When Creation was divided, so was each xelton. At first the halves remained linked across the Wall of Worlds, but through the millennia this link has stretched and attenuated as the xelton half within fell into a deep sleep. As a result, people on the Home side of the Wall are no longer aware of the existence of their xelton or their Hokano counterparts.

Another result of the Great Sundering was that human flesh was no longer immortal. It aged and decayed while the xelton within, being a fragment of the Presence itself, remained immortal. Each xelton passes through a succession of humans, being reborn immediately into a new body after an old one dies.

All the miseries that afflict humanity—war, pestilence, hunger, greed, hate, even death itself—are a direct result of our sleeping xelton and our loss of awareness and estrangement from our Hokano counterpart.

All the miseries that afflict humanity—war, pestilence, hunger, greed, hate, even death itself—can be conquered by awakening the inner xelton, reestablishing its contact with its Hokano counterpart, and fusing with it.

These Truths were unknown to Mankind until 1968 when they were revealed to Cooper Blascoe in the Black Rock desert of Nevada by a glowing Hokano traveler. The Hokano's name was Noomri and he was sacrificing his life by crossing the Wall of Worlds to bring the Good News to our side: All the Hokano people have awakened their xeltons and are anxiously awaiting contact from their counterparts in this world.

But Noomri said that strengthening contact across the Wall of Worlds requires effort on both sides. The Hokanos are alert and trying to fortify the links, but our Home world remains unaware. Without effort from our side, the links will remain attenuated.

Noomri revealed that there are ten levels of contact that if diligently pursued will result in fusion of the sundered xelton halves. The human hosting a fused xelton will experience wondrous benefits—success, happiness, long life, contentment, fulfillment, and seemingly magical powers.

But that is only a small part of the reward for fusion. Noomri foretold that once enough xeltons are reunited and fused with their missing half, once the two parts again become one, the Presence will be pleased and will remove the Wall of Worlds. Then will come the Great Fusion when the two halves of Creation will rejoin into an Eternal Paradise.

Noomri warned that those beings on either side, flesh and xelton alike, who have not yet rejoined with their Hokano counterpart by the time of the Great Fusion, will be blasted from existence and will not partake of the Eternal Paradise.

Noomri sadly added that over the millennia a certain number of xelton halves have deteriorated to a state from which they cannot be awakened. These unfortunate xeltons and the people housing them are called "nulls" and will never experience fusion. Noomri was a null, and since he would never see the Eternal Paradise, he was bravely sacrificing himself for his fellow Hokanos and the people of the Home world. His time was running out, for one cannot long survive after crossing the Wall of Worlds.

Before he burst into flame and died, Noomri begged Cooper Blascoe to carry his words to all the people of the Home side.

Cooper Blascoe has done exactly this, forsaking all his personal needs and goals to create the Dormentalist Church to carry out this sacred mission.

Jack slumped in the chair and slowly shook his head. How could people—tens, maybe hundreds of thousands of them—fall for this line of bull? It read like bad science fiction.

He knew he should read more but couldn't keep his eyes open.

Tomorrow . . . he'd try again tomorrow . . .

MONDAY

1

Jack awoke early on Halloween with vague memories of a dream about xeltons and Hokanos . . . all of whom bore strange resemblances to Abe and Mama Amalia.

He was heading for the door to grab a cup of coffee at the corner deli when his phone rang. The 305 area code on the caller ID told him who it was.

"Hey, Dad."

They'd been in touch almost weekly since their Florida escapade. The bond they'd forged then had not attenuated despite the months and miles since they'd last seen each other.

"Jack! I'd hoped to catch you before you went out."

"Good timing. Another thirty seconds and I'd have been gone. What's up?"

"I'm coming north to do some condo hunting next week."

"Oh? Where?"

Jack closed his eyes. Please don't say New York—*please* don't say New York.

As much as he enjoyed this renewed closeness with his dad, he did not want him living down the block, didn't want him in any of the five boroughs in fact. He was a good guy but he tended to be too curious about his younger son's lifestyle and how he earned his living.

"I was thinking of Trenton."

Jack pumped a fist. Yes!

"To be near Ron and the kids."

Ron Iverson was Jack's sister Kate's ex—but it hadn't been a rancorous divorce and Dad had stayed close to his grandkids, Kevin and Lizzie, all along. Even closer since Kate's death.

"You've got it. And it puts me just an hour away from the city via Amtrak." He cleared his throat. "Anyway, I've got to get cracking on finding a new place. The sale of the place down here closes in less than a month."

"The Tuesday before Thanksgiving, right?"

"Right. And I can't wait to get back."

Jack could hear the anticipation in his voice.

Dad added, "I thought maybe we could get together for dinner in Trenton. They've got some nice restaurants there. Kevin's away at college but Lizzie is still around. Maybe—"

"Might be better if you came up here, Dad. We've got the best restaurants in the world."

He didn't think he could bear spending hours at a table with Lizzie. Since Jack had been the last family member to see Kate alive, she'd have all sorts of questions about her mother, questions he couldn't answer honestly—for Kate's sake.

"You sound like you don't want to see Lizzie. You've never known her, Jack. She's a great kid and—"

"She'll remind me too much of Kate and I'm not ready for that. Not yet."

"Someday you'll tell me what happened to Kate up there, won't you."

"Someday, yeah. But I can only tell you what I know." Which was everything. "Call me when you're back in the good ol' Garden State and we'll set something up."

"Will do."

Jack hung up and let out a deep breath. Sometimes he got sick of lying. It wasn't so bad with strangers, but with family . . .

And on the subject of lying . . . he was going to have to do some to Jamie Grant. He wondered if she'd be in her office this early. Wouldn't hurt to try.

He'd realized from his stint with *The Book of Hokano* that it wasn't going to tell him about the inner workings of the Dormentalist Church. It was all doctrine. He needed someone who'd looked under the hood.

He still had his copy of *The Light* from yesterday, so he looked up the number again. He dug out a business card from the secretary's bottom drawer and dialed Grant on his Tracfone.

After working through the phone tree he heard that same gruff voice say, "Grant."

She was in. Did she sleep there?

Before she could hang up on him again he quickly explained that he was a private investigator who had been hired by the family of a missing Dormentalist to find their son.

Hey—not much of a lie. Almost true.

"Dormentalists go missing all the time," Grant said. "They get sent away on ML—that's 'Missionary Leave' to the uninitiated—and don't tell their families where they're going. Most of them pop up again a couple of years later."

"Most?"

"Some are never seen again."

"This woman's certain her son is still in New York. Said he was acting strange."

She snorted. "A Dormentalist acting strange—how ever could she tell?"

"She said he'd started wanting to be called by another name and—"

"Ah. That means he was getting into the top half of the FL situation."

"F—?"

"Fusion Ladder."

"Yeah, well, look. I think I'm going to have to go inside and I'd like to ask you a few questions about the organization first."

"What's in it for me?"

He'd figured it would come down to this.

"I'll feed you whatever I find inside. And if you want to know something specific, I'll do my best to run it down for you."

She didn't answer right away, but he could hear her puffing away on a cigarette.

Finally, "What's your name?"

Jack glanced at the business card: "John Robertson."

He'd met Robertson years ago and had not only saved his card, but printed out a few copies of his own with a business card program.

"You licensed?"

"Of course."

Well, the real John Robertson was. Sort of. He was dead now but Jack kept renewing his state private investigator's license.

"You'd better be, because I'm going to check on that. Show up here at noon. If you're legit, I'll tell the front desk to let you come up."

"Great. Thanks a—"

"You licensed to carry?"

He wasn't sure if the real Robertson was. "Why do you want to know?"

"Just fair warning: Leave the artillery home or else you're gonna have to answer a lot of questions when you set off the metal detector."

"Okay. Sure. Thanks."

Metal detector? Did newspapers now use metal detectors?

2

It was almost ten A.M. when Jack arrived at Russell Tuit's apartment. Jack had looked him up a few years ago—before his conviction—and had made the mistake of pronouncing his name *Too*-it. "Tweet," Russ had told him. "As in Tweety Bird."

"Hey, Jack," he said as he opened his door. Jack had called earlier, so Russ was expecting him. But apparently he wasn't expecting how Jack would be dressed. "Wow. Look at you. You didn't have to get all spiffed up for me."

Jack wore a blue blazer over gray slacks, a blue oxford shirt, and a striped tie—all for his meeting with Jamie Grant.

"Oh, hell! I didn't? You mean I could've worn jeans? Damn!"

Russ laughed. "Come on in."

His tiny two-room, third-floor apartment overlooked Second Avenue in the East Nineties. His five-story building looked like a converted tenement, wrought-iron fire escape and all. Even though the Tex-Mex bar and grill next door had yet to open for the day, his front room was redolent of grilled meat and mesquite smoke. Rumbling traffic from the street below provided subwoofer Muzak.

Russ himself was the quintessential computer geek: a pear-shaped guy in his early thirties, big head, short bed-head red hair, and a blackhead-studded forehead; he wore an *i-pipe* T-shirt, baggy jeans, and ratty flip-flops. Looked like he'd been designed by Gary Larson.

Jack glanced around the barely furnished front room and noticed a laptop on the desk in the far corner. He hadn't asked during their brief and intentionally oblique phone conversation, but he'd been sure Russ would have some sort of computer.

Jack nodded to it. "You're not worried your parole officer will drop by and see that?"

"No problem. My parole says I'm not to go online or consort with other hackers. But not to have a computer at all—that'd be cruel and unusual, man."

"Staying offline . . . knowing you, how're you going to survive twenty-five years of that?"

Russ had been caught hacking into a number of bank computers and coding them to transfer a fraction of a cent of each international transaction to his Swiss account. He'd been sitting back, collecting well into six figures a

year until someone got wise and sicced the Treasury Department's FinCEN unit on him. His lawyer pled him
down to two years of soft time in a fed pen but the judge
imposed a quarter-century ban on going online.

He offered a sickly grin. "Only twenty-two-point-
three-seven-six years to go." The grin brightened. "But
you've heard of cyber cafés, haven't you?"

"Yeah. You're not afraid they'll catch you?"

"I'm pretty sure they're monitoring my lines, but they
don't have the manpower to follow me every time I go out
for a cuppa." He rubbed his hands together. "So. Whatcha
got for me?"

"Well, it's what you're going to get for me."

"Long as it's not an online thing, I'll see what I can do."

"Okay. I need to find a way to erase a hard drive and
make it look like an accident."

Russ dropped into the swivel chair by his computer.
"Windows?"

Jack tried to envision the computer he'd seen in Cordova's attic back in September. It hadn't looked like a
Mac.

"Yeah. Pretty sure."

"Well, you could reformat it and reinstall Windows, but
that doesn't happen by accident. He'll know." He leaned
forward. "Why don't you tell me exactly what you want
done."

Jack hesitated on baring the specifics, then realized he
didn't have to.

"This guy's got certain files on his computer I want to
wipe out, but if just those files disappear, he'll know
who's behind it. So I want to wipe *all* his files."

"What about backups?"

"My gut tells me he stashes those someplace where,
say, a fire wouldn't hurt them."

Russ grinned. "And you want to follow him to the
backup."

"You got it."

Not exactly, but why waste time explaining it to someone who didn't need to know.

Russ thought a moment, then snapped his fingers. "Got it! HYRTBU!"

"Her taboo? I don't need voodoo, I—"

Russ laughed and spelled it for him. "It's a mischief virus. Deletes all kinds of files—docs, jpegs, waves, mpegs, gifs, pdfs, and just about every other suffix you've ever seen—without harming the programs. In fact, it doesn't just delete the files, it *overwrites* them."

Jack was relatively new to computers. He'd bought his first about a year ago and was still feeling his way.

"What's the difference?"

"When something is deleted, it's still there on the disk. You can't get to it through the operating system because its references are gone from the system tables, but it isn't *gone* until it's erased or overwritten with another file."

"But if you can't get to it—"

Russ was shaking his head. "You *can* get to it. All you need is a data recovery program, and there are dozens of them."

A scary thought, that.

"But HYRTBU overwrites every file and leaves a doc with the same name in its place."

"Doc?"

"Yeah. A document file, each with the same message: 'Hope You Remembered To Back Up!' Get it? It's an—"

"An acronym, yeah." Jack was baffled. "You mean someone sat down and spent all that time writing the code for this HYRTBU thing, just so he can screw up strangers' hard drives?" He shook his head. "Some people have way too much time on their hands."

"Guy probably justifies it by telling himself he's teaching his victims a valuable lesson: Always back up your files. I bet once you've been hit by HYRTBU you become a compulsive backer-upper."

"But still . . ."

"Hey, it's like Everest, man. You do it because it's there. Back when I was a kid, in my phreaking days, I used to break into the phone company's computers just to see if I could. And then I'd push it to see how far I could go, you know, seeking system mastery. Of course later I figured how to get myself free long distance, but that wasn't how it started."

"All right, Sir Hillary, how do we get HYRTBU into this computer?"

"Easiest way is to send it with an e-mail. Guy opens the attached file and, if he's doesn't have his AV setup to screen e-mail, *kablooey*—he's toast."

"Audio visual?"

"Antivirus software."

"I don't know the guy's e-mail address, don't even know if he goes online."

Russ looked glum. "Everybody goes online. Everybody but me." He sighed. "Well then, you've got to get to his computer and physically slip the virus into his system."

"I'm planning to visit his office."

"Perfect. What's his rig like? New? Old?"

"Unless he's replaced it, I'd say it has a few miles on it."

"Great. A floppy should do it. For a very reasonable fee I can put together a special boot disk that'll get you past any password and AV protection he's got and infect his hard drive."

"How reasonable?"

"How's a half K sound?"

"Sounds like a lot."

"Hey, I got expenses."

Jack made a show of looking around. "Yeah. I can see."

He spotted a variety of blank invoice forms on Russ's desk. He picked one up. *Yellow Pages* was printed across the top next to the walking-fingers logo in the upper-left corner.

"Oh, no. The invoice game?"

Russ shrugged. "Hey, I gotta make ends meet."

Phony invoices . . . a small-time, hit-or-miss scam. A guy like Russ would invoice medium-to large-size companies for services that hadn't been rendered. Unless someone was watchdogging it, more often than not the invoices got passed to the accounting or bookkeeping department where they were paid.

"You're on *parole,* Russ. You get caught, you're back inside, and most likely not in a country club like last time."

"Yeah, but they gotta catch me first. And then they gotta convict me. You see, nobody ever bothered to trademark 'Yellow Pages' or the walking fingers. They're public domain. Now, check out the lower-left corner."

Jack squinted at the tiny print. " 'This is a solicitation'?"

"Right. As long as I've got that there, I'm within the law—at least the letter of the law."

"So you go through the Yellow Pages and bill companies for their listings."

He grinned. "The bigger ones with the display ads are the best. They advertise in so many places they expect lots of invoices and don't look too closely. Works like a charm."

Jack tossed the invoice blank onto the desk and shook his head. "Still . . . you're on parole . . ."

"What else am I gonna do? I was a frosh at CCNY when I caught the hacking bug and dropped out. I know one thing, man, and I'm not allowed to use it. Shit, I'm not even allowed to work in Circuit City. And I need money for tuition."

"Tuition?"

"Yeah, I gotta look like I'm bettering myself, so I'm taking courses back at CCNY. Started as an English major, so I figure I'll go back to that, look like I'm trying for a degree. Makes my parole officer happy, at least."

"But not you."

He shook his head. "Taking a lit course. Now I know why I dropped out. Prof's got us wasting our time reading Marcel Marceau."

Jack blinked. "Um, Marcel Marceau was a mime. A man of few words, you might say."

"Well, then, Marcel somebody. Long-winded guy—zillions of words about nothing. The most boring shit you've ever read." He shook his head again. "My life sucks."

"If you're trying to break my heart, it worked. Five hundred for the disk. Half down, half when I know it did the job."

Russ's face broke open with a big grin. "I'll have it for you tonight. Jack, you just made my day!"

Deadpan, Jack reached for his wallet. "That's me. Jackie Sunshine. It's what I'm about. I live for moments like this."

Jack didn't feel completely naked walking through town without at least one weapon hidden somewhere on his person, merely stripped to his underwear. At the stroke of noon he arrived at *The Light* offices, just west of Times Square. A peek through the glass doors of the front entrance made him glad he wasn't carrying. Jamie Grant hadn't been kidding: An armed guard and a metal detector waited just inside.

After confirming that John Robertson was expected, the guard passed him through the detector without a hitch. He was told to wait until someone from editorial came to escort him up.

Soon a heavyset woman with short, curly ginger hair and a puffy face showed up and extended her hand. Jack immediately recognized the voice.

"Robertson? Jamie Grant."

As they shook hands, Jack checked her out: Early forties, about five- five, a large chest and bulky torso but thin arms and legs. She wore a loose white blouse over dark brown slacks. Small gold earrings, thin gold necklace, no rings. Her eyes were bloodshot and she smelled like an ashtray. Other than that she was a dream girl.

"Thanks for meeting me." He handed her one of the Robertson cards, then jerked a thumb at the metal detector. "I'd thought you might be kidding. Why the high security?"

"It's new. We've got an ongoing threat situation here. *The Light* pisses off a lot of people, so we're always getting one kind of threat or another. But nothing like what's come in since my Dormentalism article." She flashed a nicotine-stained smile. "I now hold the death-threat record. Hallelujah." She turned and motioned him to follow. "Let's retire to my boudoir."

She led him to a messy little third-floor office that looked like it had been trashed by burglars on PCP. Books, magazines, newspapers, printouts everywhere. As she lifted an elastic-bound pile of papers off a chair, Jack noticed that her right pinkie was only a stub—the last two bones were missing.

She dropped the papers on the floor. "Have a seat."

Grant plopped into the chair behind her littered desk and lit a cigarette. Jack noticed how the skin on her right index and middle fingers was the color of rotten lemon rind, but then his gaze drifted again to the pinkie stub. On the way in he'd seen one of those *This Is a No Smoking Building* signs but didn't bother to mention it now. He couldn't imagine her caring.

"So," she said, leaning back and blowing a long stream into the air, "you say you're on the trail of a missing Dementedist."

Without using names, Jack went over everything Maria Roselli had told him about Johnny.

Her smile was wry as she shook her head. "And you think you're going to find sonny boy by joining the church? Forget it—unless of course you're willing to spend lots of years and lots of bucks."

"How so?"

"You'll enter as an RC, the lowest of the low, and you'll have to climb pretty far up the FL before you can get close enough to the TO to sneak a peek at any membership files."

Jack twisted a finger into his right ear. "I thought we were speaking English here."

Grant laughed. "Dormentalese. They use initials for everything. I'll translate: You'll enter as a Reveille Candidate, and you'll have to climb a good way up the Fusion Ladder before you can get close enough to the Temple Overseer."

Jack realized he had more to learn than he'd thought.

"And the 'lots of bucks'?"

"This is what you've got to realize about the Dementedist situation: The church is set up to squeeze every last dollar from its members. They promise self-realization, maximization of potential—the goals of a million self-help books—but they go beyond that. At the end of their rainbow is a supernatural pot of gold. But there's one major catch: You can't do it alone. You need to become a member of the Church, you need Dementedist guides to help you along the ten rungs of the ladder to 'Full Fusion.'"

"That would be FF, I assume?"

"Keerect. The Fusion Ladder—that's the steps it takes to fuse your xelton with its Hokano counterpart—started out with five rungs, then it went to seven, now it's ten. The instruction sessions, the books, the tapes, and all the other paraphernalia for each new rung cost more than the last. The FAs—that's Fusion Aspirants—are promised increasing powers as they advance along the FL. And then there's the big carrot of Full Fusion where you're promised to be transformed into some sort of demigod."

"Able to leap tall buildings in a single bound?"

"Pretty much. But Dementedism differs from most religions in one important respect: Yeah, it offers everlasting happiness, but it has no good and evil, no good god versus bad god, no Jesus and Satan, no yin and yang. You've been separated from your Hokano xelton, so you can't expect perfection. If you've failed in the past, it's not your fault. All you need do is weather the long process of fusing the two halves of your xelton and your problems will be over. You'll go from homo sap to homo superior."

" 'Not your fault.' I can see how that would go over big."

"Yeah, the everyone-is-a-victim zeitgeist has swelled their ranks. But it can cost you about a quarter mil before you're through. To reach the High Council you've got to achieve the tenth level of fusion . . . hardly anyone gets past the eighth unless they're very rich, very determined, and more than a little crazy. Members get so wrapped up in the FL situation they take out second and third mortgages on their homes to finance the climb. The ones who don't have any assets either go out and recruit new members or mortgage themselves to the church as volunteers."

"What does that do for them?"

"Helps them pay the fees for their current FL rung. But they receive discounts instead of cash. They also get discounts for every new member they bring in."

"Sounds like a Ponzi scheme, or multilevel marketing."

Jamie nodded. "Amway as religion. Headhunters and staff workers paid in a currency not subject to withholding, Social Security, or Medicare deductions."

"Nice."

"But there's a more sinister side to it. Not only does this serfdom situation keep you in almost constant contact with other Dementedists—thereby reducing exposure to conflicting opinions—but the church works the volunteers till they drop, knowing full well that exhaustion makes people more susceptible to suggestion."

"They sound like swell folks. Is that why you're after them?"

Jack saw Grant stiffen. He sensed a door slamming closed.

"Is this conversation about Dementedism or me?"

"Demen—Dormentalism, of course, but I was just—"

"Just nothing! None of this is about me! And I swear, if they sent you here on a fishing expedition—"

Whoa, Jack thought. I do believe I've touched a nerve.

He held up his hands. "Hey, hey, easy. I'm not after you and I'm not after Dormentalism. I just want to find sonny boy."

She seemed to relax, but just a little. Jack realized she was stretched tight. Scared.

"Sorry for sounding paranoid, but you don't know what it's been like since that article came out. Phone calls—I had to change my home number—threats, lawsuits, people following me, every type of harassment you can imagine."

"You're not paranoid if they're really after you."

"Oh, they are. When I applied for membership I gave a phony name and address. Didn't take long before they found out. They designated me UP—that's Unwelcome Person—and kicked me out. But with that article I graduated to what's known as a Wall Addict—"

"That would be a WA?"

"Right. But I'm not just a WA, I'm also IS—In Season. That's an 'enemy of the Church' and fair game for all their smear tactics. They use character assassination to try to discredit you privately and professionally, and they're ruthless. And now I hear that some person or persons unknown have been prying into my personal situation—financials, past relationships, hell, even the movies I rent. That's why you see so few investigative pieces on Dementedism. Reporters and editors are afraid of the shit storms that follow."

"But not *The Light*."

She allowed a tight little smile. "No. Not *The Light*. That's why I stick with the small-time weekly—formerly small-time, I should say. Those exclusives we had on the Savior last June bumped our circulation and it's stayed up."

Jack wondered what she'd do if she knew she was talking to the so-called Savior.

"I've had offers from every other paper in town, plus the *Washington Post* and *Times,* even the *San Francisco Chronicle,* but this is where I stay. And you know why? Because *The Light* isn't afraid of anyone. It's not in the pocket of some larger corporation that's always trying to cover its ass. George Meschke's a tough son of a bitch of an editor, but he's fearless. Oh, he makes damn sure you've got your facts straight and your sources lined up, but if that's all copacetic, then he goes to press."

"He still behind you after the suits and threats?"

She nodded. "He's a human bulldog. He doesn't let go." She pointed at Jack and he noticed how her pinkie stuck up. "But you—" She must have spotted his stare; she pointed the stub straight at him. "Can't keep your eyes off it, can you. I'll answer your unasked question: boating accident eight years ago. Outboard propeller. Satisfied?"

"Hey, I wasn't—"

"Yeah, sure." She switched to her index finger as a pointer. "Anyway, I've got George and the paper to watch my back, but you're just one guy. For your own good, my advice is stay away."

"Can't do that."

"Listen, I told you: You're not going to find anything, and you risk making nasty enemies."

"Wouldn't be the first time. I've managed to tick off a few people in my day."

"Not like these, you haven't. These aren't just a bunch of kooks—kooks believe their nonsense, charlatans don't. Bottom-rung, true-believer Dementedists qualify as kooks, but the charlatans at the top have got tons of money, a shark tank full of lawyers, and a huge number of volunteers who will be only too glad to ruin your career, your reputation, even your marriage—if you're married. They're tenacious, relentless, vicious. Have you got a life situation that will stand up to a gang of pros and amateurs peeking into every corner of it?"

Got to find me first, Jack thought.

But the idea of a well-financed horde prying at his life, uncovering his secrets—he had so many—made him edgy. More than edgy . . .

"That would make me very upset," he told her.

Something in his tone must have caught her attention. She stared at him for a long moment.

"Are you saying you're not a nice person when you're upset?"

"I'm saying I'd appreciate it if you'd tell me the mistakes you made that got you kicked out."

She lit another cigarette. "Are you fucking deaf? I'm telling you, you can't move high enough up the ladder to get access to membership records."

"I think I might have a way to, shall we say, accelerate my progress."

Her eyes narrowed. "How?"

Jack wagged a finger at her. "Trade secret."

Her face darkened. "After all I've just given you?"

"You tell me what you know and what I should avoid, and when this is all over I'll tell you how I got in, what I saw, and what I learned—just you."

"An exclusive," she said, leaning back. "Maybe."

That surprised Jack.

"Maybe? You've got something better?"

A little cat smile here. "Maybe . . . maybe a *lot* better." The smile faded. "And maybe not. Okay. I'll trust you—to an extent. I can tell you that the intake procedure is pretty straightforward: Just fill out the forms."

"A church has forms?"

"It's only legally a church. In real life it's a closely held corporation with a CEO and a board of directors, although they don't call themselves that. I've poked at many religions and cults, but no one's come after me like the Dementedist Church. That's because it's not a church, it's a for-profit behemoth."

"I've gathered that. But do they ID you on day one?"

"No. You don't have to show ID then and there—that

would create a cloud in the relentlessly sunny atmosphere they like to present—but they'll run a background check on you within a day or two. That's how I got caught. After filling out the forms—one of those, believe it or not, is an NDA—"

"More Dormentalese?"

"No. That's a common business practice—a non-disclosure agreement. After signing that you'll be asked, very pointedly, to make a donation to the temple and pay for your first Reveille Session in advance."

"What happens there?"

"The supposed purpose of Reveille is to wake up your sleeping xelton so you can start the fusion process. It's really a cover for the RT—Reveille Tech—to pry out the most intimate details of your life. These go into a file that will be used against you should you turn against the church."

"That's it? We sit and play Q and A?"

Grant gave him the full smile this time, stained teeth and all. "Oh, no. There's so much more to it than that."

"Like what?"

"You'll see, you'll see."

Jack wasn't sure he liked the way she said it.

She reached into a drawer and took out a couple of sheets of paper.

"Take a look at these," she said, handing them across. "It's a list of the Dementedist hierarchy and all their abbreviations. Some are my work, some come right out of the church bulletins and newsletters. I've stuck in a few comments here and there."

Jack took the sheets and scanned them.

Cooper Blascoe—Prime Dormentalist (PD)
Luther Brady—Supreme Overseer (SO) and APD (Acting PD)
High Council (HC)
Grand Paladin (GP)

President of the Council of Continental Overseers
(PCCO)
Continental Overseer (CO)
Regional Overseer (RO)
Temple Overseer (TO)
Temple Paladin (TP)
Fusion Aspirant (FA)
Fusion Initiate (FI)
Reveille Candidate (RC)
Null (N)
NB:Cooper Blascoe was the first PD with Luther Brady
as his SO. When Blascoe went into suspended anima-
tion, Brady took over PD duties while retaining the SO
position.

Jack looked up. "Oh, yeah. I meant to ask about this
suspended animation thing. What's up with that?"

"He was in such close contact with his xelton that he's
immortal, and put himself into a state of suspended animation to await the Great Fusion."

"No, really."

"You're a big boy: Read between the lines."

Jack shrugged. "He's dead, right?"

"He was on in years. You can't have the founder of an
apocalyptic cult die before the apocalypse. So he doesn't
die, he goes into suspended animation to wait for it."

"In Tahiti?"

"That was where he was living. Probably where he's
buried."

Jack sensed a lack of conviction on her part.

"What's a paladin?"

"Security." Grant jetted a stream of smoke from the
corner of her mouth. "Think of them as the Dementedist
KGB. The Grand Paladin's name is Jensen; he's their
Beria."

"Sounds ominous."

"He is."

Jack read on.

Other Designations:

Fusion Ladder (FL)—The progressive steps ascending toward FF.

Fusion Aspirant (FA)—One who has passed through the FI stage and has started to ascend the FL.

Full Fusion (FF)—One who has ascended the FL all the way to the top and achieved complete fusion of both xelton halves.

Null (N)—A member of the unfortunate 7.5 percent of humanity who houses a xelton that cannot be awakened. A certain number of FAs do not learn until they are far along the FL that they are nulls and have been experiencing SF.

Sham Fusion (SF)—When a null FA's desire for fusion is so great that they enter a state of denial, believing they are achieving levels of fusion when they are not. This is a tragic occurrence.

Xelton Name (XN)—When the FA reaches the fifth level, his TO will be able to discern the name of his or her xelton. The name always contains a double-o.

Lapsed Fusion Aspirant (LFA) (unofficially called a "lapser")—An FA who progresses well, then exhibits sudden LFP (see below) tendencies. A meeting with the local temple's Fusion Progress Review Board (FPRB) is mandatory; punishment must be accepted or the LFA will be designated DD.

Low Fusion Potential (LFP)—This can be anyone deemed too skeptical, too questioning, not accepting enough. Although it's highly unlikely they'll ever achieve FF, they are allowed to take the courses but are closely monitored.

Wall Drone (WD)—Most of humanity. They are content to allow things to remain as they are. They aspire to nothing better than their present circumstances. It is the Church's mission to win them over to Dormentalism so that they may proceed with the fusion of their xelton with its Hokano counterpart.

Unwelcome Person (UP)—Anyone who unintentionally

causes ripples in the tranquil pool of Dormentalism. These are often people with disruptive personalities incompatible with the Church's goals.

Detached Dormentalist (DD)—LFAs who have become too frustrated or have lost their direction and refuse to accept their punishment from their FPRB. They are banned from all temples and no Dormentalist is allowed any contact whatsoever with them. The DD has a high potential of becoming a WA.

Wall Addict (WA)—The greatest threat to Dormentalism: These are ruthless, disturbed persons who, for whatever reason, want the Home and Hokano worlds to remain separate. They infiltrate and attempt to interfere with, undermine, and sabotage the Church's mission to break down the Wall of Worlds. They act as roadblocks on the path to maximal human potential and should be treated as enemies of humanity.

Negative Null (NN)—A WA subset; as a rule, nulls are to be pitied, but there are some nulls who, out of spite, envy, or resentment, try to undo the Church's work.

In Season (IS)—A WA, DD, or NN who poses such a threat to the Church that they must be brought down by any means necessary—lawsuits, character assassination, wiretapping, physical and mental harassment, the works.

Jack shook his head in amazement. "These folks are crazier than I ever dreamed."

"Just don't confuse crazy with stupid. Look how they've covered their asses with the Null category. If someone spends a small fortune going through a whole bunch of rungs on the FL and still isn't finding any new powers, he must be a Null. But no way he gets his money back."

"I think I'll designate myself LFP now, just to save them the trouble."

Grant's laugh broke up into a phlegmy cough.

He glanced at the two sheets again. This would save him hours and hours of reading.

"Can I have a copy?"

Controlling her cough she waved at him. "Take it. I've got it filed on my computer."

"One more thing," Jack said. "You mentioned you might have a better source. Mind telling me who that might be? Once inside, maybe I can—"

"Forget it. That's my exclusive. And believe me, it just might overturn the Dementedist rock and shine a— you'll pardon the expression—*light* on all the slimy things beneath."

Jack watched her. What—or rather, *who*—was she hiding?

"You told me *The Light* isn't afraid of anyone. How about you? These Dormentalists scare you?"

"Shit, yes. But that doesn't mean they're going to stop me. Installment two hits the stands next Wednesday."

Jack smiled and nodded. "Good for you."

This Jamie Grant was one tough broad. He liked her.

4

Jack left *The Light* and turned east, heading for Lexington Avenue. He put in a call to Ernie as he walked.

"It's me," he said when Ernie answered. "My shipment ready for pickup?"

"Not yet, sir. I have confirmation that it's in transit, if you know what I'm sayin', but it ain't here yet. I expect it tomorrow."

"What's the holdup?"

"Well, sir, this item was pretty freakin' hard to find and

took longer to track down than I originally thought. Plus it's real delicate, so the packin' has to be perfect, if you know what I'm sayin'."

Jack knew what he was saying. "Let's hope it's worth the wait."

"Oh, it is, sir. Some of my best work." Ernie's voice took on a gleeful tone. "You might even say it's a, whatchacallit, work of art. Yeah. A work of art, if you know what I'm sayin'. Should be ready first thing in the morning."

Jack kept walking toward Lexington. From what Jamie Grant had told him, he wouldn't need a full set of ID when he signed up. Might as well get the intake process out of the way so he could set up his first Reveille Session for tomorrow.

He remembered Grant's vaguely malicious grin when she'd mentioned the Reveille Session. What was he getting into?

5

When Jack arrived at the Manhattan Dormentalist temple, he had to admit it was pretty impressive: twenty-plus stories of red brick and white corner blocks, with setbacks at the tenth and twentieth floors. And spotless. Looked like it had been scrubbed with a toothbrush. No New York City building had a right to be so clean.

According to Grant's article, the Dormentalist Church owned and occupied the whole thing.

As he approached the arched entrance he saw a group of half a dozen people, four men and two women, exiting onto the sidewalk. All wore steel gray double-breasted jackets buttoned all the way up to their high military collars. Two of the jackets sported braided fronts.

Jack occasionally had seen similar uniforms on the subway and around the city, but hadn't connected them with Dormentalism. As the group approached he considered asking them whether they were going for the Sergeant Pepper or the Michael Jackson look, but decided against it. He simply nodded and they smiled back and wished him a good afternoon.

Such happy people.

He stepped through the etched glass front doors and stuttered a step when he saw the metal detector. Another one? Why hadn't Grant mentioned it? Not that it mattered; he was still unarmed.

The detector stood to the left; to his right was a turnstile. A smiling, young, uniformed woman stood behind a barrier table between them.

Jack opted for the turnstile but the young woman called to him.

"Sir? May I see you over here?"

As he turned and approached her, Jack put on an uncertain expression that was only partially feigned.

"This is, um, my first time here and . . ."

She beamed at him. "I could tell. My name is Christy. Welcome to the New York temple of the Dormentalist Church."

Jack detected an uppercase *C* in her tone.

Christy wore her dark hair long and couldn't have been much past twenty. A college girl, maybe? She had three braids across the front of her jacket. She also had circles under her eyes. Looked tired. Probably one of the volunteers Grant had told him about.

"How may I help you?" she said.

"Well, I'm interested in, um, joining the Church, or at least looking into it, and—"

"Were you at the rally yesterday?"

"Rally?"

"Sure. In Central Park. We were there to spread the word."

Jack remembered passing a cheering group on his way to Maria Roselli's.

"Oh, yes. I heard some things that interested me and I . . ." He pointed to the metal detector. "Why's *that* here?"

Her smile held. "Just a necessary precaution in this world of terrorists and fanatics from other religions who feel threatened by the miraculous spread of Dormentalism."

Jack wondered how long it had taken her to memorize that.

"Oh. I see."

"If you'll just put your keys and change into this little bowl—just like at the airport—I'll clear you through."

Just like the airport . . . Jack's last airport experience had had a few shaky moments. But he expected none here.

As he emptied his pockets, he looked beyond her and saw other gray uniformed people of all ages bustling around the two-story lobby—

Lobby . . . right. That was what it was. This place hadn't been built as a church or temple; it looked like a hotel. A balcony ran along the rear wall. A closer look revealed a lot of old Art Deco touches still hanging on; enough so you might expect to see George Raft or William Powell hanging out near the registration desk.

Instead, with all these uniforms passing back and forth, he felt as if he'd wandered into a Trekkie convention.

"Do you wear the uniforms all the time?"

"Oh, no sir. Only in the temple—and traveling to and from, of course."

"Of course."

He saw a uniformed woman enter and walk to the turnstile. She swiped a card through a slot, waited a couple of seconds, then pushed through.

Jack put on a smile. "You take MetroCard here?"

Christy giggled. "Oh, no. After you reach a certain

level, you get a swipe card that's coded into our computers. See that Temple Paladin over there?"

Jack spotted a burly man seated in a kiosk a dozen feet away. His jacket was like Christy's but deep red, almost purple.

"When you use the card your face pops up on his screen and he lets you through." She smiled apologetically at Jack. "But newcomers like you, I'm afraid, have to go through here."

For the second time in as many hours Jack stepped through a metal detector. As he retrieved his change and watch, Christy picked up a phone and mumbled something into it. She hung up and grinned.

"Someone will be here soon to escort you to one of the interview rooms."

"Who?"

"Atoor."

She said it the way some women still said "Bill Clinton."

6

A few minutes later a good-looking guy, maybe thirty, approached and extended his hand.

"Welcome to our Church," he said, smiling like everyone else Jack had seen. "I'm Atoor and I'll guide you through the introductory phase."

Jack shook the guy's hand. "Jack. Jack Farrell. Pardon me, but did you say your name was Atoor?"

"It's my xelton's name."

"He's Fifth Rung," Christy said, beaming up at him with a gaga look. "He has *powers*."

Atoor had a good build, brush-cut blond hair, a

fresh-scrubbed face, and an air of confidence and seren-
ity. If he had any *powers,* they weren't showing. But he
made an excellent poster boy for Dormentalism.

Christy gave Jack a friendly little wave. "Bye."

"Live long and prosper," Jack said.

Atoor led the way toward the left rear of the lobby.
"What brings you to our Church?"

Jack had been expecting this. On the way over he'd re-
hearsed a mixture of fact and fabrication.

"Well, I was raised Presbyterian but that never gave me
what I needed. I've tried a number of things but I still feel
walled in, like I'm marking time, not going anywhere. I
think there's more to me than what I've seen so far. I'd
like to open myself up and, you know, achieve my full
potential."

Atoor's smile widened. "Then you've come to the right
place. You've just made a decision that will change your
life forever—and only for the better. You'll be more ful-
filled, more satisfied, even healthier than you've ever been.
You're taking the first step toward unlimited potential."

Jack couldn't detect a single false note. A true believer.

"I hope so. I've tried Transcendental Meditation and
Buddhism, even Scientology, but none of them lived up to
their promises. Then I read *The Book of Hokano* and . . ."

"And lightning struck, right? That's what happened to
me. I read it and thought *here* is the answer I've been
looking for."

"But I've got questions . . ."

"Of course you do. *The Book* is confusing to those who
have a dormant xelton. But once it is awakened and
you've started the ladder toward fusion, it all becomes
crystal clear."

"I can hardly wait."

Atoor led him down a short hall, then ushered him into
a small office furnished with a three-drawer file cabinet
and two chairs flanking a small table. He closed the door
and directed Jack to a seat while he pulled a folder from
the filing cabinet. Seating himself opposite Jack, he

opened the folder and pushed it across the table.

"Okay, Jack. The first step is for you to tell us about yourself."

Nice way of saying, Fill out these application forms so we can get the lowdown on you.

Jack looked down at the forms and frowned. "I have to *apply* to join the church?"

A laugh. "Oh, no. It's just that the better the Church knows who you are, what your life is like, what your goals are, the better we can help you. We don't want people coming to us with unrealistic goals and then leaving disgruntled because we couldn't achieve the impossible."

Sounded good, but if "the Church" was already promising the sun and moon and stars, was any goal out of reach? He wondered how many were turned away for any reason.

But Jack said nothing. He wasn't here to make waves.

As Atoor watched, Jack filled in the blanks with mostly phony information. He wasn't surprised to see a box for his Social Security number—tracking down members' financial data was probably routine. He made up a number and stuck it in. The only true data was his Tracfone number.

He finished up, leaving only one box blank. Atoor tapped it with a finger.

"Did anyone refer you?"

"No. I don't know any Dormentalists."

"Well, then, might as well stick my name in there—just so all the blanks are filled."

Jack glanced up and caught a hint of hunger in Atoor's eyes. He wanted the headhunter discount.

"Should I put in your real name?"

"Atoor *is* my real name now. When you reach the Fifth Rung you learn your xelton's name and can choose to use it or not." Pride filled his voice. "I choose to use it."

Jack remembered how Maria Roselli had said that her Johnny now wanted to be called Oroont. Must have reached the Fifth Rung.

He glanced at Atoor and couldn't resist. "I can't wait

till *I* reach the Fifth Rung. I'm going to name my xelton Pazuzu."

Atoor, though still smiling, looked scandalized. "You can't *name* your xelton. It has its *own* name."

Jack shrugged. "Well then, I'll rename it."

"That . . . that isn't possible." Atoor looked like he was having a real hard time holding that smile. "Your xelton isn't some sort of pet. It's had its name for billions of years, since the beginning of time. You can't just up and change it."

"No?" Jack put on a hurt expression. "I really like the name Pazuzu." Then he brightened. "Maybe its name really *is* Pazuzu!"

"Highly unlikely. How is it spelled?"

Jack spelled it for him.

Atoor shook his head. "All xelton names have a double *O*."

"Well, maybe we could compromise and spell it with double *O*'s instead of *U*'s. You know, *Pa-zoo-zoo*?" He glanced at Atoor's strained but still smiling face. "Or maybe not."

Jack asked Atoor to spell his name, then printed it in the referral box. That form was snatched away to be replaced by another.

"And here is a simple nondisclosure agreement."

"Why . . . whatever for?"

"The Church has enemies and at this point you are an unknown quantity, so we must ask you to agree not to reveal anything of what you see, hear, or learn here. Even though you might have good intentions, your words could be taken and twisted and used against us."

Jack had to ask: "Who are you afraid of?"

Atoor's expression darkened. "Just like any movement that seeks the betterment of mankind, Dormentalism has fierce enemies in the outside world. Enemies who, for their own selfish reasons, want to keep humanity from bettering itself and reaching its full potential. A man or woman who has reached Full Fusion bows to no one. And that terrifies the oppressors of the world."

Good speech, Jack thought as he signed the form.

Jack Farrell would not disclose a thing.

He let himself be talked into donating five hundred dollars to the church and paying another five hundred in advance for his first five Reveille Sessions. Atoor was a little taken aback when Jack pulled out a roll of bills.

"We'd prefer a check or credit card."

I'm sure you would, Jack thought.

"I don't believe in them."

Atoor blinked. "But we're not set up to take cash, or make change . . ."

"Cash or nothing," Jack said, sliding one of the Roselli thousand-dollar bills across the table. "I'm sure you can find a way to handle this. No change necessary. All I need is a receipt."

Atoor nodded and took the bill. After some fumbling around in a drawer he found a receipt book. A few minutes later Jack had his receipt and his appointment for his first Reveille Session at ten tomorrow morning.

Atoor glanced at his watch. "Almost time for the afternoon AR."

"The what?"

"Affirmation Recital. You'll see." Atoor rose and motioned Jack to follow him. "Come on. You'll love this."

He led Jack back to the lobby where a couple of hundred Dormentalists, uniformed in an assortment of hues, had gathered. They all stood facing a man in a sky blue uniform on the balcony.

"That's Oodara, the TO," Atoor whispered. Before Jack could ask, he added, "The Temple Overseer."

"But what—?"

"Here we go." His eyes were alive with anticipation.

"*First*," Oodara the TO intoned into a microphone, "*there was the Presence and only the Presence.*"

Jack jumped as hundreds of fists shot into the air and

an equal number of voices shouted, "IT IS TRUTH!"

"The Presence created the World, and it was good."

Again the fists and the shout. "IT IS TRUTH!"

"The Presence created Man and Woman and made them sentient by endowing each with a xelton, a Fragment of Its Eternal Self."

Atoor nodded, and smiled and nudged Jack's right arm upward. "IT IS TRUTH!"

Jack closed his eyes. Don't tell me they're going to run through all the Pillars of Dormentalism. Please don't.

"In the beginning Man and Woman were immortal . . ."

Yep. That was exactly what they were doing. He fought the desire to run screaming for the street. He was supposed to be a Dormentalist wannabe and had to act the part. So he clenched his teeth and, when it was time for the next response, pumped his fist and shouted with the best of them.

It went on forever.

". . . forsaking all his personal needs and goals to create the Dormentalist Church to carry out this sacred mission."

"IT IS TRUTH!"

Then everyone started clapping and cheering.

Was it over? Yes. Finally.

Atoor slapped him on the back. "Wasn't that wonderful? Wasn't it inspiring?"

Jack grinned. "I can't tell you how much I enjoyed myself. How often do you have these, um, ARs?"

"Only twice a day. I wish it were more."

"More would be overwhelming, don't you think? I don't know if I could take it."

"We're going to be filming one of our ARs, you know, so Dormentalist shut-ins won't feel left out."

"Really? Too bad LR isn't alive to direct it."

Atoor's brow furrowed. "LR?"

"Leni Riefenstahl. She'd be perfect."

"I don't think I've ever—"

"Never mind. Doesn't matter."

A minute later Jack was trucking for the door. On the way out he waved bye-bye to the ever effervescent Christy.

He started humming the refrain from Richie Haven's "Freedom" as he stepped back onto the sidewalk.

Okay, check off Step One on the Dormentalist front. As for Sister Maggie's problem . . .

Before leaving home this morning he'd looked up the number of Cordova Security Consultants, Ltd. He now punched it into his cell phone as he walked up Lexington.

A woman answered. When Jack asked for Mr. Cordova he was told that he was in, but with a client. Could she take a message? Jack asked if he could have an appointment later this afternoon. No, sorry, Mr. Cordova was leaving soon. Would he like an appointment tomorrow? Jack said he'd call back later.

Perfect. Now home for a quick change, a little makeup, and a hustle to the Bronx.

7

" 'Of all these people, the Belgae are the . . . the most courageous because they are far . . . farthest removed from the . . . ' "

Sister Maggie suppressed the urge to translate the difficult word for the little girl, opting instead for simple encouragement.

"Keep going, Fina. You've got it so far."

Big brown eyes glanced up at her, then refocused on the text.

" 'Farthest removed from the . . . the culture and civilization of the Province.' "

"That's wonderful! You are *so* good at this."

And she was. Little Serafina Martinez might be only

nine but she was already reading from Caesar's *Gallic Wars*—not fluently, of course, but her grasp of Latin vocabulary and sentence structure was beyond anything Maggie had ever seen in someone her age. Knowing how to speak Spanish didn't hurt, but still . . .

And language wasn't Fina's only strong point. She was a whiz in math too, already doing simple algebraic equations.

No question about it: This girl was the brightest child Maggie had encountered in nearly twenty years of teaching. Best of all was her hunger to learn. Her brain was a sponge, sucking up everything that came within reach. The child actually looked forward to her thrice-weekly after-school sessions with Maggie.

"I think that's enough for today, Fina. You did great. Pack up your things."

She watched Fina stow her Latin book in an oversized, overstuffed backpack that must have weighed as much as she. Well, perhaps not that much. Fina still had her baby fat, but less of it this year than last. And were those budding breasts beginning to swell beneath the top of her plaid uniform jumper?

Fina wasn't one of the cool kids in school. Makeup wasn't allowed in St. Joseph's Elementary, but already some of the girls were starting to strut what little stuff they had: shortening the hems of their jumpers up to thigh level, pushing their knee socks down to their ankles. Fina remained oblivious to that. She kept her hair unfashionably short and, if anything, her jumper was overly long; she kept her socks all the way up to her knees. But she had plenty of friends; her easy smile and winning sense of humor guaranteed she'd never be a social outcast.

But Maggie worried about Fina. The child was approaching a critical juncture in her life. When her hormones kicked in and ignited a growth spurt, her baby fat would very likely rearrange into more womanly curves. If she turned out to resemble her mother, even remotely, the boys would start to circle. And then she might have to decide: Be popular or be smart.

Maggie had seen it happen so many times—bright children dumbing down to be with the "in" crowd—because cool kids found school "boring"; cool kids didn't care about anything except what was pulsing through their grafted-on headphones; and cool kids certainly didn't get A's.

If Fina stayed in St. Joe's, Maggie was sure she or one of her sister nuns could keep her on the road to academic excellence and help her reach her full potential. But Maggie feared this might well be Fina's last year here.

Maggie's too if those pictures were ever made public.

"Any word on your father?" she asked as the child began to struggle into the straps of her backpack.

Fina paused in her efforts, then shrugged the pack onto her back. Her lips trembled.

"He's going to jail."

Maggie had known this was coming. For years her father, Ignacio, had been in and out of rehab for cocaine. Last year it looked like he'd finally made it. He'd found a decent job that had eased the family's financial burdens. Even so, the tuition cost of sending four children to St. Joe's, despite the break the parish allowed for each successive child, strained their budget to the limit. But they'd been getting by. And then Ignacio was caught selling cocaine. It wasn't his first arrest, so this time he was sentenced to a jail term.

Maggie smoothed the child's glossy black hair. "I'm so sorry, Fina."

Fina's mother Yolanda was already working three jobs. Without her husband's income she was going to have to pull her children out of St. Joe's and send them to public school. They'd wind up at PS 34 up on East Twelfth. Maggie knew some good teachers there, but it was an entirely different atmosphere. She feared the public school meat grinder would chew up Fina and spit her out. And even if she did manage to keep her head, no way could she receive the one-on-one guidance Maggie offered.

She'd gone to Sister Superior and Father Ed, but the parish was tapped out. No more financial assistance available.

So Maggie had searched elsewhere for financial aid. And as an indirect result of that search, she was now being blackmailed.

How could something begun with such good intentions have turned out so wrong?

Maggie knew the answer. And hated it. She'd been weak.

Well, she'd never be weak again.

She walked Fina out to the late bus and saw her off. But instead of returning to the convent, she unlocked the door to the basement and entered the church's soup kitchen. The Loaves and Fishes served a hearty lunch every day. Volunteers from the parish ran it during the week, with Maggie and the other teaching nuns pitching in on weekends and holidays.

She wound her way between the deserted tables toward the rear. Just outside the kitchen door she grabbed a chair and dragged it through. She set it before the stove and turned on one of the burners, turning the flame to high. She removed the two-inch-long steel crucifix from around her neck, then pulled a pair of kitchen tongs from a utensil drawer. She seated herself and pulled her skirt up to the top of her thighs. Using the tongs, she held the crucifix in the flame until it began to redden. Then she took a deep breath, stuck a dish rag between her teeth, and pressed the crucifix against the skin of her inner thigh.

Sister Maggie screamed into the towel but held the cross in place as the smoke and stench of burning flesh rose into her face.

Finally she pulled it away and leaned back, weak and sweaty.

After a moment she looked down at the angry red, blistering cross, identical in shape and size to three other healing burns on her thighs.

Four down, she thought. Three more to go. One for each time she'd sinned.

I'm sorry, Lord. I was weak. But I'm strong now. And these scars will remind me never to be weak again.

8

Jack stepped up to the door and looked up at the camera as he pressed the button next to the Cordova Security Consultants label. He'd put on a black wig, black mustache, and shaded his skin with a little Celebré dark olive makeup. Getting a natural look around the eyes was a bitch, so he wore sunglasses. He'd removed his tie but left the shirt buttoned to the top; he'd kept the blazer but wore it draped over his shoulders, Fellini style.

A tiny speaker in the wall bleated a tinny *"Yes?"* in a woman's voice.

"I seek an investigation," Jack said, trying to sound a little like Julio, but not pushing it. He'd never been great with accents.

"Come in. First door on your right at the top of the stairs."

The door buzzed and he pushed through. Upstairs he opened the Cordova Security Consultants door and entered a small waiting room with two chairs and a middle-aged reed-thin black female receptionist behind a desk. Jack doubted Cordova was busy enough to need a secretary-receptionist or a waiting room—if he were he wouldn't need the blackmail sideline—but it looked good. Sam Spade had Effie Perine and Mike Shayne had

Lucy Hamilton, so fat Richie Cordova had to have a Gal Friday too.

Jack gave the inner surface of the door a good look-see as he made a point of closing it gently behind him. He noticed how the two wires from the foil strip ran off the door just below the upper hinge to disappear into the plaster of the wall. They protected the glass, but what about the door? A glowing light on the keypad beside the doorframe confirmed an active alarm system, but where were the door contacts?

"Yes, sir?" the receptionist said with a smile as she looked up at him over her reading glasses.

"I seek an investigation," he repeated. "Mr. Cordova was recommend."

"How nice." She picked up a pen and poised it over a yellow pad. "May I have his name?"

Jack shrugged. "Some guy. Look, is he in?"

He glanced around and saw no area sensors. He did spot a magnetic contact switch on the waiting-room window. It, like all the office windows, sat above Tremont. No way he was getting in through those.

But why no alarm on the door?

"I'm afraid Mr. Cordova is engaged in an investigation at the moment. I can make you an appointment for tomorrow."

"What time he come in?"

"Mr. Cordova usually comes in around ten." She gave him a you-know-what-I-mean smile as she added, "His work often keeps him up late."

"No good. Be outta town. I come back nes' week."

"I'll be glad to book that appointment for you now."

Jack noticed that the door to the rear office stood open behind her. He wandered over and gave the room the once-over. As fastidiously neat and clean as his house, but no area sensors here either. He made note of the monitor on the desk.

"Sir, that's Mr. Cordova's private office."

"Jus' lookin'." He stepped back into the waiting room,

keeping his distance. Too close and she might notice the makeup. "Bueno. How 'bout next Wen'sday? Garcia. Geraldo Garcia. Son'time in the afternoon."

She put him down for three P.M.

As he opened the door to make his exit, he stopped and crouched on the threshold, pretending to tie his shoe. From the corner of his eye he checked out the hinge surface of the molding. And thar she blew: The short plastic cylinder of a spring-loaded plunger jutted from the wood a couple of inches off the floor. These babies popped out whenever the door opened and, if the system was armed, sent a signal to the box. If the right code wasn't punched in during the preset delay, the alarm would sound.

Jack smiled. Outdated stuff. Easily bypassed as long as you knew it was there.

Down on the street again he checked his voice mail and heard Russ saying his floppy would be ready around six. Jack called back and said pickup would have to wait till tomorrow.

Tonight he had a heavy date.

9

Jack was glad the weather had turned chilly; even then, his Creature from the Black Lagoon suit was hot and stuffy. Glad too that daylight saving time had ended yesterday. If the sun were still out he'd be parboiled inside this green rubber oven.

Green . . . why did they always color the Creature green? The films were all black-and-white, so who knew his real color? Most fish Jack had seen were silvery gray, so why should the Creature be this sick green?

Another recurrent question: If Eric Clapton had to

steal one of the Beatles' wives, why the hell couldn't it have been Yoko? Imponderables like this were what filled his head when he couldn't sleep.

He and Gia were chaperoning Vicky and five of her friends—two princesses, a leprechaun, a Hobbit, Boba Fett, and the Wicked Witch of the West—along an upper-crust Upper West Side block of single-owner brownstones. Gia walked, Jack lumbered, and the kids scampered. Only Gia was uncostumed, though she denied it, saying she was disguised as a nonpregnant woman. Since she didn't look to be in a family way, Jack couldn't argue.

Through the mask's eyeholes he watched the kids run up a brownstone's front steps and ring the bell. A pleasant, blue-blazered, balding man in horn-rimmed glasses answered the door to a chorus of "Trick or Treat!" He dropped a candy bar into each kid's goodie bag, then grinned down at Jack waiting on the sidewalk.

"Hey, Creature." He gave a thumbs-up. "Nice."

"Better be, after what it cost to rent it." Jack's voice sounded at once muffled and echoey inside the mask.

"How about a snort of ice-cold Ketel One to keep you going?"

"I'd need a straw."

The guy laughed. "Not a problem."

Jack waved and started moving after the kids. "Have to take a rain check. Thanks for the thought, though."

The guy called, "Happy Halloween," and closed his door.

Vicky ran back from where her friends were climbing to the next door. With her black pointed hat, flowing dress, and warty green skin she made a great mini Margaret Hamilton.

"Look, Jack!" she cried, digging into her bag. "He gave me a Snickers!"

"My favorite," Jack said.

"I know." She held it up. "Here. You can have it."

Jack knew she was allergic to chocolate, but was

touched by her generosity. He was continually amazed at the bond they'd developed, and wondered if he'd ever be able to love his own child as much as he did Vicky.

"Thanks a million, Vicks, but"—he held out his gloved hands with their big webbed fingers and rubber talons—"can you hold it for me till we get home?"

She grinned and dropped it back into her bag as she ran after the others. Her friends were just finishing up atop the next set of steps. The door closed just as Vicky reached it. She knocked but the young woman behind the glass shook her head and turned away. She knocked again but the lady turned back and made a shooing gesture.

Vicky trudged back down the steps and looked up at her mother with teary eyes.

"She wouldn't give me any candy, Mom."

"Maybe she ran out, hon."

"No. I saw a whole bowlfull inside. Why won't she give me any?"

Suddenly it felt a lot warmer in the Creature suit.

"Let's go find out."

"Jack," Gia said. "Let it go."

"I'm cool, I'm cool," he told her, though another look at Vicky blinking back tears made him anything but. "I just want to satisfy my curiosity. Come on, Vicks. Let's go check this out."

"No, Jack. Leave her here."

"All right."

He climbed the stairs and rang the bell. The same young woman, maybe thirty, answered.

"Mind telling me something?" He pointed to Vicky standing at the bottom of the steps. "Why did you stiff that little girl?"

"Stiff?"

"Yeah. You gave her friends candy but not her."

She began to close the door. "I don't think I have to explain my reasons to anyone."

Jack held the door open with a taloned hand. "You're

right. You don't, but there's the right thing to do and there's everything else. Giving her an explanation is the right thing to do."

The woman's lips tightened into a line. "If you insist. Tell her it's because I don't approve of this so-called holiday in the first place but, just to be a good neighbor, I put up with the indignity of it. However, I draw the line at rewarding paganism. That child is dressed as a witch, a pagan sorceress. I won't encourage paganism or sorcery."

Jack felt his jaw working behind the mask. "You gotta be kidding!"

"I assure you I'm not. Now please get off my steps or I'll have to call the police."

With that she closed the door and turned away.

Jack raised his hand to knock again—cops or not he wanted to tell her a thing or two—when he heard Gia's voice.

"Jack—"

Something in her tone made him turn. When he saw how she was bent slightly forward, her hand over her lower abdomen, her face pale with pain, he ran down the steps.

"What's wrong, Mom?" Vicky was saying.

"Mommy doesn't feel too great. I think we have to go home now."

"I think we have to go to the hospital," Jack said.

Gia grimaced and shook her head. "Home. Now."

10

While Gia closed herself in the master bathroom upstairs at the Sutton Square place, Jack did his best to put aside his fears and fill the half hour until the parents of Vicky's friends showed up. He stayed in costume and told them the story of *The Creature from the Black Lagoon*. None of them had ever seen it. Jack once had persuaded Vicky to watch it but she'd lasted only ten minutes. Not because she was scared. No, her complaint was, "There's no color! Where's the color?"

He half told, half acted out the story, going so far as to lie on the floor and imitate the Creature's backstroke in its fabulous water ballet with Julie Adams.

His audience's consensus: Great performance, but the story was "just like *Anaconda*."

Finally the parents started arriving and Jack explained that Gia wasn't feeling well—"Something she ate." When the townhouse was cleared, he ran upstairs and knocked on the bathroom door.

"You okay?"

The door opened. An ashen Gia leaned on the edge of the door, hunched over.

"Jack," she gasped. A tear ran down her left cheek. "Call the EMTs. I'm bleeding. I think I'm losing the baby!"

"EMTs, hell," he said, lifting her in his arms. "I'll have you in the ER before they even start their engines."

Terror and anguish were icy fingers around his throat, making it hard to draw a full breath, but he couldn't let any of that show: Vicky stood at the bottom of the staircase, fist jammed against her mouth, eyes wide with fear.

"Mom's not feeling good, Vicks," he said. "Let's get her to the hospital."

"What's wrong?" she said, her voice high-pitched, barely audible.

"I don't know."

And he didn't, really, though he feared the worst.

11

Throughout the nail-biting two-hour wait outside the Mount Sinai ER, while interns, residents, ER docs, and Gia's obstetrician did whatever it is they do in these situations, Jack tried to keep Vicky occupied. Not necessary. Before long she found another girl her age to talk to. Jack envied her ability to strike up a friendship anywhere.

He tried to take his mind off Gia and what might be happening in that treatment room by shuffling through some leftover section of the *Times*. He spotted a familiar name in the Sunday *Styles* section: "New York's most eligible bachelor, Dormentalist Church guru Luther Brady, was observed in close conversation with Meryl Streep at the East Hampton Library Fund charity ball."

Not exactly an abstemious lifestyle.

He looked up as a nurse approached. She started to speak, then broke into a laugh.

"What's so funny?"

"I'm sorry. When your wife said to look for a man dressed like the Creature from the Black Lagoon, I thought she was kidding."

By now Jack had gotten used to the stares from the other people in the waiting room. He'd left the mask, gloves, and feet back at the house, but still wore the green, finned bodysuit.

"It *is* Halloween, you know. How is she?"

"Dr. Eagleton will tell you all about it."

They followed her to a treatment room where they found Gia propped up on a gurney. Her color was better but she still looked drawn. Vicky darted to her side and they hugged.

As Jack hung back, letting them have their moment, a tall, slim woman with salt-and-pepper hair stepped in. She wore a long white coat.

"You're the father?" she said, eyeing his costume. When Jack nodded, she held out her hand. "I'm Dr. Eagleton."

"Jack," he said. She had a firm grip. "How's she doing?"

Dr. Eagleton didn't look exactly comfortable discussing this with a man in a rubber monster suit, but she bore with it.

"She's lost a lot of blood, but the contractions have stopped."

"She's going to be okay?"

"Yes."

"And the baby?"

"Ultrasound shows no problem—good position, steady heart rate."

Jack closed his eyes and let out a relieved breath. "Thanks. Thank you very much."

"I want to keep her overnight, though."

"Really? Is there still a danger?"

"She should be fine. The further along the pregnancy, the less likely a miscarriage. Gia's in her twentieth week and it's rare after that. So I think we're in good shape. Just the same, I'd like to be sure."

Jack glanced at Gia. "What caused this?"

Dr. Eagleton shrugged. "The most common causes are a dead or grossly defective fetus." Jack's stab of alarm must have shown on his face because she quickly added, "But that's not the case here. Sometimes it's trauma, and sometimes it just . . . happens."

Jack didn't like the sound of that. For a while now it seemed that things—bad things, at least—didn't "just happen" in his life.

Jack stepped over to the gurney and took Gia's hand. She squeezed his.

"You'll take care of Vicky until I get home tomorrow, won't you?"

Gia had no family in the city. Everyone was back in Iowa.

Jack smiled. "You don't even have to ask." He winked at Vicky. "Vicks and I are going straight home to do flaming shooters of Cuervo Gold."

As Vicky giggled, Gia said, "Jack, that's not funny."

Jack slapped his forehead. "That's right! She's got school tomorrow. Okay, Vicks: only one."

As Gia went on about Vicky's schedule, Jack wondered at the awesome responsibility of caring for a nine-year-old girl, even for a day.

He'd stepped into *Family Affair*—without Mr. French.

Cordova and the Dormentalists weren't half as scary.

TUESDAY

1

Jack spent the night in the guest bedroom at the Sutton Square place. Lucky for him, Vicky turned out to be pretty self-sufficient.

More than self-sufficient.

Next morning, after showering and getting herself dressed, she insisted on making Jack bacon and eggs before it was time for the school bus. Bacon here meant strips of bacon-flavored soy.

She seemed in good spirits, not the least bit worried. Dr. Eagleton had told her that her mother was going to be fine and that was enough for Vicky. If Mom's doctor said so, that's how it was going to be.

Oh, to be nine again and have that kind of faith.

As he watched her bustle around the kitchen—she knew exactly what she needed and where everything was—and listened to her chatter, he felt his heart swell. Vicky was going to be a wonderful big sister to the new baby.

New baby . . . his appetite took a nose dive. He hadn't heard any bad news, so he gathered Gia had had a quiet night. He hoped so.

During breakfast Jack called Gia to get a progress report—and give one.

She'd had a good night but wouldn't be released until late afternoon, which meant Jack had to arrange to be home to meet Vicks when she returned from school.

No problemo.

Vicky talked to her mother for a few minutes, then it was time to run. He walked her to the bus and gave her his cell phone number, telling her to call if she needed anything—*anything*.

Then he showered, shaved, and headed across town to Tenth Avenue.

2

Pedestrians flowed around the sandwich board sign propped in the center of the sidewalk.

ERNIE'S ID
ALL KINDS
PASSPORT
TAXI
DRIVER'S LICENSE

No business at this hour, so Jack had Ernie all to himself.

"Hey, Jack," Ernie said from the rear of the tiny store. He stood maybe five-five, weighed a hundred pounds after a five-pound meal, had a droopy, hangdog face with perpetually sad eyes, and spoke at a hundred-and-twenty miles an hour. "How y'doin', how y'doin'. Do the thing with the door there, will ya?"

Jack locked it and flipped the OPEN sign to CLOSED. On the way to the rear, next to the bootleg videos, he passed a display pole festooned with high-end handbags—Kate Spade, Louis Vuitton, Gucci, Prada—none of them the real deal. Not with twenty-dollar price tags. Everything Ernie carried was a knockoff of one sort or another.

"Into women's accessories now?" Jack said as he reached the display case that served as the rear counter.

"What? Oh, yeah. Outta towners come in and buy three, four at a time. Can't hardly keep 'em in stock." He pulled a manila envelope from behind the counter. "Wait-'ll you see this, Jacko. Wait'll you see!"

He dumped the contents onto the scratched glass: a driver's license with Jack's photo and two credit cards—a Visa gold and a platinum AmEx.

"That's it?"

Jack couldn't see what all the excitement was about. Ernie furnished him with this sort of thing all the time.

"Checkitout, checkitout." He was literally vibrating with excitement. "Check the license."

Jack leaned over for a closer look, then picked it up. His picture, but the name was Jason Amurri, and the language was . . .

"French?"

"It's Swiss," Ernie said, "and it's perfect. And the credit cards are both exact duplicates of his, right down to the expiration date and the verification number. Just don't use 'em or you'll blow everything."

"And just who is Jason Amurri?"

Ernie grinned. "Lives in Vevey. That's on the Swiss Riviera—you know, Montreux, Lake Geneva, those kinda places. Céline Dion and Phil Collins and people like that got homes around there."

"Okay. He lives in a ritzy area in a foreign country. That's a good start. Give me the details."

"You're gonna be impressed."

Jack had set strict criteria for this set of ID. He hoped Ernie had come through.

"I'll decide that after you tell me."

Ernie told him.

And Jack was impressed.

"Nice work," he said, forking over Ernie's stiff fee. "You deserve every penny."

"I do." If he rubbed his hands together any faster his palms would catch fire. "I do, I do."

"Looks like I'm going to have to get a room at the Plaza," Jack said.

"Nah. Every nobody who thinks they're somebody stays at the Plaza. I mean, they got rooms for a couple hundred and change. You need better than that. You want someplace where the money that knows goes. The Ritz Carlton . . . now *there's* a hotel."

"If you say so."

Maybe Mrs. Rossi hadn't been so overly generous with her advance. This was turning out to be one expensive fix.

3

Instead of the bubbly Christy, the equally bubbly Jeanie was on duty at the Dormentalist temple's metal detector this morning. She checked her computer, made a call, then guided Jack through the detector.

"Your RT will be with you in a minute, Mr. Farrell."

"RT?"

"Sorry. Reveille Tech. Oh, here she comes now."

Jack saw a large frizzy blond woman waddling his way on legs like Doric pillars. Instead of the ubiquitous uniform, she wore a sleeveless yellow tunic that looked a size too small for her. Maybe two sizes. And of course she was grinning ear to ear.

In a high-pitched, lightly French-accented voice, she introduced herself as Aveline Lesueur and led him to the double elevator bank. When she called him "Jack" it sounded like "Jock."

In the elevator on the way up he noticed a sweaty odor about her. He was glad it was a short trip.

On the fourth floor she pointed out the Male RC Changing Room, explaining that RC meant Reveille Candidate and he should go in, pick out a locker, and change into the RC uniform he'd find there.

"Like yours?"

She shook her head. "I am afraid not. This is only for RTs, and only while we are conducting sessions."

"A gray one then?"

"Not until you qualify for FI—Fusion Initiate—status. Until then you must wear RC colors."

Although her English was good, she still hadn't mastered the "th" sound, resorting to a soft "z" instead.

In the Male RC Changing Room—he was surprised they didn't call it the MRCCR—Jack found a dozen lockers. Ten stood open, each containing a dark green jumpsuit, each with a key in its lock. He shucked his street clothes and slipped into the jumpsuit. It was too big for him but he wasn't going to bother searching for one that fit. He noticed it had no pockets—just a tiny pouch on the left breast big enough for the locker key and nothing else. He'd have to leave his wallet and effects in the locker.

Jack smiled. Perfect.

Back in the hall Aveline led him to a door labeled *RF-3*. When he asked, she explained that the RF stood for Reveille Facility.

Jamie Grant's words from yesterday, when he'd asked her if the Reveille Sessions were just a series of questions, came back to him.

Oh, no. There's so much more to it than that . . .

Her smile when she'd said it still bothered him.

RF-3 turned out to be a windowless cubicle furnished with a desk, two chairs, and a white mouse. The mouse's wire cage sat on a pedestal to the right of the desk. Aveline indicated the chair before the desk for Jack. He sat and found himself facing a horizontal copper pipe fastened to the front panel of the desk by six-inch brackets at each end. A wire ran from the middle of the pipe to a black box the size of a loaf of bread on the desk; another wire ran from the box to the mouse cage.

He didn't have to fake a baffled look. "You're going to explain this to me, right?"

"But of course," she replied as she seated herself on the other side of the desk. "As I am sure you know, if you have read *The Book of Hokano,* the purpose of the Reveille Sessions is to awaken your Personal Xelton, the hemi-xelton asleep within you."

Jack kept glancing at the mouse.

"Right. But what—?"

She held up a hand. "To awaken it, you must explore your present life and your PX's past lives." She pulled a folder from the desk's top drawer. "We do this by asking you a series of questions. Some of them will seem very personal, but you must trust that none of what you say will ever leave this room."

Not according to Jamie Grant.

Jack leaned back and rubbed his temples, using the motion to cover a look at the grille over the ventilation duct. Between two of the slats he spotted something that looked like a tiny lens pointed his way. Somewhere in the building an AV feed of the goings-on here was being monitored and most likely recorded.

"I trust you," Jack said.

"Good. This is your first step in a marvelous adventure of discovery. The memories from your PX's multiple lives will sound a reveille and awaken it. After that you will begin the task of reconnecting your PX to its Hokano half, allowing them to fuse and become whole again. It is a long process, requiring many years of classes and sessions, but in the end you will be a superior being, unafraid to accept any challenge, able to overcome any obstacle, able to cure all ills and live forever after the GF."

She threw her arms wide at the end of her recitation and Jack jumped at the sight of a sea urchin in each armpit. Then he realized it was hair.

"Wow," he said, trying not to stare. "The GF is the Great Fusion, right?"

She lowered her arms and her accent thickened. "Yes. That is when the world as we know it will reunite with the Hokano world. It will be Paradise Regained, but only those who have fused their PX with its HX will survive."

"I want to be in that number," Jack said.

But what did the damn mouse have to do with it?

"Wonderful, Jack. Let us get started then. First you must grip that bar before you with both hands. Grip very tight."

Jack did as he was told. "What does this do?"

"This makes certain that you are telling the truth."

Jack looked offended. "I'm not a liar."

"Of course you are not. But we all hide truths from our-selves, oui? Repress acts we are ashamed of. We all have 'vital lies' that get us through the day. We must pierce our self deceptions and thrust to the heart of truth. And do you know where that heart is? In your Personal Xelton. Your PX knows the truth."

"I thought my PX was asleep."

"It is, but that does not mean it is not aware. When it hears an untruth it will react."

"How?"

"You will not notice it, and neither will I. Only FAs who have reached FL-8 can perceive it unassisted."

"Then how will we know?"

She tapped the black box. "This is an XSA—a Xelton Signal Amplifier. It cannot amplify the signal enough for us to perceive it, but that mouse will know."

"Okay." Jack felt like he'd stepped through the Look-ing Glass and wound up chatting with the Mad Hatter. "But how will the mouse tell us?"

"Answer a question with an untruth and you will see." She opened the folder. "Let us begin, shall we?"

"Okay. But I've got to tell you, I lead a very boring life—boring job, no family, no pets, never go anywhere."

"And that is why you are here—to change all that, oui?"

"Oui. I mean, right."

"Well then, hold on to the XS conductor bar in front of you there and we will begin."

Jack tightened his grip. He felt unaccountably tense.

He kept his eyes on the little white mouse sniffing nervously around its wire mesh cage as Aveline asked a string of innocuous questions—about the weather, about how he arrived here today, and so on—all of which he answered truthfully.

Then she stared at him and said, "Very well, Jack. This is an important question: What is the worse thing you have ever done?"

The directness took him by surprise. "As I told you, my life's not interesting enough for me to do anything wrong."

The mouse squeaked and jumped as if it had received a shock. Jack jumped too.

"What happened?"

"You told an untruth. Perhaps an unconscious untruth," she added quickly, "but your xelton heard it and reacted."

The untruth hadn't been unconscious. He'd done lots of wrong—at least by most people's criteria.

Aveline cleared her throat. "Perhaps we are being too general here. Let us try this: Have you ever stolen anything?"

"Yes."

The mouse didn't react.

"What was the first thing you ever stole?"

Jack remembered the moment. "When I was in second grade I remember stealing an Almond Joy from a Rexall drugstore."

The mouse was cool.

"Good," Aveline said, nodding. "What was the biggest thing you've ever stolen?"

Jack put on a show of deep thought, then said, "The Almond Joy is about it."

A squeak from the mouse as it jumped two inches off its cage floor.

A queasy feeling stole over him. The XSA was right. He'd boosted plenty of things, plenty of times—usually from thieves, but it was still stealing. So far the XSA had been right every time.

Had to be coincidence. But still . . .

"You're acting like I'm a criminal. I'm not."

The mouse jumped again.

This was getting spooky. He'd lied . . . his everyday existence was a criminal act . . . and Mr. Mouse had paid for it.

Jack released the bar and waved his hands in the air. "I'm telling you the truth!"

"The truth as you know it, Jack. What you say may be true in this life, but your xelton must have inhabited the body of a thief sometime in the past."

"I don't like this."

"It is all part of the process, Jack."

Mr. Mouse had backed into a corner where he crouched and trembled.

"Please don't hurt that mouse anymore."

"He is not being hurt. Not really. But I am doing nothing to him. You are. You are in charge here. Now please grip the XS conductor bar again and we will continue."

Jack did so. He noticed his palms were moist.

"Have you ever killed anyone, Jack?"

He stared at the mouse and said, "No."

No reaction from Mr. Mouse.

Gotcha, he thought. A number of people were on the wrong side of the grass because of him.

Somehow, maybe with a floor button, Aveline was triggering an electric shock in Mr. Mouse's cage. Pretty damn potent way to mess with a new member's head. The psychological impact of causing an innocent animal harm with every untruth was enormous.

"Are you heterosexual?" she asked.

"Yes."

Mr. Mouse maintained his nervous crouch.

"Have you ever raped anyone?"

Here was another one he could answer truthfully. "No way."

Mr. Mouse's squeal of pain was a signal to end this bullshit. A tantrum was in order.

Releasing the bar, Jack shot to his feet and began pounding on the desk.

"No!" he shouted. "Impossible! No, no, no! I'd never do something like that! Never!"

Aveline's face paled. "Calm down, Jack. As I have told you, it is probably from some past life—"

He pounded harder on the desk. "I don't want to hear that! I don't want a xelton that would be party to such a thing. You're mistaken! It's wrong! Wrong-wrong-wrong!"

The door swung open with a bang and two shaved-headed, burgundy-uniformed men burst in.

The taller of the pair grabbed Jack's arm and said, "Come with us. And don't make a fuss."

"Who are you?" Jack cried, cringing.

"Temple Paladins," Aveline said. "You must go with them."

"Where?"

"The Grand Paladin wants to see you," said the shorter one.

Aveline's eyes widened. "The GP himself? By Noomri!"

"Yeah," said the taller one. "He's had his eye on you since you stepped into the temple this morning."

Just as Jack had expected. He went without a fuss.

4

"My name is Jensen." The big black man said as he loomed over Jack. Jack detected a vaguely African accent filtering through the subway rumble of his voice. "What's yours?"

The two TPs had brought Jack to the third floor, which

seemed to house the temple's security forces, and seated him in a chair in a small, windowless room. They made him wait ten minutes or so, probably looking to up his anxiety level. Jack accommodated them by fidgeting and twisting his hands together, doing his best to look like a house cat in a dog pound.

Finally this huge black guy who made Michael Clark Duncan look svelte—hell, he looked like he'd had Michael Clark Duncan for breakfast—swung through the door like a wrecking ball and stopped two feet in front of Jack. None of his bulk looked like flab. The overhead fluorescents gleamed off the bare scalp of a head the size of an official NBA basketball. His black uniform could have doubled as a comforter on a king-sized bed.

Pretty intimidating, Jack thought. If you're into that sort of thing.

He started to stutter a reply. "I-I-I'm—"

"Don't tell me you're 'Jack Farrell,' because we ran a routine check on you and learned there is no Jack Farrell at the address you gave. As a matter of fact, there isn't even a house at that address."

"A-all right," Jack said. "My real name—"

"I don't care what you're real name is. I just want to know your game. What are you up to? You work for that rag, *The Light,* is that it?"

"No, I've never even heard of whatever it is you're talking about. I'm—"

"Then why are you coming to us under false pretenses? We don't allow lies in Dormentalist temples—only truth."

"But I've a good explanation about why—"

"I don't want to hear it. As of this moment you are officially designated UP and banned from this and all other Dormentalist temples."

Jensen turned and walked back to the door.

"It's not fair!" Jack cried but Jensen didn't acknowledge him.

As soon as he was gone, the two guards who'd brought

Jack here led him back down to the Male RC Changing Room, watched him change, then escorted him out the door to the sidewalk. All without a word.

Jack stood in the late-morning sun, looking dejected, then turned and began walking uptown. Pulled out his wallet and checked the slot where he'd stowed the Jason Amurri ID. The hair he'd tucked around the top of the card was gone.

Perfect.

He hadn't gone three blocks when he spotted the tail. But he wasn't going to try to lose him. He wanted to be followed.

Let the games begin.

5

Jensen's secretary's voice rasped from the speaker on his desk. *"TP Peary on line one, sir."*

Jensen had told Peary to get into his street clothes and follow this phony bastard Amurri. At first, when the routine background check on "Jack Farrell" had come up blank—name, address, SSN, none of them had connected—he'd suspected the usual. Most troublemakers for the Church were either members of another belief system who felt Dormentalists had to be "saved," or former members with an imagined score to settle. Occasionally one turned out to be a muckraker like that Jamie Grant bitch.

Just as Jensen had expected, when he called a raid on "Jack Farrell's" locker during the Reveille Session, they came up with a whole different set of ID. But not the ID of someone who fell easily into the usual categories.

Jason Amurri. Okay. But from Switzerland? That had thrown Jensen. Why would a guy come all the way from

Switzerland to join the New York Dormentalist temple under an assumed name? Granted, this temple was the center of the Church, its Vatican, so to speak, but why the lies? And bad lies to boot. Obviously he'd never thought they'd check up on him.

Couldn't let anybody get away with that. Doesn't matter if you're from Switzerland or Peoria—you lie, you get the boot. That was the rule.

Jensen stared at the phone and frowned. Kind of early for Peary to be calling in. He'd only started tailing the Amurri guy a little while ago.

Unless . . .

He snatched up the receiver. "Don't tell me you lost him."

"No. Only had to follow him to Central Park South. He's staying at the Ritz Carlton."

Another surprise.

"How do you know he's not just visiting someone?"

"Because I called the hotel and asked to be connected to Jason Amurri's room. A few seconds later the phone started ringing."

The Ritz Carlton? Jesus. Years ago, while the luxury suites were being refurbished here in the temple, Jensen had had to book rooms in the Ritz for visiting Dormentalist celebrities. He remembered how a rear single with a view of a brick wall had cost almost seven hundred a night. And, of course, none of the visiting high rollers wanted that. No, they wanted a park view. Cost a damn fortune.

"What do you want me to do next?" Peary said.

"Come back in."

He hung up. No sense in having Peary waste his time watching a hotel. Jensen now knew where the guy was and who he was.

Well, not really who. Just his name. And home address in Switzerland. And that he was staying at just about the most expensive hotel in the city. That meant he had some bucks. This Jason Amurri was full of surprises.

A worm of unease wriggled in Jensen's gut. He didn't like surprises.

He reached for the buzzer and hesitated. What was his new secretary's name? The brainless little twits came and went so quickly. He seemed to go through them like a fox through chickens. No one applied to be his secretary anymore; they had to be drafted from the volunteer pool. Was he that hard on them? Not that he cared what they thought, it was just that some of them had long learning curves.

He decided he didn't give a shit about her name.

He buzzed and said, "Get me Tony Margiotta."

Jensen loved what computers could do for him but, beyond e-mail, he let other people deal with them. Margiotta was the computer whiz among the TPs. He'd find out what Jensen needed to know.

He just hoped it wasn't something he didn't want to know.

"Here you go," Richie Cordova said, handing a five to the kid from the mail drop.

Every time something popped into his box at the drop—hardly ever more than three times a week—the kid ran it up the two blocks to Richie's office on his break. Worth the fiver every time. Saved Richie the trip, but more important, it meant he never had to show his face down there.

A good thing to avoid. Never knew when one of the cows might get the dumb idea of watching Box 224 to see who opened it. Might see Richie and follow him back to the office, or home, and look for a chance to get even. Didn't want none of that shit.

With Richie's delivery setup, they'd be waiting till they

was dead and gone before seeing anyone so much as touch Box 224.

"So what've we got today?" Richie muttered when the kid was gone.

One manila envelope. Typed label. Hmmm.

He pulled a folding knife from a desk drawer and slit it open. He found a legal-sized envelope within. Inside that was a note in a woman's hand and a hundred-dollar bill.

A hundred bucks? What's this shit?

The note was from the nun, whining about how she didn't have no more to give. Richie smiled. Normally he'd be royally pissed at the short payment, but not with this little lady. Oh, no. He wanted her tapped out—at least personally.

But was today the right day to put the screws to her?

He picked up the *Post* and turned to the horoscope page. He'd been there once already this morning and hadn't been too crazy about what he'd seen. He folded the tabloid into a neat quarter page for a second look.

Gemini (May 21–June 21): It seems as if you have a dwindling safety margin. Don't confuse aggression with initiative. Live in the moment, follow the rules, and close the week in triumph despite these obstacles.

Dwindling safety margin . . . that didn't sound so good.

But it might not be so bad. His birthday was June 20, which meant he was officially a Gemini. But because Cancer started June 22, lots of astrology experts said people like him was "on the cusp" and could go either way.

He checked the next reading.

Cancer (June 22–July 22): It might be necessary to experience what you thought you wanted in order to better appreciate what you have. Dearest ones help you find fresh resources which might be able to hook you up in a surprising way.

He read the first sentence three times and still couldn't scope out what it was saying. As for the rest . . .

Dearest ones? That would have to be the crowd at Hurley's.

Sure as hell couldn't be a woman. He'd been split for seven years now from the stupid bitch he'd married, and his mother was five years gone. No gal at the moment—most of them were slobs anyway and the ones who weren't never seemed to stay. His mother, God love her, had left him her house in Williamsbridge and everything in it. He'd grown up there and, because it was so much better than the crap apartment he'd been living in after his divorce, he'd moved back instead of selling.

He decided what these horoscopes was telling him was that since he was going to find *fresh resources* today, his *dwindling safety margin* wouldn't matter, and he'd *close the week in triumph.*

Good enough.

He unfolded the paper and laid it on his desk with the front page up. Then he used a Handi Wipe to remove the newsprint smudges from his fingers. That done, he wheeled his chair over to the radiator and pulled a padded envelope from behind it. He added the nun's hundred to the rest of the cash. The total was up to about three thousand now. Time to make a trip to the safety deposit box. His office was alarmed, sure, but it wasn't no bank. He'd head there come Friday.

As he stuffed the envelope back into its hiding place and rose to his feet, he burped and rubbed the swelling dome of his belly. That liverwurst and onion sandwich wasn't sitting too good. He loosened his belt a notch—to the last one. Shit, if he swelled any more he'd have to buy a whole new set of clothes. Again. He already had one closet full of stuff he couldn't wear. He didn't need another.

He slipped on his suit jacket—didn't even try to button it—and straightened up his desktop. Not much there. He kept a lean look in everything but his body. He realigned the photo of Clancy so it was centered across the far left corner, then headed for the waiting area.

"Going out for a little walk, Eddy," he told his receptionist. "Be back in thirty or so."

Edwina checked her watch and jotted the time on a sticky note.

"Sure thing, Rich."

Uppity black skank, but she was good, one of the best receptionists he'd ever had. Wouldn't come across with any extracurricular activity like some of them, though. Couple that with the way business had slowed, and he just might have to let her go soon.

But he'd put that off as long as he could. A fair number of his clients had some bucks. Not big bucks, but comfortable. They came to him from Manhattan and Queens— first time ever in the Bronx for a lot of them. When they called for directions they were relieved to hear he was near the Bronx Zoo and the Botanical Garden—civilization would be close by.

The bad part about this location was that parking was a bitch and his clients wouldn't see anyone like them on the street; the good part was they damn sure wouldn't bump into anyone they knew, and that was important. Nobody wanted to run into a friend or acquaintance in a detective agency.

So they hauled themselves all the way up here, and after that sacrifice they needed the reassurance of seeing a receptionist when they stepped through the door.

He adjusted Eddy's RECEPTIONIST sign, lining it up with the leading edge of her desk, and walked out.

7

Tremont was jumping today. But nobody on the crowded sidewalk seemed to be looking for a PI. They weren't his sort of clientele anyway.

Richie didn't know why business had been off lately.

He gave good service to his clients and got a lot of referrals from them, but things had been unaccountably slow since the summer.

Which was why his second income stream had become more important than ever. The regular snoop jobs had always been the meat and potatoes, but the gravy had come from blackmail.

Blackmail. He hated that word. Sounded so dirty and underhanded. He'd tried for years to find a substitute but hadn't come up with anything that worked. *Private knowledge protection . . . secret safekeeping service . . . classified information management* . . . none of them did anything for him.

So, he'd resigned himself to *blackmail* . . . which made him a blackmailer.

Not something he talked about at Hurley's, but not as bad as it sounded. Really, when you got down to it, he was simply supplying a service: I have information about you, information you don't want made public. For a regular fee I will keep my mouth shut.

What could be fairer than that? Participation was purely voluntary. Don't want to play? Then don't pay. But be ready to face the music once your ugly little secret gets out.

Plus he had to admit he loved being able to pull people's strings and make them dance to whatever tune he felt like playing. That was almost as good as the money.

Richie rounded the corner and walked up past the newer apartment houses toward the zoo.

Yeah . . . blackmailer. Not exactly what he'd planned for himself as a kid.

What do you want to be when you grow up, Richie?

A blackmailer, Mom.

He hadn't planned on being a cop either. Cops had been "pigs" back then. But as he grew older in a crummy economy and saw his old man lose his factory job, he started thinking maybe being a cop wasn't so bad. Chances of getting laid off were slim to none, the pay was decent, and you could retire on a pension after twenty or twenty-five years and still have a lot of living ahead of you.

He'd tried for the NYPD but didn't make it. Had to settle for the NCPD—Nassau County—where the pay didn't turn out to be all that decent. Didn't take him too long, though, to find ways to supplement it.

As a patrolman first and later a detective, Richie spent twenty-six years with the NCPD, twenty-four and a half of them on the pad. That got him into a little trouble toward the end, but he'd traded keeping mum about a certain IAD guy's sexual tastes for a Get Out of Jail Free pass, and walked away with his pension intact.

That had been his introduction to the power of knowing things he wasn't supposed to. Instead of putting himself out to pasture, he applied for his private investigator license and opened Cordova Security Consultants. No big expectations, just someplace to go every day. Startup had been slow, but stuff sent his way by his old buddies in NCPD had helped keep him afloat. He found he liked the work, especially the spouse snooping. He'd got pretty good with a camera over the years and had taken some pretty steamy pictures. He'd kept a private gallery back at the house until this past September.

But often it was the bonus material he collected that paid the best. While checking out a husband or wife suspected of getting it on with somebody else, he frequently came across unrelated or semi-related dirt that he put to work for himself.

Like this nun, for instance. Helene Metcalf had traveled all the way from her Chelsea high-rise to hire Richie. Her hubby Michael was a capital campaign consultant— that meant professional fund-raiser—and had been out on the job an unusual number of nights. She was starting to suspect he might be sneaking a little something on the side and wanted Richie to find out.

Mikey's latest account was raising money for the

renovation of St. Joseph's Church on the Lower East Side. Camera in hand, Richie started tailing him and found he was indeed going to St. Joe's—but not just for fund-raising. Seemed he was also doing a little habit-raising with one of the nuns.

Richie took a few shots of the pair in flagrante delicto, as they say, and was about to show them to the wife when he realized he might be sitting on a gold mine. Normally putting the squeeze on a nun would be like trying to buy a whale steak from Greenpeace, but this nun was one of the honchos in the fund-raising project. That was how she'd got so tight with Mikey boy in the first place. Lots of cash flowing through that lady's hands, and those photos was a way to tap into that stream.

So Richie told wifey that her hubby was going exactly where he said he was—showed her photos of him entering and leaving the St. Joe's basement on the nights in question—and said he'd found no impropriety.

He put the squeeze on Mikey as well. Usually he had a rule: Never use nothing against the client. That was a no-no. Had to keep up the reputation, keep up the referrals from satisfied clients.

But Mikey wouldn't know that the guy who was milking him had been hired by his wife.

Because another rule was keep it anonymous. Never let the cow see your face or, worse, learn your name.

So Mikey Metcalf became the second cow in this particular pasture.

Up until a couple of months ago, Richie had maintained a perfect score on the anonymity meter. Then one September night he'd come home from Hurley's and smelled something funny. He raced up to his third floor and found out some guy'd poured acid over everything in his filing cabinet. The guy got away by running over a neighbor's roof.

Only explanation was that one of the cows had found out who he was. Richie had burned his gallery of photos—hated to do it but it was evidence if anyone hit him with a search warrant—and moved his sideline to his office. He'd been looking over his shoulder ever since.

He was puffing a little by the time he reached the wall of the zoo. A hot dog pushcart tempted him but he forced himself to keep moving. Later.

Call the nun first.

Kind of fun to have a nun on the hook. Back in grammar school the penguins—nuns dressed head to toe in black in those days—had always been after him, whacking him on the back of the head or rapping his knuckles whenever he acted up. Not that he'd been damaged for life or nothing. That was a crock. Truth was, he couldn't think of a single time he hadn't deserved what he got. That didn't make them any less of a pain in the ass though.

The nun thing had got to be a game after a while. A badge of honor. If you hadn't got hit you was some kind of fag.

He guessed this was sort of like payback.

He chose a public phone at random and licked his lips as he dialed the convent. He knew Sister Margaret Mary would be over at the school until three or three-thirty, but wanted to shake her up a little.

And he knew just how to do that.

8

"Got him!" Margiotta said.

Jensen had insisted he do the search for Jason Amurri in Jensen's own office. He didn't want anything they found becoming water-cooler talk around the admin floor. So Margiotta had pulled up a chair beside Jensen's desk, swiveled the monitor, moved the keyboard, and gotten to work.

"About time."

"This guy's one reclusive SOB." Margiotta shook his head. He had close-clipped black hair and dark brown eyes. "Only someone with my enormous talents could have dug him up. A lesser sort would've come up with jack shit."

Jensen decided to humor him. "That's why I called on you. Show me."

Margiotta rose and swiveled the monitor back toward Jensen. He pointed to the screen.

"You want to know about his father, I came across tons. *Tons*. But as for Jason himself, this is the best of what I found. It ain't much—like I said, he's pretty much a recluse—but I think it's enough to give you an idea who he is."

On the screen was a paragraph from a news article about one Aldo Amurri. Jensen had never heard of him. It mentioned he had two sons, Michel and Jason. Michel, the older one, lived in Newport Beach on the shore. Jason lived in Switzerland.

"That's it?"

"Did you read about the father? Check him out. That'll tell you something about this Jason guy."

Jensen scrolled back to the beginning of the article and began reading. He felt his mouth go dry as he learned about Aldo Amurri, father of the young man Jensen had booted out on his ass.

He knew he couldn't keep this from Luther Brady. Eventually he'd find out. Brady always found out. So it was better if Jensen broke the news himself.

But Brady was going to be pissed. Royally pissed.

9

The phone was ringing as Jack stepped into Gia's place. He'd just picked up Vicky at the bus stop. When he saw *Mount Sinai* on the caller ID he snatched up the receiver. God, he hoped it wasn't bad news. He'd talked to Gia just a couple of hours ago and—

"Is Vicky home?" Gia's voice.

"She's right here. Is anything—?"

"Then come and get me. *Please* get me out of here."

"Are you okay?"

"I'm fine. Really. Dr. Eagleton released me but the hospital doesn't want me going home alone. I know it's only been one night but I'm so sick of this place. I want my home."

Jack knew it was more than that. Gia skeeved out—her verb—in hospitals.

"We're on our way."

They grabbed a cab on Sutton Place, zipped up Madison into the low One Hundreds, then west over to Fifth Avenue. Mount Sinai Medical Center had a view of Central Park that the Donald Trumps of the city would kill for. Jack and Vicky found a very pale Gia perched on a wheelchair inside the front door. Jack guided her into the cab, and off they went.

Ten minutes later they were stepping through the front door on Sutton Square.

"Oh, God, it's so good to be home!"

Jack followed her down the hall. "Now you're going to be a good girl and take it easy like the doctor said, right?"

"I feel fine, Jack. Really, I do. Whatever was going on has stopped. I slept straight through the night and haven't had a hint of a cramp since."

"But you lost a lot of blood and didn't you say you're supposed to take it easy?"

"Yes, but that doesn't mean putting myself to bed."

"It means staying off your feet and that's exactly what you're going to do." He led her to the big leather chair in the oak-paneled library and seated her in it. "Now stay there till bedtime."

He knew Gia would never do anything to jeopardize the baby, but he also knew that her high energy level made it difficult for her to sit still.

"Don't be silly. What about dinner?"

"I can make it!" Vicky cried. "Let me! Let me!"

Jack knew a Vicky dinner would mean more work for Gia than if she were doing it all herself. But he had to play it carefully here. Didn't want to step on little-girl feelings.

"I was thinking of takeout."

Vicky wouldn't let it go. "Let me make it! Please, please please!"

"Gee, Vicks, I already ordered Chinese for tonight." Jack knew it ran a close second to Italian on her favorite foods list. "You know, egg rolls, wanton soup, General Tso's chicken, and even a doo-doo platter."

Her eyes widened. "You mean a *pu pu* platter?"

"Oh, yeah. Right. You know, with ribs and shrimp toast and even a fire." She loved to singe her spareribs in the flame. "But if you'd rather cook, then I'll call and cancel. No problem."

"No, I want a pu pu platter. I can cook tomorrow night."

"You're sure?"

Vicky nodded. "A pu pu platter, right?"

"Right. I've got an errand to run and after that I'll bring home the doo-doo."

Vicky giggled and ran off cheering.

Jack turned and winked at Gia. "The usual broccoli and walnuts in garlic sauce, I presume?"

She nodded. "You presume correctly. But where can you get a takeout pu pu platter?"

"I don't know, but I'll find one, even if I have to get a can of sterno and jury-rig one myself." He leaned over and kissed her. "You're sure you're all right?"

"The baby and I are fine. We just had a little scare is all."

"And you're going to follow doctor's orders, right?"

"I'm going to take a shower in my own bathroom to wash off the hospital and then I'm going to sit right here and read a book."

"Okay. But make it a quick shower. I've got some errands to run."

"Fix-it errands?"

He nodded. "Got a couple of them going."

"Nothing dangerous, I hope. You promised—"

"No danger. Really. One is just finding a missing guy for his mom. And I'm arranging the other so that the guy I'm fixing won't even know he's been fixed. No danger, no chance of bodily harm. It will be no-contact poetry."

"I've heard *that* before. You say 'piece of cake' and next you show up with a purple face and choke marks all over your throat."

"Yeah, but—"

"And you couldn't even go visit your father without starting some sort of war."

Jack held up his hands. "Sometimes these things take unpredictable turns, but the two fix-its running now are as straightforward as they come. No surprises. I swear."

"Oh, I know you believe that, but lately every time you start one of these jobs it seems to turn nasty."

"Not this time. See you in a couple of hours. I'm keeping my cell phone off for the rest of the day." When he saw her questioning look, he said. "Long story. But I'll be checking in lots." He waved. "Love ya."

She smiled that smile for him. "Love you too."

10

"You're looking better today," Jensen said as he seated himself on the visitor side of Luther Brady's helipad-sized desk.

Jensen wished he had an office like this—high ceilings, rich wood paneling, a rosette of skylights above, and a bank of floor-to-ceiling windows facing uptown with a magnificent view of the Chrysler Building. The paneling was all walnut except for a pair of chromed steel doors embedded in the south wall. That was where Brady kept a monument to his biggest secret, the one known only to him, Jensen, and the High Council: Opus Omega.

The Acting Prime Dormentalist and Supreme Overseer was a handsome man of average height with broad shoulders and a head of long wavy brown hair that he let trail over his collar. A few years ago Jensen had noticed gray creeping into that brown, but it hadn't lasted long. Today he wore one of his Hickey-Freeman or Dolce & Gabbana suits—he never wore a uniform—that he donned for public appearances. He was Dormentalism's public face and as such needed to cut an impressive figure. Luther Brady wasn't simply the Church's leader, he was its peerless PR man too.

Jensen had to admit he did a great job in both roles, but especially the latter. When he appeared on TV he was the soul of rationality, generosity, and selflessness. The MVP of the Altruism Bowl.

"Better?" Brady frowned. "What do you mean?"

"You looked tired yesterday."

Brady paused a beat, then said, "Not surprising, considering the effort it took to keep that low pressure area to the north during Sunday's rally."

Jensen remembered watching the weather reports all week, preparing for the almost certain probability that it would rain on the rally. And then, during Saturday night and early Sunday morning, the front had slid north. Jensen had written it off to good luck, but now Brady was telling him . . .

"You did that?"

"Well, not alone. I had a couple of HC members helping me. I probably could have done it on my own, but I had to give my address at the rally *some* attention. As you know, we Fully Fused may be superior beings, but we're not gods."

No, we're not, Jensen thought with a spasm of guilt. Some of us aren't even superior beings.

Brady looked apologetic and added, "I would have asked your help but I didn't want to distract you from your security duties."

Thank Noomri you didn't, Jensen thought. His sham fusion would have been revealed.

Brady leaned back in his chair. "As I'm sure you know, I spent Sunday night in the mountains, to be alone with my xelton and recharge my spirit. I needed the rest."

Jensen nodded. Brady spent a lot of Sunday nights at his place upstate in the woods.

"You must come with me sometime." Brady's eyes unfocused as he smiled. "I've moved *The Compendium* up there and was reading it again. It thrills me every time."

The Compendium . . . the most wonderful, amazing, magical book Jensen had ever seen or read or imagined. He longed to see it again, touch it, flip through its pages. In his darkest moment of faltering faith in the goals and beliefs of the Church, Luther Brady had shown him *The Compendium* and all doubts had vanished like smoke.

Jensen wanted to say, Yes, yes, invite me to see *The Compendium* again, but Brady's next words stopped him.

"After reading *The Compendium* we can float together above the forest. It's so peaceful to watch the wildlife from above."

Jensen's tongue felt suddenly thick and dry. Levitate? His heart fell. No . . . that would never do. But he had to look upbeat.

"I look forward to it."

"But let's put that aside." Brady straightened in his chair. "What did you want to see me about?"

Here goes, Jensen thought.

He recited the facts: Someone had tried to join under a false name. He turned out to be Jason Amurri, son of Aldo Amurri.

"Unbelievable! Aldo Amurri's son!"

"You've heard of him?"

"Of course. He's a very wealthy and important man. We could suffer a lot of bad press because of this. And we may have lost a well-heeled contributor to boot. Does the son have any money?"

Jensen licked his lips. "Some."

"How much?" The words sounded more like a threat than a question.

Jensen showed him the printout of the financial breakdown Margiotta had found on the Internet.

Brady went livid, right up to his dyed hairline and no doubt beyond. Jensen had known the boss would be mad, but not this mad.

"I didn't know any of this at the time," he said. "How could I?"

"You took a man worth two-hundred-million dollars and kicked him out the door!"

In addition to being the Church's APR and SO, Brady was also its CFO, and as such he was always on the prowl for cash to fund Church projects—one Church project in particular.

Were Jensen not Grand Paladin, were he not in a position to know about Opus Omega, he might have been disillusioned. But knowing about the Opus changed everything, and explained the Church's need of a constant stream of cash.

"All I knew was that he'd given us a false name and address and was causing a violent scene in his first Reveille Session. That fits the criteria for instant UP. Criteria you laid down yourself, I might add."

Brady gave him a brief, hostile look, then swiveled his chair toward the windows. Jensen let out a breath. He'd done everything by the book; that, at least, was in his favor.

Brady stayed turned for a good minute, giving Jensen time to reflect on how far he'd come from Nigeria to be sitting here with such a powerful man.

He'd been born Ajayi Dokubo and spent his earliest years in a poor village in southwest Nigeria near the Benin border; his people spoke Yoruba and sacrificed rams to Olorun. When he was five his father moved the family to Lagos where Jensen learned English, the official language of Nigeria. At age nine his father uprooted them again, this time to the U.S. To Chicago.

His old man survived long enough to see to it that his son became a U.S. citizen, then wound up the victim of a fatal mugging. Jensen survived a turbulent, fatherless, rough-and-tumble adolescence that landed him in trouble with the law. A Southside cop, an ex-marine named Hollis, had given him a choice: Join the army or go to court.

He joined up just in time to be sent to Iraq for the first Gulf War where he killed an Iraqi in a firefight and liked it. Liked it too much, maybe. Killed two more and that would have been okay except that the last one was trying to surrender at the time. That didn't set too well with his lieutenant and he was given another choice—honorable discharge or face charges.

So he returned to the streets again, this time in New York City. Being black, with no education, his options were few. So it had to happen: He got in with a rough crew that was dealing drugs, boosting and fencing electronics, smuggling cigarettes, the usual. Because of his size, Jensen became their go-to guy when strong-arm stuff was called for. Mostly it was punch-ups, maybe breaking a leg or two. But then came the day they decided someone needed killing.

Jensen had been game. So he'd found the target in a bar and cracked his skull with a pool cue. His mistake had been being so public about it. He was picked up for the murder but the cops had to release him when the witnesses developed amnesia.

Coming that close to a jolt in the joint had shaken him to the point where he decided it was time to turn his life around.

He'd lived by his wits for most of his life, never looking to rule the world, just to be comfortable without doing a nine-to-five grind. Now he was willing to get on the treadmill. But he needed direction.

He found it when he saw Luther Brady on *Oprah!*—his girlfriend at the time never missed that damn show—and the more Jensen listened, the more he knew Dormentalism was what he'd been looking for.

To seal the deal with himself to leave his old ways behind, Ajayi Dokubo changed his surname to a simple one he'd picked out of a phone book: Jensen. He never used his first name, treated it as if it didn't exist. He became Jensen—period.

As for Dormentalism, it didn't turn out to be what he'd originally thought, but it was indeed what he'd been looking for.

He might have screwed that up too if not for Luther Brady.

He still remembered the day he'd been called into Brady's office and confronted with his arrest record. He'd expected to be declared UP, but instead—because of his military experience, Brady said—he was made a TP.

Brady went even further by paying his tuition to John Jay College of Criminal Justice where he earned an associate degree in security management. Jensen was still attending part time, working toward a BA.

In the five years since Brady had appointed him Grand Paladin, Jensen had taken the job personally. Luther Brady had had more faith in him than he'd had in himself. He couldn't think of anything he wouldn't do for the man.

"Well, what do we do?" Jensen said.

" 'We'?" Brady's eyebrows levitated a good half inch. " 'We' are doing nothing. *You,* however, are going to get this Jason Amurri back here."

That wasn't going to be easy. They hadn't exactly parted buddies.

"And don't," Brady added, "let on that we know who he really is."

"How am I supposed to do that? I can't call the Ritz Carlton and get his room without knowing he's Jason Amurri."

Brady jabbed a finger at him. "I don't care. Beg, plead, go to his hotel and offer him a ride on your shoulders if you have to, but I want him back here tomorrow! Get to it. Now."

Jensen stewed as he made the trip back to his office. How the hell was he going to—?

The application! Maybe this turkey had left a working contact number.

He rummaged through the papers on his desk. Yes! Here it was, with a 212 area code.

He buzzed What's-Her-Name. "Get in here."

When she did, all buttoned up in her uniform and looking scared, he handed her Amurri's application and gave her a new version of the situation. A mistake had been made and had to be rectified. "Jack Farrell" had been declared UP and ejected in error. Apologize and persuade him to come back for another meeting.

She hurried out but returned a minute later.

"He doesn't have his phone on," she said with a trembling lower lip. For some reason his secretaries never seemed to like to tell him things he didn't want to hear.

"Then keep calling, you idiot!" he shouted. "Call every five minutes until you reach him, and then do the selling job of your xeltonless life!"

Why was it so damn near impossible to get good help these days?

11

Jack found Russ Tuit in an agitated state. He let Jack in, then started stomping around the apartment.

"Can I say, 'What the fuck?'" he shouted, waving a thick, oversized paperback in the air. "Can I just?"

Jack shrugged. "Hey, it's your apartment." Then an unpleasant thought struck. "You're not having trouble with the disk, are you? Yesterday—"

"The disk is fine. No, it's this English Lit course I'm taking. I just had to read 'Ode on a Greek Urn' by Keats and I just *got* to say, 'What the fuck!'"

"It's 'Ode on a *Grecian* Urn,' I believe, but if it'll make you feel better, sure. Be my guest."

"Okay. What the *fuck*?" He flipped through the pages till he found what he wanted. "Listen to this: 'More happy love! More happy, happy love!'" He tossed the book across the room to where it bounced off the wall, leaving a greenish scuff—the same green as the book cover. It joined half a dozen similar marks in the vicinity. "Is this guy kidding? It sounds like the Stimpy song!"

"And you sound like Ren."

"Do you *believe* the shit they want us to read? Now I remember why I dropped out and went into full-time hacking. This is worse than prison, man! This is cruel and unusual!"

"Speaking of hacking," Jack said, "the disk *is* ready, isn't it?"

"What? Oh, yeah. Sure." Simply mentioning the disk seemed to calm him. "Got it right here."

He picked up a red three-and-a-half-inch floppy and scaled it across the room.

Jack caught the little thing and said, "This is it?"

"All you'll need. Just make sure you put it in the floppy drive *before* you start the machine. That way my disk'll be in control of the startup."

"What do I do?"

"Nothing. You don't even have to turn on the monitor. The disk'll bypass any password protection. It'll disable any antivirus software he's got—Norton, McAfee, whatever—and introduce HYRTBU. All you've got to do is wait maybe ten minutes till the hard drive stops chattering, then pull out the disk—Jesus, make sure you don't leave it there—turn off the computer, and buy yourself a beer. His files are toast."

Jack stared at the red plastic square resting in his palm. "That's it?" It seemed too simple.

Russ grinned. "That's it. That's why you pay me the big bucks. Speaking of which . . ."

Jack dug into his pocket, saying, "But how will I know if it worked?"

"If you don't see him tossing his rig out a window, you'll see him down at his computer guy's place the next day asking what the fuck's going on."

Jack nodded. He planned to be watching.

But before all that he had to track down a take-out pu pu platter.

12

"Your cousin called," Sister Agnes said.

Maggie froze. She had just entered the convent's central hallway and now she felt unable to breathe.

So it begins.

Had she done the right thing in hiring Jack? She'd know soon enough. She'd either be free of this human leech or her life's work would be shattered by shame and humiliation. Either way, it had to be better than this awful in-between state of constant fear and dread.

"Maggie?" Agnes said, her brow knitting with concern. "Are you all right? You're white as a sheet."

Maggie nodded. Her words rasped over a dusty tongue. "What did he say?"

"He said to tell you your Uncle Mike has taken a turn for the worse and he'll call you back around four. I didn't know you had an Uncle Mike."

"Distant relative."

She went to her room and waited for Agnes to leave the hallway, then she darted out to a public phone two blocks west. The convent didn't allow sisters their own phones, and she couldn't discuss this on the common line in the hall, so she hurried to the one the blackmailer had sent her to the first time he'd contacted her.

It was already ringing when she arrived. She grabbed the receiver.

"Yes?"

"I thought you was going to stand me up," said that nasty, grating voice. God help her, she hated this faceless monster. "I wouldn't have been too surprised, considering how you shorted me on the latest payment."

"I don't have any more!"

Jack had told her to say that, but it was true. Her meager savings were almost gone. She'd told Mike and he'd helped her as much as he could without raising his wife's suspicions. He was being blackmailed too. But although he'd be damaged if those pictures got out, he'd survive—his marriage might not, but he'd still have his career. Maggie would be left with nothing.

"Yes, you do," the voice cooed.

"No, I swear! There's nothing left."

Now a snarl. "But we both know where you can get more!"

"No! I told you before—"

"It won't be hard." Back to the cajoling tone. "You've got all that cash coming in to the building fund. I'll bet a lot of the poor suckers in your parish don't ask for no receipts. All you gotta do is siphon off a little every time some comes through. No one will know."

I'll know! Maggie wanted to shout.

But Jack had told her to string him along, let him think she was giving in—but not too easily.

"But I can't! That's not my money. It's for the church. They need every penny."

The snarl again. "And how many pennies do you think they'll get when I start tacking up photos of you and Mr. Capital Campaign Consultant all over the parish? Huh? How many then?"

Maggie sobbed. She didn't have to fake it. "All right. I'll see if I can. But there's not much coming in during the week. What little we do get comes in on Sundays."

"I ain't waitin' till next week! Get me something before that! Forty-eight hours, or else!"

The phone went dead.

Maggie leaned against the edge of the phone booth and sobbed.

How in the world had she come to this? Never, not once, not for an instant since the day she'd joined the order had she ever even dreamed of becoming involved with a man.

If not for Serafina Martinez, none of this would have happened.

Not that she blamed the child in any way. But knowing that Fina and her sisters and brother would be forced to leave St. Joe's had compelled her to search for a benefactor.

And about that time she'd been getting to know Michael Metcalf. Bright, handsome, charming, and he was working to make St. Joe's a better place. Their positions in the fund-raising campaign put them together time and again. They became friends.

One day, out of desperation, she mentioned the Martinez children after one of the fund-raising meetings and asked if he might help. His immediate agreement had stunned Maggie, and as they continued seeing each other at the meetings, and at increasingly frequent tête-à-têtes about Fina and her siblings, she felt herself longing to touch him and be touched by him.

Then one night, when they were alone in the church basement—in the deserted soup kitchen—he'd kissed her and it felt wonderful, so wonderful that something broke free inside her, demanding more . . . and they made love right there, beneath the floor and aisles and pews of St. Joseph's Church. Beneath God's house.

Maggie had awakened the next morning ashamed and utterly miserable. Bad enough she had broken her vow of chastity, but Michael wasn't just a man, he was a man with a wife and children.

That had not been enough to stop her though. Being with Michael had lit a fire in her that she could not extinguish. A whole new world had opened for her and she thirsted constantly for him.

Seven times . . . she'd sinned seven times with him. And there would have been more if the arrival of that envelope hadn't shocked her back to sanity. Black-and-white photos, grainy and underlit, but her ecstatic face was clearly identifiable as she writhed under Michael.

She'd vomited when she saw them, and nearly passed out when she read the note with its threats.

She'd called Michael who told her he'd been sent the same photos with a similar demand for payment.

Maggie closed her eyes, remembering those photos. To see herself in the act, doing what she'd been doing . . .

It still shocked her that she'd been capable of such a thing. She'd turned it over and over in her mind, trying to understand it, trying to understand herself.

Maybe because she'd joined the convent directly out of high school. She'd been a virgin then—no experience with men, certainly not with men interested in her as a woman—and had remained so until Michael Metcalf came along. She'd found herself mesmerized by this kind, generous man. He'd awakened yearnings she'd never realized she had.

And God forgive her, she'd surrendered to them.

But never again.

Now she and Michael saw each other only at fund-raisers, and occasionally at Mass where he'd pass Maggie some cash to help her with the payments. But he could give her only so much.

She prayed that even that would end soon.

She turned and walked back toward the convent, speaking softly to God.

"Lord—the Father, the Son, and the Holy Ghost—deliver me from this trial, I beg You. Not just for my own sake, but for St. Joseph's as well. I have strayed, I know, and I am ashamed. I've repented, I've confessed my sin. I've done penance. Please forgive my one deviation from the Path of Your Love. I will never stray again. Never. Absolve me of this and let me go on serving You with love and devotion. But if I must be punished, let it be in a manner that does not reflect ill on St. Joseph's.

"I beg You to guide Jack so that he may end this threat to the parish and to myself without causing harm or sinning on my behalf."

Self-loathing choked her into silence. It was all her fault. No one else to blame. Yes, Michael was complicit, weak, and she perhaps was not his first dalliance, but she should have been strong enough for both of them. She had the Calling, not Michael.

If a few weeks from now she was still a member of the convent and the good name of St. Joseph's remained unsullied, she would know that God had heard and forgiven her.

If not . . .

13

A hand touched Jamie Grant's shoulder and she started. A quick glance in the streaked mirror behind the Parthenon's bar showed it was only Timmy Ryan.

"Hey, jumpy tonight."

Jamie shrugged.

Timmy leaned in closer, elbows on the bar, and spoke in a low tone. "Listen, Schwartz's got his kid brother along tonight. In from Duluth. We figured we'd have the usual fun with him if you're up to it."

Jamie didn't move her head. Instead she fixed her eyes on Ryan's reflection in the mirror. He had a Jay Leno situation going with his chin; he wore a dark suit, wrinkled, a striped tie, loosened, and a toothy grin, capped. He spent his days as a copywriter and his nights as a Parthenon regular, like Jamie and Schwartz, and Cassie and Frank, and about half a dozen others.

She took a sip of her Dewar's and soda. "I don't know if I'm up to it, Timmy."

She was feeling edgy. She could have sworn she'd been followed here. This comfy little bar in the West Sixties had been a nightly refuge for years. Had it been invaded? Had some Dementedists infiltrated the irregulars?

She hated to think so. A good neighborhood tavern like the Parthenon was a place to be nurtured and cherished. She liked the feel of the bar's mahogany under her elbows, the give of the leather on the chairs and stools and booths, the drama and pageant of foam rising in a draft pint of lager or stout, the smell of what's been spilled, the rattle of the cocktail shaker, the murmur of conversation, the green glow of a football game on the TV screen.

Where everybody knows your name . . . more than a theme song, it was the foundation of what made a tavern work. But Jamie didn't need everybody knowing her name to feel at home here, just a nod or a wave from a few of the regulars as she stepped through the door sufficed. And few things were better than Louie timing the preparation of her Dewar's and soda—her "usual"—so that it was homing in for a three-point landing on the bar as she slid onto her usual stool.

Maybe she liked the place too much, maybe she spent too much time here. She definitely knew she drank too much.

Which always reminded her of an old Scottish proverb: *They talk of my drinking but never my thirst.*

And that pretty much nailed the situation. A thirst for something more than ethanol in all its various and wondrous permutations drew her to the Parthenon. If getting a load on were the sole objective, she could do it quicker and far cheaper by staying home with a bottle. She came for the embrace of kindred souls—who also just happened to like to consume ethanol in all its various and wondrous permutations—and for the camaraderie . . . a potion far more potent and alluring than distilled spirits.

Timmy draped an arm over her shoulders. It felt good, a spot of warmth on this chilly night. She and Timmy had had a fling a few years ago—Jamie had flung with a number of regulars at the Parthenon—but nothing serious, just someone to be with now and then. Some nights the thought of going home alone to an empty apartment was simply too much to bear.

"Come on, Jamie. Been a while since we heard a pinkie story. They're *always* good for a laugh."

"Tell you what," Jamie said, putting on a smile. "Pay my bar tab tonight and you've got a deal."

"You're on. After Frank finishes yakking about that new Lexus of his, I'll bring the kid over. So put on your thinking cap."

He gave her shoulder a squeeze and moved off, leaving her alone.

Alone . . .

She didn't want to be alone tonight, but not for the usual reasons. Those Dementedist threats—of course, they never said they were Dementedists, but who were they kidding—and now this feeling of being shadowed were getting to her. Maybe she and Timmy could hook up for the night . . . just for old time's sake.

She'd never liked the emptiness of her apartment—that was one of the reasons she spent so much time at the office—but she'd never feared being there. Maybe she'd just spend the night here at the Parthenon . . . entertaining the troops.

Always good for a laugh . . .

Yeah, that's me all right. Jamie the Joke Machine. Quick with the quip, the bon mot, the laugh-aloud girl, the—

Christ, I hate my life.

The Dementedism stories had been the first thing in years to fire her up, but now she sensed it turning on her. How could she enjoy writing pieces that kept her looking over her shoulder? She'd expected *some* negative fallout, but figured she could handle it.

Well, you're sure doing a bang-up job handling it tonight, Jamie.

She signaled Louie for another hit of Dewar's, then stared at the stub of her right pinkie. What tall tale could she come up with tonight? Yesterday she'd given that PI—what was his name? Robinson? Robertson? Something like that—the outboard motor story. But she'd already used that here at the Parthenon. Had to come up with something new.

Only Jamie knew the real story . . . how she'd lost most of that finger to the love of her life.

Never should have married Eddie Harrison. Her mother had known her college sweetheart was bad news and had warned her, but did she listen? No way. So right after she got her journalism degree she married him. It looked like a good situation at first, but it took him only a few years to morph from sweetheart to lushheart. And one night during year five he almost killed her.

Eddie was such a sweet guy when he was sober, but the booze did something to him, made him mean, frayed his temper. Jamie had been a stringer back then, doing most of her writing at home. On the fateful night, for some still-unknown reason, the clicking of her keyboard set him off and he demanded that Jamie stop typing. When she told him she had a morning deadline and had to finish, he flew into a rage, went to the kitchen, returned with a carving knife, and tried to cut off her hands. Lucky for her he was so drunk he couldn't manage it, but the slashing blade did manage to connect with her pinkie. As she knelt on the rug, bleeding and moaning and trying to dial 911, Eddie carried the severed end to the bathroom and flushed it down the toilet. Then he passed out.

The next day he was all anguish and remorse and contrition and full of promises never ever to drink again. But Jamie was not getting on that merry-go-round. She packed up, moved out, pressed criminal charges, and filed for divorce—all in one day.

And hadn't had a long-term relationship since.

She'd seen enough depressed people in her forty-three years to know she fit the clinical picture. She spent every waking moment riding depression's ragged edge. But she wasn't into pills. Her self-prescribed therapy was work. Filling the hours with relentless activity staved off the down feelings. And she produced an amazing amount of copy—for *The Light,* for various magazines under a pseudonym, even a chapter in a soon-to-be-published journalism textbook. If she got into a pill situation—started on Prozac or Zoloft or one of those—and it did its job, would the lifting depression take the writing drive along with it?

She couldn't risk that. She'd found a formula that kept her from tumbling into the abyss: days spent either writing or researching; evenings here at the Pantheon, just a few blocks from her apartment, drinking and kibitzing with the regulars; and nights of exhausted sleep.

Jamie wasn't so sure about the sleep situation tonight, though.

She glanced around, looking for unfamiliar faces. There were always some. No secret that she was writing a derogatory series about the cult—she refused to call it a church—but did they have any idea that she might have discovered something that would embarrass the hell out of them and set their whole organization on its ear?

Might . . . that was the key word here. She hadn't confirmed her suspicions yet, and so far she'd been stymied in finding a way to do so.

But if the Dementedists knew of her suspicions, no telling what they might do. She'd have to—

She jumped as someone tapped her shoulder. Timmy again. Damn it, she was edgy.

Timmy introduced Schwartz's brother, who looked barely thirty and nothing like Schwartz. After a little small talk Timmy pointed out Jamie's short pinkie and said something about wait till you hear this . . . You just won't believe it. Schwartz and Cassie and Ralph and the others were gathered in a semicircle around her and Little Brother. She had an audience but no material.

What the hell, she thought. Wing it.

"Well, it was years ago, back in 1988, when I was in the Karakoram to—" She noticed the kid's perplexed expression, mirrored in the other listeners. Christ, was there anyone left who knew their geography? "That's a mountain range. I was in a mountain-climbing situation, preparing to tackle the Abruzzi ridge of K2—which the locals call *Chogori*—and I was looking for an ice ax . . ."

14

"I'm gonna get it from ya! Yes, I am! Yes, I am!"

Clancy growled as he gripped the rawhide toy in his sharp little teeth and tried to pull it away from his former master.

Kneeling on the floor, Richie Cordova was amazed that the little terrier still had this much play in him. He had to be ten years old, the equivalent to seventy in a man. Or so they said.

Every so often Richie got this urge to see Clancy and play with him. The divorce agreement granted him visitation rights, but supervised.

Supervised! It still rankled him. What'd the judge think he was going to do, run off with the pooch? Hardly.

The worst part was that he had to visit Clancy in Neva's apartment. She was such a slob. Look at the place. Nothing where it should be and it stank of cigarettes.

A place for everything and everything in its place, Richie always said.

"Neva!" he called.

Her scratchy voice echoed from the kitchen. "Yeah?"

"C'mere a minute, will you?"

She took her sweet time traveling the ten feet or so to the living room. She stood in the archway, wearing a housecoat and puffing a butt.

"What?"

"Don't you ever clean this place? It's a dump."

Her face reddened. "I clean it just fine. I dare you to find a speck of dust."

"I ain't talking about dirt. I'm talking about straightening things up. Everything's tossed every which way. And you've got mail on that table and keys on this table, and—"

"Cram it, Rich. You're allowed to come here to visit Clancy, not bust my chops."

"I don't think Clancy should have to live in all this clutter."

Shit, he loved this little dog! He never should have allowed Neva custody.

"Clancy's doing just fine. Aren't you, baby?" She bent and slapped the side of her leg. Immediately Clancy forgot about Richie and ran over to her. She scratched his head. "Aren't you, snookums?"

"And I don't think the secondhand smoke is good for his health."

Neva glared at him. "Up yours, Rich. Don't you remember why we split? Not some other man or some other woman: you. You and your neatnik ways. You and your need to *control*. You make Monk look like Oscar Madison. Everything has to be just so, and yet you walk around—or maybe I should say *waddle* around—looking like the Goodyear blimp."

Richie said nothing. He wanted to kill her. Slowly.

This wasn't the first time. Every goddamn time he came here it was the same thing: He wound up wanting to wring her scrawny neck. He couldn't think of anyone else on earth who could piss him off this way.

"You still studying those horoscopes every day?" she said. "What a laugh. A guy who wants to control everything and everyone around him thinks his life's being controlled by a bunch of stars a zillion miles away. It's a riot."

"You got no idea what you're talking about. I use them for guidance, that's all."

"Stars are pulling your strings. Ha! You believe in flying saucers too?"

Hauling himself to his feet took a lot out of him. He *had* to lose some weight soon.

"You're pushing it, Neva."

"Yeah, well why not? You pushed me around for five years. About time someone pushed back."

"Neva . . ."

"I ain't afraid of you, Richie. Not anymore."

"You should be." Feeling like he was about to explode, he took a step toward her. "You really—"

Clancy bared his teeth and growled. The sound pierced him.

You too, Clancy?

"Fuck the both of you."

Richie Cordova turned and left his ex-wife and his ex-dog to wallow in their shit hole.

15

After picking the lock to Cordova's office, Jack slipped a slim, flexible metal ruler between the door and the hinge-side jamb. He held the ruler against the plunger as he pushed the door open. Without letting the plunger pop, he replaced the ruler with the short length of duct tape he'd stuck to his sweatshirt. He let the outer inch of the tape stick out free in the hallway, then closed the door.

Okay. He was in. First thing he did was pull on a pair of latex gloves. Next he flicked on his penlight and stepped through the reception area into the office where he went directly to Cordova's desk. Neat as could be— even the paper clips were lined up like soldiers in review. A single photo on the desk: a terrier of some kind.

A dog . . . he kept a photo of a dog on his desk.

Jack knelt and found the computer's mini-tower on the floor at the rear of the kneehole. He noticed a CD drive, probably a burner for backup. One CD could hold a ton of blackmail photos. He pulled out Russ's HYRTBU disk, inserted it into the floppy slot, then pressed the on button.

As the computer whirred to life, Jack began exploring the office. Cordova wasn't the sharpest knife in the drawer, but you didn't need an Oxford degree to know to store a valuable backup off premises. Not just to protect against theft, but fire as well.

Jack started with the file cabinets. Just for the hell of it he checked for a folder labeled *backup* but didn't find one. So he combed through every drawer, every hanging folder in both cabinets but found no backup disk. Unlike the file cache Jack had found in Cordova's home office last September, these contained no blackmail material. Nothing but PI records. So he did a little floor crawling, looking for something taped to the underside of the furniture. Nope.

He thought he'd struck pay dirt when he found a padded envelope behind the radiator, but it contained only cash. Money he'd squeezed from his victims, no doubt. Jack was tempted to take it, just for spite, but he couldn't let Cordova know someone had been in his office. The success of this whole fix-it depended on that.

He went back to the computer. The cooling fan was running, but the hard drive was silent. Russ's disk had done its job. Maybe.

Jack removed the disk and pocketed it. He felt weird leaving the place without knowing for sure that he'd accomplished what he'd come for. Of course he could turn on the computer and, if it wasn't password protected, open a few files to check, but he might unknowingly leave some sort of trace that could make Cordova suspect someone had been here.

Better to trust Russ and leave clean.

He returned to the hallway and locked the door behind him. Then he yanked the duct tape free of the jamb. The tape would leave a little adhesive behind, but that couldn't be helped. Unless Cordova got down on his hands and knees and checked the plunger with a magnifying glass, he would never know.

Time to head back to the Ritz. He needed his beauty rest. He was expecting an important call in the morning.

WEDNESDAY

1

Jack spent an uncomfortable night at the Ritz Carlton. Not because there was anything wrong with the twelfth-floor park-view room—it was superb. The front desk manager hadn't blinked when Jack had declared that he didn't believe in credit cards and laid down three of a kind of Maria Roselli's thousand-dollar bills as an advance on his stay. But despite all the comforts he kept thinking he should be at Gia's place, watching over her, ready to jump should anything happen. By reminding himself that the Ritz was only a few blocks from Sutton Square—closer than his own apartment—he managed to drift off to sleep.

He was up early, and showered and dressed before he called Gia to make sure she was okay. She was. No surprise there. If something had gone wrong, she had his room number and would have called.

At eight-thirty room service delivered his breakfast and he turned on his Tracfone. Four minutes later, as he was digging into a pair of deliciously runny eggs Bene-dict—Gia would have made a face—the phone rang.

"Mr. Farrell?" said a woman's voice.

"Speaking."

"Oh, I'm so glad I finally contacted you. I've been calling this number since yesterday."

Jack smiled. Bet it drove your boss crazy that no one answered.

"Who are you and why are you calling me?" Jack knew the answers, but Jason wouldn't. "If you're selling something—"

"Oh, no! My name is Eva Compton from the New York City Dormentalist Temple. I'm calling from the Grand Paladin's office and—"

Jack let out a little gasp. "Dormentalist? I have nothing to say to you people! You threw me out!"

"That's why I'm calling, Mr. Farrell. What happened yesterday was a terrible mistake. Please come back to the temple so that we can rectify this unfortunate error. We're all terribly upset here."

"You're upset? *You're* upset? I've never been so humiliated in my entire life! You Dormentalists are awful, heartless people and I want nothing to do with any of you. Ever!"

With that he thumbed the off button and glanced at his watch—8:41. Jack made a mental wager that they'd call back in twenty minutes.

He lost. The phone rang at 8:52. Jack recognized the accented bass voice immediately.

"Mr. Farrell, this is Grand Paladin Jensen of the New York City Dormentalist Temple. We met yesterday. I—"

"You're the rude man who kicked me out!"

"And I'm so sorry about that. We made an error—a terrible error—and we'd like to rectify it."

"Oh, really." Jack drew out the word. He wasn't going to let Jensen off the hook easily. "You said I was a phony, that you ran a check on my name and found out I didn't exist. So why are you calling a man who doesn't exist, Mr. Jensen? Tell me that?"

"Well, I—"

"And why are you calling me 'Mr. Farrell' when you say that's not my name?"

"I-I don't have any other name to call you. Look, if you'll just come back, I'm sure we can—"

"You also said you don't allow lies in Dormentalist temples—only truth. If that's true, why do you want me back?"

"Because . . . because I was too hasty." Jack could almost hear him squirm. "After you left I did some investigating and learned that your RT made several errors. Errors which would rightfully upset anyone."

"I'll say!"

"I promise you she's being disciplined. She'll be sent before the FPRB and—"

"The what?"

"The Fusion Progress Review Board. Her behavior will be reviewed and appropriate disciplinary measures taken."

Electroshock therapy, I hope, Jack thought, remembering that hapless mouse.

He figured it was time to waver, but not before twisting the knife.

"Well, that's encouraging, but what about you? You didn't even give me a chance to speak. Are you going before this FPRB?"

"Well, ah, no. You have to understand, Mr. Farrell, that the Church is under constant assault, and sometimes we get jumpy. I realized that you had volunteered your real name but I wouldn't listen, so I discussed the matter with Mr. Brady."

Time to be impressed. "*Luther* Brady? You discussed me with Luther Brady himself?"

"Yes, and he was very upset that you'd come to the Church for help and we'd turned you away. He wants to meet with you personally when you come back."

Bump it up to breathy-voiced awe: "Luther Brady wants to meet with *me*? That's . . . that's . . ." a little catch in the voice here ". . . wonderful! When can I come back?"

"Anytime you wish, but the sooner the better as far as we're concerned."

"I'll be right down."

"Excellent! I'll have somebody meet you at—"

"Not just 'somebody,' " Jack said, unable to resist one last turn of the blade. "You. I want the Grand Paladin himself there to bring me in."

Jack heard Jensen swallow, then say, "Why, of course. I'd be happy to."

Oh, yeah. I'll bet you're just dying to be my escort to Luther Brady.

Jack considered asking Jensen to bark like a dog but canned it. He grinned as he ended the call.

Finding Johnny Roselli was turning out to be fun.

2

Grand Paladin Jensen took up most of the elevator cab. Jack managed to squeeze in beside him and find a way to stand without rubbing elbows with his black uniform, but that was it. The two of them pretty much maxed out the space. Gollum might have been able to make it a threesome, but that was iffy.

As Jensen pressed the 22 button, Jack decided to go into chatty mode.

"All the way to the top, huh?"

Jensen nodded, staring at the doors. "That's Mr. Brady's floor."

"The *whole* floor?"

Another nod. "The whole floor."

"I'm really looking forward to meeting him. Will he be waiting for us?"

Jensen had the look of a man trying to be cool while a Doberman sniffed his crotch.

"He's expecting us."

"Do you have a first name, Mr. Jensen?"

"Yes."

Jack waited a few seconds. When it became obvious Jensen wasn't going to volunteer anything else, Jack said, "And that would be . . . ?"

Jensen kept staring straight ahead. "That would be a name I don't use."

Yessiree, the size of a GE double oven but less person-ality.

"And speaking of names," Jensen added, finally look-ing at Jack, "what do we call you?"

Before Jack could answer, the cab stopped but the doors didn't open. He noticed that the floor indicator read *21*.

"Are we stuck?"

"No, merely being cleared through."

Jack checked the upper corners and spotted a mirrored hemisphere front left. Security camera. Seemed like Luther Brady didn't like drop-in company.

The cab began moving again, then stopped on twenty-two. The doors slid open onto a hallway with a gleaming parquet floor and walnut-paneled walls. Ahead a pair of doors stood open revealing a large sunny space. A young, gray-uniformed receptionist sat behind a black desk to the right.

"We're expected," Jensen said.

She nodded knowingly. "Of course. Wait here and I'll announce you."

But Jack kept going, like a moth heading for the light, ignoring calls from Jensen and the receptionist. He strolled through the doors into a high-ceilinged room clad in the same walnut paneling. He squinted in the light from the skylights and windows. To the left he noticed a pair of chromed steel doors sliding shut across a recess that contained what appeared to be a giant sphere.

A familiar-looking man rose from a huge desk by the windows. Jack knew him from TV, usually in a tape clip associated with a sound bite. But he hadn't seen that ex-pression before: Luther Brady was furious.

"I tried to stop him, Mr. Brady," said the breathless re-ceptionist behind him, "but he wouldn't listen."

The anger flashed out of Brady's face as quickly as it had come. He was smiling now as he came around the desk and started toward Jack.

"Quite all right, Constance," he said, dismissing her with a left-handed wave. He thrust out his right hand as he approached Jack. "Our guest, it would seem, has a rather unpredictable nature."

Constance left, shutting the door behind her. Jensen remained, standing with his feet apart, his hands clasped in front of him. Like some dark stone idol.

"I'm so sorry," Jack said. "I didn't mean to barge in. It's just that, well, the thought of meeting Luther Brady himself, in person, it . . . well, it just blew my manners out the window. Really, I apologize."

"Quite the contrary," Brady said. "It is I" —a quick glance at Jensen here—"*we* who should be apologizing to you for the way you were treated yesterday."

"Don't give it another thought." Jack clasped Brady's hand in both of his and gave it a hearty shake. "This is *such* an honor, sir."

Brady's supercilious expression indicated that he agreed.

"But you have me at a disadvantage, sir. You know my name but I don't know yours." He laughed. "I certainly can't call you 'Jack Farrell' now, can I."

"It's Jason . . . Jason Amurri."

"Jason Amurri," Brady said slowly, as if rolling an unfamiliar sound over his tongue.

You're good, Jack thought. Very good.

No doubt Brady and Jensen knew all about Jason Amurri by now, but Brady was putting on an excellent show.

Ernie's job had been to find a rich recluse in his thirties, someone who didn't get his pictures in the pages. He'd been justly proud of coming up with Jason Amurri.

Ernie had said Jason was the younger son of shipping magnate Aldo Amurri—not Onassis class, but up there—with a personal fortune somewhere in the couple-of-hundred-million neighborhood; nice neighborhood, but due to become lots nicer when he inherited Daddy's company. Unlike his older brother, Jason was anything but a jet-setter. He was a recluse who'd spent much of the past ten years on the continent, mostly in his chateau in

Switzerland. As such, he was not paparazzi fodder and so there was almost no public record of what he looked like.

All perfect for Jack.

Brady was milking his act. "I must say, Jason Amurri is a rather nice name. Why would you hide it?"

"Well, it's kind of embarrassing." Jack wished he knew how to blush on demand. "I've read articles that say that, you know . . . that the church is only after . . . you know . . . money."

"May their xeltons never know union!" Brady's features darkened with anger. "The Dormentalist Church has so many enemies, but not one of them will confront us on the issues—whether or not our members lead better lives because of their association with the Church, or whether or not we make the world a better place with our good works. Why not? Because they know they'd lose the argument. So they attack us with innuendo, hinting this, insinuating that, knowing we can't fight back, that we can't open our records without breaking the sacred pact of trust between the Church and its members."

No doubt about it, Brady had the gift. Even Jack found himself wanting to believe him.

"In my heart I think I knew that, but I just, well . . ." He put on his best guilty expression and looked away. "I have some money behind me and I didn't want that to be a factor or influence anyone. I just wanted to be treated like a regular Joe."

Brady laughed and clapped a hand on Jack's shoulder. "You will be. We all start out as regular Joes here. It's on the Fusion Ladder that the men are separated from the boys."

Jack shook his head despondently. "I don't know . . . that Reveille Session was so upsetting. That poor mouse . . ."

Brady's grip tightened on Jack's shoulder. "I realize that some of us are more sensitive than others, and since you've already had one bad experience . . ." He paused, looking thoughtful, then directed his gaze over Jack's shoulder. "What do you think, GP Jensen? Should I handle this myself?"

"Oh, I don't see how, sir," Jensen rumbled from behind Jack. "Your schedule is so full as it is. I don't know where you'll find the time."

Sounded as if he was reading it off a teleprompter.

"You know what?" Brady turned away from Jack and walked to the windows where he struck a wide-legged, hands-clasped-behind-the-back pose as he stared out at the city. "I'm going to *make* time."

"I don't understand," Jack said.

Brady turned and focused the full wattage of his pale blue gaze on Jack. "I am going to take you through the Reveille process myself."

Jack feigned a weak-kneed wobble. "No! I can't believe this!"

"Believe it." Brady moved closer. "With my guidance I can have you through the RC level and into an FA uniform in no time. But first you must tell me why you wish to join our Church. What do you think we can do for you that you can't do for yourself? What are your goals?"

"Well, I'd really like to become a more *effective* person. I'll be facing major responsibilities before too long and—"

"What sort of responsibilities?" Brady made it sound like a casual conversational query.

Jack cleared his throat. "Well, uh, my brother and I will be running the family business soon." He didn't expect Brady to ask what business that was; he wasn't supposed to be interested in that sort of thing. Besides, he already knew. "It's a major responsibility and I don't know if I'm, you know, ready for it."

Did that sound ineffectual enough? He hoped he hadn't overdone it.

Brady laughed. "Well then you've come to the right place! The Dormentalist Church is all about maximizing personal potential. Once your xelton half is fused with its Hokano counterpart, the world will be yours for the taking. There will be no task too difficult, no responsibility so great that you cannot handle it with ease!"

Jack grinned. "If I can achieve only a fraction of that I'll—"

"A fraction? Nonsense! With me guiding your Reveille, we'll awaken your sleeping xelton and have you on the path to Full Fusion in no time!"

Jack forced a little laugh and shook his head. "I've got to warn you. I'm a very closed-in, uptight person. You may have your work cut out for you."

Brady's expression became serious. "You forget that you are dealing with someone who has achieved Full Fusion. There is nothing I cannot do. We will conduct your Reveille right here in my little domain where no one will disturb us. It will go quickly, I promise you."

"I hope so."

Probably the first true thing Jack had said since his arrival.

3

Luther Brady arranged to meet with Jack tomorrow morning to restart his Reveille Sessions, gave him his "personal" phone number that he could call any time, then told Jensen to show him around the temple.

Jensen acted cool about it but Jack could tell he thought he had better things to do than play tour guide for some rich twit who wanted to be more *effectual*.

Jack made a trip to one of the rest rooms and used the break to put in a quick call to Cordova's office. Knowing he was probably being watched, he kept the conversation brief and oblique. In response to "Is he in?" the receptionist said she was expecting her boss around ten-thirty. A late-night investigation, you know.

A late-night investigation into the bottom of a beer glass at Hurley's, you mean.

Okay, that gave him about an hour.

The tour turned out to be about as interesting as a limited warranty statement. The whole damn building seemed little more than a collection of classrooms and offices. So far Jack wasn't seeing what he wanted: the place where the temple kept its membership records. He'd been thinking that if they were computerized and if he could persuade Jensen to give him his e-mail address, he could have Russ hack into the system and locate the whereabouts of Johnny Roselli.

Only two of the upper floors turned out to be interesting. The twentieth couldn't be accessed without a special swipe card. Here was Celebrityland. The entire floor had been converted to luxury suites for high-visibility visitors—the actors, rock stars, scientists, politicians, and so on who'd joined the Dormentalist fold.

But the twenty-first floor was altogether different. At the end of a short hallway lay a large open space with floor-to-ceiling windows on three sides.

"This is the Communing Level," Jensen told him. "FAs can come here at any time of the day or night to meditate with their xelton and, if they're far enough along toward fusion, its Hokano counterpart."

Canned patter if Jack had ever heard it.

He looked around and saw about a dozen people scattered throughout the space, most in chairs facing the windows but a few sat on the floor with their limbs folded into something resembling the lotus position.

Not a bad spot to commune with your inner xelton, or your inner coleslaw, or inner anything. The 180-degree view was spectacular. The south wall was taken up by a row of booths.

"What are those for?"

"For those FAs who wish to commune in privacy."

Privacy? Jack doubted that. Privacy seemed a rare bird in the temple. He'd spotted video pickups everywhere Jensen had taken him.

He heard a latch click and saw someone step out of one of the booths and walk their way. His hair looked oily, face unshaven, and he was dressed in raggedy clothing. Looked like a squeegee man. As he passed, eyes averted, Jack caught his scent: major BO.

He also caught sight of a long nose with a bulbous tip. Could it be?

"I didn't know you had homeless Dormentalists," Jack whispered as the raggedy man passed.

Jensen glared at him with a scandalized expression. "All Dormentalists are productive citizens. That man isn't homeless, he's a lapser."

At first Jack thought he might be referring to some sort of subsect, then remembered seeing the term on one of Jamie Grant's summary sheets. Couldn't remember what it meant, though.

"Lapser?"

Jensen sighed as if everyone should know this. "A Lapsed Fusion Aspirant. He engaged in LFP behavior and this was the punishment meted out by the FPRB."

"The same people dealing with my RT from yesterday?"

Jack congratulated himself. He was starting to get with the lingo.

"Exactly."

"That's his punishment? Sack cloth and ashes?"

"So to speak."

Just to be sure of that nose, Jack wanted another look at this seedy guy before he hit the elevators. He hurried after him.

"Wait," Jensen said behind him. "You can't—"

But Jack kept going. He couldn't let on that he recognized him—no way Jason Amurri would know Johnny Roselli—so he had to try a different tack.

He came abreast of the guy and said, "Excuse me?"

Yeah, that was the nose, and those were Maria Roselli's eyes flashing toward him, then quickly away. He'd found Sonny Boy.

Now what?

Jack was about to ask him his name, just to be absolutely sure, when he felt a big hand close around his arm.

"What do you think you're doing?" Jensen said.

Jack looked after the retreating Johnny Roselli who hadn't even broken stride.

"I just wanted to ask him what he did wrong."

Jensen shook his head. "He's not allowed to tell you, I'm not allowed to tell you, and you're not allowed to ask."

"Why not?"

"Because when you see someone dressed like that, it means they've been declared SE—a Solitarian Exile. He has to wear clothes he found in a trash heap and may not bathe or shave for the term of his punishment. He's an outcast, an untouchable who may not speak or be spoken to by another Dormentalist unless it's a Paladin or a member of the FPRB."

Jack made a face. "How long does that go on?"

"In his case, four weeks. He has about a week left."

"What's his name?"

Jensen's eyes narrowed. "Why do you want to know?"

"Just curious. I might want to look him up after he's no longer an SE and ask what it was like not to bathe for a month. Must be awful." Jack smiled. "Although not as awful as for someone who has to live with him."

Jensen didn't seem to find any humor in that. "If you see him afterward, he can tell you all about it himself, if he so desires."

Jack knew an opening when he saw one.

He'd finished the first half of the Roselli job: He'd established that Johnny was here instead of wandering around Uganda or some such place as a Dormentalist missionary. And though he looked like an SRO hotel regular, he seemed healthy enough.

To finish the job he now had to get in his face and tell him to call Mama. That would mean finding out where he lived, which might involve getting into the membership files.

So Jack jumped on the segue Jensen had presented.

"Ah, yes. Confidentiality. I'm really impressed with how seriously you take that here. I assume your membership records are computerized."

"Of course. Why do you ask?"

"Oh, you know, hackers, disgruntled employees. I'm a very private person and hate the thought of someone snooping through my file in your computer."

"Not to worry. We have state-of-the-art security and virus protection. Only Mr. Brady, myself, and the Overseers have full access."

"Excellent." He glanced at his watch. He needed to be up in the Bronx soon. "Oh, look at the time. I have a couple of family matters to attend to, so—"

Jensen held up a hand. "Before you go, Mr. Brady wanted me to register you for an EC."

"I love old comics!"

Jensen's face showed an instant of confusion. "It's an Entry Card that will pass you through the front entrance without signing in. It's highly unusual for an RC to be issued one, but Mr. Brady feels we owe it to you."

"Oh, you're too kind, but that isn't necessary."

"Oh, but we insist. Our pleasure."

Jack did not want this. It meant having his picture taken and entered into the computer. But how could he refuse without compromising his credibility?

Damn.

4

Jensen watched Jason Amurri sit for his photograph. He appeared upbeat about it, but Jensen sensed an undercurrent of unease.

Why? This was a unique privilege—one that Jensen had been against, but he'd been overruled—so why wasn't Amurri happy?

Just one more thing about this guy that didn't add up. He was supposed to be some kind of rich loner, but he didn't move like a guy who'd grown up deciding which silver spoon to put in his mouth. And his eyes . . . they didn't miss a thing. Jensen was sure he'd spotted some of the video pickups, maybe all of them, but he hadn't asked about them.

Of course he might have expected them as part of the security system, but wouldn't a guy so hooked on privacy have made some sort of squawk?

Then again, maybe Jensen was wrong. Maybe Amurri hadn't spotted the pickups.

Still, he was getting an itch about this guy—no red-flashing alarms or anything like that, just a feeling that something wasn't quite what it seemed.

He wouldn't tell Brady yet. The boss saw dollar signs when he looked at Amurri and would brush off Jensen's suspicions. So right now he'd keep them to himself and have Margiotta do a little more digging. And maybe have Peary follow him again.

Scratch an itch and sometimes you find a chigger.

5

A large Dunkin' Donuts coffee in one hand, the *Post* in the other, Richie Cordova elbowed his office door open and breezed through the reception area.

"What've we got today, Eddy?"

"New client at two."

He stopped in mid-breeze. "That's it?"

"Afraid so."

He shook his head. Christ, things were slow.

In his office he dumped his weight into the chair behind his desk, set down the coffee and paper, and pulled a bag containing a pair of glazed chocolate donuts from the side pocket of his jacket.

He hadn't been able to resist. Damn. He had everything else in his life pretty much locked down the way he wanted. His appetite was the only thing not under control.

Maybe tomorrow.

He hit the power button on his computer and gobbled one of the donuts while it warmed up.

He'd had a dream last night about that nun. A hot one. Must've been because he'd talked to her during the day. He knew what Sister Golden Hair looked like in her birthday suit and she was nothing great—sure as hell nothing like the faked-and-baked babes in the shots he downloaded from *teen-lust.com*—but she wasn't bad, and she was *real*. And he'd been there, watching in real time as he snapped shots. Last night he'd had that pale, hot little body sweating over him instead of Metcalf.

Richie entered his password and went directly to his photo files.

Photo-wise, he was moving away from film to digital. Eventually he'd be all digital, but old habits were hard to break. Photos of any kind had stopped being worth much in court these days. Too easily faked. Hell, even negatives could be faked. But things were different in the good old Court of Public Opinion. A compromising photo could still mess up a reputation. Even if you came out and swore on a stack of Bibles that the pictures were fakes, those images stuck in people's minds long after the explanations had faded away.

He opened the SIS folder and double-clicked one of the jpeg files within. But instead of an image of Sister Maggie in a clinch with her fund-raiser pal, he found only a string of flashing capital letters.

HOPE YOU REMEMBERED TO BACK UP!

Where was the photo? He closed that file and opened the next. Same message.

"Oh, my God!"

He opened more files and felt his mouth grow progressively drier as the same words popped up time after time. He moved to other folders, but all his jpegs carried the same message. He tried a couple of doc files and they were the same! Every goddamn file on his computer had been wiped clean and replaced by the same sneering message!

He was on his feet, hands clamped against the sides of his head. "This can't be! This can't fucking be!"

Eddy poked her head through the doorway. "Something wrong, Richie?"

"My computer! Someone's been in here and sabotaged my computer! Wiped out everything!"

"How is that possible?"

He went to the two windows and checked the contacts. No sign of tampering. And both were locked from inside.

"I don't know. I—" He jabbed an index finger at her. "You must've forgot to turn on the alarm."

Eddy shook her head and looked offended. "Not a chance. I put it on as I always do. And it was still armed this morning when I opened up."

"Bullshit!" he said as he charged her way. She had to back out of the doorway to allow him through. "If that's true, how did he get to my machine?"

Same story with the sealed window in the reception area. What was going on?

"Maybe he didn't," Eddy said. "Maybe he—what do they call it?—hacked into it. I've heard they can get into government computers, so why not yours?"

Richie didn't know much about hacking, but he knew one thing for sure: "A computer's got to be turned on before you can hack it, and I turn mine off every night."

He returned to his office.

Eddy said, "Well then, I don't know what to tell you besides the alarm was set." She frowned. "And then you've got to ask yourself why anyone would want to sabotage your computer? I keep all the correspondence and billing records on mine. If someone wanted to hurt your business, they'd go after my machine, wouldn't they? And mine is fine."

Richie couldn't answer that. And suddenly he was thinking about the envelope.

"Okay, okay, we've wasted enough time jawing about it. Get the number of that computer place down the street. Call him and tell him I've got an emergency here and need him ASAP."

"Will do."

As soon as the door closed, he went over to the radiator. The envelope was still there. He yanked it out and checked the money—all there. He dropped it back into its hiding place and stumbled back to his chair.

Maybe no one had broken in after all. That was a relief. He'd moved his computer here for the security system. Rudimentary but better than nothing, which was what he had at the house. And since it came with the rent here, a hell of a lot cheaper than installing one.

He grabbed the *Post* and fanned to the horoscope page.

Gemini (May 21–June 21): Win points by accepting additional responsibilities. Extra hours ensure future financial security. If you are in negotiations, you know by now that the other side may not be taking things as seriously as you are.

Well, he was always in financial negotiations, and that nun bitch didn't seem to be taking things as seriously as she should, but nothing here about bad luck or watching your back. Cusp guy that he was, he read on to the next.

Cancer (June 22–July 22): Being in the right place at the right time is your style today. You get recognition for a job well done. Balance job responsibilities with social ones. Celebrate, even if you have to invent a reason.

No warning here, either. But he liked the being in the right place at the right time part. That never hurt. No help, though, on what had happened to all his files.

He glanced at the screen where the words still flashed:

HOPE YOU REMEMBERED TO BACK UP!

Richie jabbed the off button and the screen went dark. "Fuck you!"

He *had* remembered to back up. He had a copy of every file in a safe place.

6

Jack found a small neighborhood no-name bar and earned a lot of stares as the only white face in the place. The available drafts were various Buds and Millers so he ordered a bottle of Corona—no lime—and a bar pie. He took it to the front window where he had a good view of Cordova's office across Tremont.

Traffic was thick on the sidewalks as well as the street where every third car seemed to be a black Lincoln Continental or Town Car with a livery sticker.

The Corona was good, but he barely tasted the pie. Good thing, because the backroom microwave oven had left the crust as gummy as the stingy layer of cheese. Hard to tell where one left off and the other began.

Not that he cared. He was eating simply to keep from being hungry later. Knowing that his face now resided in the Dormentalist computer had filched his appetite. Didn't want his photo anywhere.

But he hadn't been able to do anything about it. He'd considered pushing the privacy-nut persona a little further but had had a feeling that wouldn't wash with Jensen. The big guy was no dummy, and Jack sensed he could be trouble.

Maybe he was already trouble. He'd had him followed again. The same guy who'd tailed him yesterday had tried to dog him again today. Jack had lost him easily in the Rockefeller Center mob and then headed straight up here to the Bronx.

Jack read the tail as a sign Jensen might not be completely sold on his Jason Amurri persona. Maybe just his nature: He didn't seem to be a trusting guy in the first place, and no doubt a big part of his job was sniffing out trouble and heading it off at the pass. But beyond that, he appeared to have a chip on his shoulder where Jack was concerned. Probably hadn't liked looking bad in front of his boss.

So Jack had let them take his picture. Now what to do about it? He'd have to think of something. Maybe Russ could handle it, although Jack sensed he might be leery about serious hacking, considering how it could screw up his parole.

Checked his watch. Almost noon. Cordova had probably fired up his computer by now. Jack wished he could have been a fly on the wall when he'd opened his first file, then watched the growing horror on his face as he realized he'd been wiped out.

He was halfway through the pie and three-quarters done with his Corona when he spotted Cordova sidling out onto the sidewalk with his computer tower cradled against his big belly. As he started moving uphill, Jack gulped the rest of his beer and headed for the door.

It took him longer than he liked to weave through the lunchtime crowd—it looked like Sidewalk Sale Day, with more clothes and electronics and miscellaneous merchandise displayed outside the stores than in—and when he got to the street, Cordova was gone.

"What the—?"

Had he jumped into a cab? Jack was about to launch into a litany of self-excoriation when he noticed a sign just a few doors to his left: *Computer Doctor*.

"Let's hope," Jack muttered as he dodged across the street.

He stopped before the front window and pretended to be looking at the display of monitors and keyboards and various gazillion-megabyte hard drives. A quick glance up showed Cordova standing at the counter, waving his arms at the white-coated clerk.

Jack let out a long breath and retreated to the far side of the street to watch and wait.

7

"I've got your diagnosis already," said the clerk after Richie had explained what had been happening.

Richie wanted to wipe that smug grin off his pimply face—preferably with a barbed-wire washcloth. His white coat hung loose on his narrow shoulders; he had a shaved head and lots of earrings. Lots. Richie stopped counting at six.

"Yeah? What?"

"Your computer caught a cold."

What was this asshole up to? "How do you know that? You ain't even hooked it up yet."

A wider smile as the geek hooked his thumb under the name tag of the white coat. It said *Dr. Marty*.

"The doctor knows. And you've come to the right place. Where better to take a computer with a virus than to the Computer Doctor?"

"Virus?" Richie had heard of those. "How'd I get that?"

"Do you have antivirus software?"

"No."

Dr. Marty rolled his eyes. "Do you go on the Internet?"

"Well, yeah." This clown better not ask where.

"Ever download anything—programs, patches, files?"

"Yeah, sometimes."

Lots of times. Richie didn't know what a patch was, but he'd downloaded a ton of picture files of tight young bodies going hot and heavy at—

"Then that's where you probably picked it up. That or through e-mail."

"So it doesn't mean someone came into my office and put this in my machine?"

"You mean physically uploading it into your machine?" Dr. Marty laughed. "Hardly! This is the twenty-first century! You opened your computer's door and it breezed right in off the Internet."

Well, that was a relief. Sort of.

Dr. Marty then went on to explain something called the HYRTBU virus that causes exactly what had happened to Richie's machine.

"Can you fix it?"

"Of course. I'll install some antivirus software and run a diagnostic."

"How long's that gonna take?"

"Give me a couple of hours. Leave your number and I'll call when it's cleaned up." He shook his head. "Won't be able to retrieve any of your files, though. They're dead and gone. HYRTBU takes no prisoners."

"That's okay. I've got a backup."

Dr. Marty gave him a thumbs-up. "My man!"

"Hey, no chance of this HYRTBU thing messing up my backup?"

"Can't. Not if you're backed up on CD. That's ROM and you can't—"

Richie had heard all he needed to hear.

"Great. I'll be waiting for your call."

8

Jack straightened as Cordova came out. Instead of returning to the office, though, he began walking in the other direction.

A good sign. Jack was pretty sure Cordova's backup wasn't in his office; maybe he was heading for it now.

Keeping to the opposite side of the street, he followed—a whole three blocks to the local Morgan Bank branch. He followed Cordova inside, saw him pick up one of the clerks and follow her back into the rear section.

Jack nodded. Heading for a safety deposit box.

He noted the bank hours: the lobby locked up at three. Great. It would take time for the Computer Doctor to clean up Cordova's machine—too long to allow him to retrieve it, hook it up, restore all his files, and get back to the bank before closing.

So a good chance he'd leave the disk in the office overnight.

And then? Jack would break in again tonight and reintroduce HYRTBU, but what about the backup disk? He could simply steal it, but that would tip Cordova to the fact he'd been invaded.

Jack decided he could live with that if he had to, but he much preferred to leave fatso raging at the gods, believing it was all due to the dumping of the truckload of bad karma he'd been amassing.

Which meant another trip to Russ to find out how he could wreck the backup CD with no one the wiser.

But first he had to visit Beekman Place.

9

"You've seen him? He's well?"

Maria Roselli's dark eyes danced in her puffy face as she beamed at Jack.

Esteban had announced him and Benno the Rottweiler had greeted Jack at the door. She'd offered tea again but he'd declined.

"He looks healthy," Jack said. Couldn't say he'd looked clean, but he hadn't seemed malnourished. "Looks like he's working on a beard."

She frowned. "Really? He tried that once before and said the itching drove him crazy." She waved her hand. "But that's neither here nor there. What did he say when you told him to call his mother?"

"I didn't get to that. It seems he's, um, being punished."

"What?" Her hand fluttered to her mouth. "Whatever do you mean?"

"I don't know what he did, but he's not allowed to talk to other Dormentalists and they're not allowed to talk to him."

"Isn't that silly? I can't believe Johnny allows himself to be humiliated like that. He should just get out of that place."

"That would be up to him. Since I'm pretending to be a Dormentalist wannabe, I can't talk to him in the temple. So I'm working on finding out where he lives. I'll catch up to him outside the temple and give him your message."

"How long do you think that will take? Another day, perhaps?"

Jack shrugged. "I'd like that, but don't count on it."

"But you've accomplished so much so soon."

"Pure luck."

A lucky coincidence. There it was again: the *C*-word. Was this situation being manipulated? It didn't seem so, but one of those old ladies with a dog had told him there'd be no more coincidences in his life.

He rose and looked down at Maria. "Are you *sure* you don't know Anya Mundy?"

"That woman you mentioned the other day? I believe I told you no."

"Yeah, you did, didn't you." He sighed. "If I'm lucky again, I'll catch sight of Johnny and follow him home. In case that doesn't happen, I'll work on getting a peek at member records."

Jack liked the former course better. Tomorrow he'd try hanging out on the Communing level at about the same time he'd been there today. If Johnny Roselli was a creature of habit, Jack might be able to create his own coincidence.

Out front, Esteban smiled and held the front door open as Jack exited. As he started walking toward First Avenue he realized he hadn't seen Gia all day. He had a few minutes. Why not pop in?

10

Gia smiled as she glanced through the peephole. Jack. Just the tonic she needed.

She pulled open the door. "Howdy, stranger."

He grinned. "Hey, it hasn't even been twenty-four hours."

"I know." She pulled him inside and threw her arms around him. "But it seems like a week."

As they hugged she felt some of the day-long tension uncoil within her. It had been a long, long morning and she was only partway through the afternoon. She'd intended to work on her latest painting today—a new angle on her Fifty-ninth Street Bridge series—but had found herself too weak to stand at the easel for any length of time. Still feeling that blood loss, she guessed.

But even if her energy had been at its usual high level, she doubted she could have done much. She felt too down in the dumps to paint, and not just because of the blood loss.

She'd almost lost the baby. Dr. Eagleton had reassured her that everything was fine, but that didn't mean it wouldn't happen again. She'd miscarried her first pregnancy, the one before Vicky. Who said this one wouldn't wind up the same way?

This baby may not have been planned but he was here—she didn't know that he was a "he" but couldn't help thinking of him that way—and she couldn't wait for the day she could hold him in her arms and look into his little face. She'd felt his first quickening two weeks ago and he'd been kicking up a storm ever since. Especially so since the bleeding, which was wonderfully reassuring.

But still she couldn't help feeling that a sword was hanging over her.

"How're you doing?" Jack said.

"Fine. Great."

Truth be told, she was feeling a little dizzy, but she wouldn't tell Jack that. He'd be all over her, hiring a housekeeper, insisting she stay in bed. . . . She didn't want to deal with that.

"You look like a ghost."

"It's going to take me a while to build up my blood count. Dr. Eagleton's got me on extra iron." Which wasn't sitting too well with her intestines.

Concern was writ large on Jack's face. "Why don't we sit down?"

I thought you'd never ask.

"Sure. If you want."

They moved to the cozy living room, decorated in old English aunt style because the townhouse was still listed in the name of Vicky's aunts Grace and Nellie. Those two dear old souls were no longer among the living, but no one but she and Jack knew that.

"Thanks for taking care of Vicky," she said as she sat down.

"First of all, you never have to thank me for doing anything for Vicky. Anything."

"I know. I just—"

"And second, she took care of me. She's one amazing kid."

"That she is."

They snuggled together on the couch, but she sensed the tension in him.

"You've got to go, don't you."

He nodded. "Regrettably, yeah. Gotta see a man about a disk."

She hugged him closer. "Okay, but be careful."

"I'm always careful."

"No you're not. That's why I worry."

And she did. Always.

11

"You want to wreck a CD?" Russ said. He was wearing the same T-shirt and jeans as on Jack's last two visits. "Easy. Stick it in a microwave and cook till it's all cracked like an old mirror."

Jack had started the digi-head talk as soon as he'd arrived—before Russ could start bitching about his latest reading assignment. The six-pack of Sam Adams Jack had brought along further distracted him from academic matters.

"But, Russ, the idea is to make it unreadable without the owner knowing it's been tampered with."

"Oh, well, that's a different story." He sipped his beer. "I'm assuming we're dealing with a CD-R here and that's a good thing, because they're more easily ruined than the commercial kind."

"I thought a CD was a CD."

"In a way, yes. They both use a laser beam to read ones and zeroes from the disk, but—"

"What about music?"

"Same thing: ones and zeroes. Binary code, my friend."

'Wait a minute. You mean when I'm listening to, say, Jack Bruce doing his bass runs on 'Crossroads,' it's just a series of ones and zeroes?"

"Exactly. The music was translated into binary code that's inscribed on the disk, and the player translates it back."

Jack shook his head in wonder. "I always thought . . ."

And then he realized he hadn't really thought about it. He put the CD in the slot and hit play. He hadn't needed to know anything more. Until now.

"Let me give you a quick course in CDs and CD-Rs. They both have a single, uninterrupted spiral track, half a micron wide, running from the inside toward the periphery."

"The opposite of a vinyl record."

"Exactly. On a full CD, that track is three-and-a-half miles long. A commercial CD codes its ones and zeroes with bumps and lands: The bumps are ones and the lands—the flat parts—make up the zeroes. The laser reflects off the bumps onto an optical reader that sends them straight to your computer if they're data or to a digital-analog converter if music. All this at 450 rpms."

"Yow. Complicated."

"The tracking makes it even more complicated, but we won't go there."

"Thank you."

Russ smiled. "That's the commercial CD. The homemade CD-Rs use a slightly different technology. Instead of bumps and lands, they take a stronger laser and heat up a series of spots on a dye layer in the plastic. The heat changes the spots' reflectivity, creating virtual bumps."

"So where does that leave me?"

"Well, since you don't want anyone the wiser, that leaves out scratching or marking with a pen or dipping in acid. So I can see only two options. The first is to take some sort of X-Acto knife and use it to enlarge the central spindle hole—just a little. Won't take much. Just a small change in the diameter will cause a wobble in the disk as it's doing its 450 rpms, and that wobble will cause the tracking system to mess up, which will mean the laser's reading bumps and lands off multiple tracks—they're only a micron and a half apart—which will completely confuse the optical reader. The result will make *Jabberwocky* read like *Dick and Jane*."

He made a dramatic flourish with his free hand while he drained his beer bottle.

"But the data's still there, right?" Jack said. "So if someone could fix the spindle hole, they could get their data back."

"*If* they knew the hole had been tampered with, and *if* they could make a perfect restoration. Both highly— *highly*—unlikely."

"But not impossible."

Russ sighed. "No, not impossible."

"What's the other option?"

"Bring along a hot plate and heat up the disk just enough to give it the slightest warp. A sixteenth of an inch, even less, will do it. The laser beam will reflect all over the place, hitting the optical pickup only by chance."

"But what about—?"

"Fixing the warp? Never happen."

He popped the top from another Sam and offered it to Jack who waved it off.

"You're sure?"

Russ gave a vigorous nod. "Once warped, that plastic will never be perfectly flat again, the tracks in the dye layer will never line up just right again."

Jack liked it. Just his thing: simple and low tech.

"You wouldn't happen to have a hot plate sitting around, would you?"

12

Maggie moaned with relief in the dark kitchen as she removed the red hot crucifix from her thigh. She'd thought the pain might become easier to take with successive burns, but this had been the worst. And the day-long anticipation of the coming agony had been almost as bad as the pain itself.

Five now. Only two more to go. Another on Friday, and then the final—fittingly—on Sunday, the Lord's Day.

A different kind of pain pushed a sob past her throat. She looked down at her blistered thighs and prayed.

I'm doing this penance, Lord, not just for myself, but for Fina and others like her. I can make a difference in their lives, Lord. So please guide Jack. Let him destroy those pictures so that I can remain in Your service, and in service to Your children.

That's all I ask, Lord: To sin no more and be allowed to go on giving in Your name.

13

Jack leaned against the brick divider between an Italian restaurant and a bodega. He pretended to watch the up-town crawl of the rush-hour traffic on Broadway, but his real interest was the subway exit to his left on the other side of Eighty-sixth Street.

He'd adopted his John Robertson identity and called Jamie Grant to arrange a meeting. He had some questions. When she said people were watching her, he figured she wasn't being paranoid. The last thing he needed was someone from the Dormentalist temple to see them together. He told her to hop any of the Broadway line trains to Eighty-sixth Street, and gave her some tips on how to lose a tail in the subway.

And here she came, dressed in a loose jacket and matching blue slacks, with her cell phone in her hand.

She hit the sidewalk and walked east as planned. Jack

stayed where he was, watching the rest of the Morlocks climbing to the surface. Three of them—a lone woman and two men—followed Grant east. Jack trailed them through the twilight.

The woman stopped at a Chinese take-out place and the two men turned uptown on Amsterdam.

The plan had been for Jack to call her if he spotted a tail. He stuffed his phone into his jeans pocket and came up behind her.

"Looks like you lost them," he said.

She jumped and turned. "Oh, shit, Robertson! It's you!"

"You think I was a PS or something?"

"PS?"

"That's what we Dormentalists call a purse snatcher."

She smiled. "Cute. Where'd you come from?"

"Been following you. But I'm the only one."

"At the moment maybe, but not earlier. There were two of them. They were on me from the minute I stepped out of *The Light*."

Jack gripped her arm and turned her west. "We want to go this way."

"It's the oddest thing. They don't hide what they're up to. Almost as if they *want* me to know I'm being followed."

"They do. Serves two purposes: They find out where you go and who you meet, and they put you on edge, keep you looking over your shoulder. Surveillance and harassment, all in one neat little package."

"But that move you told me—you know, stand by the doors and pop through just as they're closing? Worked like a charm. And so simple."

"The simpler, the better. Fewer things that can go wrong."

She grinned in the fading light. "After I ducked out I stood there on the platform and gave them the SD salute through the windows."

"Single digit?"

"You got it. They deserved no less. You should have

seen their faces." She looked around. "Where's this bar
you told me about. I need a GDD."

"A gin and . . . ?"

"A goddamned drink."

14

A couple of blocks and a couple of turns later they were
stepping into a place called Julio's.

It reminded Jamie a little of the Parthenon—not in
looks but in ambiance. The same laughter, the chatter, the
air of camaraderie. She liked the FREE BEER TOMOR-
ROW . . . sign over the bar, and the dead, desiccated plants
hanging in the front window were a unique touch.
Robertson was obviously a regular here. Half the people
in the place waved, nodded, or called hello as he entered.

"So you're 'Jack' to your friends?"

He nodded. "You can call me that if you want."

"Maybe, if we become friends."

He smiled and pointed toward a rear table. "We can
talk over there."

She noticed that he seemed more relaxed here than
he'd been in her office. Almost a different person. He'd
gone from somewhat uptight to loose and friendly.
Maybe it was the clothes situation. He'd been wearing a
shirt and tie and jacket before. Now he was more casual.
And not bad looking. She liked the way his jeans and bur-
gundy golf shirt fit, liked the way the sleek muscles of his
forearms moved as he absently drummed his fingers on
the table.

Soon after they were seated—he with his back against
the wall, she with her back to the room—a muscular little
Hispanic with a pencil-line mustache came over. Robert-

son introduced him as the eponymous proprietor. He left with an order for a pint of Rolling Rock and a Dewar's and soda.

"I like this place," she said. "It's got personality."

He nodded. "Yeah. But not too much. Julio's gone to some lengths to keep it from becoming a yuppie hang."

Jamie glanced around at the crowd—mostly working-class types with a sprinkling of yups.

"He hasn't been entirely successful, I see."

"Well, he can't bar them from wandering in, but he does nothing to attract them. Somehow he's managed to maintain the place's original flavor."

"What is it about places like this?" she wondered aloud. "You know, bars, taverns, pubs. Empires rise and fall, religions come and go, ideologies and political philosophies wax and wane, but the tavern remains a fixed star in the human social firmament. Even when pursed-lipped, tight-assed self-righteous ninnies try to eradicate them, taverns keep popping back up."

"Sort of like GB," he said.

"Hmmm?"

"That's how we Dormentalists refer to Gopher Bash."

That threw Jamie for a moment, then she remembered: that game where you take a mallet and keep hammering a plastic gopher back into its hole only to have it pop up out of another.

She laughed. "*Exactly* like GB."

"Kind of appropriate then that it's found in so many bars, don't you think?"

Jamie smiled and nodded. "I like you, Robertson."

"Call me Jack."

"Okay, Jack."

He was kind of on the young side for her, but who knew? Some guys dug older women. She wondered if he had any plans for the rest of the night.

Julio brought their drinks then. They clinked glasses.

Jack said, "Cheers."

"FOTD."

Jack paused, then smiled. "First of the day?"

"Uh-huh." She took a sip of her Scotch—ohhh, that tasted good—and looked at him.

"So, I gather from your acronym mania that you're officially into the Dementedist situation now."

"Officially I'm an RC. I suppose that makes me a member." He drank some beer. "What do you know about Luther Brady?"

"The APD and SO? I know he graduated from Indiana University, Bloomington, in 1971 with an accounting degree. I don't know exactly how he got involved with Dementedism. At the time it was just another hedonistic California cult, although a fairly popular one. Before you know it, it's incorporated and on its way to becoming the behemoth it is today."

Jack shook his head. "A Hoosier CPA getting cozy with a California cult. How does that happen?"

"Beats me. But I doubt Dementedism would still exist or even be remembered if he hadn't. The guy's an organizational genius. Took the reins from Cooper Blascoe— left him titular head but without any power—and made all the decisions."

"But who *is* he?"

Jamie shrugged. She knew what he was asking but couldn't help much.

"I tried to interview his folks but his father died in '96 of a stroke and his mother's in a nursing home with dementia. I tried to hunt down a few people who might have known him in college but you know what the class sizes are like in those state diploma mills. Found a couple of fellow accounting majors who remembered him but hadn't been friends with him. I don't think he had any friends. I get the feeling he still doesn't have any. For more than thirty years now, this so-called church has been the focus of his life. Eats, drinks, and sleeps Dementedism. Christ, he even lives there."

"Really? Where? On the twenty-second floor?"

"Yeah. I hear he's got quite a setup there."

Jack nodded. "The view is amazing."

Jamie stared at him. "You were up there?"

A smile. "Yep. Brady invited me up for a little chat this morning."

"You apply for membership on Monday and by Wednesday you're having a tête-à-tête with the SO? Do you see a dunce cap on my head? Do you see a birth certificate with yesterday's date on it? What kind of hayseed do you take me for?"

"No kind. I worked it so he thinks I'm someone else—someone he wants to be chummy with."

"Like who? And how did—?"

He shook his head. "Sorry. Trade secret."

"If that's true, then you are one amazing motherfucker."

He wagged his finger at her. "Now, now. No sweet talk." Another quaff of beer, then, "By the way, how many RCs does Brady handle personally?"

Jamie's turn to laugh. "Luther Brady? Doing the Reveille Tech thing?" She shook her head. "I'd have to say none. If you met him, you should know that."

Jack shrugged. "He's offered to take me through the Reveille process himself. Starting tomorrow."

Jamie felt a flare of anger. "That does it. You almost had me with the bit about meeting Luther Brady. You should have quit while you were ahead." She snorted. "Hardly anyone under Overseer rank—except maybe for the GP—even *sees* him with any sort of regularity. So the idea of him acting as your RT is . . ."

The words ran out as Jamie saw the matter-of-fact look on Jack's face. He didn't *care* if she believed him.

Could it be true?

John "Jack" Robertson was either the best undercover operator she'd ever met, or the biggest liar.

He cleared his throat. "What's with that big sphere hidden away in his office?"

"The globe?" she said, feeling her skin tighten. "How close are you two?"

"Well, I'm not number one on his speed dialer, but I get the feeling he'd like to be number one on mine."

"But he showed you the globe?"

"No. I caught just a glimpse of it as I walked into his office—before the sliding doors closed it off. So it's a globe?"

"That's what I've been told. I interviewed a DD— that's a Detached Dementedist—who used to work on the temple's cleaning crew. She got a good look at it once when Brady forgot to close the doors. Told me it's about eight feet high with all the seas and continents in relief, but dotted with all these red-and-white lightbulbs and crisscrossed with lines that aren't latitude and longitude. She figured Brady wanted it cleaned—why else would he leave the doors open?—so she started dusting it. Brady came in and threw a screaming fit. He pressed some button in his desk that closed the doors, then threw her out."

"Really." Jack's eyes narrowed. "You've got to figure the lights are temple locations. But they're no secret. Why would he throw a fit because she saw them?"

"Obviously it's more than just a map of the earth. And Brady did more than throw a fit. He had this poor girl declared a lapser and had her brought before FPRB. She was so upset she quit, which means an automatic DD situation."

She watched Jack as they sat and sipped in silence. He seemed to recede.

"You're figuring how you can get a look at that globe, aren't you."

He nodded. "My curiosity is, as they say, piqued."

"But you're there to find a missing member, right?"

"Yeah, but unanswered questions tend to nag me."

"Any luck finding him?"

Jack nodded. "Spotted him yesterday, but couldn't speak to him—he was in lapser mode."

Jamie laughed. "I wonder if he got caught looking at the globe too."

"Could be."

"At least you know where he is. He could have been one of the unaccounted for. There's a certain number of Dementedists who simply vanish every year."

"Missionaries, right?"

"So we're told. But nobody hears from them again. Ever."

"Ever is a long time. They could resurface in a few years."

"Yeah. So could the *Titanic*."

But someone *had* resurfaced—at least Jamie thought he might have. She was still trying to confirm his identity.

She rattled the ice in her glass. "I could use another DS. Another RR? I'm buying."

He shook his head. "I've got an errand to run."

"At this hour?"

"It's the only hour for this particular errand. A hot date with a hot plate."

"Pardon?"

"Just kidding." He rose. "I'll get you a cab."

Jamie hid her disappointment. She was pretty good at it. Plenty of practice.

"That's all right. I think I'll hang in here awhile." She didn't feel like heading down to the Parthenon. Her Dementedist shadows would be waiting. "I kind of like this place."

"Great."

As he slipped past her she gripped his arm. "You figure out what's going on with that globe situation, you'll tell me, won't you?"

"Sure. Least I can do for all the backgrounding you've given me."

She watched him go, and thought about the fellow she thought—hoped—she'd discovered. She was going to need help nailing down his identity. Maybe Jack . . .

No. She had to keep this to herself. Besides, she didn't know yet how far she could trust John "Jack" Robertson. For all she knew he might be a Dementedist plant, trying to lure her into a bad situation.

Listen to me, she thought. Completely and thoroughly paranoid.

But still, she didn't know enough about him to trust him with what might turn out to be a major coup. Not yet.

15

Jensen stepped out onto Tenth Avenue and headed for his car, leaving John Jay College behind. He'd had trouble focusing on tonight's *Police Science 207* lecture. His thoughts kept veering toward Jason Amurri. Something off-kilter about that guy. Maybe he should have listened more closely to the lecturer—the subject had been Investigative Function, and he sensed this Amurri needed some investigating.

Jensen climbed in behind the wheel of his Hummer and sat there without starting the engine.

Nothing seemed right in his life lately. Shalla, the woman who'd been living with him for eight years, had walked out last summer, saying he spent too much time at the temple. Well, maybe he did. Still, he missed her.

Lately, without her to come home to, he'd been spending more time than ever on the job. He felt he owed it to the Church and to Brady, and not just for the nice salary they were paying him.

He owed them because he was a fraud.

When he'd reached the top of the Fusion Ladder, Jensen had had to face the devastating realization that he

was a Null. Somewhere along the way his xelton had
fallen into a coma from which it would never awaken,
and so Jensen hadn't achieved *any* sort of fusion, let
alone Full. Everything he'd experienced climbing the FL
had been Sham Fusion, a form of Null self-delusion:
He'd wanted fusion so badly he'd imagined it happening.

But he couldn't tell anyone. It would pull the rug out
from under his status in the Church. The HC might let
him go back to being an ordinary TP, but no Null could be
Grand Paladin.

He found it hard to hide his pain with Brady and the
High Council members as they sat around and traded stories about their Full Fusion powers. Jensen couldn't remain silent—they'd wonder why—so he was forced to
make up tales of levitating or leaving his body.

Fortunately no one was required to demonstrate their
powers. Luther Brady had made it clear from the outset
that exhibitionism would not be tolerated. But that didn't
lessen the deep ache Jensen felt as he listened to them.

He'd even gone through a period of doubt where he'd
questioned the whole Fusion process. What if he wasn't
the only Null hiding his Sham Fusion? What if some
members of the HC were also Nulls and not admitting it?
What if, just like Jensen, they were concocting far-out
tales to cover the truth.

Those had been dark days. He'd even gone so far as to
suggest at a meeting with Brady and the HC that they all
levitate together. The shocked looks from the HC—every
one of them—had worsened his suspicions.

Brady had abruptly adjourned the meeting and taken
Jensen to his private quarters. He'd pulled a book from
a special cabinet and placed it before him. To Jensen's
astonishment, the title, *The Compendium of Srem,* was
in Yoruba, his native tongue. He opened the cover and
flipped through.

And then another shock as Brady began translating one
of the passages.

"You speak Yoruba?" Jensen remembered saying.

Brady shook his head and smiled. "Not a word. When I look at these pages I see English. If I'd been born and raised in France, I'd see French. Whatever your native tongue, that is what you see."

Jensen had wondered about that. He'd learned English young—an almost-native tongue in his case. He squeezed his eyes shut and concentrated on memories of his early English classes, forcing that language to the front of his brain, pushing the Yoruba back, then opened his eyes.

For an instant the text swam before him in English, then transformed into Yoruba.

It wasn't a trick. But how—?

"Look here."

Brady directed him to the end, to a strange illustration of Earth crisscrossed with lines and dots.

The drawing rotated on the page.

Jensen had stared in wonder, trying not to believe, but the look and feel of this book, its uncanny lightness, the odd textures of its binding were all so strange, so unlike anything he had ever encountered in his life, that he'd had no choice but to believe.

Brady then explained what the drawing meant, told him about Opus Omega. And in that great project Jensen had seen a possibility of salvation. All who aided in the completion of Opus Omega would be saved when the Hokano world fused with this one. More than saved, they would be like gods in the new world.

Perhaps if he helped Luther Brady with this project, his Null status wouldn't matter. When the worlds merged, he might be transformed along with all the Fully Fused members of the Church. In the end, when it was over, he could join them as a godlike being in the remade world.

And so he'd become a partner in Opus Omega, doing whatever necessary to speed it along.

Jensen sighed and turned the ignition key.

But he was still a Null, with no guarantee of a future. He would go on living the lie, but he would make up for it by continuing to be the most devoted GP the Church had ever known.

Part of that effort meant keeping a close watch on Jason Amurri.

Richie Cordova sliced into the thick filet mignon still sizzling on the platter. He smiled as he inspected the purplish meat inside: black and blue, just the way he liked it.

He took a bite: as good as it looked.

He'd heard this place grilled a mean steak, and they weren't kidding. Kind of upscale for the neighborhood—which meant downscale for just about everywhere else—but it seemed to be doing okay. Just down the street from his office all these years and he'd never tried it.

Richie refilled his glass from the bottle of Merlot he'd ordered and toasted himself.

He had a couple of reasons to celebrate tonight. First off, his horoscope had told him to, even if he had to make up an occasion. Fortunately that hadn't been necessary. He'd received a cool thou in the mail today from a new cow. The first of many, if he had anything to say about it. Next was the successful restoration of his computer files.

He'd had a few sweaty moments there in the office. Sure, he'd had a backup CD. He burned a new one every time he added new material and broke the old one into half a dozen pieces—too many copies lying around could only lead to trouble—but he'd never checked to see if the files had been properly recorded. What if something had been wrong with his disk burner? What if he'd only *thought* he'd copied the files, and when he tried to restore them, they'd all turn out blank?

So he'd chewed a fingernail while waiting for the contents of the CD to pop up on the screen. But when they did, and when they proved to be perfect copies of all his lost files, he'd almost got up and danced. Almost.

By the time he'd restored all his files it was well past closing time at the bank. Rather than drag the disk along to dinner, he'd left it back in the office with the money. His original plan had been to run them up to the safety deposit box in the morning, but now he was having second thoughts.

Something wasn't right.

No matter how hard he'd tried, he'd been unable to come up with an explanation beyond simple bad luck for what had happened to his computer. The computer guy had had a good explanation of how the virus had gotten into his system. Matter of fact, he'd informed Richie that the new antivirus software he'd installed had detected a total of thirteen different viruses on his hard drive. Thirteen! That was why it had taken a couple of extra hours to get his computer back to him. But he promised he'd disinfected all the files and programs. The hard drive was clean.

Richie had to admit that it was running faster and smoother now.

So okay, his computer had been a sewer of viruses. And he hadn't found a single scrap of evidence that someone had broken in. Plus the horoscopes hadn't even hinted at foul play.

So why this bad feeling? Why this gnawing suspicion that he'd missed something? Why the prickly feeling at the back of his neck that something bad might go down tonight?

His horoscope had said being in the right place at the right time was his style today. Suddenly he knew that the right place for him was his office and the right time to be there would be right after dinner. The right place for his backup CD and his money—a pretty fair amount of cake in that envelope—was safe at his house, under his pillow.

Richie turned his attention back to the steak. He felt better already.

17

Jack closed the door to Cordova's office behind him.

The duct tape was back on the alarm plunger, the pick gun and the HYRTBU disk were in his pockets, the brand-new hot plate was under his arm, his flashlight was in his latex-gloved hand and lighting his way through the dark reception room.

So far so good. No one had seen him come in, no one else on the second floor.

The idea of searching for the backup disk in the receptionist's desk vanished almost before it arrived. Right, like Fat Richie would leave his precious blackmail photos where someone could dip into them.

No, if it was anywhere, it was in the boss's lair.

Jack laid the brand-new hot plate on Cordova's desk. What a job finding one. He'd figured someplace like Macy's would carry them in their kitchen section, but no. Not a one. He'd finally found a selection at a chef's supply shop. Of the two single-coil models, he'd noticed that one was made by Acme. Remembering a certain coyote's bad luck with that brand, he'd bought the other.

Jack squatted in the kneehole of the desk and slipped Russ's HYRTBU disk into the floppy drive. He turned on the computer and crossed mental fingers. If Cordova hadn't had antivirus software before, he surely had it now. But Russ had promised that his disk would slip past any protective program and reinsert HYRTBU. He'd better be right.

As the box beeped and the hard drive rattled to life, Jack went through the desk first, being careful to replace everything in the exact position he'd found it. Cordova might be a fat slob, but that didn't carry over to his home or office.

No luck.

He moved to the file cabinets. A lot of stuff in these. He knew from his last trip here that going through them would take a while—a long while. He hated the thought of pawing through every one of those folders again, so he decided to leave the cabinets till last.

He searched the furniture as he'd done last night—under the cushions, the undersides of the seats and drawers, between the desk and the wall. Nada.

And then a *d'oh!* moment.

The computer—what if Cordova had left the backup disk in the CD drive?

Jack quickly hit the eject button. The tray popped out, looking like a coffee-cup holder—an empty one.

That left the file cabinets. What made the prospect of rummaging through them again so daunting was the possibility that Cordova had taken the disk home with him. But why would he? In fact there were good reasons *not* to take it to Williamsbridge—like losing it along the way, for instance.

But he'd never thought of Cordova as smart. Crafty and devious, yes. But no brainiac.

He was about to pull open the top drawer on the first cabinet when he heard a noise at the outer door—a key rattling in a lock.

Cleaning service? Receptionist? Cordova? Shit!

Jack turned off his penlight and squeezed back against the filing cabinets as the lights in the reception area came on. He pulled his Glock from its holster at the small of his back—he knew Cordova had a carry permit—as he listened to the beeps of someone punching a code into the alarm keypad. Then with a gut-spiking jolt he noticed the hot plate sitting on the desk. He did a quick tiptoe out from hiding, grabbed the plate, and ducked back out of sight just as the office overheads came on.

Back pressed against the wall, he waited. He couldn't see who it was but from the wheezy breathing figured it must be the Fat Man himself.

What the hell was he doing here? He was supposed to be back in Williamsbridge, either drinking in Hurley's or at home, just like every other night.

Jack hadn't turned on the computer monitor, but Cordova might notice the glowing power light or hear the hard drive. He held his breath, waiting. When he heard a grunt on the far side of the room, he chanced a peek.

Cordova's arm was in mid-reach behind the radiator. He pulled out the padded envelope Jack had seen last time, checked inside, and smiled.

The disk—he must have put it with the money. Good thing Jack hadn't found it, otherwise Cordova would go on a rampage and find Jack in the process.

Ten seconds later the lights were out and the outer door was closing.

Jack remained where he was for a few heartbeats, wondering what to do. He needed that disk, had to get it away from Cordova before he returned it to his safety deposit box, otherwise three days of work would go up in smoke, and Sister Maggie would still be on the hook.

Jack retrieved the HYRTBU disk, turned off the computer, and moved toward the door.

Time to improvise.

Jack hated to improvise.

18

Jack gave Cordova enough time to travel half a block, then stepped out onto the sidewalk. As expected, Fatso was heading for the subway station, waddling along and playing it cool with the envelope tucked casually under his arm, like it held nothing more valuable than a home remodeling contract.

Jack stayed close behind, looking for an opportunity. He was going to have to take him before or after his ride home. Too much light on the train itself. Jack didn't want to show his face.

Only scattered pedestrians out and about at the moment, fair amount of traffic to the right, locked-up storefronts to the left. This wasn't looking good.

He realized he was still wearing latex gloves and carrying the hot plate. He was about to dump both in a trash can coming up on his right when he spotted the dark slit of an alley ahead.

Jack's heartbeat kicked up its tempo as he decided to give this a shot. He broke into a trot and intercepted Cordova just as he came abreast of the alley mouth. He gave the big man a hard shove into the darkness, then clocked him once, twice on the back of his head with the hot plate.

Cordova stumbled and landed on his belly with a *whoosh* of breath. Jack tossed the hot plate to the side and pounced on his back. Had to be quick now. He grabbed the hair at the base of his neck to hold his head in place. He didn't want Cordova to get a look at him, even in the dark.

"Gimme your wallet, Fatso," he hissed as he pawed at the man's hip.

Cordova seemed dazed, his coarse breaths rumbling in and out.

Jack took the wallet, then felt around front for a gun. When he didn't find one, he grabbed the envelope. Cordova came alert then and fought for it.

"No!"

"Shut up!" Jack shoved his face against the pavement. Hard. "Whatta ya got there? Jewelry, huh?"

"There's cash," Cordova grunted. "Take it. Go ahead, take it all, just leave me the computer disk."

"Yeah, right." Jack wrestled the envelope free. "Like I'm gonna sit here and play games."

He gave Cordova another face slam, then he was up and out of the alley, fast-walking to the first cross street where he turned and broke into a run.

As he opened the padded envelope he noticed the blood on his gloves. Looked like he'd laid open Cordova's scalp with that hot plate. At least he'd found some use for it.

Inside the envelope he found the cash—looked like even more than last night—and a CD jewel box. He snatched it out and stopped under a light. He scanned its gold surface for a label. Nothing beyond *Sony CD-R*. But this had to be it.

Yes! And though Cordova might suspect that he'd been set up, he'd never know for sure. And he'd never know by whom.

Jack went through Cordova's wallet, transferring the cash and credit cards to the envelope, then he tossed it in the gutter. He inverted his bloody gloves as he pulled them off and stuffed them into another pocket.

He remembered a subway stop on 174th Street, just a few blocks down. He'd catch the next 2 or 5 train and get the hell out of the Bronx.

But the game wasn't over. Not until Jack was sure Cordova didn't have another backup. If he did, it meant extra innings.

THURSDAY

1

Richie didn't remember the last time he'd made it to the office this early. Maybe never. He beat Eddy by ten minutes. Her surprised look at his mere presence escalated to shock when she saw his bandaged face and head. He told her what he'd told the cops last night.

The last thing he'd wanted to do was call 911, but he was bleeding like a pig from the back of his head and knew he needed stitches. He'd been straight with them, told them he'd been caught from behind by a scumbag he hadn't seen coming or going. The only thing he'd held back on was the money in the stolen envelope. Even if he was an ex-cop and getting special treatment, that much cash would lead to too many questions.

The cops found what the jerk had used to open his head: a hot plate. Assaulted with a hot plate! He couldn't fucking believe it.

So they did a search while his head was being sewn up in the ER. They found his wallet—empty, of course—but not the envelope, empty or otherwise.

Not that he'd had any hope of ever seeing it again.

Fuck, fuck, fuck!

Why'd it have to happen to him, and why when he was carrying a couple of thou? Talk about bad fucking luck.

But it was that backup disk that worried him. He didn't want anyone going through those picture files . . . it could screw up everything.

And having no backup at the moment was making him nervous as all hell. But he could fix that real quick.

He sent Eddy out for coffee and fired up his computer. He slipped a blank disk into the CD-R drive and ran the copy program that automatically copied everything out of certain folders.

When the program finished, he leaned back in his chair and took a deep breath. Done. He was protected. He felt better on that score at least. His stomach felt a little queasy, though, and he had a pounding headache that four Advil hadn't touched.

He went to remove the CD from the drive and then thought, Better check the disk, just to be sure.

He opened a file from the CD and stopped breathing when he saw:

HOPE YOU REMEMBERED TO BACK UP!

"No! No-no-no-no-no!"

He switched back to the hard drive and checked a random file.

HOPE YOU REMEMBERED TO BACK UP!

One after the other, the same message. That fucking virus had got back into his system and cleaned him out! Everything was gone!

He started kicking at the computer tower on the floor, but stopped himself after two strikes.

Wait. All was not lost. His files were gone, but the cows didn't know that. They'd already seen what he had . . . he could still string them along, keep squeezing them till they ran out of juice.

But still, this was a fucking catastrophe.

Feeling sicker than before, he flopped back into his seat. The phone started ringing but he couldn't bring himself to answer it. All that work, all that risk . . . gone. He still couldn't believe it.

Eddy popped back in then with the coffee and picked up the phone. A few seconds later she stuck her head through the doorway.

"It's the guy from Computer Doctor. Want to speak to him?"

"Do I? *Do* I?" He snatched up the receiver. "Yeah?"

"Oh, Mr. Cordova," said a prissy male voice he didn't recognize. "This is Ned from Computer Doctor. We just wanted to call and check on how satisfied you are with our service."

Richie wanted to kill him. In fact, he might just go down there now and tear his whole staff into little pieces.

"Satisfied? I'm NOT satisfied! Listen, asshole! The virus you were supposed to kill off is still there! And it wiped out all my files again!"

"Well, sir, if you want to I'll be glad to come up and recheck the hard drive. I'll even restore all the files from your backup."

"Don't bother."

"Really, sir, it will be no trouble at all. And while I'm there—"

Richie knew if he got within ten feet of this geek he'd rearrange his face. Things were bad enough at the moment; he didn't need an assault and battery charge added to the pile of shit his life had become.

"Just forget about it, okay? You've fucked things up enough already."

"Really, sir, I hate the thought of a dissatisfied customer. Just get out your backup disk and I'll—"

This asshole just wouldn't take no for an answer.

"I don't *have* a backup, you little shit! It was stolen last night! *Now* what are you going to do?"

"No backup?" the voice said. "Oh, well, then. Never mind."

And then the fucker hung up. He . . . just . . . hung . . . up!

2

Jack stood amid the surging pedestrians on Lexington Avenue and pocketed his cell phone. He smiled as he imagined Fat Richie Cordova pounding his receiver against his desktop, maybe even smashing it through his monitor screen.

Game. Set. Match.

He'd arrange a meet with Sister Maggie later. Now it was time to awaken his xelton.

Jack had dressed in his blue blazer and a tieless, button-down white oxford shirt. He entered the temple, used his swipe card for a free pass through security, then went to the information desk. It looked like an old hotel registration desk.

"I have an appointment for a Reveille Session," he told the uniformed young woman behind the counter, then added, "With Luther Brady."

Her hand darted to her mouth, covering a smile. Jack detected the hint of a giggle in her voice as she said, "Mr. Brady is going to Reveille you?"

"Yes." Jack glanced at his watch. "At nine sharp. I don't want to keep him waiting."

"No, of course not." Her lips did an undulating dance. She really, really wanted to laugh. "I'll call upstairs."

She pressed a button then turned away as she spoke into the receiver. It was a short conversation, and when she turned back, she was no longer smiling. Her face was pale, her expression awed.

She swallowed. "G-GP Jensen will be right down."

Jack figured it wouldn't take long for word to spread that he had Luther Brady as his RT—one, maybe two nanoseconds after he and Jensen stepped into the elevator it would be all over the building. A few more nanos after that it would be spread throughout Dormentaldom.

He'd had a reason for mentioning it. He planned to use his new cachet to allow him access to places that would be verboten to a regular newbie.

Jensen showed up in his black uniform, looking like the megalith from *2001*. On the trip to the top floor the two of them started off with an earnest discussion about the weather, but Jensen soon steered the talk toward Jack.

"How was your day, yesterday?"

"Great."

"Do anything interesting?"

Jack thought, You mean after I ditched your tail?

"Oh, tons. I don't get to New York that often, so I did some shopping, had an excellent steak at Peter Luger's."

"Really? What cut?"

"Porterhouse." Jack knew from a number of meals at Luger's that porterhouse was the only cut they served. "It was delicious."

"And then what? Called it a night?"

Jensen wasn't being the least bit circumspect about third-degreeing him.

"Oh, no. I went to an Off-Broadway play someone had recommended. It's called *Syzygy*. Ever hear of it?"

"Can't say as I have. Any good?"

Gia had dragged him to *Syzygy* last month and he'd wound up liking it . . .

"Very strange. Lots of twists and turns in the plot." Jack feigned a yawn. "But it didn't start till ten and I was late getting to bed."

That would jibe with the report from whomever Jensen had put on the Ritz Carlton last night.

Jensen delivered Jack to the twenty-second floor where he found Brady standing near the receptionist's desk. His suit hung perfectly on his trim frame, and not a single strand of his too-brown hair was out of place.

"Mr. Amurri," he said, stepping forward and extending his hand. "So glad you could make it."

"Call me Jason, please. And I wouldn't miss this for the world."

"Very well, Jason. Come in, come in." He led Jack into the office area. "We'll conduct the session in my private quarters and—"

"Really?" Jack said in his best gosh-wow voice.

"Yes, I thought it would offer more privacy and a much more personal atmosphere. But I have one matter to attend to before we get underway, so why don't you make yourself comfortable until I get back."

Jack swept an arm toward the enormous windows. "The view alone could keep me occupied for hours."

Brady laughed. "Oh, I assure you it will be no more than a few minutes at most."

As Brady breezed out, Jack looked around, searching for the ubiquitous video pickups. He couldn't spot a single eye, and then realized why: Luther Brady would not want anyone monitoring his meetings, recording his every word and gesture.

Jack turned away from the windows and faced the opposite wall. The mysterious globe sat behind those sliding steel panels. Jack wanted a look at it. Jamie Grant had mentioned something about a button on Brady's desk.

Jack walked over and examined the vast mahogany expanse. No button in sight. He stepped behind the desk and seated himself in Brady's high-backed red-leather swivel chair. Maybe he had a remote somewhere.

Two rows of drawers formed the flanks of the desk. Jack went through them quickly and found mostly papers and pens and notepads with *From the Minds of Luther Brady* emblazoned across the top of each page in some fancy heraldic font.

Sheesh.

The only thing out of the ordinary was a stainless-steel semiautomatic pistol. At first glance it looked like his own PT 92 Taurus, then he noticed the different safety,

making this a Beretta 92. A box of 9mm Hydra-Shok
Federal Classics sat next to it. What made Brady think he
needed a weapon?

Coming up empty in the drawers, Jack felt around under the edge of the desktop. There—a smooth nub near
the right corner. He pressed it and then heard a motor
whine to life, a soft scrape as the panels began to recede.

He rose and approached the expanding opening.
Grant's DD informant had been right. A globe of Earth,
studded with a scattering of tiny light bulbs in no dis-
cernible pattern. As he watched, the globe began to rotate. The bulbs flickered to life—not all of them, but
most. The clear bulbs held the majority, but here and
there a red one glowed.

A swirl of odd-looking symbols had been painted on
the wall behind the globe. They looked like a cross between Arabic script and hieroglyphics.

Jack stepped closer to the globe and saw a crisscrossing network of fine red lines. They seemed to radiate
from the red bulbs, circumnavigating the globe as they
passed through each of the other red bulbs and returned
home. At first glance he thought the same was going on
with the white bulbs, but a closer look showed that they
were positioned at red-line intersections. Not every intersection—only where three or more crossed. Most of the
white bulbs were lit, but a few here and there about the
globe were dark. Bad bulbs? Or, for some reason, not yet
powered up?

Jack stared, baffled. The red bulbs seemed to be calling
the shots, the white were secondary players. He focused
on the U.S. and noticed a red bulb in the northeast, near
New York City. Did the reds represent major Dormentalist temples? Was that the key? He noticed another in
South Florida. Was there a big temple in Miami? Could
be. He'd have to check.

No, wait. Here was a red bulb in the middle of the
ocean off Southeast Asia. No Dormentalist temple there.
At least he assumed not.

He backed up for a more encompassing look. Something about the display reached into his gut and scraped the lining with an icy claw . . . something deeply disturbing here, but he couldn't say what. The reason dangled somewhere in his subconscious, skittering away every time he reached for it.

Jack wrenched his thoughts away from the display and refocused on his immediate circumstances. Right now he should be ducking back to Brady's desk to hit that button again, but he held off. He was here to find Johnny Roselli and give him a message. He'd completed the first half of that task, and was sure he could finish up without setting foot inside this temple again. All he had to do was wait outside for Johnny to leave and follow him home.

But that could take forever. Jack didn't have the time or temperament to stand around and scope the temple door from morning to night, so it would have to be on a catch-as-catch-can basis. Sure, getting a peek at the membership lists would accelerate the process, but that skittish something inside him screamed from the dark that this globe was much more important.

So he stayed where he was, deciding to push his sudden elevated status to the limit.

Jack was still staring at the globe when Brady returned. He froze at the threshold, eyes wide, jaw hanging open.

"What . . . how . . . ?"

Jack turned. "Hmmm? Oh, I was just looking at this globe here. It's fascinating."

Brady's eyes narrowed as his lips drew into a tight line. "How did you open that?" he said as he stepped toward his desk.

"Oh, it was the funniest thing. I was leaning on your desk there, looking out at the city, when my fingers hit a button under the edge. Suddenly these doors opened and there it was."

Brady said nothing. He reached his desk and hit the hidden button. He was clearly upset but trying to hide it.

Jack said, "Did I do something wrong?"

"My desk is for my personal use."

"Oh, I'm terribly sorry. But it was an accident." Jack tried an offended look. "You cannot believe that I would rummage through your desk."

"No. No, of course not."

"I do apologize. I have an impulsive nature and it has created difficulties for me from time to time. I'm hoping that Dormentalism will show me how to control it."

Brady seemed to have calmed himself. "No need to apologize, Jason. It's just that I was . . . surprised to find the doors open. We don't put that globe on display."

"I don't see why not," Jack said as the leading edges of the panels clicked together. "It's so unique. What do all those lights represent?"

"I'm afraid you're not qualified to know that just yet."

"Really? When will I be?"

"When you have achieved Full Fusion. Only someone in the FF state can comprehend the meaning that globe holds for the Church."

"Tell me something about it," Jack said. "I'm dying to know. How about just a hint? What's that globe about?"

"It is the future, Jason Amurri. The future."

3

Except for two paintings—both of big-eyed waifs—the living room of Brady's personal quarters was as spare as his office. One painting was a little boy holding a wilted flower, and the other a skinny little kid in rags.

"Keane kids?" Jack said.

Brady nodded with vigorous enthusiasm. "Yes. They're originals."

Jack had always found them kitschy, and those big sad eyes monotonously repetitious. But he supposed some of the old originals might be valuable to someone.

"I know they're not considered real art, but something about them appeals to me. I think they remind me of all the sadness in the world, all caused by fractured xeltons. I look at them and they keep me going, reminding me of the Church's mission."

Jack sighed. "I know exactly what you mean."

They finally settled down for the Reveille Session—sans mouse. Brady sat on a straight-backed, cushionless chair. Jack leaned forward on the comfy sofa. A coffee table of glossy blond wood sat between them.

"What in your life do you feel guiltiest about?"

Jack had an answer ready but he leaned back and pretended to think about it. After an appropriate pause . . .

"I suppose it would be having so much more than others."

" 'So much more' ?"

"Yes. You don't know this, but I'm rather wealthy."

Brady's expression remained bland, barely interested. "Yes, I believe you mentioned something yesterday about having money. But we have many wealthy members."

"Yes, but I'm *quite* wealthy."

"You are?" Brady scratched his temple, as if this was all news to him, and uninteresting news at that.

"Filthy rich, you might say."

"You don't strike me as the 'filthy rich' type. And do I detect a note of dissatisfaction with having a lot of money?"

Jack shrugged. "Perhaps. Not that it's dirty money or anything like that. It's clean as can be, honestly earned. It's just that . . . well, I didn't earn it."

"Oh? And who did?"

"My father. And not that I don't get along with him, I do. It's just, well . . . 'from him to whom much is given, much will be expected' . . . if you know what I mean."

Brady smiled and nodded. "Ah, he quotes scripture. Luke 12:48, if I remember correctly."

If so, it was news to Jack. He'd remembered hearing the phrase, or something like it, now and again, and it seemed an apropos cliché. Had to admit, though, he was impressed that Brady could quote book, chapter, and verse.

Jack clasped his hands before him. "I know that a lot will be required of me when I take over the family business, and I want to be up to it. But I'm not interested in simply amassing more wealth. I mean, I'll never spend what I already have. So I'd like to find a way to put the wealth that will be flowing my way to better use than investing in stocks and bonds. I want to invest in *people.*"

He wondered if he might be laying it on too thick, but Brady seemed to be lapping it up.

"Well then, Jason, you've come to the right place. International Dormentalism is always reaching out to needy people in the poorest Third World countries. We go in, buy a parcel of land, then establish a temple and a school. The school teaches the Dormentalist way, but more importantly, it also teaches the locals self-sufficiency. 'Give a man a fish and you've fed him for a day; teach a man to fish, and you've fed him for a lifetime.' That's our philosophy."

Jack widened his eyes. "What a wonderful concept!"

One good cliché deserves another, he thought, and suppressed a smile as he remembered Abe's variation: *Teach a man to fish and you can sell him rods and reels and hooks and sinkers.*

"Yes. That is the Dormentalist way. You can rest assured that any contributions you wish to make to the Church will go directly toward helping the less fortunate."

"That sounds like a fine idea. You know, I don't think I'll wait till I take my father's place. I'd like to start right now. As soon as we're through here I'm going to contact my accountant."

Brady's smile was beatific. "How kind of you."

4

Luther Brady tapped his fingertips on his desktop as Jensen stood at attention on the far side. He'd known the Grand Paladin's first name once, but had long forgotten it. He wondered if even Jensen remembered.

Not that it mattered. What did matter was Jason Amurri and how he seemed just a little too good to be true.

He wanted Jensen's opinion but decided to have a little fun while he was at it.

"What does your xelton tell you about Jason Amurri?"

Jensen frowned. His answer was delayed, and drawn out when it came.

"It's suspicious. It finds inconsistencies about him."

Watching Jensen's shifting gaze, Brady wanted to laugh at his obvious discomfort talking about the perceptions of his Fully Fused xelton. He should be uncomfortable: Jensen's xelton wasn't FF. In fact, he didn't even *have* a xelton. No one did!

But no one—not Jensen nor any members of the HC—would admit it. Because each of them thought of himself as the sole Null among the elite FFs. Each hid their Sham Fusion because admitting to Nullhood would mean they'd have to leave their posts in disgrace.

Oh, it was rich to listen to them talk about levitating or leaving their bodies to wander among the planets and stars, almost as if they were engaged in an unspoken contest. And since Luther had made it implicitly clear all along that to exercise one's FF abilities in front of others was bad manners—tantamount to trivializing the wonders of FF by cheap exhibitionism—no one had to back up his or her wondrous claims.

That way, no one could say the emperor had no clothes.

"My xelton feels the same way, but for some reason it cannot pierce through and contact Amurri's. And we know what that means, don't we."

Jensen nodded. "Amurri is probably a Null."

"And that," Brady sighed, "is always tragic. I pity Nulls, but I pity even more the poor Null who's deluded himself into Sham Fusion."

He watched Jensen blink and swallow. He could almost read his mind: *Why's he saying that? Does he suspect? Does he know?*

"So do I," Jensen rasped.

"I'm sure there are members with SF in the temple, but one must restrain one's xelton from piercing their veil. That would be too much of an invasion. And unnecessary because, as you know, sooner or later all Nulls betray themselves." He cleared his throat as if clearing his mind. "But back to our friend Jason . . ."

Yes, Jason Amurri . . . after the Reveille Session was over and Amurri gone, Luther realized that he didn't know a damn thing that he hadn't known at the outset. Perhaps the man was just naturally reticent, but Luther had an uneasy feeling that he might be hiding something.

"Since our xeltons cannot yet contact his," he went on, "perhaps you had better pry a little more deeply into his background."

"I'm already on that."

Brady raised his eyebrows. "Oh?"

"My, um, PX doesn't think he acts like a rich boy. Doesn't move like one."

"And your xelton knows how the rich move?"

"I agree with my PX. I know people who move like Amurri and they're not rich. They're dangerous."

"But it's not like he showed up claiming to be Jason Amurri. He tried to *hide* that."

"Yeah, I know. That's the only thing that doesn't fit. But then again maybe he planned it that way all along— gave an obviously phony name and then—"

Luther laughed. "That's pretty convoluted, don't you think?"

Jensen shrugged. "My PX thinks there's more to him than meets the eye."

"I think you give him too much credit."

"Maybe. But if I can find just one picture of Jason Amurri, I'll feel a whole lot better."

"Knowing you, Jensen, if you found one, you'd wonder if it had been planted."

A rare flash of white teeth in Jensen's dark face—he almost never smiled. "That's my job, right?"

"Right. And one you do so well." Time to end this. He waved his hand at Jensen. "Keep checking on him. But if he shows up tomorrow with a six-figure donation, then stop. Because who he really is will no longer matter."

As Jensen walked out, Luther pressed the button under the edge of his desktop. The panels rolled back, revealing the Opus Omega globe.

He'd felt like a stunned fish when he'd walked in earlier and found the panels open with Amurri standing before it. He'd been about to shout for Jensen when he noticed that Amurri made no attempt to hide what he was doing. His lack of furtiveness had allayed Luther's suspicions. And his open curiosity about the meaning of the lights on the globe had seemed genuine.

Obviously he had no idea of the apocalyptic significance of what he'd seen.

Luther's thoughts slipped back to that late winter day in college when he first saw the globe. It had existed only in his mind then. He'd been a frosh, away from his strict Scottish-American home for the first time in his eighteen years, and making the most of the sex, drugs, and rock and roll of the early seventies. He was into his first tab of acid, with a couple of more experienced guys guiding him through the trip, when the globe had appeared, suspended and spinning in the center of the room. He remembered pointing it out to the others but he was the only one who could see it.

Not a Rand McNally globe, but a battered, pock-marked sphere with brown, polluted oceans and bilious chemical clouds shrouding the land. As he'd watched, red dots began to glow on all the continents and oceans, and then glowing red lines arced out from each to connect with the others, creating a globe-spanning network of scarlet threads. And then black circles appeared at some of the intersections of those threads. Soon after, the black circles began glowing white, one by one, and when all were lit, the globe glowed red, then white hot. Finally it exploded, but the scattered pieces returned and reformed into a new world of fertile green continents and pristine blue oceans.

The vision altered the course of Luther's life. Not immediately, not that night, but in the weeks and months afterward as it returned on a nightly basis, with or without chemical enhancement.

At first he was uneasy, thinking it was a recurring flashback and that he'd really screwed up his head. But after a while he got used to it. It became part of his quotidian existence.

But he was terrified when he first heard the voice. Never during his waking hours, only in his sleep, only during the vision. He began to think he might be schizophrenic.

At first it was an indistinct muttering—definitely a voice, but he couldn't understand a word. Gradually it grew louder, the mutterings progressing to distinguishable speech. But although he understood the individual words, they seemed disjointed and he could make no sense of them.

That too changed and by his senior year he came to understand that this world, the ground on which he stood, was destined to change and merge with a sister world in another space-time continuum. Those here who helped speed the fusion would survive the transition from a polluted planet to paradise; the rest of humanity would not. The voice told him to find the places designated by the white lights, to buy the land there, and wait.

Buy up pieces of land? He was a college student, virtually penniless. The voice didn't say how, but it implied
that his future well-being depended on it.

And then, shortly after graduation, the book arrived.
He found it on his bed in the apartment he was renting.
No mailer, no note saying who it was from . . . just this
weird, thick book. It looked ancient, but its title was in
English: *The Compendium of Srem.* The text was in En-
glish as well. He began reading.

The voice stopped with the arrival of the book. Reading it changed his life.

Toward the end of all the strange and wondrous leg-
ends the *Compendium* recounted, he found an animated
drawing of his vision globe. The text following the illustration explained Opus Omega.

And then he understood the dream and what he must
do with his life.

So Luther went hunting for the locations. By then he
had seen the globe so many times he could picture every
detail in his mind. He found those places—some of them
at least—and when he looked up the deed holders he discovered a startling trend: Many of the parcels were
owned by a man named Cooper Blascoe.

A little more research revealed that Blascoe was the
leader of a commune in northern California. Luther went
out to check on him and what he found, what he learned
there, changed his life forever.

For he realized then that the vision and the voice had
come from the Hokano world. Cooper Blascoe had stumbled on a cosmic truth; he would provide the means for
Luther to fulfill the prophecy of the voice.

Yes, the Hokano world was real, and maybe xeltons
were too—who could say for sure?—but the Fusion concept and the ladder to achieve it were all products of
Brady's imagination, all designed to aid him in completing Opus Omega.

And now, after decades of struggle, only a few more
tasks remained before completion.

Luther stepped closer to the spinning globe and reached out to it. As the ridges of its mountains and flats of its plains and oceans brushed against his fingertips, he closed his eyes. Just a few more locations and his work would be done.

But the final steps were proving difficult. Some of the needed land was terribly expensive, some simply not for sale. But Luther was sure he could overcome all obstacles. All he needed was money.

It always seemed to come down to the same thing: never enough money.

But perhaps Jason Amurri could remedy that, at least in part.

And then the final white bulbs could be lit . . . and the Great Fusion—the only real fusion in the tapestry of lies he'd created—would begin, joining this world with Hokano.

And in that new, better world, Luther Brady would be rewarded above all others.

5

Gia felt moisture between her legs. She hurried to the bathroom and groaned with dismay when she saw the bright red blood on the pad she'd been wearing.

Bleeding again.

She calmed herself. It wasn't much and Dr. Eagleton had warned her to expect some intermittent spotting for a few days afterward. But this was a little more than spotting.

She'd been tired all morning but noticed an uptick in her ambition level. She'd been planning on trying some painting, but now . . .

The good news was she wasn't having any pain. Monday night she'd felt as if someone had kicked her in the stomach. Not even a cramp now.

She'd watch and wait. She didn't want to be an alarmist, jumping on the phone for every little thing.

She'd take it slow and easy. Put her feet up and put off painting till tomorrow or the next day. Another thing she'd put off was telling Jack. He'd have a squad of EMTs here in seconds.

She had to smile at the thought of him. He was so confident and competent in so many areas of life, but where this baby was concerned, he was as jumpy as a cat. He cared so much.

Now, if he'd just find a lifestyle that wouldn't cause Gia to wonder every time he walked out the door whether this might be the last time she'd see him alive, he'd make a great father.

6

Dressed in street clothes, Sister Maggie stepped into the dimness of Julio's. Jack had said he wanted to meet with her and she felt this Upper West Side bar would be the least likely place she'd be seen by a Lower East Side parishioner.

She spotted Jack waiting at the same table against the wall and rushed over to him.

"It's true?" she said, clutching the edge of the table in a death grip. "What you said on the phone—they're gone?"

Jack nodded. "Your worries are over. I wiped out his files."

Maggie felt her knees weaken. Blood thundered in her ears as she sagged into a chair.

"You're sure? Absolutely sure?"

"Nothing's absolute, but I'm as sure as I can be without strapping him to a chair and taping live wires to delicate parts of his anatomy."

"That's . . . that's wonderful. Not what you just said," she added quickly. "What you said before."

Jack laughed. "I gotcha."

She didn't know how to ask this, and felt her face turning crimson. Finally she blurted it out.

"Did you happen to see any of the . . ."

Jack opened his mouth, closed it, then said, "You know, I was going to say yes, and boy were they hot, but I know it's not a joking matter for you. So the truth: no. He didn't keep hard copies. Why risk leaving evidence around when he could point and click and get a fresh print anytime he needed it?"

"I'm so glad, so glad."

Maggie closed her eyes. She had her life back. She wanted to drop to her knees right here on the bar floor and cry out her gratitude to God, but that would attract too much attention.

"But listen," Jack said, his voice grave. "Here's why I wanted to meet in person. I want you to realize that even though I've wiped out his files, you're going to hear from him again."

The wonderful, airy lightness that had suffused her drained away.

"What do you mean?"

"If I did my job right—meaning he thinks this was all a terrible accumulation of accidents—he'll assume that none of his victims know they've been wiped out. Which means they'll all be thinking they're still on the hook. You can't let *him* know that *you* know you're not."

"Okay."

"I'm serious about this, Sister. And you can't let your other half know either."

"Other . . . ?"

"Whoever else was in those pictures with you. Do *not* tell him."

"But he'll be forced to go on paying."

"That's his problem. Let him fix it. You fixed yours, so—"

"But—"

"No 'buts,' Sister. There's a saying that three can keep a secret if two are dead."

"But we two know."

"No. Only you. I don't exist. Trust me on this, please. This guy's an ex dirty cop, so no telling—"

"How did you learn so much about him so soon?"

"Past research from my first encounter with Mr. Slime."

"I . . ." She felt a sob build in her throat. "I can't believe it's over."

"It's not. Not yet. Like I told you, you've still got to deal with him, and very carefully. When he calls, tell him you're tapped out and will send him something as soon as you get it. Plead with him to be patient."

"But he wants me to . . . you know . . ." She lowered her voice. "The building fund . . ."

"Tell him you'll try, but it won't be easy. Because of the kind of neighborhood you're in, they watch it like hawks, yadda-yadda. But whatever you do, don't refuse to pay. You're not going to send him another damn cent, but you can't let him know that."

"But I am going to pay you. I promise. Every cent."

"No need. It's all taken care of. Financed by a third party."

Maggie was stunned. First the good news about the blackmail, and now this. But she couldn't help being a little put off that a third party was involved in this, her most private business.

"But who—?"

"Don't worry. You'll never know her and she'll never know you."

A sob burst free as tears trickled down her cheeks. What more proof did she need that God had forgiven her?

"Thank you. Thank you so much. If there's anything I can ever do for you, just say it."

"Well, there is one thing." He leaned forward. "How does such an uptight straight arrow like you let herself get involved in a situation that could ruin her life?"

Maggie hesitated, then figured, why not? Jack knew the bad part; he should know the rest of it.

She told him about the four Martinez children and how they were all going to have to leave St. Joseph's for public school by the end of the year. She explained what a tragedy she thought that would be, especially for naïve little Serafina.

Without mentioning his name she told Jack about approaching Michael Metcalf for help.

"And somehow," she said, "I found myself in a physical relationship with him. But the Martinez children are the innocent, unwitting victims. The blackmailer drained away the funds that would have gone to them. But don't worry. I'll find a way."

Jack looked as if he was about to say something but changed his mind. He glanced at his watch instead.

"I've got someplace I've got to be, so . . ."

Maggie reached across the table and gripped both his hands. "Thank you. You've given me back my life and I'm going to do good things with it." She gave his hands a final squeeze, then rose to her feet. "Good-bye, Jack. And God bless you."

As she turned and started away she heard him say, "Did you hurt your leg?"

She stiffened. The burns on her thighs ached and stung with each step, but she offered up the pain.

"Why do you ask?"

"You're limping a little."

"It's nothing. It will pass."

Maggie stepped out into a new day, a new beginning—
a redundancy she'd flag in one of her student's prose, but
at this moment it seemed right and true.

Lord, don't think I'm forgetting my promise just because I'm free of my tormentor. Tomorrow, cross number
six. And on Sunday, the seventh and last, just as I promised. And also as promised, I will devote every moment
of the rest of my life to Your works and never stray again.

She headed for the subway, for St. Joseph's Church, to
give God thanks in His house.

Life was good again.

7

Jack thought about Sister Maggie as he loitered in a doorway on Lexington Avenue and kept watch on the temple's
entrance. He'd ditched Jensen's tail—he'd put two guys
on him this morning—on his way to Julio's. After his
meeting with the nun, he'd returned to Lexington and set
up watch for Johnny Roselli.

Sister Maggie . . . he'd had an urge to grab her and
shake her and try to convince her to get out and enjoy life.
But he couldn't. It was her life, to live her way. His in-
ability to comprehend her choices didn't invalidate them.

Still . . . he didn't get it. Probably never would.

His thoughts refocused on the here and now when he
saw Roselli appear, pushing through the doors and then
trotting down the steps of the nearby subway entrance.
Jack had to do a little booking to keep from losing him.

He caught up on the downtown platform and followed
him aboard a 4 train. Johnny was still in the grungy
sackcloth-and-ashes mode and his mind seemed light

years away as the car swayed and rattled and yawed along the tracks.

Jack's mind wasn't exactly locked onto the present either. It kept straying back to Brady's office and the hidden globe. He remembered that cold feeling in his gut as he'd stared at the red and white lights and the lines running between . . .

They rode the 4 down to Union Square where Johnny hopped the L to its terminus on Eighth Avenue and Fourteenth. From there Jack shadowed him into the meat-packing district.

When Jack first came to the city, this area had deserved its name—beef hindquarters and pig carcasses hanging in doorways, burly, cleaver-toting butchers in blood-stained white aprons hustling in and out, back and forth. A different kind of hustle at night: curb clingers in hot pants and microminis—not all of them women—hawking their wares to passing cars.

Creeping gentrification had wrought its predictable changes. Most of the butchers were gone now, replaced by art galleries and trendoid restaurants. He passed Hogs and Heifers, the inspiration for the bar in *Coyote Ugly,* a charter member of Jack's Worst Movies of All Time Club.

Johnny kept walking west. What was he going to do, jump in the Hudson?

The light was fading, the wind picked up enough to make people turn up their collars. Not the skateboarders, though. Dressed in nothing more than the de rigueur baggy shorts, T-shirt, and backward baseball cap, a bunch of them were doing kickflips and railslides as Jack passed.

Eventually Johnny stopped outside a bar called The Header on the ground floor of a ramshackle building in the far, far West Village. If it called itself a dive, it would be putting on airs. The dozen or so motorcycles lined up out front left little doubt as to the nature of the preferred clientele. A neon Budweiser sign glowed in one of the two tiny windows; a handwritten placard announcing FOOD was taped in the other.

Food? Dinner at The Header ... now there was a thought. Tonight's special: ebola quiche.

But Johnny didn't enter the bar. Instead he keyed open a narrow door around the side from the entrance and disappeared inside. A minute or so later Jack saw a third-floor window light up.

He didn't get it. Why a third-floor walk-up over a biker bar? According to his mother the guy was worth millions.

Maybe he'd given it all to the Dormentalists. Or maybe he still had it but had decided to live in poverty. Jack tried to care, but failed. No explaining cult members. Waste of time to try.

And anyway, his job wasn't to make sense of Johnny Roselli, it was to give him a message from his mother. The easiest way would be to knock on his door and tell him, but he didn't like the idea of letting Johnny see his face.

Why not? After delivering the message to call Mama, Jack's job was done. If he were sticking with the Jason Amurri identity, yeah, it would matter: He wouldn't want to risk Johnny spotting him and opening his yap. But Jack had no intention of ever setting foot in the temple again ...

Or did he?

He had a feeling he had unfinished business there ... business involving Brady's globe.

Jack noted the number on the door, then turned and headed east at a comfortable pace. He pulled out his cell phone and dialed information. They had no listing for a J. Roselli at that address.

Damn. He stopped walking. He might have to show his face after all.

On a sudden whim he called back and asked for a party named "Oroont" at that address. Bull's-eye.

He smiled and said aloud, "Am I good or am I good?"

He let the operator dial for him and a few seconds later he was listening to a phone ring. A man answered.

"Is this John Roselli?"

The tone was guarded. "It was. How did you get this number?"

"Not important. I have a message from your mother. She—"

"You *what*? Who are you?"

"Someone your mother hired to find you. She's been worried about you and—"

"Listen, you son of a bitch," Roselli gritted, and Jack could all but feel the steam coming through the phone. "Who put you up to this? The GP? Are you one of Jensen's drones trying to trap me?"

"No, I'm simply—"

"Or some dirty WA trying to harass me?"

Be nice if I could finish a sentence.

"Not even close. Look, just call your mother. She's worried and wants to hear from you."

"Fuck you!"

And then the phone slammed down.

Jack tried three more times. On the first he heard the receiver lift, then clatter down again. After that all he got was a busy signal.

Okay. He'd done his job, delivered the message. Johnny apparently had big issues with Mom. Jack was sorry about that but his fix-it skills—thankfully—did not reach into family therapy.

As he kept walking east, heading for Eighth Avenue where he could catch a train, Brady's globe spun into his thoughts again . . . the red and white lights . . . the network of crisscrossing lines . . . so tantalizingly close . . . he reached for it, stretching . . .

And then Jack grasped it. But when he realized what he had hit on he instantly wished he hadn't. He stumbled as he felt the world slow around him.

The lights and the lines . . . he'd seen that pattern before . . . and now he knew where . . .

Suddenly out of breath, he stopped walking and leaned against a railing. He wasn't going to be sick, but he wanted to be.

When his heart and lungs dropped back toward their normal tempos, he pushed off and got moving again. He'd planned to stop by Maria Roselli's to tell her he'd contacted Johnny boy, and then drop in on Gia and Vicky to see how his girls were doing. But all that was out of the question now. He needed answers, needed to find someone who might have an explanation.

He could think of only one person.

8

Jamie had been working late—as usual—when Robertson called. His voice had sounded tight and he'd said he needed to talk to her. Now. Something had come up—something big and very strange.

Well, she'd been ready to leave anyway. After she assured him that the line had been checked for taps, he said he'd pick her up in his car, a big, black Crown Victoria. When she'd reminded him about her Dementedist shadows, he told her where to meet him and exactly how to get there.

So here she was at 8:15 walking west through the Forty-second Street tunnel. One of the Dementedist shadows was following her, laying back about fifty feet or so. Where was the other? They usually had a crew of two waiting outside *The Light*. It bothered her that she didn't know where he was.

Jamie was puffing by the time she reached the Eighth Avenue station. Damn those cigarettes. Had to quit some day.

Instead of heading for one of the train platforms, she rushed up the steps to the street.

Now she was really breathing hard. She spotted a big

black car idling at the corner. That had to be Robertson, but he'd told her to wait until he gave a signal. Why? She didn't want to wait with one of those nutcases coming up behind her. She wanted in that car *now*.

Suddenly the passenger door flew open and his voice called from within.

"Let's go!"

Jamie didn't need to hear that twice. She trotted over and jumped in. The car was roaring up Eighth Avenue before she closed the door.

"We've got to stop meeting like this, Robertson."

Light from passing street lamps flashed against his face. His features looked tight, tense.

"Call me Jack, remember?"

"Oh, right. Hey, tell me, why did you want me to wait by the top of the steps instead of just jumping in and going?"

"I wanted the traffic lights the right color. Not much point in burning rubber just to stop a block away. Now they'll have to find a cab before they can come after us. And they're not going to find us when they do."

"Not they—he. Only one tonight. But he probably got a look at your license plate."

The line of his mouth tightened further. "Might have got a look at more than that. While I was waiting for you a guy I'd seen in Jensen's office when I was getting my Entry Card came out of a deli carrying a paper bag. Coffee and sandwiches, probably. Walked right past the car."

"Think he saw you?"

"Looked at me but didn't seem to recognize me."

"Oh, hell. If they've got your plate numbers—"

He smiled, but even that was tight. "Won't do them much good. And they're in for a pile of trouble if they start hassling the real owner of these tags."

"So this is a borrowed car?"

"No, it's mine, but the plates are duplicates of someone else's. Someone you don't want to mess with."

"Who?"

He shook his head. "Trade secret."

That again. But he'd piqued her curiosity. "Would I have heard of him?"

"As a reporter? Oh, yeah."

The way he drew out the *oh* was enough to make her crazy. Who was he talking about? But she sensed that asking again would be like talking to a statue.

He took a left onto Fifty-seventh and headed farther west.

"Where are we going?"

"We need someplace quiet and private. Any ideas?"

"We're only a few blocks from my place but I think it's got a surveillance situation."

"Wouldn't be surprised, but let's go check it out anyway."

She directed him to her block on West Sixty-eighth.

She pointed right to the front door of her apartment building. "That's me."

Jack jerked a thumb toward his side window. "And there's the Dormentalist stakeout team."

Jamie saw a dark coupe, parked curbside, no lights on inside or out. A man sat alone in the front seat. Her stomach crawled.

"Let's get out of here."

9

Jensen was on his way out of the temple when his two-way chirped. It was Margiotta.

"Finally found a picture of him, boss."

"Amurri?"

"Yeah. You'd better come see. I don't think you're going to like it."

"Be right there."

On the contrary, Jensen thought as he did an about face and headed back across the nearly deserted lobby. I bet I'll like it just fine.

Margiotta's tone had said it all: The photo he'd found did not match the guy who'd been calling himself Jason Amurri.

He did a mini fist pump. Knew it!

His instincts had been right on target. He gave himself a mental pat on the back for his powers of observation, and for plain old gut instinct. He'd spotted Amurri for a ringer from day one.

And now we've got him.

Another chirp from his two-way. Margiotta again.

"Here's something else you won't like, Boss. Lewis and Hutchison just called in. They lost the quail."

Margiotta knew better than to mention names on a two-way. He didn't have to. Jensen knew who he meant.

Noomri's balls! How hard can it be to follow one middle-aged, overweight broad?

"They give any details?"

"No, but they have more to tell. They're waiting till they get here. They should be walking in any minute."

Jensen considered waiting and holding the elevator for them, then giving them hell once the doors closed. He decided not to. He couldn't wait to see the face of the real Jason Amurri.

Margiotta sat in the office, seated before the computer. He leaned back and pointed to the screen.

"There he is."

Jensen leaned in and saw a blurry image of a man in his thirties. He ran a mental comparison and couldn't find one point of correspondence between this man and the one who claimed to be Jason Amurri. Darker hair, darker skin, bigger nose, different hairline . . .

"You sure this is the real Jason Amurri?"

Margiotta shrugged. "It says it's him, but that doesn't mean it is."

"What do you mean? I thought you said—"

"This is the Internet, boss. What you see ain't necessarily the real deal. Anybody can post anything, true or false. No one fact checks the Internet."

"But can you think of a reason why anyone would go to the trouble of posting a fake photo of Jason Amurri?"

"I can think that a fake Jason Amurri might, just in case we checked. If it looked just like him, I'd check when it was posted. And if it was of real recent vintage, I'd say we couldn't trust it. But this is a couple years old and doesn't look at all like our guy. So I'm ninety-nine percent sure it's legit."

"What would make you a hundred?"

"Finding another with the same face."

"Okay, then. Keep looking. I want to be absolutely sure before I take this to the SO. But for now, put a flag on his pass code. Next time he swipes his way in, I want him detained at the security desk."

Lewis and Hutchison walked in then. Jensen was opening his mouth to begin charbroiling them when Lewis held up one of his skinny hands.

"Yeah, I know, we lost her, but we didn't come back empty-handed."

"It had better be good."

The heavier Hutchison told about tailing her underground and then losing her to a waiting car.

Jensen had to admire the ditch: sweet and simple.

"You are going to tell me you got the tag number, right?"

Hutchison nodded and handed over a sheet of paper. Jensen glanced at it. New York plates. Excellent. A number of Dormentalists worked for the New York DMV.

He passed the sheet to Margiotta. "Run it." He turned back to Hutchison and Lewis. "That still doesn't save your asses. I put you on—"

"There's more," Lewis said. "Just out of pure coincidence, I walked by the car just minutes before Grant jumped in and took off. I saw the driver. Thought he looked familiar but didn't pay much attention. After Grant gave us the slip it clicked and I remembered where I'd seen him before."

"Yeah? Where?"

"Right here. He's that guy the SO's been doting on. What's his name? Am-something."

"Amurri." Jensen felt a huge smile spreading across his face. "Jason Amurri." He turned to Margiotta again. "But he's not Jason Amurri, is he."

"If he's working with Grant, I think we can go a hundred percent on that, no problem."

Jensen rubbed his hands together. "We know who he's not. And before the night is out we'll know who he is."

10

"So," Jamie said. "What's the situation? Why the big rush to see me tonight? I assume it wasn't because of my great looks and sparkling personality."

Jack wore a blue V-neck sweater over a T-shirt and jeans and looked good as he gave her a wan smile.

"You never know."

Right answer, she thought.

After passing her place they'd stayed on the West Side, heading downtown. Jack found a lot in the Forties, in what used to be called Hell's Kitchen, and Jamie noticed how he gave the attendant an extra couple of bucks to park his car where it wasn't visible from the street. Attention to detail—she liked that in a man. There was a lot to like about this fellow.

A short walk brought them to this little bar off Tenth Avenue. She'd already forgotten its name. Dusty and dingy, but only a quarter full, which gave them some space in a rear booth.

With half of a Dewar's and soda making its way through her system, she felt herself begin to relax. But only a little. One thing to suspect your home is being watched; something totally other to spot the guy doing the watching.

"I saw the globe today," Jack said. His bar draft sat before him, untouched.

"Brady's globe?"

He nodded. "Got a good, long look."

If true, it was a hell of a coup. But he didn't sound too happy about it.

"And?"

"Something about the lights and all the crisscrossing lines set my teeth on edge. Didn't know why, but just looking at it struck a sour note. Took me a while to realize that the pattern was familiar. Took me a little longer to remember where I'd seen it before."

"Great! So then you know what it's all about."

He shook his head. "Still don't know that. But I'll show you where I saw it."

He lifted the small plastic shopping bag that had been sitting beside him on the bench. He'd removed it from the car's back seat when they'd parked, but had only shaken his head when she'd asked what was in it.

He pushed his beer aside and laid the bag on the wet ring it left on the table. Then he sat quietly, staring at it.

Jamie felt a rising impatience. What was all the drama here?

"Well?"

"You're not going to believe what I'm going to tell you," he said without looking up. "Sometimes I don't believe it myself, but then I look at this and know it's real."

Sounds like the opening line to a bad horror story, she thought.

"Try me."

"Okay." He reached into the bag and brought out a quarter-folded piece of thick beige fabric, maybe a foot long and a little less wide. As he began to unfold it she realized it was some sort of leather. He flattened it on the tabletop between them.

Jamie leaned forward for a better look. She saw a slightly rough surface, dimpled with pockmarks of varying sizes. The larger were a dull, dusky red, the smaller pale and slightly glossy. Connecting them all were a hundred, maybe more, fine lines, mechanical-pencil thin.

"This is what's on the globe?"

Jack nodded. "The reason it took me so long to recognize it was because the pattern was wrapped around a sphere. Even though it was rotating, I never saw the whole design at once. I mean, I would have recognized it if this"—he tapped the design—"included outlines of the oceans and continents, but as you can see, it doesn't. Still it rang a bell somewhere in my head. Took me most of the day to make the connection."

"Okay, so this is the same pattern of lights and lines as on the globe. What's so unbelievable about that?"

"That's not the unbelievable part."

"All right then, what is?"

Jack didn't answer. He simply stared at the leather and gently ran a hand over its surface.

Jamie took another sip of her Scotch. She was getting annoyed.

Her turn to tap the leather. Hmmm . . . soft. She let her hand rest on it, placing a fingertip in one of the pocks.

"Does this thing get us any closer to figuring out why he keeps the globe situation so secret?"

"No, but—"

"Then what's the point? Where'd you find it? Maybe there's a clue in that. If Brady didn't make this then someone connected to him did. If we can talk to him—"

"She's dead."

She? Dead? Jamie felt her chest tighten.

"How? Tell me she died of a heart attack or something. Please don't tell me she was murdered."

"Wish I could. This is all that's left of her."

Jamie's chest tightened further.

"I don't . . ."

"This is her skin . . . from her back."

She snatched her hand back. "You're shitting me, right?"

Finally he looked up at her. She knew even before he shook his head that he wasn't.

"The only reason I'm telling you about this is because I don't know anybody else I can go to who knows more about Dormentalism."

"You mean . . . you mean a Dormentalist flayed this off her and then sat down and *drew* on it?"

"Not at all. Take a closer look." He waved a hand over the pocks, the lines. "This isn't a drawing. These are scars. Don't ask me how, but all this was on her back before she died."

"Before? But how—? Where's the rest of her?"

His eyes were leveled at her. She saw pain there.

"Gone."

Jamie didn't know what to say, but she did know her glass was empty and she needed another—needed it big time.

"I'm going for a refill. My turn." She pointed to Jack's almost full glass. "You want a back for that?"

He shook his head.

Jamie made a quick trip to the bar.

John "Jack" Robertson hadn't struck her as a nutcase, but obviously he was. What other explanation could there be?

But he seemed so sincere. Her bullshit meter wasn't even flickering. Did he believe all this?

By the time she sat down with her fresh drink she felt a little more focused.

"Okay, the lady is gone, but while she was living, these marks appeared on her back like some stigmata. Sorry, pal, but I don't believe in the supernatural."

He leaned forward. "Jamie, I don't give a rat's ass what you believe. What I'm trying to get across to you is that we're talking about something bigger than just a money-grubbing cult here. *Lots* bigger."

She felt her spine stiffen. "Well, if you don't give a rat's ass, why show me?"

"I told you, because you probably know as much as any outsider can about Dormentalism—which may not be any-where near as demented as you think. Have you found any evidence, any hint, *anything* that might lead you to think the cult could be connected to something else? Something bigger, something darker, something . . ." His mouth twisted, as if he didn't want to say the word. *". . . other."*

"No . . . but I may have found someone who does know."

He leaned closer. "Who?"

Don't, she told herself. Don't say it.

But she was caught in the grip of the moment. This man had challenged her credulity—more like sucker punched it—and so now it was her turn.

"I think I've found Cooper Blascoe."

11

Maggie had known the call would come, but not so soon. And not on the convent phone. Her stomach quivered when she recognized the voice.

"I really can't speak now," she said, looking up and down the hall. She was alone but she'd have to keep her voice down.

"Then just listen. I want to know when I'm going to see the money you owe me."

"Owe you?" She felt a spear of anger jab through her anxiety. "I don't *owe* you."

"The hell you don't! I'm saving your holy-roller ass by keeping those photos under wraps. So you owe me. And by the way, it's a nice-looking ass you've got there."

Maggie felt her cheeks burn.

"I don't have it," she said, remembering what Jack had told her. "I'll get it for you but I need more time."

"You know where you can get it."

"I'm trying but it's not easy."

"It's easy as pie. Just start skimming a little every day."

"It's closely watched."

"Find a way, sissy, or your pretty little ass and lots more will be plastered all over the neighborhood."

"But that won't be good for you either. You'll get no more from me after that. At least this way you're getting something."

"Don't try to play games with me. You're just a tiny part of my action. I'll cut you loose without a second thought."

Maggie thought she detected a note of desperation in his voice.

"I'm doing my best," she told him, sounding plaintive. "I can't give you what I don't have."

"Then *get* it! I'm in a generous mood today, so I'll give you till next week."

"Next week?" Would she have to suffer through another of these calls next week? How long before he gave up? "Okay. I'll see what I can do."

"No, you'll *do* it. By next week. All of it."

And then he hung up.

Her hand was shaking as she replaced the receiver. He'd sounded desperate. A thought struck her like a blow: Was he calling all his victims and trying to squeeze them? That meant Michael would be on his list. She knew Jack

had said to tell no one, but . . . but how could she let
someone go on paying this serpent when he didn't have
to? She was sure Michael could keep a secret.

She headed for the street to a public phone.

12

Jack leaned back in the booth. He imagined his expression right now looked like Jamie's when he'd told her
about Anya's skin.

"Yeah, right," he said. "Now who's playing 'Can You
Top This'? He's dead."

Her eyes widened. "Yeah? Says who?"

"Says Occam's Razor."

He frowned. That particular razor had lost its edge
lately. Occam's butterknife was more like it.

She flashed a yellow smile. "I can't believe you're such
a cynic. How can you possibly have the slightest doubt
that he's in suspended animation?"

"Let's see . . . dead or in suspended animation: Which
requires the fewer assumptions?"

She shrugged. "Dead, of course."

"Exactly. How does a cult that's supposed to prepare
you to be a survivor of doomsday handle the death of its
founder?"

"Hide it. Or find a way to explain it. The Scientologists
got around it by telling their members that L. Ron Hub-
bard had 'causatively discarded' his body because it had
become an impediment to the research he was doing for
the betterment of mankind."

"So, knowing all that, why do you think Blascoe's
alive?"

Another shrug. "I agree with everything you've said. You'd expect them to cover up his death, not his longevity. Unless . . ."

"Unless he's got some terminal illness or is completely off his rocker."

"Riiiight. A dead guru is an embarrassment, sure, but one with dementia is even worse. Doesn't say much about the value of fusing your personal xelton with its Hokano half, does it?"

Jack had been watching Jamie's eyes. She was onto something. Question was, how much would she tell him?

"And you say you've found him."

"I say I *think* I *may* have found him. You see, getting kicked out of the temple made it impossible for me to investigate Dementedism from the inside, so I did it from the outside. I've learned that Brady rarely leaves the temple unless it's for a public appearance. And then he's always driven back and forth in a limo. But Sunday nights are a different situation. Sunday nights—at least three out of four as far as I can tell—he drives himself."

"Where?"

"Wish I knew. He and Jensen and the High Council guys keep their cars in a garage around the corner from the temple. I've seen him pull out a number of times and tried to tail him, but always lost him."

"He ditched you?"

"I don't think so. I'm just not very good at it. But I tailed the GP a few times and had better luck with him."

Jack had to laugh. "You've been following him too? *That's* dedication."

"That's me, all right. Dedicated to a fault."

Jack saw a strange flash in her eyes as she took a sip of her Scotch.

"It's more than professional, isn't it."

She shrugged. "A journalist's credo is impartiality and objectivity. But you might say I have a thing for cult situations. You might say I think they're poisonous, that they prey—sometimes knowingly and sometimes unwit-tingly—on confused people and exploit their weaknesses."

An idea was taking root in Jack's head. "Were you ever in one?"

"Uh-uh. No way. Never. But my sister Susie was. She died of exposure on a hilltop in West Virginia. You may have read about it a few years back."

Jack nodded. Half a dozen bodies, two males, four fe-males, found stiff and cold by some hikers. They'd been dead since New Year's Eve. It had been all over the news for a day or two, then dropped.

"She and her fellow cultists literally froze to death while standing naked in the cold waiting to be 'taken home.' So yeah, it might be personal, and my articles may have an adversarial edge. I'm looking for dirt, I won't deny that, but my facts are facts and all double- or triple-checked. That's why I follow the Dementedist big-wigs. Because that cult is dirty at the top. They're hiding something."

"Like their founder, for instance?"

"I get a feeling it's bigger than that. But getting back to Blascoe: On two occasions I followed Jensen and one of his TPs to a supermarket where they packed Jensen's car full of groceries. Then he dropped off the TP and headed for the hills—literally. I followed him up 684 and lost him the first time. But then, back in September, I managed to tail him all the way into Putnam County. Way up in the hills there I saw him unload the groceries at a house in the woods, then leave."

"Maybe it's a relative."

"An old white man with long hair and a scraggly beard came out on the front porch and shook his fist at Jensen as he was leaving. Not exactly the way I'd picture his daddy."

"Blascoe?"

She shrugged. "I don't know. In any pictures I've ever seen of Cooper Blascoe he's been a hale and hearty fel-low with this blond mane. This guy was skinny and kind of stooped. I've heard Blascoe had some kind of germ phobia, but this guy looked like he hadn't seen soap and water since the Beame administration."

"And yet . . . ?"

"And yet, something about his hairline, something about his profile . . ." She shook her head. "I don't know. Somewhere in my brain a circuit closed and lit up a neon sign that kept flashing *Cooper Blascoe . . . Cooper Blascoe . . .* and wouldn't stop."

Jack knew the feeling. His own subconscious had recognized immediately the pattern on Brady's globe, but it had taken his conscious mind a while to catch up.

"How close did you get?"

"Not close enough to be sure."

"You didn't move in for a better look?"

"No. I wanted to but . . . Want the truth? I was scared. I'm brave behind my keyboard—I'll take on anyone, anytime—but out in the real world . . . out there, I'm chickenshit." She waggled the stump of her pinkie at him. "Low threshold for pain. Maybe a low threshold for death too—like if I get too scared I'll die."

"What were you frightened of?"

She placed a mocking finger against her temple. "Oh, let's see now. How about being a woman alone at night in deep woods where I was pretty sure I wasn't supposed to be? How about I was hot and all scratched up from following Jensen's car on foot and the bugs were eating me alive? Knowing how Dementedists are about security, and this being their chief of security I'd followed, how about wondering whether or not I might be walking into a trap? Like maybe an electrified fence situation or bear traps or Dobermans? How about worrying about Jensen spotting my car in the bushes where I'd ditched it? Can you blame me if all I wanted was out of there?"

Jack shook his head. "Not a bit. Can you find it again?"

She smiled as she nodded. "I might have been scared, but not scared stupid. I made careful notes on a map as I drove back to the freeway."

"And you haven't been up there since?"

"Been meaning to. Been thinking about sneaking up there in the daytime with a telephoto lens and hanging out till I got a chance to snap a few shots. Even drove by the side road a couple of times but . . ."

"But never left your car." Jack wasn't asking. He knew the answer.

Jamie looked embarrassed as she shook her head. " 'Lacked da noive,' as the Cowardly Lion might say."

"How about if I take you up there?"

From the look on her face he guessed she'd been hoping for just such an offer.

"Great idea. What about tomorrow?" Her words picked up velocity as she went on. "I'll borrow a camera from one of the staff photogs. We should leave in the morning so we can maximize our light hours."

Jack ran his fingers lightly over the pocks in Anya's skin as he thought about Jamie's proposal. Tomorrow looked like a good day for a road trip. But first he needed to drop in on Maria Roselli. Ostensibly to tell her about Johnny, but mostly to give her a grilling. He had a feeling she knew a lot more about the pattern on this thing than she'd admitted.

He refolded the skin. "Okay, let's do it. I'll drop you off a few blocks from your place and let you walk home."

He'd probably never set foot in a Dormentalist temple again, but he didn't want to be seen yet. Always keep your options open.

He noticed Jamie's worried expression.

"Don't worry. I'll follow to make sure you get home safe."

Jamie smiled and held up her hand for a high five. "Awright!"

Jack poked her palm with the tip of an index finger. When she gave him a questioning look, he simply shrugged. It always tended to be an awkward moment. Jack didn't do high fives.

She slid out of the booth. "You know what I might do? I think I might just tap on those watchdogs' car window and ask them how their Hokanos are hangin'."

"What kind of word is 'Hokano' anyway?" he said as he bagged the skin and slipped out to join her. "Made up or from some other language?"

"Probably just made up. The closest I could find was the Japanese *hoka no*—but they don't put the accent on the middle syllable like the Dementedists do. Means 'other.'"

Jack stood paralyzed as ice crystalized along every nerve in his body.

"What . . . what did you say?"

"Other. *Hoka no* means other." She stared at him, concern etching her features. "What's wrong? Are you all right?"

Jack felt as if he'd taken a battering ram to the solar plexus. It was happening again. He was being sucked in again.

He shook it off as best he could and turned to Jamie.

"Can you find this place in the dark?"

"The cabin? Pretty sure. But—"

"Good. Because that's where we're going."

"Now? But it's—"

"Now."

No way Jack could let this sit till tomorrow.

13

Jensen was getting sick of waiting. "No word on those tags yet?"

"She's faxing it through now."

Fortunately one of the DMV Dormentalists had been on the night shift.

A few moments later Jensen had the sheet in his hand. But what to make of it?

The owner of the getaway car was one Vincent A. Donato, resident of Brooklyn. Somehow the guy pretending to be Jason Amurri didn't look like a Vincent Donato. Something else bothered him.

He looked up at Margiotta. "Donato . . . Donato . . . why does that sound familiar?"

"Rung one of my bells too, so I asked her to send over a photo." The fax rang in the other room. "That'll be it now."

A moment later Margiotta returned, saying, "Oh-shit, oh-shit, oh-shit."

Jensen didn't like the sound of that. "What's the matter?"

"You know why it sounded familiar? Vincent A. Donato is Vinny the Donut."

Jensen levered forward in his seat and snatched the fax from Margiotta.

"What? There's got to be—"

But there on the sheet was a pudgy, jowly face known to pretty much everyone in New York—at least anyone who read the *Post* or the *News*. At various times over the past ten years Vinny the Donut had been indicted for loan sharking, for prostitution, or for money laundering. But before any charges could be brought to trial, witnesses seemed to develop memory lapses or give in to an urge to visit relatives in foreign countries. Not a single charge had stuck.

"Can you believe it?" Margiotta said. "He's driving Vinny the Donut's car! Our phony is mobbed up!"

"Got to be a mistake. Lewis flubbed the tag number."

"That's what I thought, but look what the Donut drives—a black Crown Vic. And what kind of car whisked Grant off the street? A black Crown Vic. And I doubt very, *very* much that he stole Vinny's car. You do *not* steal from Vinny the Donut."

Jensen felt adrift on a rough sea. None of this made sense.

"But what possible interest could the mob have in Dormentalism?"

"Maybe they want to horn in. Maybe they hired Grant to get inside info on us."

Jensen shook his head. "No. It's got to be something else."

"Like what?"

I don't know, he thought, but I'll come up with something.

Jensen knew he'd better have some sort of explanation when he laid this double bombshell on Brady tomorrow morning.

Not only was the SO's pet recruit *not* Jason Amurri, but he was connected to the mob. Brady was going to shit a brick.

14

Jamie had to admit that her current situation had her a little scared. Here she was in the dark, heading toward the wilds of upstate New York with a strange man she'd met only days ago.

At least he wasn't driving fast or lane hopping. She hated that. She had a feeling he wanted the pedal to the metal but he'd set the cruise control to sixty-five and was sticking to the right or middle lanes. Very sane, very sensible. Also a pretty sure way to avoid being stopped by a cop.

It wasn't his driving. It was him . . . the way he'd changed when she'd told him what Hokano meant. He'd become another person. The regular fellow in the booth at the bar had become this grim, relentless automaton encased in a steel shell.

"What if it's not Blascoe?" she said.

He didn't turn his head. His eyes remained fixed on the road. "Then we've made a mistake and we've wasted some time."

"What if he *is* Blascoe and doesn't want to talk?"

"He won't have a choice."

His matter-of-fact tone chilled her.

"You're very scary right now. You know that, don't you?"

She saw his stiff shoulders relax a little. Very little. But it was a start, a hint that a thaw might be possible.

"Sorry. You've got nothing to worry about."

"Yeah, I do. I started out the night with Dr. Jekyll, and now I feel like I'm driving with Mr. Hyde."

"Did I suddenly sprout bushy eyebrows and bad teeth?"

"No. But you changed—your eyes, your expression, your demeanor. You're a different person."

She saw the tiniest hint of a smile in the backwash of light from a passing car.

"So I guess we're in the Spencer Tracy version."

Jamie had no idea what he was talking about.

"What did I say—what was it about the translation of Hokano that set you off? You were fine until then."

He sighed. "You've already heard some strange stuff tonight. Ready for something even stranger?"

What could be stranger than that piece of human skin he was carrying around? Even if it was fake, even if it was some other kind of hide, the story he'd attached to it was bizarre as all hell. How could he top that?

"Seeing as we still have some time to kill," she told him, "fire away."

If what she'd heard already was any indication, it would not be boring.

"All right. It's more than a matter of killing time. You might be getting involved—hell, you're probably already involved—and you should know what you're getting into."

"How many more preambles are you going to lay on me? Can we get to the story, I mean before morning?"

He laughed—a short, harsh sound. "Okay."

Then whatever lightness had crept into his voice in the past minute or so deserted it.

"What if I told you that there's been an unseen war going on between two vast, unimaginable, unknowable forces for eons, for almost as long as time itself?"

"You mean between Good and Evil?"

"More like Not So Bad and Truly Awful. And what if I told you that part of the spoils of this war is all this"—he waved his hand at the countryside sliding past—"our world, our reality?"

"I'd say you've been reading too much Lovecraft. What's the name of that big god of his?"

"Cthulhu. But forget about any fiction you've read. This—"

"How can I? That's what it sounds like. Earth is a jewel that all these cosmic gods with funny names slaver for."

"No, we're just one insignificant card in a huge cosmic deck. We're no more important than any other card, but you need all the cards before you can declare yourself the winner."

Was he kidding her? She couldn't tell. He sounded pretty serious. But really . . .

"No offense, but I've heard it all before and it's ridiculous. And if you believe it, that's scary."

"Trust me, I don't *want* to believe it. I'd rather *not* believe it. I was much happier knowing nothing about it. But I've seen too many things that can't be explained any other way. These two forces, states of being, whatever, are real. They don't have names, they don't have shapes, they don't have faces, and they don't dwell in forgotten jungle temples or sunken cities. They're just . . . there. Somewhere out there. Maybe everywhere. I don't know."

"And you came by this arcane knowledge . . . how?"

"I've been told. And somewhere along the way I became involved."

"Involved how?"

"Too complicated, and it doesn't bear directly on what we're talking about."

"All this informationus interruptus is starting to fray my nerves."

"Let me just say that I'm a reluctant participant and leave it at that. I'm sure I've already stretched my credibility to its tensile limit."

No argument there, Jamie thought.

She was going to ask him what side he was "reluctantly" involved with, but dropped it. She couldn't see him siding with "Truly Awful."

"All right. We'll leave it there. But what's the connection to Blascoe and Dementedism and Hokano? That one little word was the jumping-off point for this story, remember?"

"I remember, and I'm getting to it. Just listen. These two forces I mentioned . . . whatever names we might call them are human invention, because we humans like to name and classify things. It's the way our brains work. So through the millennia, the people who've had a peek at the doings of these forces, their intrusions into human affairs, have given them names. They call the Not-So-Bad force 'the Ally,' and the——"

"See?" Jamie said, exasperated. "That's where all these situations fall apart. Why should this 'vast, unimaginable, unknowable force' want to take our side? It's just plain——"

"It's *not* on our side. I didn't say it was. It's indifferent to our well-being. We're just a card in the game, remember? It keeps us safe simply because it doesn't want to lose us to the other side."

"To the 'Truly Awful' force."

"Right. And through the ages the Truly Awful force has been designated 'the Otherness.' "

"Ah. Lightning strikes. That's why you were so upset when I told you that Hokano means 'other.' But Jack, lots of words mean 'other.' It's in every language on Earth."

"I know that." He sounded a bit testy. "But here's what I've been told about the Otherness: When a world or a reality—a playing card, if you will—falls into its hands, the Otherness changes it to something more like itself. And that change will not be human friendly. If it happens here, it will be the end of everything."

Jamie's mouth felt dry. She'd just flashed on something . . . pieces had clicked together into an unsettling shape.

"The Dementedist Holy Grail—the Great Fusion—it's . . . it's all about this world commingling with the Hokano world . . ."

"Yeah. The 'other' world." He jerked a thumb toward the back seat. "The lady who used to wear that piece of skin knew all about the Ally and the Otherness. She told me she was involved in the war too, but was connected to a third player, one that wanted no part of either of them. The pattern on her back matches the pattern on Brady's globe, and since the goal of Brady's cult is the fusion of this world with the 'other' . . . can you see why I got a little shaky back there in the bar?"

Jamie's first mental impulse was to deny it all as a fever dream, a worldview even loonier than Dementedism; but a primitive part of her, a voice from the prehistoric regions of her hindbrain, seemed to know something her forebrain didn't. It whispered that it was all true.

Feeling as if she were drowning, Jamie grasped at straws.

"But . . . but you can't be buying into all their nonsense about split xeltons and such. Please tell me you're not."

"No, of course not. But maybe there's a grain of truth at the heart of their mythos. What if—now, I'm just making this up as I go—but what if Dormentalism was somehow inspired by the Otherness? For what specific reason, I don't know, but I know it can't be good. What if there's a little bit of Otherness in all of us? Maybe that's what the xelton concept represents, and the purpose of the Fusion Ladder is to identify those who carry more Otherness than most and band them into a group."

"To do what?"

Jack shrugged. "Light all the bulbs on Brady's globe? I don't know. I'm counting on Cooper Blascoe to clear that up."

"*If* he's really Blascoe."

"Yeah. If."

Jamie had been praying that the man in the cabin was Blascoe, revving her interview motor for when she finally faced him. Now she wasn't so sure she wanted to hear what he had to say.

15

Jack slowed the car to a crawl along the rutted country road.

"Where did you park when you went up to the house that first time?"

"Somewhere along here, I think. I'd know better if you had the headlights on."

"Just playing it safe."

Out of necessity he'd kept the parking lights on. If there'd been a moon out, or even stars, he could have turned off everything. But the sky had put up a low roof of clouds, leaving the woods around them as dark as Kurtz's heart.

"Why don't we just turn and roll up the driveway?" She sounded impatient.

"Like you said before, we don't know what kind of security they've got here."

"Right, and I'd rather be inside a car when we find out.

And I do not feel like pushing my way through two or three hundred yards of woods again."

"We'll compromise. We'll hide the car down here and walk up the driveway."

"How about *you* walk up the driveway and signal me when it's all clear."

"I don't mind going up there alone," he told her. "But you can forget about the all-clear signal. I'll talk to him myself and tell you what he said."

"Like hell you will!"

Jack smiled in the dark. He'd been pretty sure that would get to her.

He stashed the Crown Vic behind a stand of bushes. If it were earlier in the year, they'd be in full leaf. Now their bare branches didn't give much cover. A casual passerby probably wouldn't notice, but anyone on the lookout for a car couldn't miss it.

As they stepped out it began to rain. Nothing serious, little more than a light drizzle, but it made the chill night chillier.

They walked up a long driveway that was little more than two dusty ruts—steadily turning to muddy ruts—divided by a grassy hump. Jack took the lead, with Jamie staying close behind.

He was beginning to think that maybe this wasn't such a good idea. He could scope out the security setup—if there was one—better in daylight. Right now he felt as if he were flying blind. But he couldn't turn back. He was here and if the guy in the house was Cooper Blascoe, Jack was going to learn the connection between the designs on Anya's skin and Brady's globe. Tonight.

"So far, so good, right?" Jamie said.

"We could be walking past infrared sensors, motion detectors, you name it, and we wouldn't know."

"Let's go back."

Jack kept moving. "On the plus side, we're in the middle of nowhere. If we set off anything, it'll take time to get here. We do a quick in and out."

"But if it's Blascoe, it's going to take some time to get what we want out of him."

"We'll talk fast. Or take him with us."

Lighted windows from a typical woodland A-frame shone between the trees, and still no sound of an alarm, no blaze of light from security spots.

Jack and Jamie reached the front porch without incident. He made a quick perimeter check, looking in all the windows he passed, hunting for alarm tell-tales. He wasn't concerned with motion and infrared detectors; he was looking for surveillance cameras. He didn't see any, but noticed odd-looking metal brackets on a couple of the walls.

The TV was on and someone was splayed supine on the couch, watching. All Jack could see of him were his legs and shoeless feet resting on a coffee table.

"What's the situation?" Jamie whispered when he returned to the front porch.

"We go in."

"Shouldn't we knock?"

"Don't know about you, but my plan is to go inside whether he answers the door or not, so why waste time knocking."

He pulled his Glock from the small of his back. He'd only seen one occupant, but you never knew . . .

He pressed the pistol against his outer thigh as he grabbed the knob. If it was locked, he'd kick the door open or break through a window.

Not necessary. The knob turned and the door swung inward.

He peeked into the room, giving the walls a good once-over. Not a surveillance camera in sight. That didn't mean there weren't any, but it was the best he could do at the moment.

He stepped inside, entering a high-ceilinged great room

done up in standard Hollywood hunting lodge. Moose and deer heads stared down at him; antlers were framed here and there on the tongue-and-groove knotty pine walls; faux Indian throw rugs on the floor under rustic, rough-hewn furniture. Looked like a B-movie set. All it needed to complete the picture was John Agar entering stage right.

Keeping the Glock down, he stepped up to the couch and peered at the man sprawled on it. He looked maybe seventy, long gray hair lying on his shoulders, sunken, unshaven cheeks, oversized plaid shirt and jeans, both stained. He gripped a bottle of Cuervo Gold in one hand and a knockwurst-sized joint in the other. His eyes were fixed on the TV screen.

Jack said, "Cooper Blascoe, we've come for a visit."

The man's voice was thick, phlegmy, his words slurred. He spoke without turning his head.

"Fuck you, Jensen. Hope you brought me some good shit this time. This batch is bogus."

Jack walked past him toward the rear rooms.

"Hey!" the guy yelled. "Who the—?"

Jack waved the Glock at him. "About time you noticed. Keep it down."

"Why? Nobody here but me."

"We'll see."

Turned out he was telling the truth. The two bedrooms and littered bathroom were empty.

"All right, Mr. Blascoe," Jack said as he returned to the great room. He kept the pistol in hand for effect. "We've got a few questions for you."

The man give him a bleary look. "Who says I'm Blascoe?"

"You did when you answered to that name. And calling me 'Jensen' iced the cake."

Blascoe rubbed a hand across his mouth to hide a grin.

"Did I do that?"

"Yeah." Jack waggled the pistol in Blascoe's direction. "Let's go for a walk."

The bleariness gave way to a hard stare. Jack couldn't

be sure at this distance, but the whites of Blascoe's eyes looked faintly yellow.

"You gonna shoot me, do it here. I ain't goin' anywhere."

"No shooting, just talk."

"If we're going to talk, we'll talk right here."

Jack leveled the pistol at Blascoe's face, thinking, This is going to sound like bad-movie night, but here goes.

"Don't make me use this."

"Jack!" Jamie cried.

Blascoe pivoted and looked at her. "Hey! A babe! You brought me a babe!"

Damned if Jamie didn't smile. And was that a blush?

"Been a long, long time since anyone called me that. I—"

Jack cut her off. "This place could be lousy with AV pickups. Someone could be watching us right now. We need to quiz him somewhere else."

"You worried about cameras?" Blascoe laughed and pointed to the wall brackets Jack had noticed before. "That's where they used to be."

"Where are they now?"

"Out in the yard. I rip them out and toss them off the porch. Jensen puts them back up, and I toss them out again. Don't want nobody peepin' on me."

"See?" Jamie said. "It's okay."

Jack shook his head. "I'd still rather—"

Blascoe fixed him with a rheumy stare. "Don't matter what you'd *rather,* no way I'm leaving here. I can't."

"Why can't you?"

"Because I can't, that's all. I just can't."

We're wasting time, Jack thought as he holstered the Glock. Wrestling him outside would waste even more. He unwrapped the flap of skin and held it up.

"What do you know about this?"

The old man squinted at it. "Not a damn thing. What is it?"

As Jack was trying to decide where to begin, Jamie stepped up to him and gripped his arm.

"Let me." She held up a small digital recorder. "I'm good at this."

"But—"

"My show now."

Jack reluctantly backed off. She made her living ferreting out information. He'd learned—sometimes the hard way—to respect experience.

Jamie sat next to Blascoe on the couch and turned on her recorder.

"I'd like to start from the beginning, Mr. Blascoe—"

"Call me Coop."

"Okay, Coop. I'm a reporter for *The Light* and—"

"*The Light?* I love *The Light!*"

Why am I not surprised, Jack thought.

But Jamie was all business. "Glad to hear it. Now, what I want from you is the truth, the unvarnished, warts-and-all truth about the Dormentalism situation: How you started it and how you came to your present . . . circumstances."

"You mean why I'm not in suspended animation, and how I came to be a shell of my former self?" He leaned closer and spoke in a conspiratorial tone. "Know what? If you hold me up to your ear you can hear the ocean roar."

"I'm sure that would be very interesting, but—"

"This'll take all night," Jack said.

She looked at him. "Just let me handle this, okay. If Coop knows what you want to know, it'll come out. But this is a once-in-a-lifetime coup for me, and I'm going to squeeze all I can from it."

"See that?" Blascoe said. "She don't care about time. I like that." He leered at her. "But what if I don't feel like talking, beautiful?"

Jack cleared his throat. "Then I toss you in the trunk of my car—it's very roomy, you'll like it there—and haul your ass out of here."

Blascoe waved his hands like someone trying to flag down an onrushing car.

"No, no! Don't! I'll tell you."

Wondering why the guy was so afraid of leaving, Jack gave him one of his best glares. "Better not be bullshitting us, *Coop.*"

The old man took a slug of Cuervo and held up his dead, half-smoked joint.

"Anybody got a match?"

Jack took the joint from him. "Let's not get you any more bent than you already are."

"Hey, I've been eight miles high for most of my life."

"Still . . ." Jack held up the J. "Let's leave this as a reward for when you come through with some answers."

Blascoe shrugged. "Oh, hell, why not. They can't do anything to me worse than what's goin' on. And it might be fun to watch the shit hit the fan."

"What *is* going on?" Jack said.

"Cancer for one thing." He managed a wry smile. "My fully fused xelton is supposed to be able to cure that, but he seems to be on an extended vacation."

Jamie said, "Let's go back to the sixties, Coop. That's where it all began, right?"

He sighed. "The sixties . . . yeah, that's when I invented Dormentalism . . . the best thing in my life that turned into the worst."

16

This time Jensen made it all the way to the sidewalk before his pager chirped.

"What now?" He was afraid to hear the answer.

Hutch's voice. "We've got some activity on that place we're monitoring."

Jensen stiffened. He wanted to ask which one of the telemetries was lighting up, but not on an open circuit.

"Be right up."

This could be good, he thought as he retraced his steps across the lobby, or this could be very bad. He'd feel a whole lot better if he knew where the Grant broad was.

Up in the office, Margiotta had gone home, leaving Lewis and Hutchison to man the fort. Lewis pointed to a red blinking light on the monitor labeled PERIMETER.

"In all the time I've been here, this is the first time I've seen that go off at night."

This was looking more and more like bad news.

"What's the readout?"

Lewis squinted at the screen. "Two large heat signatures—possibly a couple of bears."

Two bears? Jensen thought. On the same night that Amurri or whatever his name was had helped Grant leave her tails in the dust?

"Could they be human?"

Lewis nodded. "I don't know much about bears, but I think they tend to scrounge around alone. So, yeah. More than likely they're human."

Shit.

Jensen gave Lewis a rough tap on the shoulder. "Up." When Lewis complied Jensen said, "You two wait outside."

He and Hutch exchanged puzzled looks but did as told. When Jensen had the room to himself he clicked his way to the AV monitors. There he entered his ID number and punched in a password. He toggled the pickups to LIVE. That turned them on and started them transmitting.

A menu popped up, offering him a choice of half a dozen views. He clicked on the great room and waited for the picture to focus.

Even though the transmission was encrypted, it hadn't made sense to keep it going twenty-four hours a day, seven days a week. Besides, in the standby state the pickups were immune to most bug sweeps.

He'd put up decoy cameras just so Blascoe could disable them. It let him think he was rebelling and gave him a false sense of privacy.

A wide-angle view of the great room, through the glass eye of the moose head, swam into view. When he saw the three figures seated in a rough circle, he realized his worst-case scenario had become reality.

He exited the program and kicked open the door to the next room.

"Hutch! Lewis! Get your stuff. Road trip!"

17

Cooper Blascoe leaned back and laced his fingers behind his head and started talking. He had a Howard Hughes situation going with the hair and fingernails, and smelled like a wet collie, but Jamie ignored all that.

"Well, seeing as you're here, and you found me like this, I guess I won't be blowing your minds by telling you that Dormentalism is all a sham, man. Just something I cooked up to get money, women, and drugs—not necessarily in that order."

Jamie checked to make sure she was recording. She prayed her batteries lasted. If she'd known she was going to wind up here tonight, she'd have come prepared with spares.

She turned her attention back to Blascoe. She still found it hard to believe that she was sitting with the supposedly self-suspended Father of Dormentalism. That was a coup itself, but to be recording the real story from the man who started it all . . .

Did it get any better than this? She couldn't imagine how.

"I wanted a rock star life, but I was a paunchy, balding thirty-year-old who couldn't play music for shit, so that was out. But it was the sixties, man, when all these nubile chicks were joining communes and that sort of shit, and I wanted in on some of that—not to be some worker drone on a commune farm or anything like that. Not me. I wanted my own.

"But I needed a hook to bring them in. I racked my brains and dropped a ton of acid hoping something would come to me—you know, pop into my head like divine inspiration—but nothing. Nada. Zilch. I was ready to give it up and go join someone else's gig when—I don't know, late in the winter of '68, maybe February, maybe March . . . all I remember is it was cold in Frisco when I had this dream about some guy from someplace called Hokano talking about—"

"Wait," Jack said. "It came to you in a dream?"

Blascoe shrugged. "I guess it was a dream. Sometimes, with all the drugs I was doing, the line got a little blurred, but I'm pretty sure this was a dream."

"Do you speak Japanese?"

He smiled. "You mean beyond *konichiwa* and *arigato*? Nope. Languages never were my strong suit. They made me take Spanish my first year at Berkeley—also my last year, if you want to know—and I flunked it miserably."

"All right then, this guy in your dream—what did he look like?"

"Like a dream guy—golden hair, golden glow, the whole deal. Like an angel maybe, but with no wings."

Jamie could tell from Jack's expression that this wasn't what he wanted to hear. It almost seemed as if he'd been expecting a certain description and this wasn't it.

"Anyway," Blascoe said, "the dream guy was talking about my inner spirit, something he called my xelton, being split, with half of it sleeping within, half of it somewhere else.

"When I woke up I knew that was it: the calling card for my commune . . . like it had been handed to me. I mean, it was all there, and perfect. Finding the Real You, the Inner You sleeping in your mind—any pitch with "mind" in it was a sure grabber in those days—and achieving some sort of mystical natural harmony. Dynamite stuff. But I needed a name. I definitely wanted 'mental' in it—you know, for mind?—and then got the brainstorm of putting it together with 'dormant'—as in *dormez vous*, because the gals were gonna have to sleep with me to wake up their xelton."

Jack shook his head. "The waking involved sleeping with you . . . and you got takers?"

"Better believe it. It was before your time, I'm sure, but we called it 'sleeping together' back in those days. Now it's just 'fucking.' But anyway I put the two words together and came up with 'Dormentalism.' Pretty slick, huh?"

"Pretty clunky if you ask me," Jack said.

"Well, I didn't ask you. But Brady thought the same thing when he came along."

Jack made a face. "Swell. Just the man I want to emulate."

"Let's not get onto the Brady situation yet," Jamie said. "You came up with the name and the concept . . . then what?"

"Like you say, I had the name and the idea, now I needed to find a place to put it to work. I found this guy in Marin County who'd let me use a corner of this big tract of land he owned. I rented it for a song, even talked him into letting me put off the first payment for ninety days. Oh, I was a silver-tongued devil then. Next came the pamphlet. I wrote up a few pages and called it *Dormentalism: The Future Resides Within*. Got it mimeoed, started handing out free copies in Haight-Ashbury, left them all over the Berkley campus. I even went to some established communes and passed them out there.

"Before I knew it, the whole thing took off, I mean, beyond my wildest dreams. People duplicated my pamphlet and sent it all over the country—there were Xerox machines back then, but no e-mail or fax yet, so they had to use the Post Awful. But that worked. And then the folks on the receiving end duplicated it, and *they* sent it around, and on and on. In no time I had hundreds of followers. Then a thousand. Then two thousand. Then . . . I stopped counting. They gave me their money—sometimes everything they had—and they helped build their own housing.

"And the sex . . . oh, man, helping those gals awaken their dormant xelton . . . so many of them." He grinned again. "I was so dedicated that I often 'helped' two, sometimes three, at a time . . . just incredible . . . in-fucking-credible."

"You had only female followers?" Jack said.

"Nah. All kinds."

"What about the men? Did you—?"

"Hell no! The 'awakened' women—the ones who'd had their 'breakthrough' with me—went out and 'awoke' the men. There was plenty to go around, believe me."

Jamie wanted to lean back and kick her feet in the air. This was dynamite. No, this was nuclear.

Jack looked at her. "Can we please get to Luther Brady?"

Before she could answer, Blascoe said, "Brady showed up somewhere in the seventies. He looked like a godsend at the time. I mean, I was spending money like there was no tomorrow. Fast as it came in, it went out. I'd been given pieces of land all over the country that I didn't know what to do with. The IRS was starting to sniff around, asking questions I couldn't answer—I wasn't a businessman, so what did I know? Anyway, I was too wasted most of the time to even care about it, let alone do anything. And then up pops Brady with his fresh new accounting degree and all sorts of ideas."

Jamie checked her recorder again—still going. She had a question and did not want to miss the answer.

"So Luther Brady joined and took part in the 'awakenings' of various female members?"

"Not that I remember. I didn't notice at the time but he

was lots more interested in getting close to me than the women."

Damn, Jamie thought. Not what she wanted to hear.

"Brady said he wanted to be my assistant. When I said all my assistants were of the female persuasion, he told me he could supply services they couldn't. Like getting me out of Dutch with the government.

"Like I cared. After my usual rant about how the government was irrelevant—the big word in those days—and how awakening your xelton was the only thing that mattered, he went on to explain how the government did matter and how I'd lose everything and do federal time for tax evasion and all sorts of other crimes if I didn't get my shit together. He said he was the man to straighten things out.

"And damn if he doesn't do just that. Sets up accounts, keeps records, writes letters to the IRS, files all the right forms, and in no time we're 'in compliance,' as the feds like to say."

Jamie watched Jack get up and walk to the front door. The rain was doing drum rolls on the roof. He opened the door and stared out at the storm for a few seconds, then closed it and returned to his chair. He reminded her of a cat when it sensed a coming storm.

She turned to Blascoe. "So now he had your confidence. What did he do next?"

"What do you mean?"

"I mean, he went from assistant to running the whole show. How?"

Blascoe showed anger for the first time since their arrival.

"How? By being a weasel, that's how! Course I didn't see it at the time. He kept coming to me and saying we needed to spread the word about Dormentalism—yeah, he hated the name but we were stuck with it. When he promised greater fame and fortune, I said, 'Cool. Do it, man.'

"And do it he did. Hired someone to expand my original pamphlet into *The Book of Hokano* and really ran wild with it. I mean, he added a shitload of new stuff I'd never heard of. I might have stopped him if I'd known, or cared. But I didn't. Not really. I was on extended leave from reality—Mr. Spaceman. But if I'd taken a gander at what he was doing, I'm pretty sure that even in my addled state I'd have squawked. It was scary."

"Scary how?" Jack said.

"All the rules, man. The rigid structure. The guy was rule crazy. I mean, he took this nice, easygoing, fun thing I'd begun and started messing it up. All these crazy acronyms and such. He codified everything into steps and procedures. It wasn't anything like what was really going on. I mean, he left out the sex part completely. He made it all self-realization and self-improvement and maximizing potential instead of getting laid.

"I didn't know any of this at the time. And for a while it looked like it wouldn't matter what was in *The Book of Hokano* because he couldn't find a publisher anywhere in the world that wanted it. But that didn't stop Brady. He made an end run by starting Hokano House and publishing it himself." Blascoe frowned and shook his head. "Hard to believe people would fall for his line of bullshit, but they did. In droves.

"With all the new converts, Brady was able to branch out. He started opening Dormentalist temples all around the country. Christ, *temples*! Back in Marin we were still doing the commune thing, you know, according to my vision, but everywhere else it was Brady-style regimentation. And on *my* land!"

"Wait," Jack said. "*Your* land? Where'd you get land?"

"Given to me. Lots of my followers gave over their worldly possessions to the movement, and pieces of land made up a fair number of those possessions. Brady would sell the pieces we had and buy others, with no rhyme or reason. Like *Monopoly* for psychos, man. Guy's land crazy. Soon he had temples in all the major cities—New York, Boston, Atlanta, Dallas, Frisco, L.A., Chicago, you name it—and they were *thriving*.

"He made his Fusion Ladder thing into a money machine. Made it so you had to take 'courses' to climb from rung to rung. He designed texts for each rung and sold them for rapacious prices. You couldn't afford the price, too bad: You had to have the text to complete the rung. A money grab, that's what it was. One big money grab.

"But he didn't stop with textbooks. He commissioned a series of personal-true-story books about how Dormentalism had changed lives. The first time I got an idea of where my happy little cult was going was when he had me read the books onto tape. I started getting a bad feeling then, but when the books and the cassettes sold hundreds of thousands of copies, and I started seeing the checks rolling in, well . . ." He flashed Jamie a quick, guilty smile. "You know how it is."

"I can only imagine," she said. But maybe she wouldn't have to imagine when she turned this series of articles into a book.

"But Brady's not through yet. The guy's got endless ideas. He hired some hack novelists to write a series of thrillers under my name starring this Fully Fused detective hero who communes with his xelton to solve crimes."

"The David Daine mysteries," Jack said. "Someone lent me one recently."

Blascoe looked at him. "How far'd you get?"

"Not very."

"Yeah, they were awful, but that didn't stop them from being best-sellers. That's because Brady issued an edict to all the temples that every Dormentalist had to buy two copies: one for personal use and one to give away. And they all had to buy them the same week. The result: instant best-sellers."

Jamie pumped her fist. "I *knew* it! Everybody figured that was the case, but no one could prove it."

And here it was, straight from the horse's mouth—or horse's ass, depending on how you wanted to look at it.

"Yeah, it all worked. Dormentalism kept getting bigger and bigger, spreading throughout the world, even to Third World countries—which may not have much money but they've got bodies and their governments practically have FOR SALE signs on their front lawns.

"Then came the time I thought Brady was gonna lose it. When he heard back in '93 that the Scientologists had wrangled themselves tax-exempt status for their church, he went after the same thing. But no way. Got us officially declared a church, yeah, but couldn't get tax-free status. Made him crazy that the Scientologists had something we didn't, but no matter what he tried, the IRS said no way. Which means those Scientologists must have had something super bad on somebody really high up to rig their exemption. So Brady had to be satisfied with starting the Dormentalist Foundation, which ain't as good a tax dodge as a tax-exempt religion, but it gets the job done."

Blascoe dropped his hands into his lap and hung his head.

"Then one day a few years ago I woke up and realized this thing called Dormentalism wasn't at all what I'd had in mind, that its natural harmony had turned into something ugly, the exact opposite of what I'd intended."

Jack shook his head. "Sort of like building a glass house and then hiring Iggy Pop to house sit."

"Just about. Even worse. At least you can fire a house sitter, but me . . . I had this high-sounding title of Prime Dormentalist, but I was a figurehead. I had no say in where Dormentalism—*my* thing—was going. Hardly anyone else did either, except maybe Brady and his inner circle on the High Council.

"Like I said, he'd looked like a godsend, but he turned out to be the worst thing that ever happened to Dormentalism. Or to me. I didn't believe in God when I started out, but I do now. Oh, not the Judeo-Christian God, but Somebody watching over things, seeing that what goes around comes around in certain cases. Like mine. I'm full of cancer because I started a cancer known as Dormentalism."

He made a strange sound. It took Jamie a few heart-beats to realize he was sobbing.

"It's not fair! I never wanted this corporate Grendel, this litigious, money-grubbing monster. I was just look-ing to get laid and have a good time." He looked up. "That's all! Is that so bad? Should I have to pay for it by being eaten alive by my own cells?"

Jack was up again, looking out the door. He turned to Jamie and made a rolling motion with his hands. She got the message: *Let's move this along.*

Jamie gave him a single nod. All right. He'd brought her up here, got her inside, and coerced Blascoe into talk-ing. She was recording the interview of her career, so the least she could do was throw him a bone.

"Of course not," she told Blascoe. "No one deserves that. But tell me: Brady is said to keep this huge strange globe hidden away in his office. Do you know anything about that?"

Jack crossed back to his seat, giving Jamie a surrepti-tious thumbs-up along the way.

Blascoe nodded. "Yeah. Enough to know he's certifi-able. You think you've heard some weird shit tonight? You ain't heard nothing yet."

18

"What's with this rain?" Hutch said, banging a fist on the wheel. They'd been sitting on 684 for what seemed like hours.

"Probably some asshole wrapped his car around an abutment up ahead," Lewis muttered from the shotgun seat. "How much you wanna bet he was yakking on a cell phone when it happened?"

"Yeah, while drinking coffee and doing eighty in the rain."

Jensen had the back seat of the Town Car to himself. He needed the space. Hutch and Lewis sat up front. Odds were they were right. Somewhere up ahead there'd be road flares and flashing red lights and glass and twisted metal all over the asphalt.

Jensen didn't care if people killed themselves on the road—probably cleaned up the gene pool a little—but even on a good day it pissed him off when they did it ahead of his car. The least they could do was wait till he'd passed.

Lewis half-turned in his seat. "Long as we're sitting here, boss, mind telling us what's up?"

"What do you mean?" Jensen said, as if he hadn't been expecting the question. The only surprise was that it had taken this long.

"This place we're going to—what are we looking at here?"

"I don't get you."

"I mean, we're loaded for bear, right? Just want to know what to expect. Who's in this cabin and why are we after him tonight?"

Besides Jensen, only Brady and a few High Council members knew the truth about Cooper Blascoe. The guy had become a real liability. Jensen had wanted him to have an accident, but Brady had vetoed that. Not that he wouldn't have liked Blascoe silenced and out of the way, but he'd said that a sudden death might cause more problems than it solved. Especially with the High Council. Even the members closest to Brady held out hope that Blascoe's erratic behavior was temporary and that he might be able to get back in touch with his xelton—obviously he'd lost contact—and turn himself around, heal his mind and his body.

Thus the cabin. Isolate him. Let him sink or swim. Jensen had arranged it. He'd also arranged a way to keep Blascoe from bolting the cabin.

The TP brigade, of course, knew nothing of this.

They'd been told they were monitoring the home of a Wall Addict who was out to destroy the Church. Nothing more. Only Jensen and Brady had the codes to activate and access the AV feeds. TPs like Hutchison and Lewis merely kept an eye on the telemetry telltales, and called Jensen when something lit up.

Like tonight.

"We're not so much after the WA himself as much as the people visiting him at the moment. One of them is Jamie Grant; the other is the guy who snatched her from under your noses."

"We're packing heat for *them*?" Hutch said.

Jensen shook his head. Packing heat . . . Jesus.

"We don't know what we're heading into. We have reason to believe the man has mob ties."

Lewis jerked around. "The mob? What the fu—?"

"Exactly what Mr. Brady and I want to know. The weaponry is just a precaution. I do not want anyone shot—I have a lot of questions for the man—but I do not want anyone getting away with a recording of whatever they're discussing up there. If—"

"Hey," Hutch said as the car eased forward. "Looks like we're starting to move."

Jensen peered ahead. The jam seemed to be breaking up. Good. They still had a ways to go.

"Think it's gonna matter?" Lewis said. "They've gotta be gone by now."

Jensen shook his head. "No, they're still up there. The WA we've been watching has a long story, and it's going to take some time to tell."

"But if they're smart they'll get him out of there and to a safe house where they won't be interrupted."

"Not if the WA refuses to leave."

And he wouldn't dare.

19

"I've gotten kind of used to weird," Jack told Blascoe, "so don't hold back. Lay it on as thick as you need."

He leaned forward and focused on the old man. A slew of questions were about to be answered—he hoped.

"It's pretty thick. I think I told you about Brady being land crazy. He's always buying or trying to buy pieces of property here and there. He sells this one to buy that one. At first I thought it was just a random shuffle, something he liked to do. Then I caught on that he was after specific parcels. I figured, well, it's as good a way as any to invest the Church's extra cash. Land prices are always going up, right?"

"Those specific parcels are indicated on the globe, right?" Jack said.

"I didn't know that back then but, yeah, right. That's why he's turned Dormentalism into a money machine: so he can buy these pieces of land. Some are cheap, but some are in prime commercial districts. Others are in countries that don't like foreigners owning their land, and so a lot of palms have to be greased. And still others . . . well, some folks just don't want to sell."

Jamie leaned forward. "What's he do then?"

"He keeps upping his offers to the point where all but a very few diehards give in."

"What about those diehards?"

"I don't know about all of them, but I can tell you about one couple. Their name was Masterson and they owned a farm in Pennsylvania that Brady wanted. Well, it had been in their family for generations and they weren't selling for any price. Brady said he'd settle for a certain piece of it but they wouldn't even sell him that. So Brady asks for a face-to-face meet with them and offers an all-expense-paid trip to the city, luxury hotel, the works, just to sit down with him. They accept."

Blascoe's comment that the couple's name *was* Masterson gave Jack an ominous feeling.

Jamie raised her eyebrows. "And?"

"And someone pushes them in front of a subway."

"Oh, jeez," Jack said. "I remember reading about that last year."

Jamie had gone pale. "I did a piece on it. They never caught the guy. Everyone assumed he was just another MDP." She looked at Blascoe. "Do you have any proof that Brady was connected?"

"Nothing that would stand up in court, but I remember Jensen telling him the news and hearing Brady say something about giving a TP named Lewis a bonus."

Jack had heard the Dormentalists were ruthless, but this, if it was true . . . it put a whole new spin on who he was dealing with.

He looked at Jamie. "We should get out of here."

"Hey," Blascoe said, "I haven't got to the weird part yet. Dig: Those white lights don't get lit when he buys the land. He powers them up only after he's buried one of his weird concrete pillars on the site."

He had Jack's attention. "What kind of weird?"

"Well, as I understand it—I'm not supposed to know this, you know; got most of it by listening while they thought I was out of it. Anyway, the concrete's gotta be made with a certain kind of sand, and the column's gotta be inscribed with all sorts of weird symbols. And then they've gotta put something else inside it before they can bury it."

"Like what?" Jack said.

"I never learned that."

"What kind of symbols?"

"I saw a drawing of a column once. Same kind of symbols as on the wall behind his globe. They're kind of like—"

"I've seen them."

Blascoe's eyes widened. "You *have*? How the hell—?"

"Not important. I need to know what Brady's trying to accomplish with these columns."

"You *need* to know?"

"Yeah. *Need*." Jack wasn't in the mood for chitchat. "So let's hear it: What's he up to?"

"I haven't a clue. He's burying the damn things all over the world and I don't have the faintest idea why."

"Didn't you ask?"

"Course I asked. Started asking a couple years ago, but Brady always dodged an answer. He was keeping stuff from me. Me! The fucking founder! When I got in his face about it, Brady tried to distract me with women and booze and drugs. But that wasn't gonna work. Hey, I'm older now. I've experienced just about everything I ever wanted to. Maybe more.

"But the globe was just the fuse that lit me up. Dormentalism was my baby but it had changed to the point where I no longer recognized it. No, forget recognizing it—I was *embarrassed* by it. Do you know that to reach the upper levels you not only have to spend a fortune, but you've got to swear off sex! Yeah, you heard me, to reach the High Council you have to become some sort of fucking eunuch—nice turn of phrase, don't you think?— which turns off all but the most fanatically devoted."

Jamie flashed her yellowed grin. "I *love* this!"

Blascoe poked a finger into the air. "Yeah, Brady's supposed to be abstinent too, but I found out he's got a place—not too far from here, as a matter of fact—that nobody knows about. And that means not even his innermost circle on the High Council. That's because they aren't looking. I was. It's a place where I'm pretty sure he does stuff he doesn't want anyone to know about."

Jack didn't give a damn about Brady's personal life. He

could be dressing sheep in black garter belts and getting jiggy with them for all he cared. It was more tasty grist for Jamie's mill but provided no answers for Jack.

"Let's get back to the columns," he said. "Brady gave you no clue as to what's up with them?"

"He did say that the globe wasn't so much a map as a blueprint. It shows where the columns must go."

"So every bulb shows where he has buried or intends to bury a column."

"All except the reds. No columns go where the red bulbs are."

"Why not?"

He shrugged. "Before I could find out, he and Jensen dumped me here."

Jack unfolded the skin flap again. He studied the pattern of red and white scars and the lines connecting them, trying to superimpose the continental outlines. But he had no reference points. He needed another look at that globe. He wanted to know what the red dots meant. He had a feeling they were key.

Jamie was speaking in her reporter voice. "You say Brady and Jensen 'dumped' you here. I don't understand. Are you a prisoner?"

Blascoe nodded. "Better believe it."

"Why?"

"Because I'm stupid. Because I'm sick. And because I thought I was too important to mess with. Wrong again. I wanted to get Dormentalism back to the simple, hedonistic, mellow, hippie thing it started out to be, but I could see neither Brady nor the High Council was going to go for that willingly, so I figured I'd give 'em a kick in the ass to get them moving. I threatened to go public with my cancer and everything I knew about their money-grubbing racket. Said I'd call a press conference to announce I'd had lung cancer but I'd been cured by radiation and chemotherapy instead of my xelton, and how my xelton couldn't cure me because there's no such thing as a xelton—I made it all up.

"So they locked me away and made up that bullshit about me putting myself in suspended animation."

"You said you were cured?"

He gave her a death's head grin. "Sure as hell don't look cured, do I. That's because the cure wasn't. The tumor's back. Now they especially don't want me to be seen. Don't want me wasting away in public."

"Isn't there anything you can do?" Jamie said. "Chemotherapy or—?"

"Too late. I figure from the color of my pee that it's in my liver—had hepatitis once so I know how that goes—and dying is better than living through more rounds of chemo with no guarantee of success. I'm just gonna let nature take its course. That's me: the original Mr. Natural."

Jamie said, "Why do you stay here? I don't see any bars on the windows, no locks on the door. Why don't you just walk out?"

Blascoe raised his head and Jack saw a strange look in his eyes.

"I would . . ." He lifted his shirt and pointed to a silver-dollar-sized lump on the right side of his abdomen, southwest of his navel. "Except for this."

Jamie craned her neck forward. "What is it?"

"A bomb. A miniature bomb."

20

Jensen leaned forward and tapped Hutch on the shoulder. "Ease back on the speed."

"Just trying to make up for lost time."

"You won't be making up anything if you hydroplane us into a ditch."

They were heading west—swimming west was more like it—on 84. The normal speed limit was sixty-five but only an idiot would try that in this downpour.

"Who is this WA anyway?" Lewis said.

"You don't need to know his name, just that he's dangerous. He knows too much dirt—*damaging* dirt."

"Pardon my saying," Lewis said, "but how bad can it be? What can he know that deserves this kind of surveillance?"

The question was out of line, but he wanted these guys in skin-saving mode—not just the Church's skin but their own as well.

"Oh, let's see," Jensen drawled. "What about the time you told that Bible thumper, Senator Washburn, that unless he directed the Finance Committee's interest away from the Church, paternity test results on tissue from his closest aide's recent abortion would be made public? Dirty enough for you? Or what about the time Hutch threatened the daughter of that DD who was going to take the Church to court? And here's the icing on the cake, Lewis: He knows about that couple you shoved onto the tracks. What was their name again?"

"The Mastersons." Lewis's swallow was audible all the way to the back seat. "Shit."

Jensen was exaggerating. Blascoe suspected a few things, and could make it mighty uncomfortable for the Church if he started speculating in public, but that wasn't the real reason he'd been isolated.

"And those are just the tip of the iceberg."

The only sound in the car was the patter of the rain and the swish of the wipers.

Good, Jensen thought. That shut them up. He glanced at the glowing dial of his watch. It was a sixty-six-mile trip from the city to the cabin. In off-peak traffic it could be done in a little over an hour. They were well past the hour mark. But even with the rain and the reduced speed, it wouldn't be long now.

21

"Get out," Jamie said as she stared at the lump under the pale, flabby skin. She saw a pink line of scar tissue next to it. He had to be running a number on them. "A bomb?"

Blascoe nodded. "Yep. If I go more than a thousand feet from the house—they've got the line marked with wire—this will explode."

"What's the point?" Jack said.

"Well, as Jensen put it, this raises a minimum-security facility to maximum."

Jamie frowned, still staring at the lump. She couldn't take her eyes off it. "How did they—?"

"Get it in there?" He shrugged. "Jensen kept me under lock and key for a while after I threatened to go public. Then one day he drugs me up and hauls me off somewhere. I don't know where exactly because I conked out before we got there. I woke up here, in one of the bedrooms. I was hurting and when I looked down I saw a bunch of stitches and this lump.

"Brady and Jensen were here. They told me this place was gonna be my home till I came to my senses. They told me about the bomb and—"

Jack's eyebrows shot up. "And you believed them? For all you know that's just a couple-three big steel washers glued together."

"It's not." Blascoe's eyes were suddenly bright with tears. "They proved that to me the first day."

"How?"

"My dog."

Jamie gasped as her heart twisted in her chest. "Oh, no. I don't think I want to hear this."

"He was a mutt I'd had since he was a pup," Blascoe was saying. "I called him Bart because he was always getting into trouble like Bart Simpson. Anyway, Jensen taped one of these bombs to Bart's collar. I was still groggy from the anesthesia so I wasn't really following. I watched as Jensen teased Bart with this ball, then threw it past the thousand-foot mark." Blascoe's face screwed up and he sobbed. A tear rolled down his cheek. "Blew poor Bart to pieces."

Jamie felt her own eyes puddling up. "Bastards."

She glanced over at Jack. He said nothing, simply stared at Blascoe with a stony expression.

Blascoe sobbed again. "Lots of times I think about crossing that line myself just to end it all, but I haven't got the guts."

Finally Jack spoke. "This means they've got perimeter sensors, and that means they probably know we're here. You can take it to the bank that someone—a *number* of someones—are on their way here." He looked at Jamie. "We've got to go."

She pointed to Blascoe. "But we can't leave him!"

"Why not? This is where he lives now." He tossed Blascoe's joint into his lap. "We'll leave him as we found him."

"But they'll kill him!"

"If they wanted to kill him, they wouldn't have bothered with this elaborate setup."

"But don't you see? Now that I've got his story, they have to kill him. Once I publish it, these woods will be crawling with people looking for him. They can't risk his being found."

Jack was staring at Blascoe. "They still won't kill you, will they?"

Blascoe shrugged. "Can't say. To tell the truth, I don't much care. Haven't got much time left anyway, and going quick sounds a lot better than getting eaten from the inside out. I think Brady would've had Jensen off me at the git-go when I started making trouble. But too many of his lackeys on the High Council knew I was alive and not so well, and after all, I *am* the Father of Dormentalism and that would be . . . unthinkable. They really believe in this shit. So he convinced them to exile me, like Napoleon. Probably rationalized it to them by labeling me with one of their stinking acronyms and isolating me for the good of the Church. I don't think his High Council cronies know about the bomb—that was Jensen's idea."

"So what you're telling me is there's a good chance they'll send you to the Hokano world for real."

Another shrug. "Yeah. I guess so. But you folks'd better go while you've got the chance, or sure as shit you'll both turn up missing."

Jack looked around. "Jensen's demo with your dog proves there's a trigger transmitter nearby. If we can—"

"Find it? Don't waste your time. I've been searching for it since day one and never found it. And I was looking in daylight, not in the dark in a rainstorm."

"Ever think about getting a knife and cutting it out?" Jack said. "It's just under the skin."

Jamie's stomach turned at the thought. The idea of cutting into your own flesh—she shuddered. Didn't want to go there.

"Can't say as I have. 'Specially since Jensen warned me about just such a thing. Told me if the bomb's surface temperature drops five degrees—*blam!*"

Jack was silent for a few seconds, then, "What if we cut it out and dunk it into a bowl of hot water?"

"Whoa," Jamie said. "What if it drops five degrees while we're doing it? Then all three of us will go."

Without taking his eyes off Blascoe, Jack reached into a pocket and pulled out a folded knife. He snapped it open with a flick of his wrist, revealing a wicked-looking four-inch stainless steel serrated blade.

"I'm game if you are."

Blascoe stared at the blade. He swallowed, but said nothing.

"Don't you want to kick their asses?" Jack said. "With

Jamie's story and you to back it up on the talk show circuit, you can nail these bozos right where they live. Slice and dice them and stir-fry them for dinner."

"Is it gonna hurt?" Blascoe said.

Jack nodded. "Yeah. But this baby's sharp and I'll be quick like a bunny."

The old man licked his lips and took a long pull on the Cuervo. "Okay. Let's do it."

Jamie tasted bile at the back of her throat. "I'm not good with blood."

Jack waggled the knife in her direction. "Don't wimp out on me now."

22

Jack stuck the blade of his Spyderco Endura into the water he'd nuked to boiling in the microwave. From the front room he heard Jamie muttering as she sloshed tequila onto the skin over the lump in Blascoe's flank.

When the water stopped bubbling he poured it into a small aluminum pot.

"Not exactly sterile conditions," he said as he carried the hot water into the other room. "But we'll go straight from here to a doctor I know who'll load you up with antibiotics."

Blascoe lay stretched out on the couch, his shirt pulled up to nipple level.

"Let's just get on with it," he said.

Jamie looked up. "What about stitches?"

Jack already had that figured. "We just tie a sheet around him. That'll hold the edges together. The doc will place the sutures."

Jamie looked pale and sweaty. Her hand shook as she swabbed on the tequila.

"I don't like this, Jack."

Not too crazy about it myself, he thought.

He'd stabbed and he'd been stabbed, but he'd never got down and made a surgical incision. He couldn't show any hesitancy or Jamie might fall apart. And if she did that it would only drag out this whole scene, and Jack wanted out of here yesterday. Every extra minute increased the chances of running into Dormentalist goons.

And he wished he had gloves. He didn't feature the idea of getting some wild-ass dude's blood all over his hands.

He looked at Blascoe. "You don't by any chance have AIDS, do you?"

"I can honestly answer that with a no. They did a shitload of tests when they worked me up for my tumor and, seeing as how I'd done a few drugs in my time, that was one of the first things they looked for. But I've never mainlined so I came out negative."

"All right then. It's time."

He tossed one of the throw pillows to Blascoe. "Bite on that." He handed the pot of water to Jamie. "Remember, if the surface of the bomb drops five degrees, we've had it. So keep that water right up next to me."

She gripped the handle and nodded. She did not look well at all.

"You sure you can handle this?"

She shook her head. "No, but I'm going to try. So hurry."

Right. No sense in drawing it out like it was some scene from *ER*.

He went down on one knee next to the couch, stretched Blascoe's skin over the lump, took a breath, and made the cut—a quick slice, two inches long and half an inch deep. Blascoe was kicking and making muffled screeching noises into the pillow, but all in all doing a pretty decent job of holding still. Next to him, Jamie groaned.

"Everybody hang in," he said. "We're almost there."

Jack hadn't been crazy about making the incision, but he didn't mind the blood. He'd seen plenty—others' and his own. Slipping his fingers under a man's skin, though, was a whole other country.

Clenching his teeth he forced his hand forward, pushed his index and middle fingers through the bloody slit while his other hand pushed on the disk from the outside. He felt it press against his fingertips, then he trapped it and began to wriggle it free. It didn't move easily. Had scar tissue formed around it? He pushed and pulled harder. Blascoe began to buck but Jack rode with him.

"A few seconds," he gritted. "Just a few more seconds."

He felt the thing move and glanced to his immediate right where Jamie held the pot of hot water.

"Get ready, Jamie. Here it comes."

And then he had it. He guided the red, dripping disk through the incision. Not a second to waste now.

"Okay. Here she comes. Where's that—?"

"Oh, God!"

He heard a gagging sound, felt hot water splash across his thigh, and looked over to see Jamie with her head turned away, quaking as she retched, the pot handle twisting in her hand, the hot water pouring over Jack and the couch.

"Shit!"

He grabbed for the pot with his free hand, caught it before it emptied, but felt the slippery disk shoot from between his fingers. It slithered across Blascoe's bloody skin, fell to the floor, and rolled away on its edge.

"Oh, Christ!"

Jack lunged for it, grabbed it, and for a second, didn't know what to do: Toss it across the room or drop it in what was left of the hot water? The disk slipped in his fingers . . . might not get a good throw . . . he shoved it into the hot water, then swung the pot around and put it down around the far corner of the couch, hoping the upholstery would absorb most of the shrapnel from the pot. He rolled back toward Jamie and shoved her away.

But no explosion. He waited a few more heartbeats, but all he heard were Jamie's gasps and Blascoe's groans.

"Sorry," Jamie said as she lifted her head and wiped her chin. "I just—"

"Forget it." Jack jumped to his feet. "Let's haul him down to the car and get the hell out of here."

"Jesus," Blascoe said. He was bathed in sweat and had his hands cupped around the bloody incision but not touching it. "Like ouch, man. That fucking hurt!"

"How's it feel now?"

A weak smile. "Compared to when you were digging into me? Not bad."

"Good. Now move your hands."

Jack had arranged a rolled-up bedsheet under the small of Blascoe's back before operating on him. Once the hands were out of the way he looped it out and cinched it around him.

Blascoe grunted. "Have to be so tight?"

"Got to keep those edges together." It was the best he could do till he got the old guy to Doc Hargus. He pulled him to his feet. "Let's go."

Blascoe swayed. "Whoa. Dizzy."

Jack didn't have to say anything. Jamie jumped in and grabbed Blascoe's other arm, steadying him. She looked better but still shaken.

"Okay," Jack said. "Straight down the driveway."

Jamie held back. "Why don't we bring the car up here? Be faster."

"But the driveway dead ends up here. Somebody noses into the lower end and we're busted. Come on. Let's move. We've wasted too much time already."

He tugged Blascoe toward the door and Jamie came along. Off the front porch, into the downpour, then down the driveway. Within seconds their clothes were soaked through to the skin. Jack found the chill refreshing.

The twin ruts of the driveway had become mini creeks. Jack sloshed down the one on the right, Jamie had the left, both supporting the rubber-legged Blascoe on the grassy median.

"This is farther than I've ever come," the old man said. "If we had light you'd see yellow ribbons tied around some of these trees. Those were the warning signs that I was nearing the thousand-foot line. Yellow ribbons! That son of a bitch Jensen thinks he's such a co-median. He—"

Jack heard a muffled explosion, felt an impact against his flank that knocked him into the brush bordering the driveway. He lay stunned for a few seconds, his ears ringing. His right hand was gripping something. He squinted at it in the dark for a few uncomprehending heartbeats, then cried out and tossed it away.

An arm. With no body attached.

But how—?

And then he knew: The bastards had stuck *two* bombs in Blascoe—just in case he ever found the nerve to remove the obvious one.

Jack slumped forward and pounded his fists into the mud. He'd messed up—no, he'd *fucked* up. The possibility had occurred to him, but Blascoe had said there'd been only one incision, and Jack hadn't felt anything unusual under the bomb he'd removed. Of course, Blascoe had been kicking and writhing at the time. Or they could have buried it way deep.

"I'm sorry, Coop," he whispered. "Christ, I'm so sorry."

And then, somewhere on the far side of the driveway, he heard a woman screaming.

Jack struggled to his feet, checked to make sure he still had the Glock, then lurched toward the sound, wiping bits of flesh from his shirt and jeans as he moved. He found Jamie kneeling in the mud and rubbing her hands up and down her arms as if she were in a shower.

He grabbed her arm. "Jamie! Jamie!"

She swung a fist at him. "Get away!" she wailed. "Get away!"

"Jamie, it's me, Jack. We've got to go!"

Her voice lowered to gasping sobs. "He blew up! He . . . just . . . blew up!"

"I know. And we could end up just as dead if we don't get out of here now."

He pulled her to her feet and into a staggering walk down the driveway.

"But . . ." She looked over her shoulder. "Shouldn't we do something with him?"

"What do you have in mind?" He propelled her along, not allowing her to slow down. "Dig a grave? Call a minister and have a funeral service?"

"You bastard!" she hissed. "You cold-hearted—!"

"I'll take that any day over stupid fuck-up, which is what I really am."

That stopped her. Her tone was softer when she spoke. "Hey, I—"

Jack shook her. "Quiet."

He pointed down to the pair of glowing lights to the right of the driveway entrance. He shoved Jamie into the brush to the right and followed her in.

"They're here."

23

"Hey," Lewis said. "There's a car."

Hutch stopped the Lincoln. "Not just a car—*the* car."

Jensen leaned close to the side window and peered through the downpour at the black Crown Vic. He took a deep breath and smiled as he let it out, fogging the window. With one delay after another along the way, his hopes of catching Grant and her mystery friend here had diminished almost to zilch. But what do you know—here they were.

"Lewis, go check and see if it's locked. If not, get inside. If yes, hide in the trees and keep watch."

Lewis stepped out and trotted over to the Vic. He tried the door, turned and dashed back to Jensen's window.

"Locked," he said as the window opened a few inches. "But if I get the slim jim—"

"Forget it. You'll set off the alarm. If we don't catch them up at the house, I want them hauling ass back down here thinking they can jump in their car and drive away. But you're not going to let that happen, are you, Lewis."

"I could just flatten the tires."

"Really?" Sometimes these guys were so stupid. "And then how do we get it out of here? Or do you think we should just leave it for some hick sheriff to find and wonder who owns it and start poking around that cabin up there? You think that's a good idea?"

He sighed. "I guess not. But why's it always me gets—"

"Shut up and listen. They show up here, you do what you have to do. I don't care about Grant. You get a chance, off her. But no killshot on the guy unless he's holding."

"Why not?"

"I've got some questions and he's got the answers."

Like who he is and how he found out about this place.

"But—"

"Get out of my face and hide. Now."

He raised the window and slapped Hutch on the shoulder.

"Up that driveway on the left there."

"You want me to turn the lights off?"

Jensen thought about that a second. A darkened approach would be good, but Hutch didn't know where the driveway curved and might land them up against a tree.

"Keep 'em on. Just take it as fast as you can."

The less time Grant and company had to react, the better.

Hutch made the turn and hit the gas. The Lincoln fish-tailed left and right.

"Damn rear-wheel-drive shit!" he said, but kept going. "How long is this?"

"About six-hundred yards. Don't slow down. Keep pushing her."

At about the halfway point, Hutch shouted, "Shit!" and slammed on the brakes.

The car swerved to the left, slamming Jensen against the door.

"What the—!"

And then he saw it.

"What the fuck is that?" Hutch shouted. "It looks like somebody's head!"

Which was exactly what it was—plus the neck, upper chest, and right arm, all connected. Wide, glazed eyes in a bearded face stared accusingly at the car from the side of the road. The pelvis and legs jutted from the brush on the opposite side. Shredded innards decorated the driveway ruts and median.

"What happened here?" Hutch's quavering voice had jumped an octave.

"I don't know. Just keep going, damn it! We've got a problem!"

Actually, a problem had just gone away. But Jensen couldn't let Hutchison know that.

No more worries about Blascoe shooting his mouth off.

But how had it happened? Had Blascoe decided to end it all? Had he been running from Grant for some reason? Or had he gambled that the lump under his skin wasn't really a bomb?

And where were Grant and the former Jason Amurri?

The cabin hove into view. He'd have the answers pretty soon.

Jensen pulled out his long-barreled .44 Magnum. Hutch and Lewis carried Colt Double Eagle .45s. None of this 9mm shit. He didn't shoot often, but when he did he wanted results. He wanted whoever he put down to stay down.

The car stopped and he heard Hutch work his slide to chamber a round.

"Safety off, be ready to fire at will," Jensen told him. Probably unnecessary, but it never hurt. "Same thing goes for you as for Lewis: Save the guy for me. Go!"

They leaped from the car and dashed up to the porch. The front door lay wide open. Jensen took the doorway while Hutch, pistol held high, ducked from window to window.

"Nothing moving in there," he said as he returned.

Probably headed down through the brush back toward their car, but he had to make sure they weren't hiding inside.

"Okay. I go in and head left, you take the right. Quick search, make sure the place is empty, then we go back to their car."

Hutch nodded and they made their entrance in a low crouch, pistols extended in the two-handed grip. They flanked the couch, checked the kitchen, then the two rear bedrooms.

Hutch stood in the center of the great room, his pistol lowered. "Nobody's home." He pointed to the couch. "But catch that. Looks like blood."

Yeah. It did. And what was that aluminum pot next to the couch? Had Blascoe, or maybe Grant and her friend, done a little surgery? Uh-huh. There was the bomb submerged in the water in the bottom of the pot. Clever. Some hot water to maintain the temperature, a sharp knife, and—

Jensen felt a draft on his face. He looked up at the open door. How long had that pot been sitting in the breeze? Long enough to . . . ?

He backed away. "Hutch, I think we'd better get—"

The pot exploded. Something sharp dug into his face above his right eye as the blast knocked him back.

24

Jamie huddled and shivered against Jack as they crouched in the brush. The car sat ten feet away. Keys in one hand, Glock in the other, Jack watched it through the downpour. The good part about the pounding rain was that it drowned out the sounds of their approach. The bad part was that he had no light, not even starlight, to scope out whoever was watching the car.

And someone *had* to be watching it.

He'd seen people do amazingly stupid things, but leaving a getaway vehicle unguarded . . . uh-uh. Jensen was calling the shots here—either on-site or over the phone—and Jensen was no dummy.

Above and behind them, the *thud!* of an explosion.

"What—?" Jamie started to say, but Jack clamped a hand over her mouth.

He tried to shut out the sound of the rain, the feel of it pelting his face and hair, tried to funnel everything into his eyes as he studied the area around the car. Movement on the far side of the road caught his eye. Was that—? Yeah, a man had stepped out of the trees and was crossing toward the car. He stopped by the hood.

His face was little more than a pale blur, but he seemed to be looking up the hill, waiting for whatever he'd heard to happen again.

It wouldn't. Jack had figured the bomb would go off sooner or later. He was glad it had happened now.

He put his lips against Jamie's ear and whispered, "Wait. Don't move."

Pulled out the car keys, then crouched and began to snake through the remaining brush toward the front of the car. The rain's loud tattoo on the hood and roof covered his approach. Reached the front bumper and moved around it until he was only a few feet from the sentry. Raised his Glock and hit the unlock button on the car remote. As the locks clicked up and the interior lights came on he leaped to his feet and caught the guy whirling toward the passenger compartment, pistol up and ready but pointed in the wrong direction.

"Freeze right there!" Jack shouted. "Freeze or I'll shoot you dead so help me!"

It sounded B-movie-ish, he knew, but what else do you say? However it sounded, it worked. The guy turned into a statue.

"Hold it just like that," Jack said as he came up behind him.

He pressed the muzzle of the Glock against the back of his neck, then pulled the pistol from his hand. It had the weight of a .45.

"Heavy artillery," he said as he stuck it in his waistband. "Who were you expecting?"

The guy had a pinched face and thin hair plastered against his scalp. He said nothing.

"Be a good TP and put your hands way up." Jack did a quick one-handed pat down but found no other weapon.

"Now . . . lie facedown in the middle of the road."

"Hey, come—"

Jack jammed the muzzle harder against his neck. "Look, Mr. Temple Paladin. You haven't done anything to me so I'm giving you a chance. One way or another you're gonna wind up facedown on the road. Now, you can be there breathing or you can be there not breathing. Makes no difference to me. Which'll it be?"

Without speaking he did a slow turn, took two steps, and stretched out facedown on the wet asphalt, arms extended at right angles from his body.

"Jamie!" he shouted. "Into the car!"

Out of the corner of his eye he saw a dim shape emerge

from the brush and make a beeline for the passenger door.

"Over here! You're driving!"

"I d-don't think I can."

"You can and you will." He held out the keys. "Here. Get it started."

Jack never took his eyes off the man in the street. He'd been a little too agreeable. You don't argue with a man with a gun, sure, but this guy was playing it a little too meek and mild for one of Brady's enforcers. Might mean a lot of things, but to Jack it meant Mr. TP had a backup weapon, one he'd missed in his pat down. Probably in an ankle holster, just like Jack's AMT .380, but he hadn't wanted to risk squatting to check.

He felt the keys tugged from his hand, heard the car door open and close, the engine start.

He opened the rear door behind Jamie, found the window button and lowered it.

"Don't do anything stupid," he warned the guy, privately hoping he would.

Jack backed behind the door and moved his pistol into the open window space. He knelt on the back seat and slammed the door, keeping the TP covered all the time.

"Go!"

As soon as the car began to move the TP rolled over and—sure enough—reached for his ankle. Jack fired off three quick shots, hitting him twice. He kept an eye on his thrashing form until the car rounded a bend and he was out of sight.

"You shot him?" Jamie said.

"He had a second gun. Probably going to try for our tires."

"Did . . . did you kill him?"

"Hope not. Better for us if he's alive."

25

Ears ringing, Jensen regained his feet. He wiped his eyes and looked at his hand. It glistened with red.

"Shit!"

A spot on the front of his scalp, just where his hairline would have been if he'd had any, stung when he touched it. He looked around and saw Hutch, on his feet and looking fine.

"You okay?"

Hutch nodded. "I ducked behind the couch. But you . . ."

Jensen touched the spot again. "Yeah, I know. How bad is it?"

Hutch stepped closer and peered at the wound. "Not bad. Maybe an inch at most."

Jensen moved into the kitchen area and grabbed a roll of paper towels. He ripped off a sheet and pressed it against his scalp.

Cut by his own bomb. Shit, this was embarrassing. When he got his hands on this son of a bitch . . .

Hutch said, "Hey, what's the story with that guy in the driveway—or what's left of him? Who—?"

Jensen stiffened. Through the ringing in his ears he thought he heard three pops from somewhere outside.

He turned to Hutch. "Were those—?"

Hutch was already on his way to the door. "Damn right!"

Jensen followed him to the car where Hutch got back behind the wheel and Jensen squeezed into the front seat.

The good news was that Lewis had found the pair; the bad news was he'd had to do some shooting. Jensen hoped the mystery guy was still breathing.

They backed around and roared down the driveway. As they again passed the scattered remains of Cooper Blascoe, Jensen made a mental note to get back here ASAP with some garbage bags and clean up whatever parts of the old fart hadn't already been carried away by the local wildlife.

Hutch skidded the car to a stop as they hit the pavement. Someone was writhing in the middle of the road.

"Hey, that looks like Lewis!" Hutch said. He pushed open the door and started to get out.

Alarm flared through Jensen as he scanned the area and didn't see the Crown Vic.

"The car's gone! Shit! They took off! Get back in here and go after them!"

"But Lewis—!"

"Damn asshole let them get the jump on him. He's on his own!"

"Fuck that!" Hutch said. "He's one of us. A few minutes ago you didn't want to leave a car in the bushes, but now it's okay to leave a bleeding guy? Where are you coming from? What's a cop gonna do if—"

"All right, all right!" He was right. "Drag that sack of shit over here and put him in the back."

Jensen sat and fumed. Lewis had been wounded and left here to slow them down. But they still had a chance to catch them if they drove like hell.

A slim chance, but a chance.

FRIDAY

1

"We've got a problem."

Luther Brady had already guessed that. A call from Jensen on his private line at this hour of the morning could mean only trouble. Serious trouble.

"Go ahead."

Luther listened with growing dismay as Jensen described the night's events. His stomach was burning by the time the man had finished.

"You've got to find them."

"I'm full into that right now. But I have to ask you something: After all the face time you spent with this guy, why didn't your xelton pick up that he was a phony?"

The question stunned Luther. The audacity! How dare he?

And yet . . . it was a question he had to answer.

"I don't know," Luther said as his mind raced around for a plausible explanation. He tried to buy some time by acknowledging the problem. "My xelton has no answer, and I'm baffled as well. A Fully Fused xelton such as mine should have been able to pierce his masks in a moment, but it didn't. That's virtually impossible . . . unless . . ."

"Unless what?"

Brady smiled. He'd just come up with an explanation. A doozy.

"Unless this man has achieved FF."

"That's impossible!"

"No, it's not. How many temples do we have? Do you know every man worldwide who's reached FF? Of course you don't. He's a rogue FF. It's the only explanation."

"But why would an FF try to harm the Church?"

"Obviously his xelton became corrupted. If it can happen to our PD, of all people, it can happen to a lesser man."

He let that sink in. That was the same line he'd fed Jensen and the HC when Cooper Blascoe became a risk: The PD's xelton had gone mad and, as a result, Blascoe had gone even madder. The corrupted xelton had allowed him to get sick and was refusing to heal him. Just as a human could become a WA, so could a xelton.

Far out, *far* out, but they'd all believed. Because they *wanted* to believe. To doubt would destroy the foundation on which they'd all built their lives. They *had* to believe.

"You mean—?"

Luther had had enough of this.

"Forget him for now. He and his corrupted PX don't worry me half as much as Grant. She's had it in for the Church and now you can bet she knows everything. Well, almost everything. She can't know about Omega because Blascoe didn't. Noomri, what a mess! We've got body parts up at the cabin and a muckraking reporter with a tape of Blascoe saying who knows what. You've got to stop her before she talks."

"I'm on it. I have a clean-up detail heading for the cabin. They'll remove what needs to be removed and burn the rest. As for the tape, can't we say it's a fake?"

"A voiceprint analysis comparing her tape to Blascoe's voice on one of our own instructional tapes will make us liars. She's got to be stopped, Jensen."

"I know. I'm—"

"I mean *stopped*—as in, I do not want to hear from this woman again. Do you hear me?"

"Loud and clear."

"Find her."

Luther hung up and rose from his bed. Sleep now was out of the question. He strode into the office area, sat at his desk, and pressed the button for the globe.

He stared at its glowing lights, twinkling in the darkness of the office, and wanted to cry.

So close. He was so close to completing Opus Omega, to fulfilling all the required tasks. The end was in sight. A year . . . he needed just another year or so and all would be in place. Everything had been going so smoothly . . .

Until now.

Damn that woman. Ruination. Disaster. Cooper Blascoe, the beloved PD, not in suspended animation but held prisoner and fitted with a bomb, and then . . . blown to pieces.

The Church would deny everything, of course, but the tape would damn them.

Luther groaned and closed his eyes as he envisioned the fallout: Members fleeing in droves, recruitment coming to a standstill, revenues constricting to a trickle.

Revenues . . . he needed money, lots of it, to acquire the final sites. Final because they either were prime real estate or the owners refused to sell. They couldn't all be pushed in front of subway trains.

As a matter of fact, the new column was scheduled to be planted on the Masterson property tomorrow night.

But if that woman exposed the Blascoe debacle, it might be the last.

Luther slammed his fist on the desktop. He could not allow one lousy woman to threaten the greatest project in the history of mankind.

Yes! The *history* of mankind.

For Opus Omega had not begun with Luther Brady. Oh, at first he'd thought it did, but he had soon learned otherwise. He remembered the day in England when he'd begun to excavate a patch of moor he'd purchased in York. He'd found a bare spot in a field of wild rape and decided that would be as good a place as any to bury a pillar. But after digging only a few feet into the soft earth his crew discovered the top of a stone column. As they excavated around it Luther was stunned to see the symbols carved into its granite flanks—identical to the ones on the concrete column he'd prepared for this site.

Someone had been there ahead of him—hundreds, maybe thousands of years before. The conclusion was inescapable: Opus Omega had begun long, long ago. It was not Luther Brady's exclusive task, as he had thought. He was merely another man chosen to continue an ancient undertaking.

No, more than continue. He, Luther Brady, was determined to finish Opus Omega. The ancients had been at a disadvantage, lacking the means to travel to the necessary sites, let alone transport huge stone pillars. He was positioned to use all the modern world's learning and technology to bring Opus Omega to its fulfillment.

But one woman could bring his life's work to a grinding halt.

One woman.

Jamie Grant had to be stopped.

"I understand, Jack," Jamie said, "and I appreciate your concern, but I know what I'm doing."

Like hell you do, Jack thought.

He was driving through Midtown, heading east along Fifty-eighth, and they'd been arguing for more than half an hour.

Jamie had done pretty well behind the wheel, racing the Vic down the winding mountain road and speeding them to the highway. Jack would have preferred to be in the driver's seat but didn't want to waste the seconds it would have taken to switch places. When they'd reached 84 he'd made her turn west instead of east. He'd guessed that Jensen would expect them to head back to the city, so they went the other way.

It had worked. No sign of pursuit, even though he'd had Jamie set the cruise control at sixty-five and stick to it. Under any circumstances, Jack feared being pulled over, but more than ever tonight. Not having a valid identity would be small potatoes compared to explaining how they'd wound up splattered head-to-toe with blood and tissue from Cooper Blascoe.

Jamie had held up until they pulled off the interstate at Carmel and waited to see if Jensen would show. The meltdown occurred a few seconds after she stopped the car. First a sniff, then a tear, and then Jamie Grant, hard-nosed investigative reporter, was sobbing in his arms. Jack held her, patted her back, told her what a great job she'd done, and that she'd be okay, everything would be okay.

Eventually she regained control and seemed embarrassed. The good news was that throughout the long wait by the exit ramp he'd seen no sign of Jensen and company. Heading the wrong way had worked.

They'd found an all-night Wal-Mart and bought clean clothes. Jack grabbed the wheel then and took the long way home.

They'd been arguing since they hit North Jersey about where Jamie would spend the night. Her place was out of the question—probably had half a dozen TPs glued to it—as was Jack's. He hadn't let her know his name, and he sure as hell wasn't letting her know where he lived. So he'd been pushing for a hotel room somewhere in the wilds of Queens. He'd sleep outside her door if necessary.

Jamie wanted none of it. She insisted that he drop her off at *The Light*.

"You think they won't be watching your office too?" Jack said. "It's stupid to go back there."

"Jack, I'll be under guard. You've seen the security there during the day, and it's even tougher at night. You've got to be buzzed through the door, and Henry, the night guy, is armed."

Jack shook his head. "I don't like it."

She reached over and patted his hand. "I'll be fine. I'll take a cab and get dropped off right at the door. What are they going to do—grab me off the street in front of Henry? He'll buzz me in and I'll be safe for the night. I can work on transcribing the interview without worrying."

"I think you should call the cops. You're a taxpayer—get some of it back in protection."

She looked at him. " 'You're a taxpayer' . . . kind of an odd turn of phrase, don't you think? I mean, so are you."

Jack could have told her how he'd never sullied his hands with a 1040, but didn't want to get into that.

"Let's forget turns of phrase. Call the cops."

"No way. Not yet. I want to get this story filed first. If I call in the gendarmes now, I'll have to tell them about Coop and—"

" 'Coop'?"

She blinked and Jack noticed her eyes glistening. "He wasn't a bad guy, just an old hippie. A gentle hedonist. He didn't create Dormentalism as it is today, he isn't responsible for what Brady's done to it. He didn't deserve to die . . . to be blown up . . . and I can't help thinking how he'd still be alive if I'd just left him alone . . ."

Her voice choked off in a sob, but only one.

Jack thought about asking her if her meltdown in Carmel was the reason she was being so hard-nosed about not hiding out or getting help. He decided against it. Probably only get her back up.

"The cops, Jamie? What's wrong with getting them involved now instead of later?"

"Because in order to get protection I'll have to tell them why I'm in danger, and that means telling them what happened to Coop. And once they hear that, I'll be trapped in an interrogation-deposition situation for hours, maybe days, during which—"

"At least you'll be safe."

"—the story of what happened up there will leak out, and every paper in the city will be screaming their takes while mine remains unwritten and unfiled."

"Yeah, but the stories will be about you. You'll be famous."

"Like I care. *I* want to break the story—me. Nobody else. Where I come from, that's important. I'll be safe. Really."

"Really? Remember Coop? They blew him up."

She threw up her hands. "Look, I'm through talking about it. Stop someplace where I can get a cab."

Jack sighed. He knew an immovable object when he saw one—Gia could be just as intransigent. His instincts urged him to head straight for the on-ramp to the Queensboro Bridge and cross the East River. He wanted to find a motel room and lock her in it until she saw the light.

But he couldn't do that. He'd fight tooth and nail if someone tried to lock him up, so how could he do that to her? It went against everything he believed in.

And yet . . . how could he let her put her life on the line just to be first to file a story?

Let her . . . listen to me . . . like I own her.

He didn't. Jamie owned Jamie, and so Jamie had to be allowed to do what she felt she had to, even if Jack thought it was insanely risky. Because in the end all that mattered was what Jamie thought. It was her life. And so what mattered most was what mattered to Jamie.

Jack turned downtown, away from the bridge.

"Shit! This is idiotic, Jamie! You're going to get yourself killed. And me with you."

"How's that?"

"Well, you don't think I'm going to let you go alone."

She placed a hand on his arm. "I appreciate that, but you don't need to come along. Just cover my back till I'm inside. After that I'm home free: locked doors, an armed guard."

"I do *not* like this."

"I'm not crazy about it either, but a gal's gotta do what a gal's gotta do."

"Not funny."

"Wasn't meant to be," she said.

3

Jamie waited in the rear of the cab until she spotted Henry through the glass doors of *The Light's* front entrance. There he was, sitting behind his kiosk, just where he was supposed to be. Time to move. Heart pounding, she hopped from the cab and raced across the sidewalk.

As she jammed the ringer button, her head snapped left and right—would have rotated full circle had her neck allowed—looking for Dementedist goons. She knew Jack was somewhere nearby, hiding in the shadows. Still, if a couple of TPs suddenly jumped out and pulled her into a van, was he close enough to help?

She heard a noise and jumped. About a hundred feet to her left two men in raincoats were gliding from a parked sedan.

Oh, God!

She started hammering on the glass and at just that moment the door swung open. She leaped inside and elbowed Henry out of the way to pull it closed behind her. As it latched she peered through the glass and saw the two men standing on the sidewalk, halfway to the door, staring at her. She resisted the urge to give them the finger.

Henry laughed. "What's the hurry, Ms. Grant?"

Jamie figured if she told him that people were after her because of a story she was about to write, he'd call the cops.

She turned and smiled. "Got a big story to write, Henry."

"Must be a whopper to bring you in at this hour. I mean, this is early even for you." He leaned closer and looked at her. "Or is it late?"

She glanced up. The lobby clock showed ten after two.

"Late, Henry," she said as she started for the elevators. "Very late."

She hadn't slept well Wednesday, finally giving up on the possibility around four A.M. Thursday. She'd hauled herself out of bed and headed for the office. Here it was, Friday morning, which meant she'd been going full speed for over twenty-two hours. Yet she didn't feel the slightest hint of fatigue. She was jazzed. Adrenaline strummed heavy-metal power chords along her axons.

Good thing too, otherwise the horrors of the night— cutting through Coop's skin... his body blowing to pieces—would have reduced her to a trembling basket case by now.

But she couldn't dwell on that.

On the third floor she turned on all the overhead lights and wound through the deserted cubicle farm to her office. She paused on the threshold and looked at the comforting confusion of strewn-about books, newspapers, printouts, and scribbled-up yellow notepads.

Bless this mess, she thought. I'm home.

She dropped into her desk chair, lit a ciggie, and turned on her terminal. She'd rewound the tape during the trip back, so all she had to do now was pull the recorder from her shoulder bag and hit PLAY.

She had a bad moment when she first heard the murdered man's voice begin to speak to her from the tiny speaker...

"You mean why I'm not in suspended animation, and how I came to be a shell of my former self? Know what? If you hold me up to your ear you can hear the ocean roar."

... but she held herself together and began to transcribe.

4

Jensen eyed the front entrance of *The Light* from the rear seat of the Town Car.

"That's the only way in?"

Hutch the hulk was still behind the wheel. Davis, a twitchy sort who'd been watching *The Light*'s granite office building since Jensen had called in an alert, sat in the front passenger seat.

"The only way worth mentioning," Davis said. "The side entrance is a steel door. Unless you want to get into some acetylene action, this is it."

Jensen's head throbbed, especially around the scalp cut. They'd never caught up to Grant and Mr. Whoever, so when they got back to the city Jensen called a Dormentalist doctor who did work for the Church on the QT—anything for the cause and all that. The doc had said bring him to his office where he'd see what he could do. One look at Lewis's ass—he'd been shot in the thigh too, but the ass wound was really messy—and he said he needed a hospital. He'd try to admit him as a car accident to avoid a gunshot wound report to the police, but couldn't guarantee he'd be successful.

He'd wanted to stitch up Jensen's scalp but Jensen couldn't spare the time. He let the doc butterfly it closed and then he was on his way.

He leaned over between the seats for another quick look at his forehead in the rearview mirror. The three beveled strips of tape gleamed like white neon against his black skin. Didn't anyone make black butterflies? Or at least dark brown?

Why am I thinking about this shit when everything's poised to slide into the crapper?

He needed a way out and needed it bad. If the Blascoe story got out, he'd have to hit the road. The cops—maybe even the feds—would be grilling everybody in the Church, and sure as shit one of them would crack and start pointing a finger at him as the guy responsible for Blascoe's death. Another murder rap would put him away for good. No way he was going back to the joint. Not even for a minute.

Hutch said, "How about just going up to the door and ringing the bell? Get him to open up and speak to you and then you're in."

Davis shook his head. "At two-thirty in the morning? Wouldn't catch me opening that door for anybody I don't know."

Davis had a point. Then Jensen remembered a couple of props he had left over from an investigation they did into a state assemblyman who was making trouble for the Church a few years back.

"What if you two showed up at the door flashing metal?"

"You mean guns?" Hutch said.

Jesus! How thick was this guy?

"No. I'm talking police detective shields."

"That'll get us in. Yeah, that'll do it."

Jensen lowered his voice. "Thing is, you'll have to take out the guard."

Davis turned in his seat. "Take out . . . as in permanently? Why?"

"Because we can't risk even the tiniest chance of this leading back to the Church. And you know the rules: Grant has been officially declared IS, and that means anyone protecting her is IS too."

"In Season." Hutch shook his head. "We haven't had one of those in a while."

"Well, any IS you've dealt with in the past is nothing compared to this one. Grant and her pal are the biggest threat the Church has ever faced. A lot's riding on you guys tonight. Question is, are you up for it?"

Right off, Hutch said, "Sure."

Good old Hutch. Not so bright, but he'd do anything for the Church.

Davis hesitated, then finally nodded. "To save the Church, I guess I am."

"No guessing, Davis."

A sigh, then, "Give us the badges and we'll get this over with."

He tapped Hutch on the shoulder. "Get us over to the temple." That was where he kept the badges. "And when we get back, I want Grant in one piece. The guard goes, but I need to talk to Grant."

Did he ever. Because one way or another she was going to tell him all about her boyfriend.

Jack had promised to cover Jamie until she got inside, but he'd hung on after that when he spotted Jensen's Town Car idling across the street from *The Light*. If he and his goons made a move on the front door, Jack would have to act. Didn't want that, because it most likely would involve gun play. He didn't know what kind of marksmanship he'd be up against, but even if he got off unscathed, gunshots tended to attract cops.

So he crouched in a shadowed doorway and waited.

After five or ten minutes, the big car shifted into gear and roared off. Jack allowed himself to relax, but not too much. They might be simply driving around the block looking for another way in.

But when thirty minutes had passed and they didn't show, he called it a night. Jamie was safe behind locked doors and an armed guard. Jack didn't see what he could add to that.

6

Jamie lifted her head and looked around. She thought she'd heard a noise. Like maybe the elevator. She went to her door and stared out at the cubicle sea. She waited to see if anyone came through the hallway door. She supposed it would be way too much to expect Henry to stop by with a much-needed cup of coffee, but it didn't hurt to indulge in a little of that stuff that springs eternal.

Nope. Nobody showed. Maybe after she was done with the transcribing situation she'd head downstairs and grab a cup.

She was almost done. She'd typed in only Coop's remarks, leaving out Jack's comments, and hers as well. As soon as she finished she'd e-mail it to her Hotmail account—just in case some Dementedist hacker got into *The Light*'s system and started messing with her files.

After that, the writing would begin. She'd cull out the good passages, the really damning ones, and begin to shape her article around them.

She was nearing the point where the interview stopped and the surgery began when she heard the scrape of a shoe. She looked up in time to see a big man in a wet overcoat hurtling through her doorway. She tried to dodge a black-gloved fist swinging toward her face, but couldn't move fast enough. Pain exploded in her cheek as he connected.

The blow knocked her out of the chair. She sprawled on the floor, dazed, trying to muster a scream through the disorienting haze. As she opened her mouth she felt a sweet-smelling cloth clamped over her lips and nostrils. The fumes burned her eyes.

"We've been trying to get to you all night," said a voice.

Where was Henry?

She held off as long as she could but finally had to take a breath. As soon as the fumes hit her lungs she felt an oddly pleasant lethargy begin to invade her limbs. Her vision fogged but she still could see. And she saw another man, smaller than the first, seating himself at her desk.

She watched him grab her tape recorder and hold it up.

"Got it!" He pocketed it and stared at her monitor. "Now let's see what she's been writing."

"Jensen told you not to read it. If you—"

"Hey, she mentions Cooper Blascoe here. This must be it. The bitch is writing shit about the PD!" He started hitting the keys. "Well, we'll just have to get some deletion action going, won't we."

Jamie felt her consciousness ebbing. The voices started to fade away, echoing down a dark, bottomless canyon.

Had she e-mailed the file to herself as she'd planned? No . . . hadn't had the chance. Everything she'd done, the whole transcription was right there on the screen. All her work . . .

Work? screamed a voice in her head. *Forget your damn story, these guys are going to kill you!*

With panic welling in her, Jamie tried to struggle free but her limbs had become stretched-out rubber bands.

"Okay, that's done," said the one at the desk. "And the program says that's the only thing she's worked on since yesterday." He rose and turned toward Jamie. "Okay, let's bag her up."

Bag . . . ?

Seconds later the cloth was removed from her mouth and nose and fresh air flooded her throat. But only for a heartbeat before a coarse can-vas sack closed over her head and down along her body. She felt herself lifted and twisted and jostled into something that seemed like a huge sail bag.

"Don't forget her handbag," the big guy's voice said. "Jensen said to make sure we didn't forget that."

She opened her mouth to scream as she was lifted free of the floor, but her voice hadn't returned. She heard an *umph!* as she was slung like a sack of wheat over someone's shoulder. Probably the big guy's. And then she was on the move, bouncing along to who knew where. The point of his shoulder jabbed into her stomach with every step.

She tried to scream but again her voice failed her. She heard the elevator doors slide open. A moment later the car lurched into motion—downward motion. Did they think they could carry her out like this right through the lobby? Henry would—

Oh, no. Had they done something to Henry? Please, God, make it so they just tied him up. Please!

As soon as the elevator doors opened she made another try at a scream. This time she managed a faint squeak, like a kettle readying to boil.

No one bothered them as they passed through the lobby and out the front doors. They stopped moving and she was dumped off the shoulder onto a hard surface. From the way it bounced she knew it was a car, but it wasn't upholstered.

Another attempted scream and this time she achieved conversation-level volume, but before she could try a second, a door was slammed down over her and the faint sounds of the city were abruptly shut off.

That sound . . . not a door. It could only be a trunk lid.

No! They'd locked her in a car trunk!

As the car lurched into motion, Jamie began kicking and screaming, but knew with a despair as black as Luther Brady's soul that no one was going to hear her.

7

"The problem is partially solved."

Luther Brady felt the muscles that had been wound spring tight since Jensen's last call begin to unwind.

"Partially?"

"We have Grant. The former Jason Amurri is still out there."

"Did you get to her in time?"

"I believe so."

"Believe isn't good enough."

"I'll ask her. Then we'll know."

"How will you be sure?"

"She'll tell me."

The finality of that simple statement sent a warm glow of reassurance through Luther.

Jensen added, "What do we do after that?"

Luther had been thinking about that, and had an answer ready.

"We're pouring a column tonight. Bring her there. I'll have the volunteer notified that she'll have to wait till next time."

"You'll be there?"

"Have I ever missed? Ten o'clock. And who knows? Maybe you'll have the other half by then."

Luther hung up and allowed himself a smile. A tiny one.

Two in one pillar . . . an intriguing possibility.

8

Jack had brought Entenmann's crumb donuts to the traditional Friday morning perusal of the latest film reviews before the Isher Sports Shop opened for business. The papers were spread on the counter, collecting the crumbs, but only briefly: Parabellum was on clean-up duty, and he was devoted to the task.

Jack had checked in with Gia earlier. She'd said she was doing fine but he sensed something forced in her tone. He planned to stop in later.

He was halfway through a review of the latest Robert Rodriguez film when Abe spoke around a mouthful of Entenmann's.

"Nu? Haven't you been talking to someone at *The Light* lately? What do you think about that murder there last night?"

Jack almost choked as his throat clenched.

"What? There's nothing in the paper about—"

"Happened too late for the paper. It's all over the radio this morning. Don't you listen?"

Aw, no. A shattering rush of guilt paralyzed him. He hadn't been persuasive enough. He hadn't watched *The Light* long enough. He'd failed her.

Jack didn't want to hear the answer but had to ask: "Did they say anything about how she was killed?"

"She? No, a he. The guard at the front desk. Shot in the head. I hear the police suspect an inside job because there was no sign of a break-in or a struggle. Probably someone he knew."

Jack's burst of relief was short-lived. That poor

unsuspecting guard's death—Jamie had called him
Henry— had to be related to what they'd learned last night.

Jack yanked his phone from his pocket and called information for *The Light*'s number. A few seconds later the
switchboard was putting him through to her extension.

But a man answered, his voice gruff, sounding annoyed. "Yeah?"

"Jamie Grant, please."

"Who's calling?"

"A friend. Is she there?"

"Not at the moment. Give me your name and number
and I'll tell her you called."

Jack cut the call. If that wasn't a cop, he'd eat a pair of
Abe's roller blades for lunch.

This was looking very bad.

He checked his voice mail—he'd given her one of his
newer numbers because the one on the Robertson card
was purposefully obsolete—but no message from Jamie.
He couldn't imagine her being stupid enough to go home,
but he called her apartment anyway. Her answering machine picked up on the second ring.

He left a cryptic message: "Jamie, this is Robertson.
Call me at that number I gave you."

No sense in leaving Jensen even the faintest of trails.

He gave Abe a quick rundown on what had been going on.

"You think this Jensen's got her?"

Jack shrugged. "The only other possibility is that they
botched an attempt to grab her and she's gone to ground.
But I'd think she'd have called the police then."

"How do you know she didn't? Maybe that coplike
person answering her phone is there because she's under
protection."

"Since when are you such an optimist?"

"What—I should play Eeyore my whole life?"

Jamie with the police . . . a possibility, but somehow . . .

"I have to operate on the assumption they've got
her."

"Got her where? I can't imagine they'd risk taking her back to the temple."

"No, she's someplace else. I'm sure they're not stashing her back at the cabin, so . . . where?" He looked around. "Got any hats?"

"Hats I've got tons of. What do you want?"

"Something big. The bigger the better."

9

Gia checked her pad for the third time this morning. Still no blood.

See? Nothing to worry about. Dr. Eagleton had been right.

Relieved, she stepped out of the bathroom and just missed colliding with Vicky who tended to go wherever she was going at a dead run.

"Mom! Can Jessica come over?"

Jessica had been one of the princesses on Halloween. Good kid and not at all high maintenance. But Gia didn't feel up to overseeing two ten-year-olds.

"I'm still feeling kind of pooped, Vicky." Four days since the Big Bleed. She'd have thought she'd be bouncing back by now. "But you can go over there if you like."

Vicky grinned. "I'll call her!" She ran for the phone.

Gia would take advantage of the free time by keeping her feet up and taking it easy. One more day. If nothing else bad happened, she'd get back to a more normal routine tomorrow. Much more of this forced inactivity and she'd be ready for the loony bin.

Jack was stopping by later this morning. It would be good to slip a movie in the disk player and hang out, just the two of them.

The phone rang. It was Jack.

"Hi, hon. Look, I'm going to have to put off my visit."

She hid her disappointment.

"Something come up?"

"Yeah. Sort of."

Something in his tone . . .

"Anything wrong?"

"Not sure. Talk to you about it later, okay?"

"Okay. Keep in touch."

She hung up and wondered what he was up to.

10

Jack slouched in the back of a taxi heading west along Jamie's street. He wore sunglasses and an oversized khaki boonie cap pulled low on his head. As the cab approached her apartment house he scanned the parked cars and found one occupied by two men. Their eyes were locked on Jamie's door.

This could be a good sign. If they were watching for Jamie it could only mean they didn't have her and were still after her.

But then he thought of another reason for the ongoing surveillance. What if they weren't watching for Jamie . . . what if they were watching for him?

11

Jamie squinted in the sudden glare as the trunk lid popped open. Not that the light was all that bright—just an overhead incandescent—but after all those hours in total darkness, it looked like a supernova.

Her joints creaked in protest as she struggled to her knees. Her bladder was screaming for release. She'd wormed her way out of the canvas bag as they drove her around for what seemed like half a day. The car had stopped and started twice during the journey, but hadn't budged for hours now. If the purpose of all that had been to break down her resistance with prolonged terror, they'd succeeded. In spades.

She began to cry. She hated to let anyone see her like this but she couldn't help it. She'd never been so frightened in her entire life.

She tried to blink her surroundings into focus. Light filtered through a couple of dirty windows in a folding metal door. She seemed to be in a small garage. But in what state? She felt so disoriented.

"There, there," said a deep voice. "No need to be upset."

It came from her left. She looked up and cowered back from the blurred image of a huge black man in jeans and a black T-shirt. She didn't need the extra blinks that brought him into focus to identify him.

Jensen.

She opened her mouth, then closed it. She'd been about to ask why he'd kidnapped her and brought her here—wherever here was—but she knew the answers. She had a far more pressing concern.

The words clung to her throat but she forced them through. "You're going to kill me, aren't you."

Jensen laughed like the guy who used to do the "Uncola Nut" commercials. "Don't be silly! You've been watching too many bad movies. We have the tape, we erased your word processing file. If we wanted to kill you, you'd be dead by now."

Jamie glanced around. " 'We'?"

His smile remained fixed. "Just an expression. I'm the only one here."

"Well, know this: I made a copy of that tape." She hated the way her voice quavered.

He smiled. "Oh? And when and where would you have made such a copy? And where did you stash it? In a safety deposit box? Not at that hour. In your desk? No. In your purse? No. In your apartment? No. At—"

"My apartment? How—?"

"When we got your purse we got your keys. Apartment 5-D, right? We know you haven't been home since this morning, but we searched it anyway."

Christ, he'd covered all the bases.

She clenched her trembling hands and decided to go the disarming route and 'fess up.

"All right, you caught me. But I lied because I'm scared."

"No need to be. Just give me the answers to a few questions and you can be on your way."

"You're not going to let me go. I've seen you, and kidnapping is a federal offense."

He laughed again. "Rest assured that I'll have a perfect alibi. I'll simply say it's all something you cooked up to sell more papers. You've already gone public with your rabid hatred of Dormentalism—or 'Dementedism,' as you like to call it—and since you couldn't dig up any real dirt on the Church, you pulled this stunt. Remember Morton Downey when he faked an attack by skinheads? Making that sort of crazy claim will hurt you, not us. You'll be the new Morton Downey. No one will ever believe you again."

Jamie doubted that. Doubted it big time.

"What about Henry?" she said.

Jensen's brow furrowed. "Henry? I don't believe—"

"The night guard at the paper. Was he in on it?"

"Oh, yes. Henry. I didn't know who you meant at first because that's not his real name."

"What?"

"He's a Dormentalist, you know."

"Bullshit. He's been with the paper for years."

"He's been with the Church even longer. Of course, you'll have no way of proving that since our membership rolls are sealed."

Did he really think they could pull this off? She wasn't about to disabuse him of that particular illusion.

For the first time since the trunk lid had slammed closed over her, Jamie Grant saw a glimmer of hope that she might come out of this alive.

And if that was the case . . .

"Let me out of this trunk. I have to go to the bathroom."

"In a minute."

"I have to go *now*." God, she didn't think she could hold it another second. "I mean *right* now."

"After you've answered a question or two." His smile broadened. "Consider bathroom privileges part of an incentive plan."

When she got out of here, was she ever going to nail their asses to the wall.

She pressed her thighs together and said, "Doesn't look like I have a choice. What do you want to know?"

Jensen's smile faded. "Who is the man you were with at the cabin?"

She could pretend she didn't know who he was talking about, but Jensen would know it was another lie. All she'd accomplish was wasting more time—time she could be spending relieving herself in the bathroom. Bladder spasms or not, though, she didn't want to give up Robertson's name.

Jensen took the choice out of her hands by holding up Robertson's card.

"We found this in your pocketbook. It says that John Robertson is a private detective. When did you hire him?"

Jamie had no problem answering that.

"I didn't. He came to me. He'd been hired to find one of your members who'd gone missing—as a fair number of them seem to do. He read my article and came to me for advice on how to sneak in. He knew I'd been kicked out and didn't want to make the same mistakes."

Jensen stared at the card, nodding slowly. "He didn't." His head snapped up. "How do you know he's John Robertson?"

"I checked out his PI license. It's current."

"True, but Mr. John Robertson is not."

"What do you mean?"

"I mean he's dead. Died of cancer in Duck, North Carolina, three years ago."

Jamie couldn't believe that. "You're lying."

Jensen fished a piece of paper out of his back pocket, unfolded it, and held it out to her. A Xerox of an obit. She caught a flash of a grainy photo of an old guy in a Stetson hat before the paper was snatched away. He looked nothing like the man she'd been working with.

Jensen angrily balled it up and hurled it across the room. She sensed his pent-up fury, felt it radiating from his soul like heat from an oven, and it frightened her.

"But his license—"

"—is current. Yes, I know. But obviously someone else has been renewing it." Jensen snarled as he poked a finger against the card. "The address here is a mail drop. And the phone number belongs to a hair salon." His rage seemed to build with every sentence. "Who is this man? I want to know and I want to know *now*!"

Jamie couldn't believe it. "His name's not Robertson?"

"No, and it's not Farrell and it's not Amurri either."

What was he talking about?

"Then—?"

He jabbed a thick finger at her. "He must've given you a number."

His blazing eyes frightened her.

Jamie shook her head. "No. He always called me. No, wait. He gave me a cell number. It should be in my purse."

"There is no number in your purse."

Oh, God, had she lost it?

"Then . . . then . . ." What could she say? "Wait a minute. I have caller ID on my office phone. It would still be there on the call list. I'm always getting grief for leaving so many numbers in the list."

Pure bullshit, but maybe Jensen would go for it.

His eyes narrowed. "Then you would have seen the number. What was it?"

"I couldn't possibly remember. I get so many calls. I vaguely recall a 212 area code, but that's it. I can check it out for you if—"

Another Uncola Nut laugh. "If I let you go back to your office? I don't think so. Not quite yet. But maybe we can figure out some way for you to find that number from here."

Her bladder shot a quarrel of pain into her lower back.

"All right then, if I'm not going to my office, can I at least go to the bathroom? *Now?* I can't think straight with my bladder killing me like this."

"Of course." Jensen pointed toward the front end of the car. "It's right through that door."

She raised herself on one knee, slipped an unsteady leg over the trunk lip, past the bumper and down to the floor. When both feet were back on the ground, she straightened slowly, carefully, her back protesting all the way.

She looked around and saw an unfinished, uninsulated garage. To the car's left sat a chair and an old table with a couple of nails driven into its thick, scarred top. A pile of heavy chain sat on the table next to a folded green towel. And just past the front bumper, a closed, unmarked door.

"Is that it?" she said.

He nodded, but as she turned away she felt her shoulders grabbed from behind. She was twisted and shoved into the chair and, before she could react, Jensen was wrapping the chain around her waist and chest.

"What are you *doing*?"

His face was set in grim lines and he didn't answer. She tried to wriggle free but he was too strong for her. Finally, when Jamie couldn't move, Jensen spoke.

"Time to test your memory."

"About what?" Her pounding heart threatened to break through her chest wall. "Not the phone number! I told you—"

"We have 2-1-2 so far. Only seven more to go."

"But I don't *know* the rest!"

Jensen grabbed her left hand and flattened her palm on the tabletop. He maneuvered her little finger until it was fixed between the two nails.

"What are you going—"

"I hate when things are unbalanced, don't you?"

Jamie sensed where this was going and it doubled her terror.

"No, I—"

"Your right pinkie, for instance. It's so much shorter than the left."

"No." She remembered the pain, the blood when her darling husband had chopped it off. She heard herself sobbing. "Oh, please, please . . ."

"Perhaps I can overcome my dislike of an unbalanced body by hearing a phone number. A *complete* phone number. One that will connect me to the man I'm looking for. If not . . ."

He lifted the towel to reveal a heavy, rust-rimmed meat cleaver.

Jamie's struggling bladder gave up. She felt a warm puddle spread across the seat of the chair.

Jensen picked up the cleaver and hefted it, then raised it over her finger.

"We'll call this an exercise in memory stimulation."

Jamie could barely speak. Her words gushed out in a high-pitched rasp.

"Oh, God, Jensen, please, you've got to believe me! Please! I don't know the number, I swear, I swear, I swear I don't!"

He looked at her. "You know, the sad thing is, I believe you."

And then he swung the cleaver.

12

Gemini (May 21–June 21): You see what you want, and you know what to do to get it—give a fair dose of your winning attention, and then confidently walk away! Being too enthusiastic about a new prospect could scare him or her off or weaken your position.

Richie Cordova's office chair groaned as he leaned back, and screeched when he jerked forward. He'd rested the back of his head against the chair and his sutured scalp had let him know it wasn't too happy with that.

Goddamn, that still hurt.

He resettled his weight and looked over the Gemini reading again. He liked the part that said, *You see what you want, and you know what to do to get it.* Damn right about that.

Except about whoever had sent him that fucking virus. And who had split open his scalp. He knew what he wanted to do to those guys, but didn't have no way to track them down.

He lifted the paper off the mound of his belly and checked the other side of the astrological cusp.

Cancer (June 22–July 22): A small but satisfying victory is the beginning of a lucky streak. Do what you must to get a good deal—a little financial wrangling won't make you look bad. Tonight, lots of action with you at the center is your idea of a good time.

Well, well, well. This was looking better all the time. He had a good day ahead of him. And why not take advantage of that? He'd been thinking about that nun and how the prospect of hitting a decent payday from her was looking dimmer and dimmer. She was tapped out and wasn't going to get much from that building fund—if anything.

But her boyfriend, Metcalf . . . why not hit him up for the difference? He owed the nun. Owed her big time.

He told Eddy he was going for a walk and headed for the street.

He traveled away from the park this time, searching for a phone he hadn't used in a while. He'd thought of getting one of those prepaid cell phones, but he'd still have to leave the office. Couldn't risk Eddy overhearing him putting the teat squeeze on one of his cows.

He found a phone in a shady spot. The air was still humid after last night's downpour and Richie had worked up a sweat during the walk. Had to lose some of this weight, get back into shape.

Yeah, right. *Mañana.*

He tapped in his prepaid calling card numbers, then Metcalf's office number. He wasn't in, so Richie tried his home and caught up to him there.

"You know who this is?" Richie said when Metcalf picked up the phone.

"Unfortunately, yes."

"Good. Then listen up. I—"

Metcalf's voice dropped to a harsh whisper. "No! *You* listen, scumbag. I'm through playing your game. Do what you want. I'm not paying another cent."

For a few seconds Richie found himself speechless. Had this jerk called him a *scumbag*?

"I guess you musta forgot about the photos. They'll—"

"I don't care. Let the chips fall where they may. And don't try harassing me with more calls because I'll report you to the police and have them trace your calls. This ends it. I'm leaving town today, taking my family away on a vacation, and putting this whole thing behind me."

Richie couldn't believe what he was hearing. Had Metcalf gone bugfuck nuts?

He forced a growl to his voice. "Vacation, ay? Well, enjoy it, because married life ain't gonna be so hot when your wife and kids come home and find the neighborhood plastered with bare-assed pictures of you and your little fuck-buddy nun."

"I guess that's just a risk I'll have to take." And then Metcalf laughed—*laughed!*—and said, "Outfoxed by a nun. Some criminal mastermind you are. Good-bye, loser."

He hung up, leaving Richie staring at the handset in slack-jawed stupefaction.

Had Metcalf said what Richie thought he'd said?

Outfoxed by a nun . . .

What the hell did that mean?

And then he saw it all. Everything clicked into place. The virus hitting his computer not once but twice . . . and then the little nun giving him the runaround on payments . . . and finally Metcalf stiffing him, all but daring him to expose the photos of him and Sister Mary Margaret.

Why? Because he knew the photos were gone!

Outfoxed by a nun . . .

They'd hired someone to wipe his computer clean and—

Goddamn! It must have been the same guy who mugged him and stole his backup disk! Blindsided from two different directions.

He rammed the handset against the face of the pay phone, slamming it against the switch hook again and again until the receiver end shattered. He dropped it and turned away, ignoring the frightened look from an old woman who shied away as she passed.

Somehow they'd found out who he was. That made twice in the past few months—September and now. Where was he slipping up? The kid in the mail drop? Had he ratted him out? Richie'd look into that later.

He knew neither Metcalf nor the nun had the stones or the know-how to break into his operation. So who'd they hire? Another PI like himself? Richie wanted the name so he could even the score and—

Wait a minute . . . why was he assuming Metcalf knew who he was? Maybe he didn't know. Metcalf had just warned him he'd have the police trace his calls. Why would he say that if he knew who Richie was? Obviously he didn't.

But the PI they'd hired did. Had to. And who else? Sister Maggie?

Outfoxed by a nun . . .

Metcalf was giving Sister Maggie the credit. That could mean only one thing: It was the nun who'd found someone to track him down and ruin his operation—and do it in such a way that Richie wouldn't know he'd been sabotaged. Pretty smooth. It had almost worked.

This guy knew who Richie was. Now Richie needed to know who he was. That would level the playing field. Then he could take action. Metcalf probably knew the guy's name, but he was on his way out of town—or so he said. Richie would check on that. But if true, that left the nun. He needed a little face time with her.

What had his Cancer horoscope said?

Tonight, lots of action with you at the center is your idea of a good time.

Oh, yeah. Tonight . . . if he could work it. If not, to-morrow for sure. Get some answers, and maybe grab a lit-tle payback along the way.

No, not a little. She and her boyfriend and whoever they'd hired had screwed up his entire operation. Richie was going to need a *lot* of payback.

13

Jack was having no luck on the phone today. Repeated calls to Jamie's house and office had left him no wiser as to her well-being or whereabouts.

Same with Maria Roselli. After two calls this morning, and two more this afternoon, all unanswered, Jack had decided to visit Beekman Place in person.

He wore a blue sweater this time, but looked pretty much the same as before. One difference was the small shopping bag he carried. Anya's map was folded within. He'd started thinking of it as Anya's "map," preferring that to Anya's "skin."

A woman with a dog had sent him on a mission into the Dormentalist temple, which housed a replica to the skin map from the back of another woman with a dog.

He'd been told that there would be no more coinci-dences in his life; but even if he hadn't, he'd have known this was no coincidence. Maria Roselli had more on her agenda than finding her son, and now Jack had to know what. He also wanted to know her connection to Anya.

The only one who could fill in those blanks lived in the brick and granite building he was approaching.

He found the uniformed Esteban in the white marble atrium.

"I'm a little concerned about Mrs. Roselli," Jack told

him. "I've been calling her all day and she doesn't answer."

Esteban smiled. "The lady, she's fine. She's been in
and out—in fact, she's out now—and probably missed
your calls."

"No answering machine?"

Esteban smiled. "Mrs. Roselli doesn't like them. She
told me if someone wants to talk to her about anything
important, they'll call back."

"Would you ask her to call me when she comes in? The
name's Jack and she has my number. It's urgent that I get
in touch with her."

"Jack." Esteban nodded. "I will tell her."

Back on the sidewalk, Jack decided if he couldn't
speak to the mother, he might as well have a chat with the
son. Maybe Oroont could fill in a few blanks.

Oroont . . . sheesh.

Richie Cordova had positioned his car where he could see
the front doors of both St. Joe's church and the convent.
He had the windows rolled up against a chill breeze and
the doors locked against a chance visit by one of the locals. The Lower East Side's slow gentrification hadn't
reached this area yet. He'd left the driver's window open
an inch or so to vent his cigar smoke.

This afternoon he'd been all revved at the prospect of
grabbing Sister Maggie and hauling her off to an old
abandoned warehouse he'd scouted in Flushing. But sitting here outside her church had cooled him. Blackmailing a nun was one thing. But staking her out and

snatching her if she showed . . . that would be a big step where anyone was concerned. But a nun . . .

Must be all those years in Catholic school, he thought.

He wished he was outside Metcalf's place instead. But Metcalf had been telling the truth: He'd skipped town with his family. A call to his office confirmed that he'd be gone for a week.

That left Sister Golden Hair. If she didn't show tonight he'd be back here tomorrow, and the day after that. Sooner or later he was going to catch up to her.

And then he'd treat her to a showing of *The Catholic School Kid Strikes Back*.

15

Jack had cabbed home and changed into something more suited to the far West Village—black jeans, a faded White Stripes T-shirt, and Doc Martens. He'd finished it off with an oversized black bomber jacket, big enough to hide the Glock in his SOB holster.

He took a couple of trains down to the West Village. There, in the fading light, he stood on a narrow, debris-strewn street across from The Header and kept an eye on Sonny Boy's window as an uneven stream of bikers pulled up and swaggered into the bar.

He gave it ten minutes, letting the light dim more. No sign of life up there, so he crossed over and went to the side door where the apartment dwellers entered and made quick work of the lock with his autopick. On the third floor he found the apartment he assumed to belong to Johnny, and knocked. Picking the lock of an occupied apartment could be, well, embarrassing.

No answer, so he again put the autopick to work and let himself in.

Dark inside. He flicked his flashlight on for seconds at a time. The place seemed neat and clean, but stank from the rare delicacies nuked or fried in the bar kitchen two floors down. He spotted a poster of a robust-looking Cooper Blascoe on one wall and a shelf stacked with Dormentalist tracts on the other.

Okay. This was the place. All he had to do now was wait for Johnny "Oroont" Roselli to show his face.

A partially packed duffel bag sat on the bed. Planning a trip, Johnny?

Maybe half an hour later footsteps in the hallway stopped outside the door. As a key rattled in the lock, Jack stepped behind the door and waited. Johnny flipped on the light as he closed the door behind him. Jack didn't give him time to turn. He grabbed him from behind and took him down.

"Not a sound!" he said into Johnny's ear as he strad-dled his back. Jeez, his ratty clothes were filthy and he stank. "I'm not here to hurt you, just to talk. Keep it down and we both end up healthy. Start calling for help and one of us winds up hurting. And it won't be me. Got that?"

Johnny nodded, then whispered, "If all you want is to talk, why didn't you just call me on the phone?"

"I did, but you started calling me strange names and hung up."

"That was you?" He started to twist his neck, turning his scraggly-bearded face toward Jack. Jack pushed it back.

"No peeking. You see my face, I'll have to kill you."

Johnny pushed his nose against the floor. "For Noomri's sake, what do you *want*?"

"I was hired to deliver a message. Here it is: Call your mother."

"What? That's crazy. You were hired? By who?"

"Your mother. She's—"

"That's impossible!"

"She's worried about you and—"

"My mother's dead!"

Jack opened his mouth but closed it after a second or two. He felt his shoulders slump. He should have seen this coming.

The problem now was how to salvage the situation.

"Impossible. I spoke to her just the other day."

"You couldn't have. She's been dead four years."

"Skinny old lady with bad arthritis?"

"Not even close. She was an Old World Italian mama."

"Shit. Perhaps I've made a mistake."

"Perhaps?"

"Well, she told me her son was a Dormentalist."

"Well, at least you got *that* right. You—hey!"

Jack was digging into Roselli's back pocket. "Just checking some ID. How do I know you're not lying?"

"I'm not. Who are you looking for? Maybe I can help."

"Can't mention names. Professional ethics."

The expired driver's license in the wallet showed a more clean-shaven John A. Roselli.

"Okay. You're not him. My bad. Sorry."

"Can I get up now?"

"No. Remember what I said I'd have to do if you see my face?"

Next to the license was Johnny's temple swipe card. Jack glanced at the clothes-stuffed duffel on the bed. An idea began to take shape.

"I see you're packed for a trip. Skipping town?"

"No. Going camping, if you must know. It's the only place a person in my state of . . ."

"Ripeness?" Jack said.

"Well, yes. Plus being alone in the wild helps me commune with—oh, never mind. You wouldn't understand."

"You never know."

Jack quickly pulled out his own wallet and extracted his temple entry card. No name on either card, no way to tell one from the other. He looked around and spotted a couple of magnets—with the Dormentalist logo, for Christ sake—on the refrigerator door. He leaned to the side and plucked one off.

"What are you doing?" Roselli said.

"Don't worry, I'm not stealing your money."

He began rubbing the magnet along his card's magnetic strip.

If Jensen was worth a damn as security chief, and Jack believed he was, he'd have either inactivated the Jason Amurri entry code in the computer or tagged it with a detain-on-sight warning. Either way, it was useless for getting Jack into the temple. He hadn't planned on going back, but now with Jamie incommunicado, it might prove necessary.

Which meant he needed a working model.

He slipped his card into Johnny's wallet and pocketed the other, then dropped the wallet on the floor next to Johnny's face.

As much as Jack wanted to move a good six or ten feet away from this smelly clown, he couldn't let him up yet. Also he was curious as to what Roselli had done to deserve being declared a lapser.

Jack made a loud sniffing noise. "You ever hear of soap? Or dry cleaning maybe?"

"Of course. Normally I'm a very clean person."

"Yeah?" What had Jensen called his punishment? Oh, yeah. Solitarian Exile. "So how long are you stuck in SE mode?"

He felt Roselli tense beneath him. "How do you know about that?"

"I know a lapser when I see one. Used to be in the church myself. That's why I was hired to find this missing FA."

"Used to be?"

"Yeah. Got out years ago." He needed to stick to the Dormentalist patois here. He tried to picture the list Jamie had given him. What the hell did they call ex-Dormentalists? "They started saying I had Low Fusion

Potential and wanted me to take all these extra courses to raise it. But I couldn't afford it so I went DD on my own before they could kick me out."

Roselli laughed—a single, bitter bark. "That's pretty close to why I'm not allowed to bathe or shave or change my clothes for a month."

"LFP too?"

"No. Because as soon as fall rolled around the Church raised the fees on every course for every step of the FL. I said it was too much, that it would hold too many people back from FF. That was an unpopular position with the FPRB, so I wound up LFA for objecting."

"And you just take it? They say go make yourself dirty and stinky and you do it?"

"I have given myself to the Church and must abide by its decisions."

"Does that also mean you've given up the right to your own opinion? Your pride? Your self-esteem? I once saw this film of thousands of Shiites whipping themselves bloody in the streets of Teheran during Ramadan. If the FPRB told you to do something like that, would you?"

"I . . . I don't—yes, yes, I would. The work of the Church is far more important than one man's foolish pride."

Jack could only shake his head. True Believers never failed to amaze him.

But on a more practical level, he wondered if Roselli was as rich as his ersatz mother had said.

"Well, seeing how you live, I can see why you'd object to rising prices on the Dormentalist menu."

Roselli tensed again. "Too many creature comforts are distracting and clutter the road to Full Fusion. Money is *not* a problem for me. I live this way because I choose to."

"Yeah, right."

"I have a decent amount in the bank, enough to support me, but I gave all the rest—a small fortune, if you care to know—to the Church."

"And this is how they thank you?"

"I didn't give it for thanks. I wasn't looking for special treatment. I gave it to further the Church's mission."

Jack wished he could open this turkey's eyes.

"So after they pretty much sucked you dry, they gave you the shaft by raising the fees."

"No, that doesn't affect me. I gave the Church so much that I'll never be charged FL fees, no matter how high they go. It wasn't—*isn't* myself I'm concerned about, it's the others who aren't so lucky."

"Not so lucky? I'd say their luck will change for the better when they get booted from the church for not being able to come up with the necessary jing to stay in."

"So, that's it. You've become a WA. Lots of DDs do."

"Wall Addict? Out to destroy Dormentalism? Not likely. You have to care about something before you want to destroy it. I don't even think about the church these days."

That would have been true last week, even early yesterday. But after what had happened to Blascoe last night, and with Jamie missing, nothing would please him more than seeing Brady and Jensen and their whole crew brought down. Way down.

But he couldn't let Roselli know that. Blindly loyal Dormentalist that he was, he'd go running to Jensen.

Jack rose to his feet and placed one of his Docs on Roselli's back.

"Don't move."

He reached over to the wall and flicked off the lights. Then he paused, searching for the right parting note as he left this loser in his self-imposed filth.

"Looks like I made a mistake about you. You're not the guy I was looking for. We'll let bygones be bygones, okay? I'll keep looking for the right guy, you keep avoiding soap. And hey . . . sorry about your mother."

Jack slipped out, closed the door behind him, and hurried down to the street. On his march back to the subway

station, he placed another call to the lady who called herself Maria Roselli. Still no answer.

Are you avoiding me, lady? he thought. Hope not. Because I need to talk to you. I mean, we *really* need to talk.

16

Jack saw no sense in going back to Beekman Place, especially dressed as he was. Even if the mystery lady were
home, the doorman wouldn't let him past the front door.

He picked up the late city issue of the *Post* before getting on the train. He paged through it on the uptown ride.
His heart fell as he came across the piece he'd been looking for but hoping he wouldn't find.

Jamie Grant, reporter for *The Light*, was missing. Police were speculating whether her disappearance might
be related to the murder of the night security guard.

Shit. Jensen had her. No question.

Instead of going home, Jack got off at Columbus Circle.

The first thing he did when he hit street level was dial
911 on his Tracfone. He hated to turn to the cops, but it
was time. He was one man and Jamie could be anywhere
in the five boroughs, maybe beyond.

"Listen up," he said when the emergency operator
picked up. "I just read in the paper where the cops are
looking for a missing reporter named Jamie Grant. She
was kidnapped by members of the Dormentalist Church
for writing exposés about them."

"What is your name, sir, and where can we reach you?"

"Never mind that. Listen: She was kidnapped by a guy
named Jensen who's the Dormentalist head of security.
Keep an eye on him and you'll find Jamie Grant."

"Sir—"

"Got that? Jensen. Dormentalist Church."

He broke the connection. Maybe they'd write off his call as the ravings of an MDP, maybe not. Jamie had been very publicly at odds with the Dormentalists, so the charge wouldn't sound complete blue sky. Jack hoped they'd focus at least some of their manpower and re-sources on Jensen and his church.

He walked down to the Avis place on West Fifty-fourth. He'd been using the John L. Tyleski identity for the past few months, and since he was a paid-up Visa Card holder with a current driver's license—courtesy of ID-maestro Ernie—he was allowed to cruise away in his usual rental—a Buick Century.

Jensen and his TP crew would be on the lookout for Jack's Crown Vic. This would give him a different look.

Jamie had said the Dormentalist bigshots kept their cars in a garage around the corner from the temple. Jack found a spot on the street downstream from the exit and parked. He checked his watch. Almost eight. He'd give it four hours, then call it quits.

Could be a long night.

But half an hour later, as he talked on his cell to Gia, he was pleasantly surprised to see a black Mercedes pull out of the garage. As it passed, Jack recognized Brady behind the wheel. Jamie had said he drove himself only on special occasions. Could this special occasion be a meeting with Jamie Grant?

Brady stopped at the red light at the end of the block. Jack waited for it to go green, then pulled out and followed.

17

Fog . . . the world was fog . . . all fog . . .

And pain. A dull pain in her left hand . . . her left little finger. It throbbed and burned and—

Then Jamie remembered. Jensen. The cleaver. Her finger. The indescribable pain as the blade sliced through skin and bone and tendon and nerve.

Bad as it was, the pain hadn't lasted too long. The sweet-smelling cloth had been jammed against her face again, taking away the world and the pain.

For a while.

Now both were back.

And other sensations . . . chill air on her skin . . . bands about her arms and legs and body, tight against her stomach and especially her chest, making it hard to take a deep breath. She open her mouth for more air and realized she couldn't. Some sort of cloth had been shoved between her teeth and taped into place.

Gagged!

Fighting panic, she forced her gummy lids open and blinked her eyes into focus. Whatever light there was came from above. Images formed slowly. First came the lines, vertical and horizontal, all around her. For a moment she thought she might be dreaming . . . a nightmare in which she'd fallen into a Mondrian painting. But as the lines became clearer she made out their ribbed surfaces and recognized them as steel reinforcing rods, welded into a heavy-duty lattice.

What was she doing in a steel cage?

And beyond the rods loomed the inner surface of a giant metal tube.

She felt a cool draft against her skin and looked down

at herself. Shock blasted away the lingering effects of whatever they'd drugged her with.

She was naked.

Oh, God, Jensen or one of his drones must have stripped her while she was out. She wondered if they'd done anything else to her, but she didn't feel as if she'd been . . .

Her mind froze as she realized she was bound hand, foot, and body to a dozen or more of the reinforcing rods . . . bound and suspended half a dozen feet off the ground . . . inside a tube . . .

Jamie tried to calm herself. This had to be a dream, a very bad one, because it couldn't be real. Things like this didn't happen to people, especially her. It was surreal, had no basis in the real world . . .

Check out the inner surface of the cylinder, for instance . . . all those strange looking, sharp-edged, geometric projections running up and down and around. She'd never seen anything like those before.

A dream . . .

But dream or not, something about the oddly unsettling shapes poured a stream of acid into her already quaking stomach.

What *was* this? Where *was* she? And *why*?

And then a part of her interview with Blascoe tumbled back to her. The part about the pillars Brady was burying all over the world. It seemed like years since she'd typed the words into her computer . . .

. . . the concrete's gotta be made with a certain kind of sand, and the columns gotta be inscribed with all sorts of weird symbols . . .

She'd been tied up and suspended inside one of Brady's columns. But why on Earth would—?

Blascoe's next sentence provided a chilling hint.

. . . And then they've gotta put something else inside it before they can bury it . . .

The old man hadn't known what that something else might be, but now Jamie did.

The gag muffled her screams.

18

"Where the hell are we?" Jack muttered as he followed Brady along a dark, twisting road through the Jersey sticks.

Seemed to be a pretty popular back road, which was good. Jack had kept his distance as he'd followed Brady off the Parkway. His Mercedes was now riding behind a battered old pickup and ahead of a Taurus. Jack kept behind the Taurus.

He was pretty certain they were in Ocean County, although they could have been at the lower end of Monmouth. He hadn't seen a sign either way. Not that it mattered. He wasn't too familiar with either.

Not so Brady. He seemed to know where he was going. Not a hint of hesitation in the way he negotiated the hilly curves and turns since the Parkway.

The next turn took Jack by surprise. As the road crested, Brady hung a sharp left and disappeared. Jack slowed as he reached the spot but didn't stop in case Brady was checking for tails. He caught a glimpse of an opening through the trees, a concrete skirt abutting the road's asphalt, and then nothing but open night sky.

He doubted Brady had driven off a cliff, so he continued on for about a quarter mile until he found a spot wide enough for a U-turn, then doubled back. He killed his headlights as he turned onto the skirt and stopped. He faced a wide expanse of starry sky as he sat overlooking some sort of pit, a huge excavation maybe seventy or eighty feet deep, with a cluster of odd-shaped buildings nestled against the near wall. Light glowed through a few windows in one of the taller structures where three or four cars were parked.

Jack backed up and drove downhill to where he'd made the U-turn. He pulled the car off the road and parked it between a couple of pines, then walked back. He hugged the wall of the pit as he made his way down the steep concrete driveway.

At the bottom he came upon a small fleet of cement mixer trucks. Each had printing on the cab doors that he assumed to be the company name. Something about the design above the name drew him to the trucks. He sidled over to one. Keeping its bulk between himself and the buildings, he risked a quick flash of his penlight.

Centered on the door was something that looked like a black sun or black sunflower. Beneath that . . .

WM. BLAGDEN & SONS, INC.

He'd seen that design and that name before. But where?

And then he remembered: a couple of months ago, in Novaton, Florida, on the cab door of a dump truck.

The driver had said he was hauling sand to New Jersey. Jack had thought it strange at the time—no shortage of sand in Jersey—and had meant to check it out when he got back. But with so much happening in his life these days, he'd never gotten around to it.

And yet here he was, standing in the yard of Blagden & Sons.

A familiar heaviness settled on Jack. This was no coincidence. No more coincidences in his life, and here was further proof.

In September a Blagden & Sons sand-hauling dump truck had been stolen and used to run down his father. And now in November he'd followed Luther Brady here, to the Blagden & Sons factory or mill or whatever a concrete making-mixing place was called.

And the sand? Sand was a major ingredient in concrete, and just twenty-four hours ago the late Cooper Blascoe had spoken about Brady's life project, the one he'd been funneling church funds into, and how it involved burying concrete pillars in specific locations around the globe . . . in the same pattern as that on the skin from a dead woman's back.

Connect the dots and form a picture. But only part of one. Most of the big picture remained obscured.

Jack knew he wouldn't be part of this particular dot right now if another woman, the one on Beekman Place, hadn't involved him with the Dormentalists.

Manipulated at every turn . . .

He saw his life becoming less and less his own, and loathed the idea. But despite his growing fury he couldn't seem to do a damn thing about it.

He banked his burning frustration and focused on his mission: Was Jamie Grant here?

Keeping an eye out for any security, Jack stayed in the shadows as he crept closer to the building. No sign of guards. Too bad. He would have liked to get his hands on one of Jensen's TPs and wring Jamie's whereabouts from him.

When he reached the building he recognized Jensen's Town Car next to Brady's Mercedes; the cops obviously hadn't latched onto the GP yet—if they ever would. A big Infinity and a Saab he didn't recognize were also parked before the door. Jensen and Brady here but without a squad of TPs. Not what Jack would have expected.

He found a dirt-caked window around the corner. Using the heel of his hand he cleaned a patch large enough to spy on the interior but too small to be noticed.

His attention was drawn immediately to the metal column braced upright under a chute on the far side of the vaulted space. He spotted a group of people on a walkway ten feet off the floor. Jensen was the easiest to recognize. And here came Luther Brady walking toward them.

If only he could hear what they were saying.

19

Luther nodded and greeted the four High Council members who had come along: Glenn Muti, Marissa Menendez, Dick Cunningham, and of course, Bill Blagden. Why did some of the HC feel they had to be present at every pouring? He still hadn't figured out whether they were motivated by a sense of duty or sheer morbidity.

He pulled Jensen aside and lowered his voice.

"Everything ready?"

The big man nodded and rumbled, "All set."

"What about the man? Any trace of him?"

Jensen's already dark face darkened further. "It's like he's vanished off the face of the Earth."

"Well we both know he didn't do that. He has to be somewhere."

"But to find him I've got to know who he is. He's an onion. Every time I peel away one bogus identity, I find another."

"Please keep it down. I don't want the HC to know about this."

He could sense Jensen's frustration, but it was his rising volume that concerned Luther.

Jensen lowered his voice. "Okay, but who *is* this guy? It's like he doesn't exist. How can I find a guy who doesn't exist?"

"Stop obsessing. I have a feeling he'll come to us. Are you fully ready for him?"

"Of course."

Jensen opened his coat to reveal his omnipresent .44 Magnum in a shoulder holster. He had the size to carry the big weapon without showing a bulge.

Luther wondered if he should have brought his Beretta. He was licensed to carry and was an excellent shot. But he doubted he'd have to call on that skill. Especially here. Jensen had wanted to bring along a few of his TPs as security, but Luther had vetoed that. The fewer people who knew the final disposition of Jamie Grant, the better.

"Just be patient," Luther told him, "and it will all work out."

"Let's hope so."

Luther flicked a glance at the HC contingent, then at the cylindrical mold. "They don't know who's inside?"

"No. They think it's just another Null."

"And the original Null has been notified?"

Another nod. "She was heartbroken."

"She'll get over it."

"I promised her next time for sure."

The Compendium had been very specific: In order for a pillar to be valid, to be able to move Opus Omega closer to completion, someone had to die within it. A cadaver would not suffice. The person's life had to be extinguished within the pillar.

In the old days the pillars were solid stone that had to be quarried from specific locations—from stone found near nexus points. In those times a chamber would be hollowed out and a living person sealed within it.

Luther had modernized the process. Instead of stone he'd switched to concrete, but made with sand taken from areas close to nexus points. The sand in tonight's mixture had been taken from an Everglades cenote that housed a nexus point; it was particularly rich in Hokano influence.

He'd fashioned a mold of the proper size that would imprint the symbols in the surface of each pillar. All he had to do was fill it with the special mix Bill Blagden whipped up for him on demand and—*voilà*—a new pillar.

Well, not quite. He needed that final, critical ingredient for each.

When he'd assumed the task of completing Opus Omega, he'd thought to look outside the Church among human flotsam and jetsam for lives to extinguish within the pillars, but that struck him as wrong. He would not sully Opus Omega with worthless lives.

To that end he had created the concept of the Null—the FA whose personal xelton had died. Without a viable PX within, fusion with the Hokano counterpart would be impossible.

Of course, Null status was never identified until the FA had invested a good amount of cash in climbing the FL. Luther made a point of selecting Nulls from the most devoted, most vulnerable—as determined from the interviews conducted after the completion of each rung—most cash-strapped FAs. Invariably they were crushed by the news and devastated by the realization that they would not survive the Great Fusion when this world joined with the Hokano world.

But wait . . . all was not lost. The Church had found a way to reanimate a dead PX. But Xelton Resurrection would require boundless faith, devotion, and courage. XR was being offered only to a few select Nulls deemed worthy of salvation. The XR process would not only revive their PX, but bestow immediate Fusion. They'd achieve FF status without climbing the FL, and be ready to face the GF with heads held high.

Every Null approached over the years had jumped at the chance.

Jensen was always the bearer of this good news. The chosen Null was not told the specifics of the XR process, just that he or she would be traveling to a secret destination for a special kind of missionary work, and would be absent for an indefinite period.

The members of the religion Luther had invented rarely failed to amaze him. A startling number of the XR Nulls climbed right into the cylinder and allowed themselves to be strapped in as if they were going on an amusement park ride. Not all, of course. The ones who developed cold feet when the moment arrived had to be drugged before they were placed in the mold.

Jamie Grant would have the honor of being the first non-Dormentalist to give up her life for the cause since Luther had taken over the Opus. He didn't want the HC members to know that, though. He didn't want to be bothered with their questions or have them start second-guessing him.

"I suppose it's time," he told Jensen. He nodded toward Bill Blagden, the owner of the plant. "I hope Bill remembered to add the accelerator. It's cold in here."

"All taken care of. He told me he added enough calcium chloride to cut set time by two-thirds."

"Excellent. Let's get it done then. But I want to pull the lever this time."

"Any special reason? You know Bill sees the lever as his duty."

"I know. But this woman insulted the Church in print—called us 'Dementedists,' remember?—and was trying to destroy all that we've worked for. Decades of struggle would be negated if she'd been allowed to go public with what she'd learned. She has been a thorn in my side since she first darkened the temple's doorway. I claim the honor of sending this dangerous WA to her destiny."

Jensen nodded. "I'll tell Bill."

Luther had tried not to take Grant's ravings too personally. He didn't *need* to pull the lever himself. He could let Blagden have his usual fun. After all, the important thing was knowing that the bitch would never write or utter another critical word about the Church. That should have been enough.

But it wasn't.

20

Jamie heard a noise above as a shadow fell over her. She craned her neck and saw that a large chute had swung over the opening of the cylinder. She screamed through her gag and ducked her head as she saw the thick, wet, gray concrete begin to sluice toward her.

The pasty, lumpy stream missed her by inches, splattering and clattering instead against the cylinder wall before sliding to the floor.

As she watched it begin to collect just a few feet below her and rise like a riptide, she knew she had only seconds to live. A part of her had accepted the inevitable, but another part refused to give up. So she struggled against the ropes that bound her to the reinforcing rods, trying to slip one of the loops, but they'd been expertly tied . . . by someone who knew what he was doing . . . someone who'd done it before . . . and more than once . . .

Frantic, she looked around. On either side she saw a vertical seam. This cylinder wasn't a single piece, it was two half cylinders bound together. If she could push the side of one of those seams outward, bulge it just a little, maybe the rising concrete would seep through it, and maybe the increasing weight behind would further bulge the cylinder wall, maybe split the seam wider until the cement flowed out rather than up.

She stretched her arms wide, to their limits, straining her weight back and forth against the coils around her torso, inching her fingers toward the seams.

The concrete lapped against her feet, oddly warm, almost comforting.

She pushed harder. Somewhere a knot slipped along one of the reinforcing rods. Not much, but enough to allow her to touch the seams on either side. Her left hand was still exquisitely tender but she pushed through the pain, forcing every fiber of her strength and will into the effort.

The warm cement tide rose to her thighs, her waist.

She moaned behind her gag as the stub of her left pinkie began to spurt blood again. She ignored the agony and pushed hard left and right and—it gave! A small section of the right seam bulged outward, letting in a thin shaft of light.

The concrete was caressing her bare breasts now and moving toward her throat.

Push! *Push!*

Jamie was still pushing when the lumpy tide swirled to her chin, then engulfed her head, filling her nostrils and sealing her eyes.

21

Not much of interest going on in the plant, at least not that Jack could see. Brady and Jensen had had a little tête-à-tête apart from the rest, then rejoined the other four. A little discussion—more like an argument—and then Brady had stepped over to a wall and pulled a lever. A few seconds later, cement started running down the chute and pouring into the tube.

No, not cement—*concrete*. A landscaper Jack worked for in his younger days had always corrected him whenever he made the mistake: cement was only part of concrete, the binding compound. When you added sand and gravel to cement, you ended up with concrete.

Looked like there might be a little defect in the tube. Jack spotted a trickle of thick gray fluid leaking through one of the seams, like brains through a bullet hole. But the trickle never graduated to anything more, and soon it stopped.

Still no sign of Jamie Grant.

While all inside were intent on their pillar manufacture, Jack went over to the cars. He flashed his light into each, front and back—empty—then tried the doors. Jensen's Town Car and the Infinity were unlocked. He popped the trunks on those, but no Jamie.

He thumped on the trunks of Brady's Mercedes and the Saab, saying, "Jamie? It's Jack. If you're in there, kick something, make any noise you can."

Not a sound.

Jamie could be inside the plant, but Jack doubted it. The place looked like a going concern. She'd been gone all day and he couldn't see them stashing her here all that time. Too high a risk of someone seeing her and recognizing her. Her face was all over the news.

No, they'd have brought her somewhere else, someplace isolated.

He just hoped they hadn't hurt her.

He headed back up the hill to the road and his car. When the Dormentalists left, he'd follow Jensen this time. If anyone knew where Jamie was, and if anyone was going to lead Jack to her, it was the GP.

He reached his car, then sat in the dark and waited.

SATURDAY

SATURDAY

1

"Jack, could you please sit down," Gia said. "You're making me nervous."

"Sorry." Jack forced himself to perch on one of the chairs at her kitchen table.

"Have a donut. You haven't touched one."

When their schedules permitted, Jack liked to stop by Gia's early on a Saturday or Sunday with a box of donuts.

He picked up a brown-sugar cruller, crispy on the outside, soft and white within, and nibbled. He wasn't hungry.

"You're looking good this morning, mama," he told Gia.

And she was. Her color was better and she seemed to have more energy.

She smiled. "Thanks. I'm feeling better. I run out of gas sooner than usual, but I should do better as my blood count gets back to normal."

He heard Vicky laugh and looked up. She sat on the far side of the table, reading a book Jack had bought her last month. The sugared crème donut she'd just finished—her favorite—had left her with a snowy mustache. Appropriately she was reading, for the umpteenth time, Ogden Nash's *The Tale of Custard the Dragon*.

"What's so funny, Vicks?"

"Listen," Vicky said, grinning at him. " 'Meowch!' cried Ink, and 'Ooh!' cried Belinda, for there was a pirate, climbing in the winda.' " She laughed again. "*Winda!* I love that part!"

Vicky loved wordplay, which was why Nash was perfect for her.

"I'll get you the sequel. Something about Custard and a Wicked Knight."

"Another Custard book? When are you getting it?"

"Soon as I can find a copy."

As Vicky went back to reading, Jack looked up and found Gia staring at him.

"She's on your mind, isn't she." She spoke in a low tone with a glance across the table. "And I don't mean Miss Big Ears."

Jack had told her about Jamie Grant.

"Yeah. Not only do I not have a clue where she is, I don't even know if she's still, um, with us." He pounded a fist on his knee. "I shouldn't have let her go back to her office."

"And just how were you going to stop her? She's a grown woman who's got a right to make her own decisions. You of all people—"

"I know, I know. It's just . . . I can't help it, I feel . . . responsible."

Jack knew he shouldn't. What could he have done? Abducted her and tied her up in his trunk?—which was probably just what Jensen had done. But if he had done it first she'd be safe right now.

Gia was staring at him. "I thought we agreed that you were going to avoid rough stuff."

"This started off as a missing person thing and I—"

"Missing?" Vicky said. "Who's missing?"

"It's okay," Jack said. "No one you know. And he's been found."

"Oh, good." She went back to her book.

"But the problem," Gia said, speaking barely above a whisper, "is that you've traded one missing person for another. And she may be more than missing, she may be . . . like that poor security guard at the paper. This is not what I call avoiding rough stuff."

"Wasn't supposed to be like this." He sighed. "At least that blackmail fix-it's over with. No rough stuff there."

Clocking a mook over the head with a hot plate didn't really fit Jack's definition of no rough stuff, but he decided not to mention it.

He stifled a yawn. He hadn't gotten much sleep last night. Following Jensen had turned out to be a waste of time. He'd looked for a chance to get in the GP's face—like maybe at a rest stop—and pull a little carjack action. Force Jensen to drive him to Jamie.

But the opportunity had never presented itself. Jensen drove nonstop to a garage on East Eighty-seventh, disappeared inside. He reappeared a few minutes later and entered the apartment building next door.

Home? Probably. Holding Jamie there? No way.

So he'd driven over to the West Side where he spotted the Dormentalist surveillance team still on the job.

Again the question: Watching for her or him?

"Where is she?" he said, thinking aloud.

Gia sipped her tea. "Kind of hard for me to speculate about someone I've never met, but from what you've told me about her, she doesn't sound like a person who'd slink away in silence."

"You've got that right. Even if she was hiding in some kind of foxhole, she'd still be sending dispatches from the front." He balled a fist. "They've got her, damn it. They've got her and I don't know where."

Gia covered his fist with her hand. "You've done all you can. The police are on it, and you pointed them in the right direction. It's out of your hands."

"I suppose it is." Easier to say than accept. "But I've got a bad feeling that this story is not headed for a happy ending."

Gia gave his fist a squeeze but said nothing.

"And on the subject of missing women," Jack said, digging his Tracfone out of his pocket, "I still haven't been able to touch base with the lady who got me involved in this mess in the first place."

He punched in the number for Maria Roselli—the only name he had for her—and listened to her phone ring and ring.

"Still not answering." He stabbed the END button. "I'm going to take a quick walk down to Beekman." A ten-block trip; wouldn't take him long. "She may be there and just not answering."

Jack had told Gia that he'd been hired by a mother to locate her Dormentalist son. It had always been his practice never to mention names, even to her. Gia understood that. He'd felt free to discuss Jamie Grant with her, though, because she hadn't hired him.

But names weren't all he kept from Gia. He never mentioned details that he knew might upset her. Like the flap of Anya's skin, for instance. That was a little too gruesome to share.

He had it folded in the pocket of his jacket now. If he got to see the lady known as Maria Roselli, maybe it would shock her into answering a few questions.

"Be back soon."

"Be careful."

"I was born careful."

Gia rolled her eyes but couldn't hide the hint of a smile. "Oh, puh-*lease*!"

Esteban shook his head. "She's out shopping."

"You're sure?" Jack said.

The two of them stood in the white marble lobby that was becoming familiar to Jack. Too familiar.

"Put her in the cab myself. Mrs. Roselli goes shopping every Saturday morning. She and Benno."

"She takes that big dog shopping?"

Esteban smiled. "Benno goes wherever Mrs. Roselli goes."

"And you gave her my message—about calling me?"

"Of course." He looked offended. "I not only told her, I wrote it down and handed her the note."

"Okay, well do it again. And this time tell her I have something she needs to see."

Esteban nodded. "Something she needs to see . . . I'll tell her."

Jack stepped onto the sidewalk and started walking back uptown. Frustration burned like a furnace in his belly.

Nothing was happening. *Nothing.*

Maybe he should just go with it for now. Kick back and hang with Gia and Vicks for the day and wait for something to break. But he knew he'd be lousy company, his attention constantly wandering elsewhere.

He had to do something.

Maybe go for a ride. To Jersey, perhaps. To a cement plant where they poured concrete into a strange mold.

It was a Saturday in mid-fall. The place might not even be open.

All the better.

He sighed. Probably a waste of time. Certainly nowhere near the fun of making fatso Cordova's life miserable. Jack almost wished he hadn't finished the blackmail fix so quickly.

3

"Sister Maggie?"

"No, this is Sister Agnes. Sister Margaret Mary isn't available at the moment. Can I help you?"

"Oh, hi, Sister. This is Maggie's cousin. I was just calling about Uncle Mike."

"Not bad news, I hope."

"Well, it isn't good. Do you know when she'll be back?"

"She's working in the soup kitchen in the basement of the church. She'll be there until after the midday meal. I can give you the number if you want to call over there."

"No, no, that's okay. Don't even tell her I called. You know how she is. She'll just worry. I'll catch her later."

Richie Cordova hung up the phone.

"Yessiree," he said. "Catch her later."

Jack parked his rented Buick in the same spot as last night, identifiable by the crushed brush and weeds between the two trees. A good spot in the dark but kind of obvious in daylight.

Yeah, well, so what? He'd looked around and hadn't found anyplace better, so this would have to do. Frustration on the Jamie Grant front had made him edgy and grumpy and a little reckless.

The afternoon sun was fading behind a blanket of low clouds as Jack reached the lip of the Wm. Blagden & Sons driveway. He looked down on the plant and its sandy, barren grounds, virtually devoid of vegetation beyond patches of scrub brush and clusters of the ubiquitous and fearless ailanthus.

The place looked more deserted than last night. Not a car in sight. Apparently Blagden & Sons took weekends off—at least this particular weekend.

Figuring the less time out in the open the better, Jack broke into a trot down the steep slope of the entry drive, slowing to a walk when he reached the fleet of silent trucks. He wound through them cautiously. Just because the place looked deserted didn't mean it was.

He made his way to the tall building and found his window with its clean corner of glass. He peeked through. Light filtering through dusty skylights lit an interior much changed since last night. The tall metal cylinder was gone, replaced by a winch-equipped flatbed truck. A large concrete pillar, etched with the angular symbols he'd seen on the cylinder, lay on the truck's bed. Chains and straps locked it down.

This is what they'd been pouring last night. Here was one of the columns Luther Brady was burying all over the world. Was he nuts? It was a hunk of doodad-decorated concrete.

Jack knew there had to be more to it. Brady had to think it was part of some grand plan, a means to some momentous end, else why go to the trouble and expense of building that illuminated globe in a closed-off alcove?

Jack needed a closer look at those symbols.

He rounded the corner to the door where the cars had been parked last night: locked. He'd left his kit of B-and-E tools in the trunk of the rental. He could run up and get them, but hated wasting the time.

Out of curiosity, he stepped around the next corner to a pair of truck-sized double doors and found them unlocked. A thick chain and heavy-duty padlock lay in a bucket to the right.

Jack slipped between the doors and stood in the high, open space, listening. Silence. On guard, he approached the truck and its cargo.

As he stood beside the bed and looked up at the column, studying the symbols, he wished he'd planned this better. He should have brought a camera to photograph the thing. Someone at Columbia or NYU might be able to translate the symbols. He thought again about going back to the car, this time to hunt up a 7-Eleven or drugstore that sold those dinky little disposable cameras. Pick one up and bring it back here and . . .

His scanning gaze passed and then darted back to a small brownish area that bulged amid the unbroken gray of the rest of the column. Enough out of place to pique Jack's curiosity.

He moved to his left until he was directly opposite it. He leaned on the bed of the truck for a closer look. Reddish brown . . . almost like . . .

A chill like cold, wet concrete sludged down Jack's spine.

He levered himself up to the truck bed where he went down onto one knee for a closer look. It did look like blood. If this was part of the design, it was the only one like it that Jack could see.

He pulled out his Spyderco Endura and flipped out the blade. After a quick glance around—still no one coming—he began chipping at the concrete. It took only a few short quick jabs to loosen a dime-sized flake. As it dropped to the bed Jack touched the newly exposed gray surface.

It gave—just a little. It was soft, firm, definitely not concrete. This was flesh. This was someone's hand.

His intestines wound themselves into a Gordian knot as he chipped away more of the thin concrete overlaying the knuckles, revealing more gray flesh. The thumb, the index—this was a left hand—then the middle finger, then the ring, then . . .

The pinkie was a stub . . . a bloody stub.

Jack dropped his other knee to the bed and sagged.

"Oh, shit," he whispered. "Oh, goddamn."

Unlike Jamie's, this one had been recently amputated. And Jamie's shorty had been on her right—

Christ!

Jack crawled over the column and checked the opposite side. There he found a symbol that looked out of place. All the others had been molded into the surface, this one bulged. He began chipping away . . .

. . . another hand . . . and this one with a short pinkie as well . . . an old amputation.

Jamie Grant . . . they'd killed her, drowned her in concrete last night . . . and Christ, he'd stood outside and watched the whole thing. That little leak he'd noticed along the seam . . . had that been Jamie trying to break out? Had she worked her fingers to the edge before her air ran out?

Jack felt a pressure build in his chest. He pounded his fist against the pillar's cold rough surface below the hand.

He'd failed her.

If only he'd known. Maybe he could have saved her . . . or at least tried. Maybe . . .

The sound of a car engine outside stopped the growing string of maybes and pulled Jack to his feet. He looked around at one of the windows and spotted a car pulling up. He jumped down from the truck bed and hid himself behind an array of metal drums stacked against the wall.

The frustration at being unable to locate Jamie was gone, overwhelmed by a black rage that pounded against the inside of his skull. He hoped, *prayed* this was Brady or Jensen—or, better yet, both. He could hear his molars grinding. He wanted to hurt someone connected to the Dormentalist Church. And the higher up, the harder the hurt. Give him the right guy and he might not be able to stop once he got started. Might hurt them to death. Which wasn't so bad. Certain people had it coming.

As he peeked between a pair of drums he saw two men push open the big doors at the opposite end. It wasn't Brady or Jensen, or any of the other four he'd seen up on the catwalk last night.

Shit.

These two didn't look like Dormentalists of any stripe. In fact, Jack thought he recognized the one on the right, the guy wearing the cowboy hat.

Then he remembered. The cowboy was the big-gutted driver of the sand hauler that had damn near killed his father down in Florida. He hadn't been behind the wheel when that happened; his job had been to drive a load of

Otherness-tainted sand from the Everglades nexus point to this plant . . . sand that Jack was sure had been used to make the concrete that entombed Jamie.

Jack reached back and removed the Glock from his SOB holster.

Only two of them. He could take them, even if they were armed. But were they the only ones here? Could be a couple more outside.

He decided to wait and see.

Turned out to be a short wait. The two guys climbed into the truck cab, started her up, and pulled the truck outside. One jumped out to close the doors, and then they were driving away.

Jack eased back outside. The Suburban they'd pulled up in was empty. Just two of them.

He waited until the truck rumbled up to the road and disappeared, then he headed for his car at an easy trot. No need to rush. That big rig couldn't move fast on these winding back roads, and it sure as hell wouldn't be hard to spot.

Jack wanted to see where they intended to inter Jamie Grant. And then they were going to have to answer some tough questions.

5

"Body of Christ," Sister Maggie said as she took the host from the gold-lined pyx and, holding it between her right thumb and forefinger, raised it before Amelia Elkins's wrinkled face.

Amelia responded with a hoarse Amen and opened her mouth.

Maggie placed the wafer of bread on her tongue, and

then they said a prayer of thanksgiving together, Amelia in her wheelchair, Maggie kneeling beside it.

Genny Duncan, the Eucharistic Minister who usually brought Holy Communion to the parish's shut-ins, was ill today, so Maggie had offered to take over for her. She was tired after the long day of working over the ovens and steaming kettles in the Loaves and Fishes, but that didn't mean these poor homebound souls should be denied their weekly communion.

When they finished the prayer, Amelia grabbed Maggie's hand as she rose.

"Can I fix you some tea, sister? I have some brownies my daughter dropped off. We could—"

Maggie patted her hand and smiled. "I wish I could stay, Amelia, really I do, but I have another stop to make."

"Oh. Yes, of course. I'm not the only one who needs communion, I suppose. I was just hoping . . ."

Poor thing, Maggie thought as she replaced the cover on the pyx. So lonely.

"Tell you what I *can* do, though," she said. "I can stop by tomorrow around midday and we can have lunch together. I'll bring—"

"Sunday lunch!" Amelia said, beaming. "And you won't bring a thing. I'll fix us some nice sandwiches. Do you like tuna fish salad?"

Maggie wasn't fond of anything made with mayonnaise, but she put on a brave face. "I'll bet you make a delicious one."

"I do. These old legs may be unreliable, but I can still whip up a mean salad. What time can you be here?"

"How does one o'clock sound?"

"One o'clock it is!" She looked years younger. "I'll have everything ready when you arrive."

A few minutes later Maggie was hurrying down the rickety stairway from Amelia's third-floor apartment, wondering if she might be spreading herself too thin. She had such trouble saying no to people in need.

She stepped out onto the sidewalk and looked around. The light faded so early these days. She checked her watch. Just five o'clock and already the sun was down.

Well, only one more stop to go. She checked her list. Mr. Whitcolm lived just a few blocks away. Wonderful. She'd be back at the convent in time to set the dinner table.

She took two steps toward Fourth Street, then stopped.

"Thank you, Lord," she whispered. "Thank you for this second chance to do Your will, and to help those who can't help themselves."

As she started walking again a car pulled into the curb beside her. She angled closer to the buildings. The neighborhood was a lot safer than it used to be, but still had more than its share of drug dealers and other unsavory types.

"Miss?" said a man's voice.

Maggie slowed but didn't stop. She saw only one person in the car. A very large man, taking up most of the front seat as he leaned across from the driver's side. His features were indistinguishable in the waning light, his face little more than a pale moon floating just inside the front passenger window, but she was sure she didn't know him.

"I'm lost. Can you help me?"

The car wasn't flashy like the ones the drug dealers drove, and not a rattletrap like some of their customers'. Just a normal, everyday, respectable-looking Jeep. A family car.

Still, you had to be careful.

"I've been driving in circles down here," he said, a plaintive note in his voice. "All I need is someone to point me in the right direction."

She'd had to say no to Amelia. The least she could do was help out this lost man. She stepped closer to the car.

"Where do you want to go?"

"One of the housing projects."

"Which one? Jacob Riis? Lillian Wald? There's more than one down here."

"I'm not sure. My wife wrote it down for me but she has terrible penmanship." He thrust his arm out the window. A slip of paper fluttered in this hand. "Can you make sense of this chicken scratch?"

Keeping her distance from the car, Maggie pulled the slip from his fingers and squinted at it in the twilight. He hadn't been exaggerating about the penmanship. It was terrible. Obviously his wife hadn't attended Catholic school. She thought she could make out an uppercase *M* and *T* on two adjacent words.

"It might be Masaryk Towers."

"That sounds right. Where are they?"

"Farther downtown. Are you sure . . . ?"

"Something wrong?"

She'd never been inside the Masaryk Towers but had heard them referred to as a "vertical ghetto." It did not seem the kind of place a middle-class white man would want to go.

"Well, it has a rough reputation."

"Really? Maybe I'll just drive by. If it looks too rough I'll just keep on going and come back during the day."

"That might be a good idea." She pointed east. "Go up here, make a right on Avenue C, and take it down to East Houston. You can't miss it."

"Thank you very much. Are you going that way? The least I can do is give you a lift."

Yes, Maggie was going that way, but no, she didn't want to get into this stranger's car.

"That's very kind of you, but I have just a little ways to go and I need the exercise."

"Okay," he said. "I thought it only fair to offer." He held his hand out the window, not quite as far as last time. "Thanks for your help. I just need that address back."

"Oh, of course."

She'd forgotten that she still had it. She stepped closer, holding it out. But instead of taking the paper, the man grabbed her wrist. As he yanked her forward, his other hand darted from the window and grabbed a fistful of her hair. Her scalp burned and she cried out in pain and terror. He pulled her arm and head through the window and into the car. Maggie screamed and then something hard and heavy slammed against the back of her head. Her vision blurred. She opened her mouth for another scream but then something hit her again, harder this time.

Twilight became night.

6

Traffic had been awful. Everything seemed to be under construction. Three-and-a-half hours since leaving Jersey and rolling onto the Pennsylvania Turnpike, and they were only in the Reading area. Where in hell were these guys going?

Jack saw the truck's turn signal begin to flash and he followed it into a rest area. About time. He needed to make a pit stop and get some gas. But first . . .

He watched the driver and his buddy get out of their truck and head for the restaurant area. They locked the cab doors but left the big diesel engine running. Jack hurried around to his trunk and pulled the slim jim from his duffel bag of tools. Then he made his way to the passenger side. The truck cab was old and beat up. Probably didn't have a working alarm system, but you never knew.

Jack stepped up on the running board and looked around. The lot was mostly empty and quiet except for the rumble of traffic. Turnpike rest stops did not seem a popular Saturday night destination.

He slipped the slim jim down between the window and the door panel, moved it around in a circular motion until it caught. Jack took a breath, then pulled up. The lock knob on the other side of the window popped up.

No alarm. But now the real test: He removed the slim

jim and opened the door. The courtesy lights came on, but again, no alarm.

Great.

He leaned inside and pawed through the papers piled at the center of the bench. Mostly toll receipts and maps. He picked up a Pennsylvania map and noticed that someone had crisscrossed it with red lines. A place where three of those lines intersected, out past Harrisburg and Camp Hill, was circled. A piece of plain white paper was clipped to an upper corner of the map. Jack scanned the typewritten note and realized it was a set of directions from the Turnpike to "the farm."

He wondered how much these two drivers knew. Were they just doing a job, just making a delivery? Or did they know what lay inside that hunk of concrete? Their lack of furtiveness led Jack to suspect they knew nothing, but the only way to be sure was to ask.

He refolded the map and slipped out of the cab, relocking the door as he went.

Still a fair number of miles ahead of them. Jack would definitely need a full gas tank. He'd also need a little food and drink before he set out again.

Looked like it was going to be a long night. He wanted to see this "farm" and find out what they planned for Jamie's remains.

And then he'd get answers to his questions.

7

Richie Cordova looked down at Sister Maggie where she sat tied to a nice, sturdy oak chair, looked into her eyes and saw the fear and confusion there.

He reveled in the moment. Hard to believe that less

than an hour ago he'd been terrified, ready to call the whole thing off.

All well and good to work up a plan to snatch a nun off the street, but getting down to the job of doing it . . . that's a whole other story. He'd smeared mud on his plates so no one could report the number, he'd had the sap ready, he'd juiced himself with fury, but when he'd spotted her walking and pulled into that curb . . . man, he'd switched from being pissed to almost pissing his pants.

But he'd made himself do it. It was pretty dark, no one around with a clear line of sight—now or never. And he had to do it right. If he blew it, he'd never get another chance.

He'd pulled it off, clubbing her unconscious and then speeding away with her slumped and huddled on the passenger side floor. But even then he hadn't been able to relax. What if someone had seen? What if some nosy old bitch had been watching out her window and reported it? Not that it was likely or would even matter. He was driving a nondescript Jeep—had to be a million of them in the city—with unreadable plates.

Still . . . you never could tell. Driving along he'd spent so much time looking into the rearview mirror he almost ran down a pedestrian.

But no one gave him a second look on his way to this urban wasteland west of Northern Boulevard in Flushing. And now he was here, hidden away in a rundown warehouse he'd sniffed out yesterday, where no one would interrupt him.

And now that he had her here, securely trussed up like a prelibato salami, his fear was gone, evaporated, replaced by a strange elation. He'd always got a kick out of how the blackmail game let him call the shots and generally mess up people's lives. But that had always been a long-distance involvement, with contact limited to phone calls and mail.

But this . . . he'd never experienced anything like *this*.

Sister Margaret Mary was his to do with as he pleased. He wasn't just pulling her strings, he *owned* her.

God, it was like sex.

And he hadn't laid a finger on her. Yet.

He was learning things about himself, things he'd never imagined. This was turning out to be more that just payback, it was a voyage of self-discovery.

But maybe he shouldn't go all that deep about it, seeing as what today's Gemini horoscope had to say.

You may feel compelled to overanalyze things at work, but resist. A colleague becomes more expressive when you talk first. In time, you'll see that problems at work were a godsend.

He was kind of awed by that last part. His problems at "work" were already becoming a sort of "godsend." And when he thought about it, Sister Maggie was a colleague in a way. At least they'd worked together. Sort of. For sure she was going to become more expressive, and he was definitely going to talk first.

"Do you know who I am?" he said, moving closer and standing over her. "Do you have any idea the trouble you've caused me?"

She shook her head and made begging sounds through her gag.

Even though no one would hear her even if she screamed at the top of her voice, Richie decided to leave the gag in place. He didn't want to listen to no bullshit. It was his place to do the talking, and hers to listen.

"I'm the guy who took those pretty pictures of you and Metcalf."

The way her eyes went wide, showing white all around, shot a bolt of ecstasy toward his groin.

"That's right. Me. But guess what happened? Someone came around and messed up all my files . . . destroyed them. Ain't that a pity? I don't know who that someone was, but I think—no, I'm *sure* I know who sent him. And you're going to tell me all about him."

He savored for a moment the tears that filled her eyes
and ran down her cheeks to the gag, then he rummaged
through the toolbox he'd brought along. He wanted the
straight dope when he asked a question. That might require a little softening up. Or it might not. He wouldn't
know until he removed the gag, and he didn't plan to do
that for a while.

A boy's gotta have his fun, right?

He found the ice pick and held it up where she could
see it.

"But first, a little truth serum."

Jack wasn't sure how to play this.

Here he was, following the Blagden truck down this
bumpy country road in the dark. The very dark. The
moon hadn't risen, not a street lamp in sight, and he and
the truck were the only vehicles on the road.

They'd turned off the Turnpike miles ago, then wound
into these low hills. No way they couldn't know someone
was coasting along behind them. But did they care?

That was the question. If they knew they'd been hauling a murdered woman's body across state lines, they'd
be more than a little paranoid and watching their
rearview mirrors. They might even pull over to let a following car pass.

But if they believed they were hauling a weird chunk
of concrete and nothing more, they wouldn't care who
was behind them.

Although the truck had made no evasive maneuvers,
Jack decided to play it safe and proceed on the assumption that the drivers knew the score.

So when he saw the truck slow and make a cautious turn onto an even narrower road, Jack drove on by. He spotted two sets of headlights sitting atop a rise. Through his rearview he watched the truck climb to the top of the rise and stop by the headlights.

Jack killed his own lights and pulled over. He stepped out of the car and found himself facing what looked like an open field, overgrown and bordered by a rickety wire fence. He checked the sky. Broken cloud cover blocked most of the starshine. He looked around for signs that the moon might be rising but found no telltale glow. Good. The less light the better.

He hopped over the wire and made his way in a crouch through the tall grass toward the lights.

He dropped lower as he neared the top of the rise, then stopped and squatted just out of reach of the headlights.

The flatbed and two pickups sat angled around a pit that looked maybe seven or eight feet wide. From the size of the mound of excavated dirt piled to the side, Jack guessed it was a pretty deep hole.

Deep enough to swallow Jamie's concrete sarcophagus.

Four men with shovels, plus one of the drivers, stood around the rim showing not a hint of furtiveness. That persuaded Jack that they probably wouldn't be able to add anything to what he already knew. He'd made the trip for nothing.

No . . . not for nothing. He'd learned where they were burying Jamie Grant.

The driver on the ground made a signal to his partner in the flatbed's cab. As Jack watched, the truck's winch began to raise the forward end of the pillar, tilting the butt over the black maw of the hole.

Jack's instincts spurred him to put a stop to this now. Jamie deserved better. But he'd be taking on six men; some of them could be armed. Better to let them complete their work. This way at least he'd know where to find Jamie when the time came to arrange for a proper burial.

And another reason for holding back: As long as he knew where to find the pillar—literally where the body was buried—it remained a potential weapon against Brady and Jensen. What he had to do now was figure out how to use it to inflict maximum damage.

So he held his place and his breath and watched the pillar angle up, up, up, then slip off the truck bed and into the hole.

9

In Midtown Manhattan an old woman cries out and clutches her back as pain lances through her. Her dog, a Rottweiler, stands beside her, legs stiff, body tense, barking in sympathy.

She knows the cause of her suffering.

Another one . . . they've buried another one. They must be stopped before it's too late.

But she can't do it. Someone else must act on her behalf.

10

Jack's thoughts raced ahead of his car as he cranked east-ward on the Penn Turnpike. How to get the most out of that pillar . . .

Nothing was coming. He was dry . . . dry as the earth they'd backfilled into Jamie's grave.

East of Harrisburg he gave up and switched on the radio. Maybe he could zone out on music for a while, then tackle the problem with a fresh head. But he couldn't find anything he felt like listening to. He wished he'd brought along some of his CDs, but realized he probably wouldn't want to listen to them either.

The problem wasn't with the music, but with him. He wouldn't feel right, wouldn't be himself until he'd fixed this.

He switched to AM and picked up a strong, clear signal from WABC in New York. He hung on through a commercial to see which one of their stable of talk show geeks had the mike tonight, but instead wound up in the middle of the top-of-the-hour news update. He was reaching for the SEEK button when he heard . . .

"No word yet on the missing nun. Sister Margaret Mary O'Hara was last seen being pulled into a car from a Lower East Side sidewalk earlier this evening. The witness did not know the make or color of the car, and couldn't read the license plate. If you have any information on this incident—any information at all—please call . . ."

Feeling as if his bones were dissolving, Jack veered through the right lane and onto the shoulder where he stopped and set the shift into park.

He leaned his head back and closed his eyes, his
hands squeezing the steering wheel as if trying to stran-
gle it.

He's got her . . . the son of a bitch has got her.

But how could he have known it was Maggie?

An instant of self-doubt pierced him, but then faded as
he reviewed all the moves he'd made in the Cordova fix.
He was certain—*knew*—that he hadn't left the faintest
link to Maggie.

She must have made a slip talking to him.

Jack pounded the steering wheel. "Shit! Shit! Shit!"

All that effort to make the fix look like an accident—
for nothing. Cordova knew, and he had her. God knew
what he was going to do with her. Or was doing to her. Or
had already done to her.

A slimeball like Cordova . . . didn't deserve to live . . .
shouldn't have bothered finessing the fix. Oxygen waster
like him . . . best thing to do—for his victims and for the
human gene pool—was to walk up to him and deliver a
hollowpoint between the eyes.

But Jack hadn't wanted to set himself on that road.
Feared once he started traveling it he might not be able to
step off. He'd approached Cordova as a guy who wasn't
doing anyone physical harm—his bloodletting was emo-
tional and financial—so Jack had taken a parallel approach. Cordova was hands off, so Jack had gone the
hands-off route.

He realized now that was a mistake. A bullet to the
brain would have solved the Cordova problem. Quick,
clean, easy. No more blackmail, and sure as hell no worry
about a good-hearted nun being abducted.

A mood cold and black settled on Jack as he threw the
Buick back into drive and merged with the eastbound
traffic.

He knew where Cordova lived, where he worked. He'd
find him. And if that fat slug had done anything to Sister
Maggie, if he'd harmed her in any way . . .

11

Richie Cordova wiped the blood from his shaking hands. His hands weren't all that was shaking. His whole body was twitching. Like someone had shoved a live lamp cord up his ass.

Richie knew a few guys who might think that felt good, but he felt sick.

He turned toward the nun—or what was left of her—still tied in the chair, and quickly turned away. He couldn't look at her, couldn't believe how he'd let himself get so out of control.

No . . . not out of control. *In* control. Complete control. Of her. It had thrown some sort of switch in him, made him do things he'd never dreamed he was capable of thinking up, let alone doing.

He'd planned to kill her. That was a sure thing. Ain't no way she was leaving once he got her here. But he'd wanted to punish her some first, for ruining his game, and to get her to tell him all about it, sing the song he wanted to hear.

And she'd sung. Held out for an amazingly long time, but finally she'd started to sing. Oh, how she sang. Told him all about meeting a guy named Jack in a place called Julio's and hiring him to get back the pictures of her and Metcalf, how Metcalf didn't know nothing about it, how she'd called him and told him not to worry no more. She'd sung about how she hadn't known Richie's name. Only this guy Jack knew that and he wouldn't tell her.

Richie should have stopped then and ended it. He had what he wanted, so the thing to do was slit her throat and call it a night. He'd had the razor all set. Unlike the .38s in his pistol, a razor couldn't be traced.

But he hadn't used it. Because he couldn't stop—didn't *want* to stop. He had control, he was in the driver's seat and he didn't want to use no brakes, didn't want to let go of the steering wheel.

Only when the last of her life had leaked away did he come out of it. Then he'd stepped back and looked at what he'd done. And blew lunch.

He felt a little better now, but not much. It suddenly came to him that this was partly Neva's fault. A lot of the time he spent working on the nun he'd been thinking of his ex-wife, seeing her face. Yeah. Her fault. If she hadn't been such a . . .

Anyway, it was over. At least this part of it. He'd hide the body, try not to think about what he'd done, and move on to the next step.

And that was finding this Jack guy. That was real important, because this Jack knew who he was. Once he was out of the way, any connection between Richie Cordova and the missing Sister Margaret Mary would be gone.

But the nun couldn't remember his phone number—oh, she'd *wanted* to remember, Richie made sure of that, but it wasn't there.

Which left him with the name of an Upper West Side bar called Julio's. Richie wasn't sure how he was going to work this. He was at a disadvantage not knowing what this Jack looked like. The nun had given him a description but it sounded like any one of a zillion guys. He'd sleep on it and see if he came up with anything.

Sleep. Yeah, that would be good. He was dead on his feet.

But first he had to deal with the body.

Steeling himself, he turned and walked toward it . . .

12

Jack wasn't dressed for Beekman Place but he was in too foul a mood to play games.

He'd been to Cordova's house—picked his way in and searched it from basement to attic. Not a trace of Sister Maggie.

Next stop was Hurley's. If Cordova had snatched her, chances were slim that he'd be hanging out at his favorite bar. Then again, if he'd killed her and dumped her body, he might feel the need for a few drinks, and maybe an alibi as well. But Jack couldn't find him at Hurley's either. Even checked out the men's room. No Cordova.

Last stop had been the office: same story.

Jack had made another swing by Cordova's house—just in case he'd returned in the interim—but it looked as empty as when he'd left it. He'd parked down the street and watched the place.

Where *was* the fat slimeball? Jack's mind shied away from imagining what he'd done to Maggie. If Jack could find him, Cordova would tell him where she was. Jack would see to that.

But after an hour of sitting, Cordova hadn't shown. Good chance he might not show at all.

So Jack decided to pay a visit to the third woman who'd entered his life this week.

Esteban wasn't on the door and his late-shift coworker, a brawny black guy, wouldn't let Jack into the lobby.

His arm blocked his name tag as he opened the glass door six or seven inches and eyed Jack's wrinkled jeans and sweatshirt. "Are you on Mrs. Roselli's visitor list?"

"I don't know about the list, but she's expecting me. Just call her and say Jack's here for a follow-up chat."

"I don't know. This is pretty late for her."

"Just call her and see. I'll wait out here."

He nodded. "I know you will."

He closed the door and went to the lobby phone. Jack leaned close to the gap between the glass door and glass wall. He blocked his street-side ear and listened.

"Mrs. Roselli? Sorry to bother you, but there's a man here. He says his name is Jack and that you're expecting him . . . Pardon me? . . . Oh, I see . . . I'm sorry to hear that . . . is there anything I can do? . . . Are you sure? I can call a . . . Yes. Yes, I see. I'll tell him. And remember, if you need anything, anything at all, I'm right here . . . Right. Good-night. Feel better."

Jack backed off a step as the call ended. Sounded like the old lady was sick.

The doorman returned to the door. Jack saw now that his tag read *Louis*. He opened it wider this time. Apparently his talk with the old lady had reassured him about Jack.

"She's not feeling well. Says to come back tomorrow."

"She okay?"

"She doesn't sound too hot, but she didn't want a doctor, so . . ." He shrugged. "I'm here if she needs me."

"Good. I don't want anything happening to her."

Jack turned and walked off. Half a block away he hunched his shoulders against a sudden chill. He'd met three new women this week. Now, in the space of twenty-four hours, one was dead, one was missing, and the other was sick. Was he carrying a curse? Had he become some sort of Jonah?

What the hell was going on?

SUNDAY

1

The news came a little after nine.

With nothing better to do with his pent-up energy, Jack had been cleaning his apartment. He yearned for a cleaning service, but they might come across things they weren't meant to see. Gia sometimes helped, but today he was on his own.

He had the tuner set to 880 AM, an all-news station. Usually he cleaned to the gentle refrains of ZZ-Top or the Allman Brothers, but today he was looking for updates on the missing nun story. The morning papers had nothing new. If news hit, the radio would have it first.

Jack was mopping the linoleum floor of his kitchen when it came. It wasn't good.

The body of Sister Margaret Mary O'Hara had been found in Flushing—a guy chasing his runaway dog had discovered it. No other details were available. Police would not discuss the state of the body or anything else.

Sickened, Jack put down the mop and dropped into a kitchen chair. Two of the three women were dead. He knew each of their killers. Brady and Jensen had buried Jamie Grant alive. And Cordova . . . Jack wasn't an eye-witness, but he didn't have to be. He knew.

Question was . . . what should he do about it? How should he deal with them two without exposing himself?

He closed his eyes and rolled the people and the circumstances around and around in his brain . . . like a concrete mixer.

Brady, Jensen, Cordova, Blascoe, the temple . . . Blascoe, Brady, the temple, Cordova, Jensen . . .

And slowly, painfully, a plan began to form.

2

Goddamn stupid dog!

Richie Cordova sat in Hurley's and wanted to rip the TV off the wall and boot it through the front window.

He'd stashed the nun's body where no one would find her—at least no human—until she began to stink. He hadn't counted on no runaway dog.

He sat at a corner table and stuffed another donut into his mouth. Hurley's put out coffee and donuts and bagels on Sunday morning. Of course the bar was open too in case you wanted a Bloody Mary or something. But Richie had been feeling so good he didn't need no drink. Not anymore.

Shit, he thought as he washed the donut down with black coffee. This complicated things. The Jack guy she'd told him about already had the advantage of knowing what Richie looked like, while Richie didn't know him from Joe Blow. Richie's one advantage had been surprise—Jacko wouldn't have had a clue someone might be looking for him. But now he'd be on guard. That was, if he connected the nun's death to Richie. If he didn't, well, that would be great, but Richie had to assume the worst.

He'd awakened this morning feeling lots better than last night—over the shakes and actually feeling kind of good. Almost like he'd feel after a night of sex. Kind of peaceful inside. At ease. Like he could go for a Sunday morning drive and not get pissed at the other drivers.

But all that was ruined now. The stink of spilled beer cut through the smell of the coffee and Richie lost his appetite. Hurley's wasn't so inviting no more.

Richie paid up and stepped out into the bright morning sunlight. Now what?

He thought about heading for the Upper West Side and finding this Julio's. The nun had said she'd met Jack there twice, both times in the day, and that the guy had been alone at a table near the back wall.

So why not check out Julio's? Hang out on the street and watch the comers and goers, maybe peek through the window and see who's got a table by the back wall.

Richie liked the idea. Sort of preliminary surveillance. Get to know the lay of the land.

He turned and headed toward the subway.

3

Ron Clarkson twitched like an ant who'd found coke in a sugar bowl. If he'd had antennae he'd have been hovering a couple feet off the ground.

"I gotta be crazy for letting you in here," he said as he led Jack down a fluorescent-lit corridor. Tiled walls, drains in the concrete floor. "I'm gonna lose my job, I just know it."

Ron was rail thin with pale shoulder-length hair and a goatee. He earned his daily bread as an attendant at the City Morgue in the basement of Bellevue Hospital. He didn't owe Jack any favors, he simply liked cash under the table. Every so often—rare, but it happened—Jack had need of a body part. He'd place an order with Ron and they'd agree on a price. They'd usually meet off campus, say at a McDonald's or a diner, and make the exchange.

Today was the first time Jack had asked for a viewing. And he'd handed over a stiff price for it.

He didn't want to be here. He simply knew he had to be. He felt he owed it to Sister Maggie.

"You're not backing out, are you?" Jack put a menacing edge on his voice. "You took the dough, you do the show."

"Never should have said yes. Man, this is so crazy."

"Ron . . ."

"All right, all right. It's just . . ."

"Just what?"

"It's just that this case is hot—I mean it's steaming. Cardinal Ryan is all over City Hall, the mayor's all over the commish, the commish is all over the ME and crime scene crew. We got maybe a half hour before they start posting her—on a Sunday, can you believe it?—and here I am bringing you down for a look-see. I must be crazy."

"If you'd have gotten it done instead of running your mouth, I'd be on my way out by now."

"Yeah, but—"

"Just one quick look. A peek. That's all I want."

"I never figured you for getting off on something like that."

They passed some empty gurneys, and one not so empty. A green sheet covered a still form. Jack was about to ask if that was her but Ron wasn't slowing. Guess not.

"I knew her."

"Oh, shit. Then maybe you don't want to see her. I got a glimpse and . . ." He shook his head. "It ain't nice."

"All the more reason."

But he didn't want to see her. He felt as if his legs were slowly turning to stone, refusing to move him down the hall. He forced them forward, one step after the other after the other . . .

"I don't get it. Why?"

Because I need to do this to make sure I don't hesitate when I do what has to be done.

"None of your business, Ron."

"Okay. But you'll be sorry."

I know, he thought. But not as sorry as someone else.

Ron pushed through a set of steel double doors into a green-tiled room where a guy who looked like Malcolm X was studying a chemistry book.

"Crime lab," Ron said, jerking his thumb at Jack. "Needs another look. She still in 12-C?"

The black guy nodded and went back to his chemistry.

Through another set of double doors and into a big white-tiled room that felt like a refrigerator. Latched drawers lined the walls. Ron made a beeline for a drawer near the floor. The rollers screeched as he pulled it out.

"Needs a little lube," he said with a quick, weak smile.

A black body bag lay on a steel tray. Ron made no move. Jack looked up and found him staring at him.

"Well?"

"You're sure?"

No. Not sure. Not sure at all. But he nodded.

"Do it."

Ron grabbed the zipper, pulled it halfway down, and spread the flaps.

Jack caught flashes of a crimson mosaic of torn flesh, then turned away.

"Jesus God!"

Probably could have stared indefinitely if he hadn't known her. But he had. A sweet woman. And someone had turned her into . . . a thing.

"Told you, man."

Jack spoke past the bile collecting in his throat. "Close her up."

"What? That's it? I risk my neck bringing you down here and—"

"Close. Her. *Up*."

After he'd heard the zipper, Jack turned around and stared down at the glistening surface of the body bag.

You poor woman . . .

He tried to imagine how she must have suffered before she died, but it was beyond him. He felt the blackness he kept caged in a far country of his being break free and surge through him.

He looked up and Ron jumped back.

"Hey, man! Don't blame me. I didn't do it!"

Jack voice was a metallic rasp. "I know."

"Then don't look at me like that. Shit, for a second there I thought you were gonna kill me."

"No . . . not you."

4

"You locked the door?" Abe said as Jack approached the rear counter.

Jack nodded.

The Isher Sports Shop was otherwise empty, but it could have been any day of the week. Traffic in Abe's store was never exactly heavy.

The darkness still suffused him, but he had it under control. At least for the moment.

Abe was leaning on the counter, wearing what he wore every other day.

"I need some hardware."

"So you said. Hardware I got. What kind?"

"A Beretta 92."

It would have been so much easier to discuss this over the phone, but one never knew when the Big Ear might be listening. And the code Jack and Abe had developed wouldn't cover the specifics of this particular purchase.

Abe frowned. "You've already got a PT 92 Taurus. It's the same pistol. Except for the safety, of course."

"I know, but I need a Beretta."

"Why?"

"I'll explain later."

Abe shrugged. "Okay. You're paying. I'll call around tomorrow and see who—"

"I need it today, Abe. And in stainless steel."

"Stainless steel? *Gevalt!* Impossible! You're asking me to move mountains, and believe me, my mother didn't name me Mohammed. You want a Glock 19, fine; you want an HK-MP5, that I can do. But a stainless-steel Beretta 92 on a Sunday? As my Italian neighbors in the Bensonhurst of my boyhood used to say, Fuhgeddaboudit."

"Got to have it before tonight, Abe. Really important. I'll owe you."

"Already you owe me." When Jack said nothing, Abe shrugged again. "All right, and I owe you too, but . . ."

His voice trailed off as he stared at Jack. It made Jack a little uncomfortable.

"But what?"

"But nothing. I'm seeing that look on your face."

"What look?"

"I know it, Jack. I've seen it before. And more often than not, when I see it, someone winds up shuffling off their mortal coil."

Jack knew he tended to let his guard down with Abe, but even with reins on the darkness, was it that obvious? He'd have to watch himself.

"Maybe it's because it's not yet noon and I've had a very bad day."

"Something's wrong? Gia and Vicky—?"

Jack held up a hand. "They're fine. It's no one you know. At least personally."

Interest lit in his eyes. "And that means?"

Abe knew Jamie Grant from reading *The Light*. Maybe Jack could use her as a carrot.

"The Beretta, Abe? Get me that Beretta before tonight and I'll tell you what happened to Jamie Grant."

"*The Light* reporter?" Abe made a grumbling noise. "You make your best friend in the whole world *earn* a little news?"

"In this case, yes. Here's the math: Beretta equals story. Because without the Beretta there won't be any story to tell. At least not this week."

"For next week I can't wait. I'll start making calls. And then you'll tell me?"

Jack nodded. "If it goes down, yeah."

He had to position the pieces where he needed them, otherwise he'd lose this week's window and have to move it to next. Didn't want to do that. He wanted this to go down *tonight*.

5

Jack closed the top drawer of Cordova's receptionist's desk. He now had the fat man's phone numbers—home and cell. Next stop, the filing cabinets.

He leafed through the folders in the top drawer, checking out age and sex of the clients. Some contained photos. Jack pulled out males in their thirties until he had a stack of six. Then he started dialing, pretending to be calling from the electric company.

All of the first batch were home. So he went back to the cabinet. One in the second batch didn't answer. Lee Dobbins. Jack studied his picture and vital statistics. Lee lived and worked in Queens. He'd suspected his business partner in their real estate firm of dealing with the competition. The wad of photos in the file—taken by Cordova, no doubt—had confirmed his suspicions. Jack memorized the salient points, then filed Dobbins back with all the others.

He then turned on the computer. He typed a note and printed it out under the Cordova Investigations Ltd. letterhead. He tri-folded it and stuck it in a pocket.

Hey, Lee Dobbins, Jack thought as he exited the office. You just got yourself a new best buddy. Me.

Jack knew he'd have to tread carefully here. Had to assume that Sister Maggie had told Cordova everything she knew—which wasn't much beyond Julio's and how Jack looked. He'd have to alter his appearance some.

The other possible hitch was Cordova calling to check Jack's story and finding Dobbins home. Jack could finesse that by calling Dobbins just before he met Cordova. If still no answer, he was golden. If he picked up . . . well . . . forget finesse then.

6

Richie Cordova jumped when his cell phone started ringing. Who'd be calling him on a Sunday afternoon? Sure as hell wouldn't be Neva. Eddy?

He'd been chilling—in the physical as well as the slang sense—outside Julio's for a couple of hours. The place wasn't real busy but had a steady trickle in and out. Richie had taken a couple of peeks in the front window. From what he could see through all the dead hanging plants—what was up with that?—it looked like a typical neighborhood bar. Reminded him of Hurley's, and how he wished he was nursing a shot and a beer there instead of hanging out here on a street far from home. He'd promised himself to stay around until three or so, then head back to do just that. The Giants had the four o'clock game against Dallas and he didn't want to miss it.

Hours of watching and still nobody sitting at one of the rear tables. Everyone clustered around the bar where the TV was.

And now someone was calling him. He pulled out the phone, flipped it open, and thumbed the SEND button.

"Yeah?"

"Mr. Cordova?" said a funny-sounding voice he didn't recognize.

"Who's this?"

"My name's Louis Gorcey and—"

"How'd you get this number?"

"I was just about to tell you that. I'm friends with Lee Dobbins and he gave it to me. He recommends you very highly."

Dobbins . . . Dobbins . . . Oh yeah. The real estate guy. But he didn't have Richie's cell number. Or did he? Richie sometimes gave it out to clients when he needed to stay real close to a situation.

"That's nice of him, but—what did you say your name was?"

"It's Gorcey. Louis Gorcey."

Something about the way he said his *s*'s . . . he sounded like a fag.

"Well, Mr. Gorcey, I'm glad Lee recommended me, but this is Sunday. My office is closed. If you want to call back first thing tomorrow morning—"

"It can't wait till then. The window of opportunity is tonight. It *has* to be tonight."

"Sorry, I—"

"Please hear me out. This is very important to me and I'll make it well worth your while."

Well worth your while . . . he liked the sound of that. But it *was* Sunday . . . and the Giants were playing Dallas . . .

"I'll pay you a thousand dollars cash just to meet with me and listen to my problem. If you aren't interested, then the money's yours to keep."

"This must be one hell of a problem."

"It's not so much a matter of magnitude as timing. We have to meet this afternoon because the window opens tonight."

A thousand bucks . . . that would be the best hourly rate he'd ever earned. And an hour was all it would be.

Richie had already decided to get the money up front, listen, and say no thanks. Then he'd head for Hurley's and the game. Worst-case scenario was he'd miss part of the first quarter.

"Okay. You've got a deal. You know where my office is?"

He didn't, so Richie gave him the address. They'd meet there in half an hour.

A nasty suspicion crawled up his back as he thumbed the END button. What if this was the nun's Jack? What if he'd heard about Sister Maggie and decided to give Richie a dose of the same medicine?

He shook it off. Crazy. The nun had hired the guy to do a job and he did it. End of story. If something happened to the client afterward, so what? Not his business, not his worry.

Besides, not only did this Gorcey sound like a fag, but he knew Dobbins and had Richie's cell number.

Still, maybe he should do a little checking up before the meet.

7

Jack finally found Preston Loeb's number in an old notebook. They'd met in a martial arts class back in their twenties. Preston had been involved in one of Jack's early fix-its.

The second ring was answered by a soft, "Hello, Preston speaking."

"Preston? This is Jack." When silence followed he added, "From Ichi-san's class, remember?"

"Jack! How've you been, dearie? You never call, you never write—"

"I need a favor, Pres. A little sartorial guidance."

"You? Oh, don't tell me you're finally going to get with it! At your age? Well, better late than never, I guess. And you want me to do the *Queer Eye* thing for you? I'm flattered."

Even if he had the time—which he didn't—Jack was not in the mood for banter. But he tried to keep it light.

"I need help looking like someone who might be a friend of yours."

A pause, and then, "Now *that's* interesting. When would you want to—?"

"Now. As in right away. You free?"

"Just working on some sketches, and you know I don't like football, so, why not? Meet me at . . . let's see . . . how about Praetoria on Green Street?"

Way downtown in SoHo. He'd have to hurry.

"I'm leaving now."

"And now tell me, dearie, just *why* you of all people would want to look queer? You haven't crossed the street, have you?"

Preston Loeb stood six-one with a slim build; long, curly black hair—in the old days it had been straight— framed his handsome face. He wore a snug, vaguely fuzzy, short-sleeve, baby-blue sweater. His cream-colored slacks were tight down to the knees where they flared into outlandish bellbottoms. A black alligator shoulder bag completed the picture.

They stood just inside the entrance to Praetoria, a men's store with a twenty-foot ceiling and front windows nearly as tall. The wan afternoon light filtering through them was swallowed in the glare of the bare flourescents high above. Everything was white except the contents of the clothing-filled racks and shelves that stretched ahead of them.

Jack shook his head. "Nope. Still hetero. And I don't want to look like a flaming queen. More like someone who's, say, just a couple of inches outside the closet."

"Well, as I'm sure you know, a couple of inches can make a world of difference."

Jack closed his eyes and shook his head. "Preston . . ."

"I know what you're thinking, Jack. That I'm more outrageous than I ever used to be, that I'm *such* a cliché. Well, you're right. I am. Deliberately. And do you know why? Because I love it. I . . . *love* . . . it. It's my way of thumbing my nose at all the uptight straights wandering this earth. But you know what? My clients, straight or gay, they love it too. They think a guy this flaming has to be a *great* interior designer. So allow me my fun, okay? Life should be fun. Although looking at you I can see you're not having much."

Jack sighed. He was right.

"You might say that. And soon I'm going to have even less. I've got to meet with a slimeball who might be expecting trouble from a stranger. I want to—How shall I say it?—put him at ease."

Pres put a hand on a hip. "And *you* think that if *he* thinks you're queer, *he'll* figure he's got nothing to fear."

"That rhymes, you know, and yes, that's the way his kind of mind works."

"But you know better, don't you."

"Oh, yeah."

Pres might be an interior designer and might look like a featherweight pushover, but Jack had trained with him; the guy had lightning reflexes and was a nunchuck wizard.

"Okay, then." Pres clapped his hands and looked around. "Let's get started, shall we?" He pointed to the right. "There. Shirts. Always a good place to start."

Jack followed him to a rack and watched him fan through a rainbow of shirts. He stopped and pulled out something Jack could only describe as turquoise.

"Look at this. Isn't it scrumptious?"

"What's that stuff up and down the front? Looks like someone spilled spaghetti on it."

"It's embroidery, dearie. Embroidery is always fun."

"Never thought of clothes as fun."

"Oh, you'll never change: functional, functional, functional. Clothing should be an expression of the inner you."

Jack spread his arms. "And what do my clothes say about the inner me?"

"You really want to know, Jack? I mean, I don't want to hurt your feelings or anything."

"Don't worry. You can't."

"All right, then: The way you dress, it's like . . . it's like there *is* no inner you."

Jack allowed himself a smile. "Cool."

"How can you say 'cool'? That was *not* a compliment. I offered it with only the best intentions, but some—myself included—might consider it an insult."

"Don't worry about it. Empty is exactly how I like to look."

"Jack, dearest, you *do* know that you're a very odd man, don't you. I mean very, *very* odd."

"So I've been told."

He handed Jack the shirt. "Okay. We'll keep this as a possibility. I'll pick out some others and . . ."

He was staring at Jack's hair.

"What's wrong?"

"With the way you look? Everything. But especially that hair." He pulled a phone from his bag and hit a button. "Christophe? I need you, baby . . . No, not for me. It's for a friend . . . I *know* you're busy"—he looked at Jack and rolled his eyes as he made a chitterchatter sign with his free hand—"but you've just *got* to squeeze him in. It's an emergency . . . I *never* exaggerate!" A quick glance at Jack's hair. "You'll understand when you see him. . . . Okay, we'll be over in half an hour."

"Who's Christophe?"

"He does my hair."

"You have your barber on speed dial?"

"He's not a *barber*." Pres pulled at his curly mop. "Do I look like I go to a *barber*? Christophe is an artiste, an *architect* with hair. He's agreed to see you as a personal favor to me."

"I don't have much time, Pres. Supposed to meet this creep—"

"Christophe can't *give* you much time. Sunday is one of his busiest days. But I understand." He started fanning through the shirts again. "Come over here. We haven't a moment to lose."

9

Richie sat at his office desk studying his horoscopes for the day. He'd been too dazed this morning to pick up the paper. But he'd fixed that and now he was staring at the readings with pure wonder. He'd read and reread them and could find no way to doubt that he'd made the right choice about meeting Gorcey.

First came Gemini: *Brighter financial horizons can only be met with diligent planning. Do what it takes to keep work fresh and surprising. Be enthusiastic about how much you appreciate your current position, and it only gets better.*

Could anything be better or clearer than that?

And then Cancer: *Engaging conversations improve your financial status. Focus intently on your communication skills.*

This was just too much. One mentioned "brighter financial horizons" while the other said "conversations improve your financial status." And here he was, waiting to take money from a guy just to listen to him talk.

How could Neva keep on saying astrology was junk?

Richie heard the expected knock on the outer door. That would be Gorcey.

As soon as he'd got in the office he'd looked up Dobbins's number and called to check on this guy. But Dobbins wasn't around. Too bad. He would have felt better if he'd been able to talk to him, have him vouch for Gorcey. But since that wasn't gonna happen, Richie would just have to take some precautions.

As he pulled his .38 from its shoulder holster, he called out, "Come on in! It's open!"

The pistol gave him comfort and he'd have liked to keep a hold on it, but he was going to have to shake hands. So he slipped it under the newspaper on his desk and pushed himself to his feet.

"Hello?" said a voice from the outer office.

"Back here!"

A guy of average height and build stepped through the door. He was maybe twenty years younger than Richie and wore black-rimmed sunglasses. He had a newspaper folded under his arm, and that was the last normal thing about him.

His spiky brown hair was just too perfect and he had this dainty little mustache crawling along his upper lip. The nun hadn't said anything about no mustache on Jack. As for the rest of him, well, *queer* was the only way Richie knew how to describe the coat and pants he was wearing. And he was carrying a fucking pocketbook to boot.

Shit, the guy looked even faggier than he'd sounded on the phone.

"Mr. Cordova?" He extended his hand over the desk. "Louis Gorcey. Thanks so much for seeing me."

"My pleasure, Mr. Gorcey."

Yeah, right, he thought as he got a dead-fish handshake.

"Call me Louis."

This guy looked about as dangerous as somebody's crippled grandmother, but that didn't mean he couldn't be carrying. A couple of times, Richie had learned the hard way how looks could deceive.

"Fine. But before we go any further, I'll need you to take off that fancy coat."

Gorcey's brows knitted under his perfect hairdo. "I don't understand."

"Humor me, Lou. I'm in a business where you can't be too careful. You call me up on a Sunday and you've just gotta see me, can't wait till tomorrow, and I start to wonder. I ain't no whacko paranoid, but I ain't no fool neither."

"Really, I don't think—"

"Don't get all huffy with me, Lou. It's a simple thing: You gonna take the coat off or ain't you?"

For a second or two, when Richie thought he wasn't going to do it, he tensed and slid his hand toward the newspaper. His fingers were almost to the gun when Gorcey let out this big sigh.

"Oh, very well. If you insist."

He untied the belt, shrugged out of the coat, folded it, then draped it over the back of the client chair. He raised his arms and did a slow, graceful turn.

Richie gaped at Gorcey's shirt. What the hell was it made of? It looked like the tablecloth his mother had brought back from her trip to Venice about three hundred years ago, the one she picked up on some island called Burano or something like that. Except this one looked like it had been dunked in blueberry Kool-Aid. The guy was wearing a fucking tablecloth.

But what he was *not* wearing was lots more important—no shoulder or SOB holster. Richie let himself relax a little.

"There. Satisfied?"

"Almost," Richie said. "One more thing: Empty your bag on the desk."

"Really, Mr. Cor—"

"Do that and we can get down to business."

Another sigh. "This is very unusual, and if I didn't need your help I'd refuse. But I guess it doesn't matter."

He upended the bag and out tumbled a set of keys, a cell phone, two eyeglass cases, and a couple of legal-sized envelopes.

Richie took the bag from him and shook it.

Gorcey gasped. "Careful! That's a Marc Jacobs!"

Like I care, Richie thought as he checked the inside. Nothing hiding in there. He handed it back to Gorcey.

"That's it? You carry that big thing around and that's all that's in it?"

With floppy wrists and raised pinkies, Gorcey started putting the stuff back into his bag. "Sometimes there's more. But even so, I don't like to distort the lines of my clothing with bulging pockets."

"What? Afraid someone'll think you're glad to see them?"

Richie thought that was a good one but Gorcey didn't even smile. Instead he slid one of the envelopes across the desk.

"As promised."

Richie casually picked it up with his left hand. He didn't want to look too eager but he wasn't about to get suckered either. It wasn't sealed. He flipped up the flap with a thumb and glanced inside. He quick-counted a sufficient number of hundreds.

He relaxed. Okay. Louis Gorcey seemed like the real deal. He'd passed up a chance to go for a gun and his envelope contained the right stuff. The only thing that would remove the last suspicion was if he could see the guy's eyes. You can tell a lot from eyes. But he was keeping his shades on.

Richie shoved the envelope into his top drawer and gestured to the chair on the far side of his desk.

"Have a seat, Lou." When they both had their butts settled, he said, "What can I do for you?"

Gorcey pushed his newspaper across the desk. A copy

CRISSCROSS 395

of *The Light,* opened to page three. He jabbed at a photo of a middle-aged man who looked vaguely familiar—jabbed him right in the eye. Richie noticed that his finger was trembling. He also noticed that Gorcey was wearing nail polish. Clear nail polish, yeah, but still polish. These queers . . .

"Do you know who that is?" Gorcey said.

Richie did a quick read of the caption and reworded it.

"That's Luther Brady, isn't it? The head of that crazy Dormentalist Church?"

Maybe he shouldn't have called it crazy. This guy could be some sort of Dormentalist holy roller.

"Crazy?" Gorcey's manicured finger shook worse as his voice rose. "I wish that were the only thing wrong with the Dormentalist Church! It's worse than crazy! It's destructive and conniving and vicious and malicious and it's all this man's fault! He's . . . he's . . ."

He sputtered to a stop.

"He's what, Lou?"

Gorcey's hands flapped in the air. "He's a monster. He stole a small fortune from me, but worse than that, he stole years from my life. *Years!* I can always earn more money, I'm good at earning money, but how do I get back those years?"

"I don't know, Lou. You tell me."

Richie had found this to be the best approach with upset clients. Let them talk till they ran out of steam.

Gorcey slumped back in the chair. "It's impossible, of course." His brow furrowed. "But I can get even."

Again Richie wished he could see Gorcey's eyes.

"How do you plan to do that?"

"With your help, I hope."

This was getting interesting. A faggot like this Louis Gorcey thinking he could get even with an international figure like Luther Brady. Richie had expected a deadly dull hour, but this was kind of fun. Like getting paid for being entertained.

"Why tell me this?"

"Because I want to hire you."

"To do what?"

"Lee told me you're a wizard with a camera."

Richie fought the smile that wanted to bust out on his face. Dobbins said that, huh? Well, why not. Richie did know his way around a camera, and was good at low-light photography. Damn good. Just ask the cows he was milking.

He gave a little laugh and did the modesty thing. "Well, I don't know about the wizard part, but—"

"He told me all about how you caught his partner dead to rights, and I want you to do that for me. I want you to catch Luther Brady in the act."

"In what act?"

Gorcey's shoulders slumped. "I'm not sure. But I know he sneaks off every Sunday night and heads upstate into the hills. He lives at the temple on Lexington Avenue. Every other time he leaves the temple, on every other day of the week, he has a driver. But not on his Sunday night trips."

Richie smiled. "You've had him under surveillance, then."

"Well, yes. I've even followed him a few nights but I've lost him every time."

"Tailing should be left to a professional."

"That's why I've come to you."

"But what makes you think these trips involve anything wrong?"

"Because it's the only time he ventures out alone. That tells me he's up to something he doesn't want anyone to know about."

"Could be," Richie said. "Could also mean he just wants to be alone."

The hands fluttered again. "That's always a possibility, but with a man as ruthless as Luther Brady, I doubt it. And if he's involved in something that will not stand the light of day, I want pictures of it."

. . . will not stand the light of day . . . Was this guy for

real? No, of course he wasn't. He was a queer.

"All right, Lou. Let's just say he is. And let's just say I do get pictures. What do you intend to do with them?" He shot up a hand in a stop gesture. "Don't tell me anything illegal, like blackmail. I can't be a party to blackmail. It's against the NYAPI code of ethics."

Gorcey blinked. "Ny-ya—?"

"The New York Association of Private Investigators."

Richie had joined NYAPI when he opened his office, paid dues for one year—just long enough to earn a membership certificate to hang on his wall—then tossed all further mailings into the circular file. But claiming to follow a professional organization's code of ethics never failed to impress prospective clients. It assured them that they were dealing with a man of principle.

Gorcey mumbled, "That's good to know . . ."

"If you're planning to use these photos—assuming there's something worth photographing—to expose this man as a fraud and a charlatan, then that's fine. That's performing a public service. But blackmail? No, count me out."

That was the speech, and convincing as usual. Should be. Richie had given it enough times.

"No . . . no, I'm not looking to blackmail him. I want to, as you say, expose him for the money-grubbing mountebank he really is."

Mountebank? What the hell was a mountebank? Some kind of a queer word or something?

Gorcey leaned forward. "Will you help me? Tonight?"

Richie thought about that. Yeah, he wanted the work, but he preferred not to rush things. He liked to max the billable hours. And he had a feeling it wouldn't hurt to play hard to get.

"Why's it got to be tonight? What's wrong with next Sunday?"

"Because I want him now." Gorcey was looking a little agitated, his sissy voice growing louder. "I don't want to allow him another whole week of defrauding people like me. I want to bring him down now. Do you hear me?" He slammed both fists on Richie's desk. *"Now!"*

Richie held up his hands. "Okay, okay. I get the picture."

This guy was really steamed. Richie fought back a smile. How'd that saying go? Hell hath no fury like a woman scorned? Or something like that.

Gorcey leaned back. "Sorry. It's just . . . look, I'll pay you another two thousand just to follow him tonight and see what he's up to. Is that fair?"

Fair? For four, five hours work? Damn-fuck right it was fair. This must be one rich queer.

Richie had heard they tended to have bucks. No kids and all that . . .

He put his head back and rotated it a little to the left and a little to the right, trying to look like a man wrestling with a decision. He'd already made up his mind, but he wasn't ready to say yes. Who knew? If he stalled, maybe Gorcey would up the ante to three thousand.

The act worked. Gorcey piped up and said, "I'll add another thousand if you get pictures I can use."

You mean, Richie thought, photos you *think* you can use.

By all rights he should tell the dumb schmuck that catching Luther Brady meeting with a girlfriend or even a boyfriend wasn't going to put much of a dent in his reputation. Not these days.

Damn shame too. It made Richie long for the fifties. He'd been just a little kid at the time, but he remembered how uptight everyone had been back then. Those were the days when even a so-called breath of scandal could sink a career or a reputation. His sideline business would be so much easier and more profitable now if America hadn't changed. But it had. The new attitude was pretty much anything goes. Damn hard to shock people these days.

He sure as shit wasn't telling Gorcey that, though.

But if he did come up with something juicy—really juicy—he could always snap some extra shots—innocent ones—and tell Gorcey that all Brady did up there in the woods was sit alone and meditate.

He'd keep the real deals to himself . . . and add Luther Brady to his herd of cows. Brady controlled millions. His milk would be extra rich and creamy.

"Okay, Lou," Richie said. "I'll do it. Normally I lay a lot of groundwork—you know, thorough backgrounding and such—before I make a move, but I sense your urgency, Lou. I feel your pain, and so I'll make an exception in your case."

Gorcey beamed and fluttered his hands again—higher this time. He looked genuinely delighted.

"That's wonderful. I'll meet you tonight at—"

Richie waved a hand. "Wait, wait. What do you mean, you'll meet me?"

"I'm going with you."

"Ohhhh, no. I work alone."

Gorcey's lips tightened into a thin line. "Perhaps, but I expect you to make an exception this time. Especially considering the amount of money I'll be paying you."

"Sorry. Can't allow it. You've got no experience in this sort of thing. You could blow the whole operation. And why would you want to come along anyway? That's what you're hiring me for."

And besides, I don't want to be sitting in some car half the night with a queer.

"I want to see for myself."

"You will," Richie told him. "In the photos."

Gorcey shook his head and his lips tightened further. "I'm going along, Mr. Cordova, one way or another. Either in your car, or in my own, following you as you follow Brady."

Richie recognized a note of unswayable finality in Gorcey's voice. Shit. The last thing he wanted when he was working was a tag-along amateur. Especially if said amateur was queer. And double especially if it turned out Brady had a bona fide dirty little secret.

But it didn't look like he was going to have much choice.

He sighed. "Okay, Lou. I'll take you along. But I won't

be able to guarantee success. And I'll want the money up front."

Gorcey relaxed his rigid posture. "Of course. That's only fair."

"By the way, what's your sign?"

Gorcey's eyebrows rose as he smirked. "I'm usually in a bar when I'm asked that question."

Richie felt heat in his cheeks. "Don't be a wise ass. I want to check to see if our signs are going to be compatible tonight."

"I'm a Taurus." His smile changed. "And don't worry, Mr. Cordova, I won't get in the way. I promise." Something strange about his new smile . . . unsettling. "You'll hardly know I'm there."

10

When Jack checked his voice mail outside Cordova's and heard Abe's message—"Your package has arrived"—he hopped a cab to Manhattan.

He entered the shop, locked the front door behind him, and headed for the rear.

"Did you really find one?" he said as he approached Abe in his customary spot.

Abe said nothing, merely stared.

"Abe?"

"Jack?" His gaze ranged from Jack's hair to his glossy, wheat-brown loafers, to his man bag, then back to his hair. "This is you?"

"It's part of a fix."

"On Christopher Street you're working maybe?"

"I'll explain later. Did you get the gun?"

And still Abe stared. "Your hair . . . it's wet?"

"Nah. Just some sort of gel. The Beretta, Abe?"

"And your coat. Like a robe it looks with that tie thing around the waist."

All this scrutiny was making Jack uncomfortable.

"Earth to Abe. Did——?"

"Has Gia seen you like this?"

"No, and she's not going to." She might like it and want him to dress like this all the time. "I'll spell it out for you: B-E-R-E——"

"Yes-yes."

Abe shook himself out of whatever transported state he was in and reached under the counter. He came up with a brown paper lunch bag and slid it across the counter.

Jack slipped his hand inside and removed a stainless-steel 9mm Beretta 92. It was beautiful. It was perfect.

"Abe, you are amazing," he said, turning the gleaming pistol over and over in his hands. "Truly amazing."

"I am. Yes, I am." When Jack glanced at him with a wry smile he added, "What? I should pretend to be humble? Hours on the phone I spent. No one else in this city could have found such a thing for you on a Sunday. No one."

"I thank you for this, Abe. Really. If you hadn't found it, this whole afternoon spent setting up the fix would have gone down the drain." He looked around. "Where are your cotton gloves?"

Abe pulled an oil-smudged pair from under the counter and handed them across.

"Want some oil?"

"No. Just need to wipe it down. Don't want our finger-prints on it."

"Certainly not."

He slipped on the gloves and polished the pistol's shiny planes and bevels, its Brazilian walnut stocks. Then he pushed a release button, rotated the cam, and pulled the slide assembly off the frame in one piece. He wiped the barrel and underside of the slide.

"It's used," Abe said, "but well kept."

"I see that. Used is better than new. I just want to

double-check there's no serial number on the slide."

"With a Beretta, only on the frame."

"Perfect." He replaced the slide assembly, then ejected the empty magazine from the grip. "Got those Hydra-Shoks?"

Again Abe's hand disappeared under the counter, returning this time with two boxes of 9mm rounds, each with the familiar red *Federal* across the top.

"Federal Classics, as requested. Grain-wise I've got one-twenty-four and one-forty-seven."

"The one-twenty-fours should do."

He intended to be up close and very personal when he pulled the trigger, so he preferred a lower muzzle velocity. Jack slipped open the box and removed ten rounds. He rubbed each carefully with his gloved fingers before pressing it into the magazine.

"A CSI team you're expecting?"

"You betcha."

"And you won't tell me about it?"

"After I'm through, I'll fill you in on every last detail."

"The clothes too?"

"Everything."

"So till then I must hang?"

"But you won't be hanging alone," Jack said. "Trust me on that."

11

As he walked back toward his apartment Jack realized he had just enough time to pay a visit to the ersatz Mama Roselli. He dialed her on her cell.

A weak, raspy voice said, "Hello?"

"Mrs. Roselli? This is Jack. I stopped by last night but I heard you weren't feeling well. Are you okay?"

"I'm better, thank you."

"I was wondering if I could come over to give you an update. I found Johnny and—"

"Can this wait until tomorrow? I don't think I'm well enough yet for company."

Yes, it could wait till tomorrow, although Jack would have liked his questions answered tonight. But if she was feeling as bad as she sounded—if she was faking it she deserved an Oscar—then giving her more time to recover made sense.

"Tomorrow then. I'll see you about noon or so?"

"I'll be here."

Jack cut the connection. Her sudden frailty bothered him. He'd suspected her of being kin to Anya, a tough old bird who looked like she hadn't had a sick day in her life. The only time he'd seen her not in control was when she'd had that sudden sharp pain in her back. Took her a day or so to get over it. And the next day he'd seen an oozing sore on her scarred-up back . . . on what she'd called "the map of my pain" . . . the map of where Brady was burying his pillars.

Could it be . . . ?

He'd find out tomorrow. Tonight he had to share a car with Cordova and somehow keep himself from strangling him.

12

They sat parked east of Lexington, where Jack had waited Friday night. Cordova had insisted on using his aging, smelly Jeep Laredo, saying he had all his equipment stowed in the back, plus they might need the four-wheel drive.

So Jack had parked his rental a couple of blocks from Cordova's Williamsbridge house and cabbed to Tremont Avenue. They'd met in front of Cordova's office and driven downtown together.

"What's with the gloves?" Cordova said. "It ain't *that* cold."

Jack looked down at his hands, tightly swathed in black leather driving gloves. "My fingers are very sensitive."

Cordova snickered. "Why am I not surprised?"

"Pardon?"

"Never mind."

Probably thought he was funny. A real comedian.

Jack eyed his suet body, his suet face with its suet cheeks, his suet hands resting on the steering wheel, and wondered if this was the same car he'd used to snatch Sister Maggie.

Be so easy to reach over and grab his suet throat and squeeze . . . squeeze until he passed out. Let him wake up, then start squeezing again . . . and then do it again . . .

Jack wondered how many hours he could keep it up, how many times he could—

"Hell-o-o?" Cordova said. "Did you hear me?"

Jack shook his head, not trusting himself to speak at that moment.

"I said, What time's Brady usually head for the hills?"

Jack stared at the garage exit. Eight o'clock already and so far no sign of Brady. Jack remembered Jamie telling him about Brady's Sunday night trips, but had she said anything about time? He didn't think so. Had to improvise here.

"Varies. Sometimes early, sometimes late. But always after dark."

"Well, it's already after dark, so let's hope this is an early night. I hate stakeouts anyway. And to be frank, Lou, you ain't much of a conversationalist."

"I'll have plenty to say once I have Brady where I want him," he snapped. "I gave you your money. Don't expect chitchat too."

He noticed Cordova's quick, sidelong glance and reminded himself to remain in character.

He let out a long sigh. "Oh, I'm sorry, Mr. Cordova. I'm usually quite a talker. Sometimes I swear I just can't shut up. But tonight I'm a little tense. No, I'm a lot tense. I mean, this just might be the night I get something on him." He reached over and laid a gentle hand on the fat man's suety shoulder. "You simply have no idea how badly I want this."

Cordova shrugged off his hand. "Easy with the touching stuff. I ain't into touching."

Jack snatched his hand back and dropped it into his lap. "Sorry."

Cordova's laugh sounded forced. "Hey, relax about the rest. If there's something to get, I'll get it."

Jack hoped they got something—the bigger the better. He had three scenarios planned. Plan A was the one most fully worked out, and would kick in if they hit pay dirt scandal-wise. If not—if Brady was involved in nothing blackmail-worthy—then Jack would go with Plan B. Plan C was the simplest and the least appealing: If Brady didn't show up tonight, Jack and Cordova would return next Sunday.

The thought of allowing Richie Cordova to go on

breathing for another week made him queasy. And to have to spend another night with him in this car . . . that might just be too much to bear. Might force Jack into doing something rash.

"Hey," Cordova said, pointing across the street to where a black Mercedes was pulling out from the garage. "Is that our boy?"

Jack squinted at the plates. "Yes! That's him! Go! Go!"

"Just take it easy," Cordova said, singsonging as if addressing a child. "A professional doesn't tip his hand like that. We'll wait a few seconds, let another car get between us, *then* start after him."

Jack wrung his hands. "But we'll lose him!"

"No we won't. I guarantee it."

13

Jack had to admit that Cordova was good at tailing. It didn't hurt that Jack knew the Thruway exit Brady would be taking. At least he hoped he knew. Blascoe had said Brady owned a place not far from his, so Jack assumed he'd use the same exit Jamie had when she took him to Blascoe's. He told Cordova that he'd followed Brady twice to that exit and lost him afterward. That allowed Cordova to pass Brady and wait for him near the off-ramp. If Brady was watching his rear, he'd see no one follow him off the Thruway.

Jack had a bad moment or two, sitting there with the pressure of the Beretta against the small of his back, wondering if he'd made the wrong choice. But then Brady's black Mercedes came down the ramp and stopped at the light.

After that it was a trip up the same twisty road Jack and Jamie had traveled just three nights ago. Was that all it had been? Just seventy-two hours?

Brady passed the driveway to Blascoe's place without even slowing. Two miles beyond he turned onto a dirt path and headed uphill. Cordova cruised farther on for a mile or so, then turned, killed the lights, and headed back.

After he'd backed the Jeep deep into the brush about a hundred yards away from the mini-road, Cordova turned to Jack.

"Sit tight and I'll go see what's up."

Jack popped open his door. "No way. I'm going with you."

"Lou, are you crazy? You don't have any experience—"

"I'm going."

Cordova cursed under his breath as he pulled his cameras and lenses from the back seat. He continued grumbling and muttering as they made their way up the hill through the brush. Jack was struck by a strong sense of déjà vu: He and Jamie had made the same sort of trip on Thursday night just a few miles back down the road.

Cordova turned and said, "Hey, almost forgot: If you got a cell phone, turn the goddamn thing off."

"I already did."

Jack wondered about perimeter security devices but decided not to worry about them. If Brady was into something shady up here, he wouldn't want to draw attention to the place by linking it to a security monitoring company, and especially not to the Dormentalist temple.

"There's a cabin," Cordova said, pointing ahead to where lights glowed through the trees. "Time to slow down and keep it quiet as possible."

Soon they reached the edge of a clearing. The cabin—made of real logs as far as Jack could tell—stood at its center, windows aglow. A plank porch ran across the front and around the left side.

Cordova motioned Jack to wait and slunk into the clearing. Jack followed. When Cordova noticed, he waved him back, but Jack kept coming. The fat man's annoyance showed in the slope of his shoulders. Jack didn't care. He wasn't going to wait for Cordova to develop his film to see what Brady was up to.

As they neared a side window Jack began to hear music. All the doors and windows were shut, so the volume had to be near max. Sounded classical. Jack couldn't identify it. Didn't even try. Except for some Tchaikovsky, he found most classical music unlistenable.

They reached the side window and peeked through. The interior was similar to Blascoe's. So similar that Jack would bet they'd been built from the same design. The major difference was the collection of maybe half a dozen full-length mirrors spaced around the great room.

"Must love to look at himself," Cordova said.

And then the man himself appeared, wrapped in a big white terry cloth robe. He strode to the kitchen counter and poured himself some Glenlivet on the rocks.

Shit, Jack thought. This wasn't quite what he'd been hoping for.

Cordova's snide tone said he agreed. "Oh, yeah," he whispered—probably could've yelled, considering the volume of the music inside—"shots of this are gonna do *real* damage."

"The night is still young."

"Yeah, but he's alone."

"For the moment."

"You know something?"

"No. Just hoping."

"Yeah, well keep on hoping. Because even if we get shots of him whacking off or doing himself with a dildo, it's no big deal. You can embarrass the hell out of him, maybe, but you ain't gonna bring him down with stuff like that."

But it'll be something, Jack thought. All I need is one thing . . . anything . . . just one little thing, and Plan A goes into effect.

They hung around the window, Cordova calibrating and testing the low-light image intensifiers on his cameras, Jack studying Brady through the window. He watched him leaf through some big, antique-looking book, a hungry look in his eyes. What was it? Ancient porn?

Unlike his burning rage against Cordova, Jack felt cold, clinical, almost detached about Brady. He could torture Cordova, do to him what he'd done to Sister Maggie, and not feel an instant's regret or remorse. But that wouldn't do for Brady. Jack had other plans for him, plans that Brady might well find worse than torture.

"I say we give it an hour or so," Cordova said, now that his cameras were ready.

"We stay until we get something or he goes to bed, whichever comes first."

"Lemme tell you something: I ain't standing out here freezing my ass off till God knows when."

Jack put a hand on Cordova's shoulder, just as he'd done back in the car.

"Please, Mr. Cordova. I told you how much this means to me."

He leaned away from Jack's hand. "And I told you how I feel about being touched. Now lay off, got it? If we—"

Through the window Jack saw Brady pull a cell phone from the pocket of his robe.

"Hey. Looks like he's getting a call."

He and Cordova watched Brady go to the stereo and turn down the volume, then smile as he spoke on the phone. When the call ended, he upped the music again, and closed the big old book he'd been reading.

"This could be it," Jack said.

Cordova grunted. "And it could be nothing. But he sure do look happy, don't he. Wouldn't be surprised if—oh, shit!"

Brady had carried the book to the center of the room where he knelt and pulled up a trapdoor that perfectly matched the rest of the floor. He started down into the basement.

"If he stays down there we're fucked," Cordova said.

Jack kept silent, watching. Moments later Brady reappeared and closed the trapdoor. What was down there? A secret library of some sort? Something that could be used against him? If the photos didn't work out, then maybe—

"Oh, man!" Cordova said.

Brady had tossed off his robe to reveal a well-toned, well-tanned body.

"Buffed and baked," Jack said. "This is good. This is very good."

Cordova was already snapping pictures. "Don't get too excited now."

Jack put on a huffy tone. "I beg your pardon?"

"I mean, this kind of beefcake ain't gonna hurt him. Might get him lots of calls from the ladies, though. Or the guys. Maybe even—holy shit!"

Jack watched, fascinated, as Brady placed a feathered mask over his head, leaving only his eyes and mouth exposed. He examined himself in one of the mirrors, then slipped back into his robe.

Cordova's shutter was clicking like mad. "I got a feeling we might be heading for pay dirt."

"Shhh!" Jack whispered as he raised a gloved finger to his lips. "Is that a car?"

Cordova cupped a hand around an ear. "Damn right it is." He picked up his cameras and began moving away. "Let's ease back into the bushes and wait."

Jack followed him. They crouched in the brush as a pair of headlights became visible through the trees. Before long a Chevy van pulled up and stopped before the front door.

"Get a shot of the plates," Jack told Cordova. "I want those plates."

But Cordova already had his eye to the viewfinder. "So do I."

A gray-haired man about Cordova's age, but whippet lean, was illuminated by the courtesy lights as he stepped out of the van. He opened a rear door and out hopped two boys, maybe twelve years of age, fourteen tops. He ushered them up to the front door where Brady was waiting. After the boys were inside, the man returned to the car and drove away.

As soon as the car was out of sight Cordova was on the move toward the cabin, chortling. "Ho-ho-ho! The plot sickens!"

Jack hesitated, then followed.

Back at the window, he saw Brady offer the boys beers, then light up a joint and pass it around.

"Giving beer and pot to minors," Cordova said. "That's a good start."

The kids looked fairly comfortable, as if they were used to this sort of thing. Jack knew what they were: male prostitutes. Teenagers. "Chickens" to the trade. Usually kids kicked out of their homes because they're gay; they gravitate to cities but can't support themselves, so they wind up fodder for chicken hawks. And Brady was a chicken hawk.

Jack had hoped for something big to use against the man, but never imagined . . .

As Brady threw off the robe and the two boys began to undress, Jack moved away.

"Hey, where you going?" Cordova said.

"Back to the car."

Cordova's tone was mocking. "No jacking off now."

Jack wanted to kill him right there. Do an HVAC job on his skull, then burst through the door and do the same to

Brady. But that wasn't in the plan. And it wouldn't change the lives of those two boys. They'd spend some time in the state child-welfare mill, then wind up back on the street.

The night sky seemed bright compared to the darkness in Jack's heart.

14

While Jack waited in the Jeep he got the Mikulski brothers' phone number from information. Brad, the older one, answered.

"It's me: Jack."

"Hey. What've you got for us?"

Jack never made social calls to the Mikulskis. This was no exception. But he wanted to be careful since he was on a cell phone.

"Got a New York license plate for you. Write this down." Jack recited it from memory. "You might want to do business with the guy."

"What's he into?"

"Chickens. Export and import, I believe."

"That so?"

"And I also believe he's ripe for a takeover bid."

"How ripe?"

"ASAP."

"All right. We'll get on it tomorrow. Thanks for the heads-up, man."

"My pleasure."

Jack ended the call, then leaned back in the passenger seat. Calling the Mikulskis in made him feel a little better. Weird pair, those two. Had a real jones for pedophiles. Didn't know what was in their past to make them that way, and didn't want to. But he did know they'd track that van, and if they witnessed what Jack was sure they would, a certain chicken runner would be out of business. Permanently.

Jack wanted him gone before the shit hit Brady's fan.

He shifted in the seat and felt something jab him in the thigh. He reached down and came up with a crucifix on a broken chain. Just like the one he'd seen hanging around Sister Maggie's neck.

Jack closed his eyes and tried to stay calm. The only thing that worked was repeating . . . *it won't be long now . . . won't be long now* . . . over and over.

Cordova showed up a few minutes later. He placed his cameras in the rear, then rolled onto the driver's seat. He laughed as he started the car.

"What's so funny?" Jack said.

"We got him! We got him six ways from Sunday! He's as good as dead! Even if those pictures don't land him in the slammer, he'll never be able to show his face again! He's gonna have to hide away in his little love nest and never come out!"

He laughed again and bounced in his seat like a kid who'd just been told that Christmas had been extended to 365 days a year.

Jack said, "I'd almost think that you had as much against him as I."

Cordova immediately sobered. "Oh, well, no, I mean I'm just always happy when an investigation comes through for the client. And you gotta admit, this puppy came through in spades. I can't wait to see those photos."

"Neither can I. Where do you get them developed?"

"I got a little lab in my house."

Jack knew that. He'd seen it. Just a converted closet, but a small-time operator like Cordova didn't need more.

"Wonderful. Let's go. And don't tell me I'm not coming along, because I am. I paid for those photos and I want to see what I've got. If they're what I need to bring

Brady down, you'll get the extra thousand I promised right then and there."

"What? Come to my place? I never . . ." He paused for a few heartbeats, then, "Well, I guess it would be okay. I mean, seeing as you're laying out all this money and all. Yeah. Sure. Why not."

Cordova had agreed just a little too easily. Jack had known he'd go along eventually, but had expected him to play a little harder to get.

15

Sweet Jesus, Richie thought as he arranged the prints across his desktop. They were . . . *fantastic* was the only word for them.

He sat in his darkened attic office and stared. The only sound was the breathing of the guy leaning over his shoulder. Gorcey had insisted on printing every frame. Immediately. He wanted them now. Not tomorrow or the next day. *Now*.

That was okay by Richie. The prints wouldn't go to waste. He'd scan them and copy them onto a CD. Then he'd stick them in an envelope marked *Personal & Confidential* and address it to Luther Brady.

He wanted to get up and dance. This was the mother lode. This was the California gold rush and the key to De Beers rolled into one.

Even though he'd had to take the photos through a screened window into a moderately lighted room, the images were clear enough to detail the goings-on in that cabin. Brady without his mask before the boys arrived; Brady putting on his mask; Brady making the boys earn their pay—really earn it.

Brady, Brady, Brady.

Richie had been a little sickened by the stuff that went down in that room, but he'd hung in there until he'd had enough. More than enough.

Luther Brady, you are my meat, you are my bitch. From this day forward, I *own* you.

Only one thing stood in the way: the guy behind him. Louis Gorcey.

He couldn't let him walk out of here. The only way Gorcey was leaving this house was horizontal and feet first.

But he couldn't risk giving Gorcey even a hint of what was coming.

He spoke without looking up. "See anything you like?" he said, knowing it could be taken two ways.

"I like none of it. I am appalled. I was hoping for something scandalous, but this . . . this is unspeakable."

Gorcey sounded offended. That surprised Richie. After all, didn't gay guys like young stuff? He knew he did. Girls, of course. Not boys. But teen girls, with the way they dressed these days in their tight tops and low-riding jeans leaving their smooth, rounded bellies showing, it just wasn't fair to a guy who wasn't getting much. How he'd love to pull down a pair of those hip-hugging jeans and put his face . . .

Fat chance. Like one of them would go for a guy forty years older—older than their dads, probably. And fat to boot.

Richie sighed. The closest he'd ever get to one of those was on the Internet. But he could dream. Oh, yeah, he could dream real good.

He tore himself away from young girls and got back to these pictures of young boys.

"Well, did I earn the extra grand?"

"Yes. You earned your bonus."

"Great. Now, what do we do?" When Gorcey didn't answer, Richie looked up at him. "Hello? Did you hear what I—?"

Gorcey's face looked strange. He'd finally taken off his sunglasses. Left his gloves on but had to remove the shades, what with the room being kind of dark. His brown eyes were scary. Murderous, almost. Richie's heart stopped for a second when he thought that look might be for him. But how could it be? They'd only met tonight, and it was Brady that Gorcey was after.

Gorcey nodded. "I heard you. But I'm thinking."

"About what?"

"Blackmail." His hand did a quick wave. "I know what you said about your code of ethics, but I'm sure Brady would pay almost anything to keep these out of the public eye."

An alarm bell sounded in Richie's head. What was going on here? Almost like this guy was reading his mind. A bowel-clenching thought wormed through his head: What if he was sitting next to the guy the nun had hired to fuck up his operation?

His hand crept toward the .38 in his shoulder holster . . .

Hey, wait. That didn't make sense. Gorcey had just led him to a goose that was going to lay a steady stream of golden eggs. And besides, if Gorcey was carrying—and Richie was pretty damn sure he wasn't—he'd had a million chances on the way upstate and back to do whatever damage he might have come to do.

No . . . Gorcey wasn't Jack, wasn't the guy from Julio's the nun had told him about. He was just a fag with a hard-on for Luther Brady.

Soon he was going to be a dead fag.

"Blackmail's illegal, Lou. Don't tell me any more. I could lose my license for not reporting you."

"You wouldn't need a license with what we could squeeze out of Brady."

" 'We'?"

"Well, blackmailing him would require a certain amount of toughness that I'm not sure I have. But you seem tough, Mr. Cordova."

Richie wasn't sure how to play this. Gorcey was pro- posing a partnership. It was tempting in a way. It meant he wouldn't have to kill him. Disposing of a body was no easy thing—as the quick discovery of the dead nun proved. Forensic crime labs were getting better and bet- ter. Some simple little thing could fuck him up royally.

But bringing Gorcey in would mean splitting the milk from Brady, and Richie didn't even want to think about that. But even so, he didn't think a queer like Gorcey had the stuff to stay the course. And worse, he might spill to one of his lover boys, either while whispering sweet nothings or trying to impress some stud he was courting. That would queer—he hid a smile and thought, *Oh*, par- don me!—that would queer everything.

Okay. Let's look at the situation. I've got a gun, he don't. The shades are already pulled. My house is sealed up, and so are all the neighbors'. Nobody around here will be out on the street on a cold Sunday night like this. I can put a couple of quick ones into Gorcey's chest and no one'll be the wiser.

That would work. Then he'd wait till the dead dark hours of the morning and tote the body out to the car. He could dump Gorcey under an overpass or someplace like it and forget about him. There wasn't no connection be- tween the two of them.

But he had to go about this real careful like. Keep Gorcey nice and relaxed so he wouldn't see nothing com- ing. Richie didn't want no tussle—even a pansy man could get lucky. Just a quick, clean kill.

Sticking to the upright, uptight, ethical PI role seemed the best play.

"Yeah, I'm tough enough," Richie said, "but I'm hon- est. I'll give you the prints and negatives and then we'll both forget we ever had this conversation." He patted the area around his desk. "Oops. No envelopes. Have to get one out of the closet."

Out of the closet . . . *ha!*

As he pushed up from the seat, he snaked one hand into

his coat and pulled the .38 free of the holster. He held it chest-high. All he had to do now was make his turn and—

A gloved hand came out of nowhere and grabbed his wrist while another shoved a big shiny pistol against his cheek.

"Wha—?"

"What were you planning to do with that, Richie?" said a hard voice that didn't sound at all like Louis Gorcey's.

Moving only his eyes, Richie looked. It was Gorcey, all right. He looked the same, and yet everything about him was different. Gorcey wasn't Gorcey no more.

Richie's knees went soft as he realized he might have made a terrible mistake.

"I-I-nothing. I was just taking it out to lay it on my desk. It's heavy and it, you know, gets in the way."

Richie tried to twist his hand free but the grip on his wrist tightened, became crushing, and the muzzle pressed deeper into his face.

"Yeah, I know. Drop it on the floor."

"Hey—"

In the space of a second, the muzzle left his cheek, slammed against his nose, and then rammed into his cheek again.

Richie let out a yell as pain shot straight through his skull and bright flashes sparked in his vision. "All right! All right!"

He dropped the gun.

"Sit."

He eased himself back into the chair. He looked up and saw Gorcey staring at him. He realized that the murderous look he'd thought was for Brady was for him.

"W-what's going on, Lou?"

"Name isn't Lou. It's Jack."

Jack? Oh-no-oh-God-oh-no! The nun's Jack!

But he couldn't let on that he knew.

"Jack, Lou, what difference does it make? You didn't

have to lie about your name. All secrets are safe with me."

He saw Jack's face twist with fury, noticed that he'd reversed his grip on the pistol and was holding it by the barrel. Richie watched it rise above him, then swing down, saw the nubs of the rear sights falling toward his scalp. Tried to duck but wasn't fast enough.

Pain bloomed in his skull and the world swam around him as he heard an echoey voice say, "Shut up."

The icy, matter-of-fact tone made his bladder clench.

Another blow wiped out all sight, all sound.

16

"Hey!" someone was saying. "Hey, wake up." A foot nudged his leg. "Wake up, Fatso."

Richie forced his eyes open. The room did a half spin, then settled, then spun again. His head felt like it had exploded and then been put back together by someone who'd never seen a human skull before.

He groaned and tried to raise his right hand to his aching head but it wouldn't move. He looked and saw that it was wired to an arm of his chair. So was his left.

And then he saw that his chair had been wheeled away from the desk.

"Whuh . . . ?"

Jack glanced at him. "Oh, good. You're awake. About time."

It looked like he'd divvied up the prints into a couple of piles. The negative strips lay tangled among them.

"What're you doing?"

"Sorting."

He stepped over to Richie's chair and stood staring

down at him. The room spun again as Richie looked up. He looked away real quick when he saw what was in the guy's eyes.

"What're you gonna do?"

"If I had the time and inclination, I'd like to do to you what you did to Sister Maggie. Remember her? You threatened to ruin her life, and you did."

So here it was, right out in the open.

"You're the one she hired to mess up my computer, right?"

The guy nodded. "And you're the one who messed up Maggie."

"You gotta lemme explain. It's not how you think. I didn't—"

A black-gloved hand backhanded him across the face. "Don't waste my time."

Richie spat blood. "Okay, okay."

"How'd you find out?"

"About what?"

"About Maggie hiring me."

"Why do you care?" Another backhand across the face made Richie's head spin. "All right, all right. It was her boyfriend, Metcalf. He cracked wise about me being out-foxed by a nun. That's when I knew."

The guy sighed and said something under his breath that sounded like "Nobody listens." But he looked like he was relieved or something. Maybe this was Richie's chance.

"So it's not all my fault. It's Metcalf's too. I shouldn't take all—" He cringed as he saw that gloved hand wind up for another shot. "Don't, please! Just answer one question, will you?"

"What?"

"You her brother or something?"

Please say no, he thought. Please say no.

The guy shook his head. "Never met her before she hired me."

Relief flooded him. Maybe he could reason with him, operative to operative.

"Then why?"

"Why what?"

"Why come back? You got hired, you did the job—did it real good, I gotta tell you—and that's it. You walk away. It's over. Done. End of story. No reason to come back into the picture."

The guy stared at him like he was looking down at a splash of fresh vomit. After too long a time he took a breath and pointed to Richie's wired wrists.

"I wanted to use duct on you like you did on Maggie, but I couldn't risk carrying a roll in case you searched my bag again. Wire takes up much less space." He held up a silvery roll of duct tape. "But look what I came across in one of your drawers."

With a single swift move he ripped off a piece and slapped it across Richie's mouth.

Panic ripped through him. He tried to kick out with his feet but his ankles were wired down as well. When he saw the guy pick up the pistol from the desk Richie began to scream, but nothing got through the tape and the noise coming through his nose sounded like baby pig squeals.

"Let me introduce you to Mr. Beretta." He put the shiny barrel of the pistol against Richie's palm. "Shake hands with him. You're about to interface."

Richie wrapped his fingers around the barrel. No way he could get it away, but if he could just keep a grip on it—

The guy twisted it free like he was taking a rattle from a baby. Then he stuck it in Richie's other hand. "Feel that? Like it? You and Mr. Beretta are going to get real friendly."

Richie screamed again as the guy picked up a beige cushion. Where'd that come from? Looked like one from the couch downstairs. What was he gonna—

Oh no! The cushion pressed against Richie's stomach as the guy buried the muzzle in the fabric.

NO!

A slightly muffled *BLAM!* and then searing pain shot through his gut. He screamed against the tape and writhed in agony. He'd never imagined anything could hurt like this. Never. Vomit rose in his throat but he swallowed it back. If he puked he'd suffocate, though maybe that wouldn't be so bad. At least it would stop the pain.

"I hear nothing hurts worse than being gut shot," the guy said in a cold, dead voice. "I hope I heard right."

Richie watched through eyes blurred with pain and tears as the guy turned back to the desk and began shoving all the photos into an envelope. The negatives as well.

The room got gray around the edges and he thought he was going to pass out—if only he would!—but then things came back into focus.

Richie began to sob from an excruciating spasm, the noise snuffling in and out through his nose. Felt like someone had a pitchfork in his gut and was twisting, twisting . . .

And now the guy was stuffing everything into his shoulder bag.

Richie wailed into the gag. He wasn't going to leave him like this! He couldn't!

Then the guy picked up the cushion and the gun again and stepped up in front of Richie.

"You don't deserve this," he said in that dead voice as he placed the cushion over Richie's chest.

What? No! *NO!*

17

After putting two Hydra-Shoks into Fatso's chest, Jack stepped back and watched him buck and spasm, then go still. His wide, bulging eyes lost focus and his lids dropped to half mast.

The only regret he felt was at not being able to leave Cordova alive. He'd heard it sometimes took three days to die of a gut shot. Three days of constant agony. Barely a tenth of what he deserved.

But sooner or later, when Cordova didn't show up at his office tomorrow morning, and didn't answer his home phone, his receptionist would call someone to check on him. And that might give the fat man a chance of surviving.

No survival for Cordova. Jack not only wanted him dead, he *needed* him dead.

He stared at the fat, bloody corpse a moment longer. Maggie . . . she hadn't died because of some mistake on Jack's part, she'd died because of her own good heart. Despite Jack's warning, she must have felt a duty to let Metcalf know that he didn't have to pay any more blackmail money. And Metcalf, not knowing the level of scum he was dealing with, had opened his yap.

All of this . . . so unnecessary . . . so goddamn unnecessary.

Jack reholstered the Beretta, then retrieved two of the three ejected shell casings from the floor. He kicked the third into the darkroom. He hefted his shoulder bag and did one more sweep of the area. All clean. Nothing to identify him.

All right.

He loped downstairs and headed for his car. On the way home he'd call 911 and report hearing what sounded like gunshots from Cordova's house.

MONDAY

1

Jack paused outside the front entrance of the Dormentalist temple.

He'd stopped home and dropped off all the photos he'd
taken from Cordova's house. Then he'd changed into the
third-hand clothing store rejects he'd picked up yesterday
after his visit to Roselli. He'd used rubber cement to at-
tach scruffy black hair to his face, then pulled a knit
watch cap over his head down to the tops of his ears.

He wouldn't fool anyone who knew Johnny Roselli; he
doubted even a stranger would be fooled by the beard if
he got close enough.

But he wasn't planning on letting anyone that close.

His main concern was whether Roselli had skipped his
camping trip and returned to the temple since Jack had
left him. If so, his entry card wouldn't have worked and
he'd have been issued a new one. Using his old card now
could raise an alarm and wreck Jack's plans.

His other concern was Brady. Jack had no idea how
long he usually carried on with his hired boys, or if he
came home when he was through. The later the better, as
far as Jack was concerned. Best case would be if he slept
over till morning, which would be the wise thing to do after a night of Scotch and ganja.

But it was all guesswork at this point. He hated it when
a fix depended on something he couldn't control, and
could be sent off track by someone's whim.

Only one way to find out . . .

Jack took a breath and opened the door. As he stepped
into the unmanned security atrium, he bore right, away
from the metal detector and toward the members-only

turnstile. The deep-shadowed lobby was deserted. A few
bulbs in sconces lit the periphery and the elevator area
where one set of doors stood open, waiting. A dozen feet
beyond the turnstile a lone burgundy-uniformed TP sat in
a pool of light behind his marble kiosk.

Jack gave the guard a friendly wave as he made a show
of fishing the card from a pocket. The TP gave a wary,
noncommittal nod, watching him.

Jack kept the EC in his left hand, leaving the right free
to go for the pistol nestled in the small of his back. After
positioning it at the end of the slot, he trained his eyes on
the guard and swiped the card through.

He waited as the TP checked the computer. Hopefully
a photo of Johnny Roselli was popping onto the screen
with the message that he was a lapser—thus explaining
his scruffy attire. If the guard's expression changed or he
reached for the phone, Jack was out of here. He did not
want to be placed in a situation where he'd have to use his
weapon.

But the TP's expression didn't change. He looked up
from the screen and gave Jack a perfunctory smile and a
wave. The turnstile's mechanism clicked, allowing Jack
to push through.

Jack released the breath he'd been holding as he waved
back and headed straight for the elevators. He kept his
head down as he stepped into the open car. Before pressing 21 with a knuckle, he glanced back at the guard and
saw him reading from a tabloid newspaper. Probably not
The Light.

Okay, he thought as the doors pincered closed, I'm in.

Now came the tough part.

He looked at the unlit 22 button and wished he could
make the elevator take him there without leaving a record
of the trip in the computers. That was something he
needed to avoid at all cost.

Still . . . it would be so much easier than what he had
planned.

Jack figured he was pretty much in control from here on in. Success or failure depended on him, not chance or circumstance. Even so, he knew he had a hairy hour or so ahead of him.

2

Jensen sat in his third-floor office gazing over Tony Margiotta's shoulder. The only light in the room came from the computer screen. These things were a pain in the ass but in the right hands, they were amazing. Margiotta had been doing an online search for anything—*anything*—about John Robertson. Even though the guy had been dead two years and retired for years before that, this Google thing had come up with almost a thousand hits. But the hits, a thousand or not, weren't proving very useful.

"This is all shit," Margiotta said.

"Maybe, but keep at it. I want every one of them looked into.

"But what am I looking for?"

Margiotta hadn't been told any more than he needed to know. He already knew that Jason Amurri had been an impostor, and Jensen had told him that an outside investigation had linked him to Robertson. Any connection or reference to the missing Jamie Grant had been left out of the story.

"Find me something, anything that connects Robertson to New York City—and I don't mean just Manhattan—or to our Church or to any other church or organization that might have it in for us."

Margiotta looked up at him with an anguished expression. "This could take me all night."

Poor baby, Jensen wanted to say, but resisted. "It's already taken half the night. Consider yourself on the homestretch. Besides, you're getting time and a half."

"Yeah, but I've got a wife and a kid—"

"Who'll be glad for the bigger paycheck. Now keep at it."

Margiotta grumbled something unintelligible as he returned to the keyboard.

Jensen gave him a comradely clap on the shoulder as he rose.

"Good man. I'm going to take a stroll around to stretch my legs, maybe get a coffee. You want one?"

Margiotta looked surprised at the offer. And well he should be. Jensen didn't play gopher for anyone. But he wanted Margiotta to stay alert as he followed those hits.

He stepped out into the hallway and began making the rounds.

The elevator stopped on the twenty-first floor. As the doors slid open, Jack pressed the lobby button and stepped out of the car—just barely. He stopped as close to the doors as he could without trapping the back of his shirt when they closed.

On his previous tour of the temple he'd noticed stationary visual surveillance cameras in the elevator area of every floor, high in the corners above the doors, facing out. The TPs—if they were of a mind to do so—could watch you in the elevator car and then catch you again when you stepped out onto the floor. The meditation floor was no different.

But Jack had noticed that the fixed angle needed to capture the longest view of the hallway inevitably left a blind spot just outside the elevator doors.

Right where Jack was standing.

He looked longingly at the EXIT sign over the door to the stairwell on his right. That way would be so much simpler but the security cameras covered the approach and he was sure opening the door would be flagged in the security computer.

He slipped on a pair of latex gloves, then fished out the big screwdriver and heavy-duty coat hanger hook he'd brought along. He'd freed the hook from its wooden hanger, then tied and glued a length of sturdy twine to its straight end. He hoped he'd done it right. He hadn't had time to call on Milkdud Swigart for a refresher course on how to hack a building.

Back in December he and Milkdud had hacked a Midtown building through the elevator shaft so that Jack could eavesdrop on a conversation in one of the offices. Jack hadn't attempted anything like that since. This would be his first solo hack.

He worked the hook through the space between the top of the elevator door and the lintel. Keeping a grip on the string, he let the hook drop on the far side of the door.

Now the hard part: catching the lever that would open the door.

He fished the hook around, twisting the twine this way and that, then pulling up. If he found no resistance, he went through the process again.

He began to sweat with frustration and maybe a little anxiety. Jack remembered Milkdud saying that old buildings with old elevators had the easiest doors to open. Well, this former hotel was an old building, so why—?

The twine resisted his pull—the hook had caught something.

He sent up a prayer to the goddess of building hackers: Please, let this be the lever.

He tugged and saw the doors move—just a fraction of an inch, but enough to tell him he was in the right place. Pulled a little harder and the doors spread farther, allowing enough space for Jack to slip the screwdriver through. He let go of the string and used the screwdriver to lever the doors open until he had room for his fingers in the gap. He slipped them through, then forced the doors apart. Once past a certain point, they opened the rest of the way on their own.

The open elevator shaft yawned before him. Thick cables ran up and down the center of the shaft, their coating of grease reflecting the glow from the caged incandescent bulb set above the doors.

Jack poked his head into the shaft and looked down. Bulbs lit the way into the dimness below. He couldn't see his elevator car, but the other, marked with a "2" on its roof, waited midshaft about ten floors down.

He looked to his right and found what he wanted. Between the two sets of doors a row of rusty metal rungs had been set into the wall. They ran the length of the shaft.

He pocketed the screwdriver, the hook, and the twine. He grabbed a rung, placed the ridged rubber sole of his work boot on another, lower rung, and swung out into the shaft. He brushed against a spring switch along the way and was startled by the *ding!* of the elevator bell.

So that's what makes it ring.

He would have expected a more sophisticated system, but then again, these elevators were antiques.

He grabbed the lever and pushed down to close the doors, then began the short climb to the top floor.

Brady's floor.

No problem opening the elevator doors from this side: A simple push on the lever admitted him to floor twenty-two.

The only question was whether or not he was alone up here. The lights were on, but that didn't mean much. He listened. Not a sound.

Jack closed the doors but left the screwdriver between them. He stepped through the deserted receptionist area and crossed the office, passing Brady's huge desk as he made his way toward the living quarters.

He tried the door—locked. He knocked, a series of triplets, waited, then repeated. No response. He pulled out his cell and dialed the "personal" number Brady had given him last week. A phone began to ring on the far side of the door. On the fifth ring a voice—not Brady's—told him to leave a message. Jack was reasonably sure Brady would have answered a call at this hour.

So . . . nobody home. But that could change any minute. Jack turned and hurried to Brady's desk.

"All quiet on the Western Front?"

The TP in the lobby kiosk jumped as if he'd heard a shot. He dropped his newspaper and blanched when he saw who was speaking.

"Sir!" He shot to his feet. "You startled me, sir!"

"At ease," Jensen said, holding back a laugh.

He rarely used the elevator when he traveled from his office to the lobby. He'd found it much faster to take the stairs from the third floor. He'd eased through the stairway door at the south side of the lobby and silently made his way toward the security kiosk. He'd wanted to see how close he could get before the TP on duty realized he wasn't alone.

It had been easy. Too easy. The TP, whose name was Gary Cruz, had been so engrossed in the Sunday paper's sports section that Jensen had had to announce himself.

Jensen should have been angry, but he was too pleased with his own stealth to take Cruz's head off.

"Everything under control?"

The TP nodded. "Only one mouse in the house."

That wasn't unusual, even at this hour. A certain number of FAs would stay late or come in early to study, or catch up on assigned duties, or simply spend time on the Communing Level. The busiest after-hours periods tended to be Friday into Saturday, and Saturday into Sunday. The early hours of Monday usually found the Temple deserted. Except, of course, for the security detail.

"Thought he was a homeless guy at first," Cruz added.

"You're *sure* he wasn't?" This TP had better be damn sure.

"His card read him out as LFA, so that explained his looks."

"A lapser?" A sour note chimed in Jensen's head. "What's his name?"

Cruz sat and tapped at his keyboard. "John Roselli, sir. Came in about twenty minutes ago."

Roselli . . . he knew that name. He knew all the lapsers. He kept an eye on them to make sure they were complying with their punishment. But that wasn't the only reason. He'd kept a special watch ever since Clark Schaub. He'd been depressed because he thought his LFA designation was unjust—they *all* thought that—and killed himself.

A Dormentalist suicide was news under any circumstances, but when it happened in the Temple itself, and when the member did it in such dramatic fashion, it created a field day for the press. And not just rags like *The Light*—all the papers.

Schaub had seated himself in the center of the Great Room on the twenty-first floor, removed a straight razor from his pocket, and slit his own throat.

Covering it up had appeared impossible at first, but Jensen found a way. The only witnesses had been devout Dormentalists and they took a vow of silence to protect their Church. Jensen and Lewis and Hutch moved the body to a grove in Central Park. A police investigation listed Schaub as murdered by an unknown suspect. The case remained unsolved.

"Where'd Roselli go?"

Cruz checked his screen again. "Straight to twenty-one."

Shit. Like any other LFA, Roselli thought he'd gotten the shaft. He'd always struck Jensen as pretty stable, but you never knew. And the last thing Jensen needed now was a replay of the Schaub mess.

"Access the cameras up there. Let's see what our lapser is up to."

Cruz complied with practiced efficiency, alternating between mouse and keyboard. But as he worked, his brow began to furrow; a puzzled expression wormed onto his face.

Jensen didn't like that look. "What's wrong?"

"I can't find him."

"Well, then he must have left the floor."

Cruz pressed a button under one of his screens. "Not by the elevators. They haven't moved."

"Check the stairwell doors."

Jensen's mind raced. Each floor had access to the north and south stairways, but the doors were monitored. Access to the twenty-second floor from the stairways was blocked by password-protected steel doors that would have been at home in a bank vault.

"No record of either being opened."

"Then rerun the tapes, damn it. Let's see where he went when he left the elevator. No, wait. Do the elevator first."

Like a giant TiVo, the security computer stored each of the digital feeds on huge hard drives that made them accessible at any time.

Jensen moved behind Cruz and waited as he fiddled with the monitoring system. A bank of eight small screens arced across the inner front of the kiosk, just below the counter. Images from each security camera were supposed to rotate through the screens. The rotation had been halted while Cruz accessed specific cameras.

"Coming up on screen eight," Cruz said.

The black-and-white image of an elevator interior lit the screen. *Car 1* blinked in the upper-left corner; a digital clock ran in the upper right. The camera showed the knit-capped head of a scruffy-looking guy staring at his shoes. Jensen got a glimpse of beard but never the face.

According to the clock, Roselli stepped off the elevator onto twenty-one at 11:22:14. Something about the way he kept his head down bothered Jensen. But no problem. The other cameras would provide a good head-to-toe look.

"Roll the floor cameras back to 11:21."

Cruz did just that and Jensen watched as he scrolled through every feed from the twenty-first floor.

John Roselli didn't appear on one.

Cruz kept shaking his head as he made a second run through the feeds. "This is impossible! Something's got to be wrong!"

Jensen looked toward the elevator doors.

No, it wasn't impossible. Every surveillance system had blind spots. And yes, something was definitely wrong. Because whoever had gone up in that car had taken advantage of gaps in the system. Jensen doubted very much that John Roselli had the know-how or even the inclination to do that.

A thought hit like a horse kick in the chest.

Roselli—the Farrell-Amurri-Robertson guy had seen him during his tour . . . tried to talk to him . . . even asked questions about him . . .

Could it be him? But even so, Jensen didn't know what the guy hoped to accomplish up on twenty-one.

But the floor above . . .

"The elevators—did either go to twenty-two?"

Cruz looked up at him. "How could they? Mr. Brady left around—"

"Since Roselli checked in."

Cruz manipulated the mouse, then, "No, sir. Nothing's gone to two-two since Mr. Brady called for it earlier."

Jensen hid a sigh of relief. And yet . . .

What if this Farrell-Amurri-Robertson had somehow

got hold of Roselli's card? And what if he'd found a way to twenty-two?

Jensen cursed Brady for not allowing surveillance on twenty-two. He understood it—after all, Brady lived there—but it left a major gap in security.

"Call Roselli's home. See if he's there. And if he is, ask him if he's still got his swipe card."

"But—" Cruz began, then the light dawned. "Oh, I get it."

He placed the call, waited a long time with the receiver against his ear, then hung up.

"No answer, not even voice mail."

Okay. Then it was probably Roselli up there. He could have stepped out of the elevator, sat himself down right in front of the doors, and killed himself: knife, poison, whatever.

But then again, it was possible, just possible, that it was someone else.

"I'm going up for a look."

"I'll go, sir."

"No. You man the fort."

Either way, a dead Roselli or a live mystery guy, Jensen wanted to handle it alone.

But he hoped—no, he *prayed*—it was the mystery guy. He needed to slip his hands around the bastard's scrawny neck and watch his eyes bulge out of his head.

5

Jack pressed the button under the lip of Brady's desktop. As the doors on the opposite wall began to slide open, he pulled the Beretta from the desk drawer. He ejected the magazine from the grip and inspected it. Full. He thumbed out three rounds—not too easy wearing latex gloves—then slipped it back into its well. Next he removed the slide assembly, which included the barrel and the firing pin. He put the frame back into the drawer and placed the slide assembly on the desktop.

Then he pulled his new-bought Beretta from the small of his back and removed its slide assembly as well. This he fitted onto the frame of Brady's. That done he closed the drawer and fitted Brady's slide onto his own Beretta.

As he holstered his hybrid pistol he walked over to the now exposed globe. The little lights where pillars had been buried winked on automatically as it started its slow rotation. Was someone buried, like Jamie, in each of those spots?

Jack wanted to smash it—knock it over, pull it apart, and shatter every single one of those glowing bulbs. But he held back. He couldn't leave a hint that he'd been here.

He returned to the desk, pressed the button to close the doors, then headed for the elevator bank. After levering the doors open with the screwdriver, he swung back onto the rungs, closed the doors, then began his descent.

He'd gone two rungs when he heard the pulleys above begin to spin. He looked down and saw an elevator car with "1" on its roof moving his way.

Jack chewed his lip as he watched it rise, urging it to stop on one of the lower floors. But it kept coming. And coming.

Brady? Was the bossman home from his night of pedophilic debauchery?

Okay. No problem. Jack had done what he'd intended. He could return to the Communing Level and hang out for twenty minutes or so, then take an elevator down and stroll back through the lobby to the real world.

Expecting the car to pass him, Jack leaned away from its path. To his horror it began to slow as it approached the twenty-first.

Shit.

He hurried down the rungs and reached the door level

just as the car stopped. He peered through the gap between the car doors and the floor doors to see who was
trying to rain on his parade.

When he saw the black uniform and glistening chocolate scalp, he stifled a groan and pressed his forehead
against the cold steel of one of the rungs.

Jensen . . . what the hell was the Grand Paladin doing
here at this hour?

But the question vanished as he felt a scarlet rush
flash through him, saw Jamie's mutilated finger protrud-
ing from the concrete. Here was the guy who'd helped
bury her alive.

After coming down off the black fugue that had propelled him through his night with Cordova, Jack had been
cool, almost detached in dealing with Brady. Maybe that
was because he was miles away.

But Jensen . . . Jack had been planning to catch up with
him eventually to settle Jamie's score. Now Jensen was
here, within reach.

But Jack had to hold himself in check. This wasn't the
time or place. This was Jensen's home field. As much as
he hated to, Jack would have to wait. And improvise.

Jack hated to improvise.

Jensen held his pistol against his right thigh as he walked
through the Communing Level.

"Mr. Roselli?" he called, keeping his tone gentle.
"John Roselli?"

Come out, come out wherever you are . . .

. . . if you're here at all.

Not many places to hide on this level. He obviously

wasn't in the big open area; that left the private Communing Booths along the south wall. Jensen would have to check them one by one . . .

And if he found no one . . . what then?

Jensen had no idea.

❖

Jack watched Jensen's elevator car descend on its own to maybe the tenth or eleventh floor and stop. It had started down a minute or so after Jensen stepped off. Apparently the cars were programmed so that one waited at lobby level and the other stayed midshaft when not in use.

If nothing else it gave him some room.

To do what?

One thing he knew: He couldn't hang on these rungs till dawn.

The omnipresent surveillance cameras on the floor limited his options. Brady's lair and this elevator shaft were the only places he could move about unobserved. He could climb down to the base of the shaft and hide there until he could figure an escape route. Or . . .

Or what?

Jack noticed a metal inspection plate in the wall between the elevator doors. Desperate for some direction, for any sort of plan, he pulled out his screwdriver and went to work on the rusty screws. When he pulled off the plate he found half a dozen or so wires running to and from a pair of switches embedded in the opposite side. It took him a moment to realize he was looking at the rear innards of the elevator call buttons.

Fat lot of good that did him.

And then . . . an idea . . .

Jack had planned to catch up with Jensen later. But maybe he could do that now and then simply walk out of here.

He went to work on the wires.

❖

"Where the fuck *is* he?" Jensen muttered.

He pulled his two-way from a pocket and called the lobby.

"Cruz? Any sign of Roselli?"

"No, sir. He's not up there?"

"Haven't you been watching me?"

"Yessir."

"Well then you know the answer to your question."

He was about to add "you moron" but bit it back. Wrong thing to show frustration with an underling. Always stay in control.

"But, sir, that's impossible," Cruz yammered. "He hasn't used the elevators or the stairs and—"

"Speaking of the stairs, did the doors register when I opened them?"

"Yessir."

Damn. He'd been hoping that was it: a faulty sensor on one of the doors. But then the guy should have shown up on the Communing Floor and stairway cameras.

One fucked-up situation here.

"I'm going to do a little more looking around," he told Cruz, then thumbed the two-way off.

He strode to the elevators and hit the DOWN button. As he waited for the car he turned and surveyed the wide-open space of the Communing Level and the city towers beyond its floor-to-ceiling windows, many lit up even at this hour. But he was not in a mood to enjoy the view.

This temple was his turf. He was responsible for its integrity. Last week a man using three false identities had infiltrated his turf and burned him. He was still stinging with embarrassment. And now another—or perhaps the same man—had invaded his space and disappeared.

Jensen had to find him.

That meant searching the temple from top to bottom—

literally. He'd start with Brady's floor. He couldn't imagine how *anyone* could have reached twenty-two. Only he and Brady knew the access code. Without it you could press 22 all you wanted, but the car would stop at twenty-one and go no farther unless someone already on twenty-two—Brady or Vida, his receptionist—overrode the autostop.

Someone on twenty-two? No chance.

But the seemingly impossible had already happened, so . . .

He'd have to search twenty-two alone. Couldn't allow a squad of TPs to poke through Brady's quarters. But when he'd determined that the floor was deserted, he'd call the next shift in early and start an organized gang-bang search from twenty-one down. He'd bring in a pack of fucking bloodhounds if he had to. Nobody disappeared on his watch. Nobody.

The elevator dinged behind him and he heard the doors slide open. He turned absently and stepped toward it. Too late he realized that no car awaited him, only cables and empty space.

He let out a terrified bleat as he tilted over the chasm. His heart pounded as he flailed his arms trying to catch the doorway. The fingers of his right hand caught the lip of the molding. Not much to hang on to but enough to stop his forward motion. He teetered there, looking down at the top of the elevator car ten floors below, then began to pull himself back. He was just starting to congratulate himself on his quick reflexes when an arm shot out from the left, grabbed his tunic, and yanked him into the void.

He screamed, turning and windmilling his arms as he began to fall. He twisted far enough around to grab the floor of the doorway, first with one hand, then the other. He hung by his fingertips, kicking his feet back and forth in search of a ledge, a girder, even a loose brick, anything to help support his weight.

But he found nothing.

And then movement to his right as a man swung out of the elevator shaft and crouched before him on the edge. Jensen looked at his face and knew him. Even with his crummy fake beard and his low knit cap and his dirty clothes, Jensen knew him.

Farrell-Amurri-Robertson-Whoever.

The guy.

"Help me!" Jensen said, trying to keep from screaming. He hated pleading with this son of a bitch, but . . . "Please!"

Then he looked up and saw his eyes, brown and cold as dirt from the bottom of a grave, and knew he was as good as dead.

" 'Please'?" the guy said in a low voice, barely above a whisper. "Is that what Jamie Grant said when you were about to cut off her finger?"

Jensen's intestines clenched, sending a wave of terror through his belly.

How could he know? How could he *possibly* know?

And now the guy had a knife in his latex-gloved hand. He opened it.

"Oh, please! Oh, please don't!"

"I bet Jamie said that too. But what if I were to do some of the same to you? What if I start cutting off *your* fingers, one at a time?"

He drew the blade lightly across the knuckle of the right little finger, then the left. The steely caress sent a tremor through Jensen's tortured arms.

"Please!"

"Let's make this a game. How many fingers do you think you can spare before you can't hold on any longer? I'm thinking three—a pinkie on each side, and then when you lose a ring finger on, say, the left side, you'll fall. You're a strong man, Jensen, but you're heavy." He nodded and smiled—not a nice smile. "Yeah. I think three will do it."

"No! No, please!"

The eyebrows lifted. "No? Okay. If you say so, then no it is."

And then, miraculously he was folding the knife and leaning away.

He means it?

"Hey," the guy said. "Just kidding about that amputation thing. Had no intention of doing something like that." He drew back his right leg. "Haven't got *time*!"

The leg shot out and Jensen caught a flash of a rubber sole just before his nose and left cheek exploded in pain. The blow jerked his head back and that was just enough to loosen his grip on the threshold.

His fingers slipped and grabbed empty air. He screamed as he tumbled backward.

❖

Jack watched Jensen's twisting, kicking fall come to an abrupt end atop car one. He'd twisted around in midair to land face first, denting and cracking the roof but not breaking all the way through.

Jack stared down at the scene for a while. He didn't see how anyone could survive that kind of fall, but he'd heard of people who'd lived through worse, and with a guy that size—

Jensen's chest moved.

Jack stared, thinking his eyes were playing tricks. Then he saw him draw another breath.

Christ, what did it take to be rid of this guy?

Right now the fall looked like an accident—Jack *needed* it to look like an accident. But if Jensen lived . . .

Couldn't allow that.

Steeling himself for what he was about to do, Jack climbed down the rungs toward the car. Jensen's hands were beginning to move, his arms too. But not a twitch from his legs. Back was probably broken . . . spinal cord injury.

Well, his spinal cord was about to get worse.

Jack stopped his descent about six feet above Jensen and car one. He turned and clung precariously with his back to the rungs. He hesitated, something holding him back. Then he thought of Jamie Grant having her finger amputated, being buried alive, how it must have felt to be engulfed in concrete . . .

He jumped, aiming his boots for the back of Jensen's neck. He heard the vertebrae crunch as he hit with enough force to ram the bald head through the roof of the car.

For an instant Jack teetered backward, but he managed to grab one of the cables to steady himself. The palm of the glove was black with grease. He knelt next to Jensen and removed it, inverting it as he pulled it off, pocketing it, and replacing it with a fresh one.

Then he wormed a couple of fingers through the opening around Jensen's head and felt his throat for a pulse. Nada.

Jack straightened and took a deep breath. Two of three scores settled. Only Brady remained.

He climbed back up to the twenty-first, reattached the call-button wires, and replaced the inspection plate. Then he stepped through the doorway and hit the down button. He removed his gloves as the pulleys whirled into motion. Seconds later he was looking at the inside of cab one, with Jensen's glazed eyes staring back at him from a hole in the ceiling. Slow drops of blood dripped from his nose.

Keeping his head down, Jack stepped in and knuckled the lobby button. Jensen's head lay above the angle of the surveillance camera, so as far as any observer could tell, the bearded, knit-capped guy was alone in the car.

When the car stopped, Jack pressed a knuckle against 10 as the doors opened, then stepped out into the lobby.

"Roselli?" the TP at the kiosk called. "Is that John Roselli?"

"No, I'm *LFA* Roselli," Jack said, making for the front

door. He added some attitude. "You got a problem with that?"

This was the last hurdle. If he could get past this guy without too much fuss, he'd be home free.

"Just hold on there. Where have you been?"

Jack didn't break stride. "On the Communing Level."

"No, you weren't. You didn't show up on the cameras so the GP went looking for you and—"

Keep moving . . . keep moving . . .

"I just left Jensen. And he didn't mention cameras."

The guard had a two-way up to his lips. "GP Jensen? GP Jensen?" He lowered the two-way and looked at Jack. "He's not answering. Where did you see him?"

"I left him upstairs. He's going to hang around awhile."

As Jack reached the doors the TP came out from behind his kiosk and hurried toward him.

"Wait! You can't go yet!"

"No? Watch me."

Jack pushed through the doors, hit the sidewalk, and began walking uptown. The guard stepped out behind him.

"Hey! Come back! The GP will want to talk to you."

Jack ignored him and kept walking. He was heading home. He needed sleep something awful. He found his car two blocks away where he'd left it, parked on a side street. After checking to make sure the TP hadn't followed him, he slid behind the wheel and hit the ignition.

He drove a dozen blocks then pulled over and threw the Buick into park. He put his head back as far as the headrest would allow and took a few deep breaths. A tremor shuddered through his body. That cold black rush was fading, leaving him shaky and exhausted.

He scared himself when he got like this. Not while he was in the dark thrall—he feared nothing then—but in the low aftermath it unsettled him to know what he was capable of. Sometimes he'd swear never to let it loose again, to push it back next time it lunged for freedom. Yet inevitably, when the moment came, he'd embrace and ride it.

But he never wanted another episode like tonight. It would take him a while to forget this one.

7

As per usual, Luther Brady had awakened early and driven in from the hills. He'd started the day with a slight headache—not unexpected after a night of carousing—but that was gone now. And as always after a bout with the boys, he felt rejuvenated. Give him the right playmates and he'd never need Viagra.

He liked to arrive before seven, when the temple was relatively deserted, and slip up to his quarters.

But this morning he found chaos—flashing police cars and ambulances outside, bustling cops and EMTs within.

One of the TPs recognized him and came rushing up.

"Mr. Brady! Mr. Brady! Oh, thank Noomri you're here! It's terrible! Just terrible!"

"What's happened?"

"It's GP Jensen—he's dead!"

Shock passed through him like a cold front. Jensen? Dead? He'd been Luther's most valuable asset—loyal to the Opus, fearless and relentless in pursuing its completion. What would he do without him?

"How?"

"An accident. He fell down the elevator shaft. It was awful! TP Cruz found him. His head . . . his head had smashed through the top of one of the elevator cars!"

An accident . . .

Already Luther could feel a small sense of relief tem-

pering the shock, a slight loosening of his tightened muscles. For a moment there, and he couldn't say exactly
why, he'd feared that Jensen had been murdered. Bad
enough that he'd lost his right-hand man, but a
murder . . . that would cause a storm in the media. An accident, however . . . well, that was a nonstory. Accidents
can happen anywhere, to anyone, at any time. No reason
the Dormentalist temple should be expected to be any
different.

"This is terrible," Luther said. "This is tragic. I must
get to my quarters to commune with my xelton."

"The police may want to talk to you."

"I'll speak to them in a little while. Right now I'm too
upset."

Too true. He'd invested a lot of time, money, and effort
in Jensen. He'd been one of a kind. How was he going to
replace him? Worse, this was going to set back the Opus
Omega timetable.

Damn it to hell! Just when the end was in sight.

He'd worry about a replacement later. Right now he
had to get Vida working on a press release, and have her
prepare some public remarks about what a kind, gentle,
wonderful man Jensen was.

Oh, yes. And he needed her to look up Jensen's first
name. He should know the first name of the man he'd be
publicly mourning.

8

The clock radio woke Jack at nine. He lay in bed listening to the news about a murder in the Bronx and a fatal
accident in the Midtown Dormentalist temple. He shook
off the memory of Jensen's dead eyes staring at him from

the ceiling on the elevator ride down to the lobby and got to work.

Wearing boxers and a T-shirt, he dug out his X-Acto knife kit and seated himself at the round, paw-foot oak table in his front room. He pulled on a pair of latex gloves—man, he was going through these things like chewing gum—and got to work.

He removed the stack of Cordova's photos from the envelope and shuffled through them a second time. Familiarity did not make the task any less nauseating. Last night, while Cordova was unconscious, Jack had sorted them into three stacks: Brady alone, Brady pulling on the mask, and the masked Brady with the boys. He'd picked one at random from each of the first two, but it had taken him a while to find three from the third with the boys faced away from the camera. He'd cut off the corners where the camera had imprinted the date and time, and left them all with Cordova.

On this new pass through the stacks, Jack culled the most damning examples from each pile, then set to work with the X-Acto, cutting out the centers of the boys' faces. No need for something like this to follow them the rest of their lives. Again he cut off the camera's date-and-time imprint.

That done, he placed them in a FedEx envelope along with the letter he'd printed out from Cordova's office computer.

> *If you're reading this, I am dead, and this is the man who did it. Please don't let these pictures go to waste.*
>
> *Richard Cordova*

He sealed it and addressed it to *The Light*. He made up the return address.

Then he picked up his cell phone for the first of two calls he had to make. Information connected him to the Pennsylvania State Police. When he said he wanted to report a crime, he was shunted to another line. He told the officer who answered that they needed to go to a certain farm where a concrete cylinder had been buried, and that within that cylinder they'd find the remains of the missing New York City reporter, Jamie Grant. He also told them where they could find the mold used to make the cylinder and that the symbols on it were strictly Dormentalist.

The officer wanted to know who he was and how he knew all this.

Yeah, right.

The second call went to Mrs. Roselli-Not. She picked up on the second ring.

"Good morning, Jack."

That startled him. He had no name listed with his phone. Even with caller ID, how could she . . . ?

Maybe she recognized his number. Or maybe she didn't need electronics.

"Good morning. Feeling well enough for company today?"

"Yes. Finally. You may come over now if you wish."

"I wish. See you in about half an hour."

He got dressed, switched his latex gloves for leather, and headed out. He had the overnight envelope in hand and Anya's skin in the pocket of his coat. One he'd mail along the way. The other was for show and tell—he'd show and the old lady would tell.

He hoped.

Gia stood at the corner of Second Avenue and Fifty-eighth and marveled at how good she felt today. She seemed to have regained most of her strength and ambition. She'd even done some painting this morning.

But now it was time for some fresh air. This was the first time she'd been out of the house in almost a week. It was good to know the city was still here. It even smelled good. A fall breeze was diluting the fumes from passing cars and trucks. And most amazing of all: Traffic was moving.

She planned to walk up to Park, maybe head downtown for a few blocks, then circle back home. As she waited for the light to change, she felt the baby kick and had to smile. What a delicious sensation. Tomorrow she was scheduled for another ultrasound. Everything was going to be fine, she just knew it.

Finally, the walking green. She took one step off the curb but froze when she heard a blaring horn. She looked up and saw a delivery van racing toward her along the avenue. Gia heard a scream—her own—as she turned and leaped back onto the sidewalk. One of the front tires bounced over the curb just inches from her feet. The side-view mirror brushed the sleeve of her sweater as the truck slewed sideways and slammed into the rear of a parked UPS truck.

The rest of the world seemed to stand silent and frozen for a heartbeat or two as glittering fragments of shattered glass tumbled through the air, catching the sunlight as they showered the impact area, and then cries of shock and alarm as people began running for the truck.

Gia stood paralyzed, feeling her heart pounding as she watched bystanders help the shaken and bloodied driver from the car. She looked back to where she'd been standing and realized with a stab of fear that if she hadn't moved, the truck would have made a direct hit. At the speed he'd been going, she could not imagine anyone, especially her and the baby, surviving an impact like that.

She looked back and saw the driver shuffling toward her across Fifty-eighth. Blood oozed from the left side of his forehead.

"Dear lady, I am so sorry," he said in accented English—Eastern Eu-rope, maybe. "The brakes, they stop working . . . the steering it no good. I am so happy you are well."

Unable to speak yet, Gia could only nod. First the near miscarriage, now this. If she didn't know better she might think somebody up there didn't want this baby to be born.

10

Sitting at his office desk, Luther Brady studied the printout as TP Cruz stood at attention on the other side. Cruz looked exhausted, as he should: He'd been up all night and had lost his boss to boot.

"So the elevator records show this John Roselli going to the twenty-first floor and nowhere else."

"Yessir. At least not by elevator. GP Jensen used it next."

The printout showed the elevator going directly to twenty-one a second time. The next use after that was when it was called back to twenty-one and taken to the lobby.

"And this time?" He tapped the paper.

"That was Roselli again, sir. He's on the tape. But there was something strange going on with Roselli and the tapes."

"For instance?"

"Well—"

"Excuse me?"

Luther looked up and saw his secretary standing in the office doorway.

"Yes, Vida?"

"I just got a call from downstairs. The police are here again and want to see you."

Luther rubbed his eyes, then glanced at his watch. Only ten A.M. When would this morning end?

"Tell them I've already given my statement and have nothing more to add."

"They say they're here on a murder investigation."

"Murder?" Did they think Jensen was murdered? "Very well, send them up."

He dismissed Cruz, then leaned back in his desk chair and swiveled it toward the morning sky gleaming beyond the windows. Jensen murdered . . . Luther remembered his impression when he'd first heard the news. But who could survive a confrontation with that human mountain of bone and muscle, let alone hurl him down an elevator shaft? It didn't seem possible.

Minutes later Vida opened the door and looked in on him. "The police are here."

"Send them in."

Luther remained seated as she stepped aside and admitted a pair of middle-aged, standard-issue detectives. Both wore brown shoes and wrinkled suits under open, rumpled coats. But they weren't alone. A trio of younger, more casually dressed men followed them. Each carried what looked like an oversized toolbox.

Alarm at the number of invaders and the looks on the detectives' faces drew him to his feet.

"What's all this?"

The dark-haired detective in the lead had a pock-marked face. He flashed a gold badge and said, "Detective Young, NYPD." He nodded toward his lighter-haired partner. "This is Detective Holusha. We're both from the Four-Seven precinct. Are you Luther Brady?"

The detective's cold tone and the way he looked at him—as if he were some sort of vermin—drew the saliva from Luther's mouth.

He nodded. "Yes."

"Then this"—Young reached into his pocket, retrieved a folded set of papers, and dropped them on Luther's desk—"is for you."

Luther snatched it up and unfolded it. His eyes scanned the officialese but the meaning failed to register.

"What is this?"

"A search warrant for your office and living quarters."

The three other men were fanning out around Luther, opening their tool-boxes, pulling on rubber gloves.

"What? You can't! I mean, this is outrageous! I'm calling my lawyer! You're not doing anything until he gets here!"

Barry Goldsmith would put them in their places.

"That's not the way it works, Mr. Brady. You have the right to call your attorney, but meanwhile we'll be executing the warrant."

"We'll just see about that!"

As Luther reached for the phone the detective said, "Do you own a nine-millimeter pistol, Mr. Brady?"

My pistol? What do they want with . . . ?

"Yes, I do. Licensed and legally registered, I'll have you know."

"We do know. A Beretta 92. That's one of the reasons we're here."

"I don't under—" And then it hit him. "Oh, no! Was Jensen shot?"

The other detective, Holusha, frowned. "Jensen? Who's Jensen?"

"My chief of security . . . he died this morning . . . an accident. I thought you were here about—"

Young said, "Where is your pistol, Mr. Brady?"

"Right here in the desk." Luther reached toward the drawer. "Here, I'll show—"

Holusha's voice snapped like a whip. "Please don't touch the weapon, Mr. Brady."

Luther snatched his hand back. "It's in the second drawer."

"Step away from the desk, please."

As Luther complied, Young signaled one of the

younger men. "Romano." He pointed to the drawer. "Gun's in there."

Luther felt as if reality were slipping away. Here in his building, his temple, his word was law. But now his office, his home, his sanctum, had been invaded. He was no longer in control. These storm troopers had taken over.

And no one was saying why. He felt as if he'd fallen into a Kafka story.

It had to be a mistake. Did they think he'd shot somebody? Who? Not that it mattered. He'd never even *aimed* that pistol at a human being, let alone shot one.

This mix-up would be straightened out, and then someone at the District Attorney's office would pay. Oh, how they'd pay.

"What . . . ?" He swallowed. "What am I supposed to have done?"

Holusha pulled an index card from the breast pocket of his shirt.

"How well do you know Richard Cordova?"

"Cordova?"

Luther ran the name through his brain as he watched the man called Romano lift the Beretta from the drawer. He held it suspended from a wire he'd hooked through the trigger guard.

Cordova . . . he was drawing a blank. But how could anyone be expected to think under these circumstances?

"I don't believe I've ever heard of him. It's quite impossible for me to remember the name of every Church member. We have so—"

"We don't think he was a Dormentalist."

Was?

"What happened to him?"

"He was murdered late last night or early this morning. He was pistol-whipped, then shot three times with a nine millimeter. When was the last time you fired your pistol, Mr. Brady?"

Luther relaxed a little. Here was where he'd turn the tables.

"Four, maybe five months ago, and that was on a shooting range at a paper target, not at a human being."

Romano sniffed the muzzle and shook his head as he looked up at Young.

"Beg to differ. This was fired recently. Very recently." He lifted the pistol farther, twisting it this way and that as he inspected it. He stiffened. "My-my-my. If I'm not mistaken, we've got blood and maybe a little tissue in the rear sight notch."

Luther watched in uncomprehending horror as Romano dropped the Beretta into a clear plastic evidence bag. This couldn't be happening! First Jensen, now—

"Wait! This is a terrible mistake. I don't know this Cordova person! I've never even heard of him!"

Holusha smirked. "Well, he's heard of you."

"I . . . I don't understand."

"You probably thought you'd cleaned out his house pretty good, but you missed a few."

"A few what?"

Holusha only shook his head in reply. Luther looked to Young for an answer but all questions dissolved when he saw the detective's hard look.

"We'll need you to come up to the Four-Seven for questioning, Mr. Brady."

Luther's stomach plummeted. "Am I under arrest?"

"No, but we need some answers about your pistol and your whereabouts last night."

That was a relief. The thought of being led through the temple in handcuffs was unbearable.

"I want my lawyer along."

"Fine. Call him and have him meet us there."

He hadn't done anything wrong, but he wanted Barry along to keep everything on the up and up.

They had to be mistaken about his pistol . . . had to be.

That reddish-brown stain he'd spotted in the rear sight couldn't be blood. But if not, what was it?

11

"What should I call you?" Jack said. "I mean, since your name isn't Roselli?"

The old woman looked up at him from the seat of a Far Eastern fan-backed armchair. Her gnarled hands rested on her silver-handled cane. Her face was still round and puffy, her sinophilic apartment as crowded as ever with screens, statues, and inlaid tables. She wore a red turtle-neck and blue slacks this time.

She cocked her head. "What makes you think it's not?"

Jack had run the gauntlet of Esteban the doorman and Benno the Rott-weiler—who'd subjected him to an un-comfortably thorough inspection of his crotch—and de-murred the offers of tea and shortbread cookies. Now, finally, he stood before the old lady who'd told him she was Maria Roselli.

"Because I found Johnny Roselli and he says his mother's been dead four years. You look pretty alive to me, Mrs. . . . ?"

"Why don't you just call me Herta."

"Is that your name?"

A small smile. "It's as good as any."

Swell. "Okay . . . Herta. I can go with that. But—"

She lifted one of her thin, gnarled hands from atop her silver-headed cane in a stop motion. "Just let me say that Johnny was both right and wrong when he told you his mother was dead. That may be true of his birth mother, but not of me. For I am his mother too, just as I am yours."

Jack felt as if a great weight had been lifted from his shoulders. He wasn't going to have to argue with her. She'd just—in so many words—admitted who she was.

He sank into a chair opposite her.

"So there it is: You're one of them."

A small smile stretched the tight skin of her moon face. "And who would 'them' be?"

"The ladies with the dogs. The ladies who know too damn much. You're the fourth."

The first had been the Russian lady with the malamute in June. The next had been younger, wearing a sari and leading a German shepherd. And the last had been Anya with Oyv, her fearless chihuahua. They'd all claimed to be his mother.

He had no idea who these women were, or how many more of them existed, but somehow they represented a mysterious third force in the eternal tug of war between the Otherness and the Ally.

"Yes, I suppose I am."

"On our first meeting you told me you didn't know Anya Mundy. But obviously you do. How many other lies have you told me?"

Under different circumstances he might have been angry, but now he was too tired.

"I did not lie. You said, 'Do you know an older woman named Anya?' I did know such a person, but she is gone. You should have asked me, 'Did you *ever* know an older woman named Anya?' Then I would have given you a different answer."

Annoyed, Jack leaned forward. "Okay, let's bypass the wordplay and cut to the chase: You manipulated me into getting involved with the Dormentalist. Why?"

Herta reached out and stroked Benno's head. The dog closed its eyes and craned its neck against her hand.

"Because it must be destroyed. Or barring that, it must be damaged, crippled, driven to its knees."

This lady didn't mince words.

"Because it's connected to the Otherness?"

She nodded. "It was inspired by the Otherness, and has become its tool."

"How does a cosmic force inspire a cult?"

"Through a man whose drug-addled mind was open to influence when the Adversary was conceived—or I should say, *reconceived*."

The Adversary . . . also known as the One . . . who moved about under even more identities and names than Jack . . . the Otherness's agent provocateur in this world . . . whose True Name Jack had learned only a few months ago . . .

Rasalom.

And Jack was pretty sure he could name the owner of that drug-addled mind.

"Cooper Blascoe told me he got the idea for Dormentalism from a dream back in the late sixties. Was that when Rasa—"

Herta's hand shot up. "Do not say his True Name! I don't want him to know where I am. And neither do you."

Jack hated to admit it, but she had that right. He'd had a taste of what this Rasalom guy could do. Pretty scary.

"What do you mean, 'reconceived'?"

"After millennia of striving to maximize the human misery that fed him, he was permanently eliminated shortly before World War II. At least that was what was thought. But in 1968, through a freak set of circumstances, he contrived to be reconceived in the womb of an unsuspecting woman."

The date rang a bell . . . Jack had been to a town where a "burst of Otherness" had occurred in 1968 . . . been there a number of times. None of his visits had been pleasant, and he'd nearly lost his life there.

"That wouldn't have been in Monroe, Long Island, would it?"

She nodded. "It would. And that was not the first time he came back from the dead."

"Anya mentioned that he'd been reborn a number of times. But look, I've got to tell you, Cooper Blascoe didn't seem like a bad guy. Hard to believe a hippie like him was working for the Otherness."

"He was merely a pawn. His dream of the Hokano world that he turned into a pamphlet was Otherness-inspired. He planted the seed that Luther Brady later twisted into the monstrous entity of his church, to use as a tool to help the Otherness dominate this sphere."

Jack shook his head. "But as I understand it, the Otherness means to change everything here, make our reality living hell. Brady doesn't seem the type who'd try to screw himself. Unless of course he's insane."

"He is quite sane, but is possessed of the notion that the one who completes the Opus Omega—"

"Opus . . . ?"

"Opus Omega: the Last Task, the End Work—burying those obscene columns in all the designated spots."

"You mean . . ." Jack pulled the flap of Anya's skin from his pocket and unfolded it for Herta to see ". . . in a pattern like this?"

A cloud of pain passed across the old woman's puffy face.

She sighed. "Yes. Just like that."

"So it all comes together. 'No more coincidences,' right? The flap of skin I can't throw away, your hiring me to infiltrate the Dormentalists where I'd get a view of Brady's globe and recognize the pattern . . . everything's been carefully orchestrated."

He felt like a goddamn puppet.

"'Orchestrated' gives me too much credit. No one—not the Otherness, not the Ally, and certainly not I—has that much control. People and objects are placed in proximity in the hope that certain outcomes will ensue."

"Is Brady in the same boat?"

"Luther Brady is driving himself. I doubt he has any concept of what the Otherness's new world order will be like, but I have little doubt that he believes that the man who completes the Opus Omega will be rewarded with an exalted position in it."

"But how does he even know about this Opus Omega?"

"He too had a dream, but his was of a map of the world. It showed the nexus points around the globe, each radiating lines toward the others. Wherever three lines crossed, the intersection glowed. He had no idea of its significance until a forbidden book, *The Compendium of Srem,* was delivered into his hands."

"Forbidden, huh? How exactly does a book become forbidden? Like banned in Boston?"

She offered him a tolerant smile. "In a way. It was banned in the fifteenth century by the Catholic church."

"Six hundred years . . . pretty old book."

"That was merely when it was banned. It's much older than that. No one is quite sure *how* old. *The Compendium* first came to the church's attention during the Spanish Inquisition when it was discovered in the possession of a Moorish scholar whose name is lost. He was put through unimaginable agonies before he died, but either could not or would not say who had given it to him.

"The Grand Inquisitor himself, Torquemada, is said to have been so repulsed after reading only a part of *The Compendium* that he ordered a huge bonfire built and hurled the book into the flames. But it would not burn. Nor would it be cut by the sharpest sword or the heaviest ax. So he dropped it into the deepest well in the Spanish Empire; he filled that well with granite boulders, then built the monastery of St. Thomas over it."

Jack gave a low whistle. "What the hell was in it?"

"Many things. Lists and descriptions of unspeakable rites and ceremonies, diagrams of ancient clockwork machines, but the heart of *The Compendium* is the outline of the Opus Omega—the final process that will assure the ascent of what it calls 'the Other world.' "

Jack felt a chill. "The Otherness. Even back then?"

"Surely you realize that this cosmic shadow war is about far more than humanity. The millions of years since the first hominid reared up on its hind legs are an eye blink in the course of the conflict. It began before the Earth was formed and will continue long after the sun's furnace goes cold."

Jack did know that—at least he'd been told that—but it was still hard to accept.

"And as with all forbidden things," Herta went on, "*The Compendium* could not stay buried. A small subsect of monks within the monastery spent years digging tunnels and secretly excavating the well. They retrieved the book, but before they could put it to use they were all slain and the book disappeared for five hundred years."

"If a boulder-filled well with a monastery overhead couldn't keep it out of circulation, where did it hide during those centuries?"

"In a place built by the Ally's warrior—"

"You mean the one Anya told me about—the one I'm supposed to replace? He's that old?"

Here was another thing Jack couldn't or wouldn't accept: Like it or not, he'd been drafted into this cosmic war.

"Much older," Herta said. "Almost as old as the Adversary. More than five centuries ago he trapped the Adversary in a stone keep in a remote pass in Eastern Europe. He sealed away many forbidden books there as well, to keep them out of the hands of men and women susceptible to the Otherness. But the fortress was broached by the German Army in the spring of 1941. Fortunately the Adversary was killed—albeit temporarily—before he could escape."

"But this *Compendium* thing made it out?"

"Yes. It and other forbidden books ended up in the hands of a man named Alexandru, one of the keep's caretakers. After the war he sold them to an antiquarian book dealer in Bucharest who in turn sold *The Compendium* to an American collector. A quarter of a century later, the collector was murdered and the book stolen."

"Let me guess who was responsible for that: Rasa—I mean, the Adversary, right?"

"Not personally. He was a child at the time. But his guardian then, a man named Jonah Stevens, committed the crime and saw to it that *The Compendium* reached a recent college graduate named Luther Brady."

"And the book told him to start burying concrete columns at these spots around the globe?"

Herta shook her head. "Not start—finish. The Opus Omega had been begun long before, but there was no way for those ancients to reach certain parts of the Old World, let alone the New. Remember, *The Compendium* was already sealed in the Transylvania Alps when Columbus set sail for the Americas."

"So Brady picked up where they left off. But why Brady?"

"Because he's the sort who is highly susceptible to Otherness influence. He was and still is inspired by dreams of power—of literally changing the world."

"I didn't mean Brady specifically. I mean, why work through someone else at all? Why doesn't the Adversary just go out and bury these pillars himself? This Opus would probably be finished by now, and he wouldn't have to deal with all this Dormentalist bull along the way."

"But that would mean revealing himself, something the Adversary does not want to do."

"Why not?"

"Fear. He avoids drawing attention to himself for fear of alerting the Ally's champion. So he must work behind the scenes."

"I've seen some of what the Adversary can do, and if he's afraid . . . well, this champion must be one tough cookie. Do you know him?"

Herta nodded. "I know him well."

"What's his name?"

Herta hesitated, then, "His mother called him Glaeken."

12

Luther Brady leaned toward Barry Goldsmith, his personal attorney for the past dozen years. Barry had met him here at the Forty-seventh Precinct house and the two of them had been sitting alone at this battered table in this stuffy interrogation room for what felt like hours.

"How long can they keep us here?" Luther whispered.

He was sure they were being observed through the pane of mirrored glass set in the wall before them.

"We could leave now. I could demand that they either charge you and arrest you, or we walk."

"Arrested . . . I don't want to be—"

"Don't worry." Barry patted his arm. The gesture retracted the sleeve on his charcoal Armani suit, revealing his glittering Rolex. "I don't do criminal defense, but I know enough to tell you that they'll need a *lot* of evidence to put the cuffs on someone of your stature and pristine record. And we know they don't have that evidence— *can't* have that evidence, right?"

He sounded as if he wanted reassurance. Well, Luther would give it to him.

"Barry, listen to me and trust me when I say that I have never even *heard* of this Richard Cordova, let alone done him harm. And they say it happened up here in the Bronx. I don't know if I've ever in my life even set foot in the Bronx."

Another pat on the arm. "Well, then, we've nothing to worry about. They need motive and, considering that you've never heard of the man, you have none. They need opportunity, and a man who's never been to the Bronx could not have committed a crime here."

"But they took my pistol . . ."

Barry frowned. "That bothers me a little too. Was it out of your possession at any time during the past twenty-four hours?"

"I haven't been carrying it around, if that's what you mean. It's been in my desk."

"Which is in your office, and we both know what a fortress that is."

Yes, a fortress to which only he and Jensen—

Jensen! He could have taken the pistol. Luther couldn't imagine why, but—

No. He remembered seeing a report this morning from the Paladin office tracing Jensen's whereabouts last night. Nothing about going to the twenty-second floor. In fact, *no one* had entered the top floor last night—neither by elevator nor the stairway.

So it couldn't have been Jensen. But could his death be in some way connected . . . ?

"The pistol will vindicate you," Barry was saying. "That's probably why they've kept us waiting: ballistics tests. They'll compare slugs from your gun to the ones in the murdered man. When they get no match, they'll have to apologize. And that's when I'll go to work. They'll regret they ever heard your name."

"But that's the big question: Where did they *get* my name? There must be thousands and thousands of nine-millimeter pistols registered in this city, and who knows how many unregistered. But detectives from the Bronx show up on *my* doorstep. Why?"

Barry frowned again and shrugged.

Luther pressed on. "What worries me more is that one of the cops said my gun had been fired recently. And that there was blood and tissue in the rear sight. And I looked as he was bagging it and . . . and I thought I could see a brown stain there."

Barry's frown deepened. He appeared to be about to speak but stopped when the door next to the mirror opened.

Detectives Young and Holusha entered. Holusha carried a manila folder. He dropped it on the table as he and Young took seats opposite Luther. Young's expression was neutral, but Holusha's sent a spasm through Luther's bowels. He looked like a chubby cat contemplating a trapped mouse.

"I'll cut to the chase," Young said. "The ballistics people say the slugs that killed Cordova came from your pistol."

"Yeah," Holusha added. "Got a perfect match on the grooves, and guess what—you missed one of your brass. We found it in the darkroom. Tests show your firing pin fired that round."

A spasm again ran through Luther's gut. "That's impossible!"

Young ignored him and picked up without missing a beat. "The lab found blood on the rear sight that matches the blood type of the victim. DNA results are weeks away, but . . ." He left the rest to the imagination.

This couldn't be! It wasn't possible! This had to be a nightmare and he'd awaken any minute now.

"He's being framed!" Barry cried. "Can't you see that?"

"Two sets of fingerprints were lifted from your pistol," Young said, his gaze never shifting from Luther's face. "Yours, Mr. Brady—which we have from your gun permit application—and the victim's." His eyes narrowed. "Anything you want to tell us, Mr. Brady?"

"He has *nothing* to tell you except that he's being framed!" Barry said, slamming his palm on the table. "The pistol was stolen from his office, used to murder a man he's never heard of, and then returned! It's the only explanation!"

"A man he's never heard of?" Holusha said through a tight smile. "You're sure of that?"

"Damn right, he's sure of that! You may have a weapon, detectives, but you do *not* have a motive!"

"No?" Holusha opened the folder and arranged three photos in plastic sleeves before him. Then he slid them across the table. "I'd say these were motive, wouldn't you? *Mucho* motive."

Luther's blood turned to ice when he saw them.

13

"Glaeken . . ." Jack rolled the unfamiliar name over his tongue. "Strange name."

"It is ancient. He goes by another name these days."

Don't we all, Jack thought.

"Well, then, why don't you tell Glaeken what's going on?"

"He knows."

"He knows!" Jack leaned forward. "Then why isn't he out there kicking Adversarial butt?"

Herta sighed. "He would if he could, but Glaeken no longer has the powers he once did. He was relieved of his immortality in 1941 after the Adversary was killed, and has aged since."

"But that was over sixty years ago. He must be . . ."

"Old. Still quite a vital man, but he could never stand up to the Adversary in his present condition. That is why you have been . . . involved."

Involved, Jack thought. Nice way to put it. Dragged kicking and screaming into something I want no part of is more like it.

Slow nausea curdled his stomach as he began to realize there might be no way out for him. The Ally's torch was going to be passed his way, no doubt sooner than later if Glaeken was as old as Herta said.

Then he thought of something else . . .

"The Adversary is hiding from a frail old man . . . that means he doesn't know." He barked a laugh—first laugh in a couple of days. It felt good. "Oh, that's rich!"

"This is not a laughing matter. As long as the Adversary remains unaware of Glaeken's circumstances, he will be cautious in his doings. He will work through surrogates to prepare the way for the Otherness. But should he learn the truth . . ."

"The gloves will come off."

"As far as Glaeken is concerned, yes. He hates Glaeken. And he should, for Glaeken has killed him more than once. The Adversary will hunt him down and destroy him."

"And when he's finished with Glaeken, what happens to me?"

"You'll take his place. But don't worry about that now. It hasn't happened yet. It may never happen."

"But—"

She waved a hand in the air. "There is no point in worrying about events and situations over which you have no control."

No control . . . that's the part I worry about.

"Can I ask an obvious question: Why doesn't the Ally just step in and squash the Adversary and these Otherness ass-kissers like the bugs they are?"

"First off, you must remember—and this is always a blow to the human ego—that we are not that important. We are a mere crumb of crust on the edge of the pie they are vying for. Secondly . . . I don't know this for sure, but from what I've observed I sense a certain game play in the conflict. I sense that *how* one side increases its share of the pie is almost as important as the securing of the extra piece itself."

"Swell."

"That's just my sense of it. I could be wrong. But I can assure you that the Ally is active here in a limited way, and that's good, I suppose."

"You *suppose*?"

"Well, it counterbalances the Otherness, but I'd prefer that this world, this reality, had been left out of the conflict altogether." She raised a fist toward the picture window. "Take your fight somewhere else and leave us alone!"

"Amen to that."

"The Ally's presence, though minimal, will prevent the Adversary from becoming too bold even should he learn the truth about Glaeken."

"Which brings us back to Brady and Dormentalism and buried pillars. What's the story there?"

"*The Compendium* laid out the requirements of the Opus Omega: Find each site as laid out on the map, and there bury a thirteen-foot column of stone quarried from a site proximal to a nexus point. Luther Brady improvised a method of substituting concrete that included some sand or earth from within or around a nexus point. But special rock or sand isn't all that is necessary. Each column requires one more indispensable ingredient: a living human being—at least living when the column is sealed. Dormentalist "martyrs"—missionaries who go missing while spreading the Dormentalist gospel in Third World countries—aren't missing at all. They're buried in cylindrical tombs all over the globe."

"Not all of them are Dormentalists," Jack said, feeling a heaviness settle on him.

Herta nodded. "Yes, I know. Your friend, the reporter. I'm sorry."

Friend . . . we didn't know each other long enough to be close friends. But still . . .

"That is what Dormentalism is all about," she said. "Luther Brady turned a silly, hedonistic cult into a money-making machine to finance Opus Omega. Brady knows that fusion is a hoax. No powers are achieved at the top of the Dormentalist ladder. But the exercises practiced along the long slow road to the upper rungs do have a purpose: They identify people susceptible to Otherness influence. The aspirants may believe the nonsense about getting in touch with their inner xelton, but what they're really doing is more finely attuning themselves to the Otherness. Luther Brady reveals Opus Omega to the select few who reach the top of the ladder, telling them it will bring about the Grand Fusion—never mentioning the Otherness. He then appoints these sick folk as his Continental and Regional Overseers to further the Opus."

"Let's just say he completes this Opus Omega. What then?"

"When pillars are buried in all the designated sites, the Otherness will become ascendant. The Adversary will then come into his own and the world will begin to change."

The world changing into a place hospitable to those creatures he'd fought down in Florida . . . he didn't want to picture that.

"Okay, then. At Brady's current rate of pillar planting, when do you think he'll be done?"

"In about a year. Perhaps less."

Jack closed his eyes. A year . . . his child would be here by then. Neither the baby nor Gia nor Vicky would have a future if Brady succeeded.

And then the solution struck him. So obvious . . .

"We'll dig them up! I'll put an excavating crew together and we'll yank them out faster than Brady can bury them. We'll make his . . ." Herta was shaking her head. "No? Why not?"

"Once they are inserted into the ground, the damage is done. It's too late. Digging them up will accomplish nothing."

Damn. He'd thought he was onto something.

"That's why you want the Dormentalist Church, as you said, destroyed . . . damaged, crippled, driven to its knees."

She nodded.

Jack rubbed his jaw. "Destroying it . . . that's a tall order. It's everywhere, in just about every country. But crippling it . . . that might be possible. Let's say Brady gets kicked out of the driver's seat. What will that do?"

"It won't stop Opus Omega—his High Council will carry on without him—but it will slow it down. And that will buy us some time."

"For what?"

She shrugged. "Time for the Ally to realize the extent of the threat to its interests here. Time for the Adversary to make a mistake—he's not infallible, you know. He's made mistakes before. And he's eager, so eager for his promised moment. After millennia of struggle, his time is almost within reach, and he's impatient. That may work to our advantage."

"I think we may just get that extra time."

Her eyes brightened. "You do? How? Why?"

"If things go the way I've planned, Mr. Luther Brady should be doing a perp walk sooner rather than later."

"A perp . . . ?"

"Just keep watching your TV." Jack stood and noticed Anya's skin flap still folded in his hand. He held it up. "What do I do with this?"

"It was meant for you to keep. Don't you want it?"

"It's not exactly something I care to frame and hang over my bed. Why don't you take it. You know, as a reminder of Anya."

Herta rose and began unbuttoning her blouse. "I need no reminder."

"What—?" Jack said, startled and embarrassed. "What are you doing? Wait a second here."

Her twisted fingers moved more nimbly than perhaps they should have, considering her swollen knuckles.

She glanced up at him. "A second or two is all this will take."

As she undid the bottom button she turned away toward the picture window and let the back of her blouse drop to her waist.

Jack gasped. "Holy—!"

"There is nothing holy about this, I assure you."

He stared at her damaged skin, at the array of cigarette burn–sized scars and the lines crisscrossing between them. Except for one fresh wound, slowly oozing red to the left of her spine, her back was an exact copy of Anya's.

"What's going on here?"

"It is a map of my pain," she said over her shoulder.

"That's just what Anya said. She called it a map of the Adversary's efforts to destroy her. Why?"

"Because he cannot win if I am still alive."

As crazy as that sounded, Jack took it at face value.

"But who are you?"

"Your mother."

Jack fought an urge to scream and kept his voice low. "Not that again. Look—"

"No. You look. Look more closely at my back."

"If you mean that fresh wound, I see it." Realization clubbed him. "The pillar out in Pennsylvania! You mean, every time Brady and his gang buries one of those pillars—"

"I feel it. I bleed."

Jack sat again. "I don't understand."

"You do not need to. But look closely and tell me if you see any other difference."

Jack stared and noticed something else Anya hadn't had: a deep depression in the small of her back, big enough for, say, two of Jack's fingers. He reached toward it, then snatched his hand back.

Herta backed toward him. "Go ahead. Touch it. It's healed now."

Jack felt a touch of queasiness. "No, I don't think—"

"Place your fingers in the wound. It will not bite you."

Jack reached out again and slid his forefinger to the first joint into the depression. It was deep; he could feel nothing against his fingertip. He eased his finger farther in, to the second knuckle. And still nothing against his fingertip.

Jack couldn't bring himself to push farther. He withdrew and leaned closer to see if he could get an idea of how deep it was. Maybe then—

He jerked his head back. "Jesus Christ!"

"He had nothing to do with this either."

Had he seen what he'd thought he'd seen? No. Not possible.

But then, "not possible" had lost all meaning some time ago.

Jack peered again into the opening. He saw a scar-lined tunnel and, at its far end, light. Daylight. A circle of blue sky and distant buildings.

Christ, he was looking at the Queens waterfront on the East River, viewing it through a hole that ran clear through Herta's body. Jack backed away and leaned to his right, looking past Herta at a wider view of the same scene through the picture window. It was as if Herta had been run through with a spear and the wound hadn't closed—it had healed along the walls of its circumference, yes, but left an open tunnel through her body.

"What—what did that?"

"Anya's passing," Herta said, pulling her blouse back up over her shoulders.

"That must have been—"

"It was beyond anything I have ever experienced. Far beyond the agony each pillar inflicts."

Jack spoke slowly, feeling his way along. "Why should these pillars wound you? Who are you?"

"I've told you: I'm your—"

"Please don't say 'mother' again."

"Then I shall say nothing, for that is the truth."

He tried another tack. "If every pillar wounds you, I can see why you want Brady stopped. But if he finishes the Opus, that in a way benefits you too. I mean, no more pain from new pillars."

Herta nodded and turned as she finished rebuttoning her blouse. She fixed him with her dark eyes.

"Yes, I suppose that is true about no more pain. Because I will be dead. The whole purpose of Opus Omega is to kill me."

14

The interrogation room was silent, breathless while Luther Brady stared at the photos and felt as if his bones were dissolving.

This couldn't be! These photos . . . him with the two boys from last night. At least he thought it was last night. He didn't hire the same boys every time and couldn't make out their faces. But yes! That was the mask he'd used last night. He rotated through a series of them for variety. But last night or last month didn't matter. The very existence of these photos was a horror, but even worse, they were in the hands of the police.

How? Who?

Petrovich! He'd delivered the boys as usual. This time he must have stayed around and shot these! The greedy little shit! He—

But how did they wind up with this Richard Cordova they were talking about? And who had used his pistol to kill him?

"Wh . . . wh . . ." His dry tongue seemed unable to form words.

"Fakes," Barry said in a dismissive wave of his hands. "Very obvious fakes. I'm no computer whiz, but even I know what can be done with Adobe Photoshop. They've even put a mask on the guy in these photos! Give me a break, will you? The whole thing is ludicrous!"

"Where . . ." Finally Luther could speak. "Where did you get these?"

Holusha tapped the center photo. "We found them under the cushion of the victim's desk chair. The chair where he was killed." The finger moved to a brown stain along the edge of the photo. "That's some of his blood that leaked around the cushion."

"You must believe me," Luther said, leaning forward and covering the photos with his hands. He didn't want anyone, especially Barry, looking at them. But he had to convince these detectives. "I did not kill that man! I swear it! I am being framed for something I did not do!"

Young hadn't broken his relentless stare. "Why would someone want to do that, Mr. Brady?"

"The Dormentalist Church has more than its share of enemies," Barry said. "Mr. Brady is the Church's spiritual leader, its public face. If this plot to disgrace and discredit him succeeds, the Church will suffer irreparable damage."

"Well, then," Young said, "the solution is very simple. If you weren't at Mr. Cordova's house last night, Mr. Brady, where were you?"

With those boys!

But he couldn't admit that. And what good would it do? He'd never allowed any of the boys to see his face. Not even Petrovich knew what he looked like.

"I was in my cabin upstate."

"Can anyone vouch for your presence there?"

"I . . . no, I was there alone. I go there every Sunday evening to escape the pressures of the Church and the city so that I can commune with my xelton."

Holusha snickered. "Your xelton or whatever it is looks an awful lot like a couple of teenage boys."

"No one to verify your presence at the cabin last night?" Young said.

"No."

"I didn't think so." Young withdrew some folded papers from his inner coat pocket. "I have here a warrant for your arrest."

As he handed it to Barry, Holusha pulled out a pair of handcuffs.

"Luther Brady," Young said, "I'm arresting you for the murder of Richard Cordova. I know your attorney is already present but I'm going to read you your rights anyway: You have the right to remain silent . . ."

The rest of the words faded into the roaring in Luther's ears. He'd heard them on TV so many times he knew them by heart. But never in his darkest nightmare had he imagined that someone would be reciting Miranda to him . . .

He glanced at Barry, who'd grown awfully silent, and saw him staring at the photos.

"Barry . . . ?"

The attorney looked up at him and shook his head. He seemed to have receded to the far side of the room.

"You need more help than I can give you, Luther. You need a criminal attorney. A good one. I'll start making some calls right away."

"Barry, you've got to keep these photos from the public. They're fakes, Barry." He turned to Young and Holusha. "I swear they're fakes, and I beg of you, don't let word of them get out. Once something like this gets around, you're forever marked. Even after you've been proven innocent—which I *will* be, I assure you—you never lose the taint."

"We'll do what we can," Young said. "We're more interested in the murder right now."

Luther fought to keep his knees from buckling as he felt the cuffs snap around his wrists. Yesterday he'd been on top of the world, the Opus Omega all but completed.

Now he was being arrested for murder and his life was swirling down the toilet.

How? How had this happened?

15

Jack nodded to Esteban as he walked through the lobby and out to the sidewalk.

Beekman Place was quiet, as usual, but not as quiet as Herta had been when Jack tried to squeeze more information out of her. The Opus Omega was designed to kill her? What the hell?

Why? How? She wouldn't say.

Who was she that Rasalom and the Otherness wanted her dead? Beyond her usual I-am-your-mother line, she wouldn't say.

What she did say was that she was tired and he should go. They'd talk another day.

He walked uptown toward Gia's. Vicky would be in school, but he hoped Gia was home. He needed a dose of sanity.

TUESDAY

1

The news broke overnight.

When Jack awoke he flipped on MSNBC. He wasn't sure why. Maybe because the channel had had Brady on as a guest so many times. But *Imus in the Morning* was playing—who was the genius who'd dreamed up broadcasting a radio program on TV?—so he switched around until he saw Brady's face.

It was a photo and the voiceover was going on about how everyone was shocked—*shocked!*—that Luther Brady had been arrested for murder. Then they switched to a live feed from outside the Bronx House of Detention for Men where Brady had spent the night. A pretty, blond news face was standing on the curb while a hundred or so protesters shouted and waved signs behind her.

After some prefatory remarks she motioned a young woman onto the screen. Jack recognized the eternally cheery Christy from the temple. Only today she wasn't cheery. She stood there in her gray, high-collared jacket with the braided front, tears streaming down her cheeks as she blubbered about the injustice of it all. That a wonderful man like Luther Brady, who'd bettered so many lives the world over, should be accused of murder, it just . . . it just wasn't fair!

"Fairer than you'll ever guess, my dear," Jack muttered.

Next the blond reporter brought on another familiar face—the Aryan poster boy, Atoor. In contrast to Christy's grief, Atoor was angry. Color flared in his scrubbed cheeks as he denounced the police, the DA, and the city itself.

"It's a witch hunt! It's religious persecution! We all know that the old-time entrenched religions call the shots in this town, and obviously they've decided that Dormentalism is becoming too popular for its own good. So the solution is to trump up charges against the head of our Church and throw him in jail. What next? Burning him at the stake?"

Jack applauded. "Well said, young man! Well said! But let's not burn him at the stake yet."

If the Penn cops were earning their pay, there'd be lots more shit raining on the Dormentalist roof real soon.

With that in mind, he headed out the door for Gia's. The baby was scheduled for a follow-up ultrasound in just over an hour.

2

"I can't believe it!" Luther said.

This whole situation was a horror, and it worsened at every turn.

Bail denied . . . the gavel bang after those shocking words still rang through Luther's head like a slammed door.

Arthur Fineman, the criminal attorney Barry had referred him to, didn't appear too worried. He seemed so out of place in this dingy meeting room in the detention center, like a Monet that had somehow fallen into a garbage dump. His suit looked even more expensive than Barry's, and his Rolex flashier. Considering his hourly fee, he could well afford both.

Luther, on the other hand, felt dirty and disheveled.

And humiliated . . . forced to walk a gauntlet of reporters and cameramen as he'd been led—handcuffed!—

to and from the Bronx courthouse on Grand Concourse.

"Don't worry. We'll appeal the denial of bail."

Luther tried to contain his outrage, but some of it seeped through.

"That's all well and good, fine for you to say, but meanwhile I'm the one who stays behind bars. Every day— every *hour*—that passes with me locked in here, unable to defend myself to the public, only makes it worse for my Church. Only one side of the story is getting out. I need to be free to present my side to the media."

Fineman shifted in his seat. He was deeply tanned and combed his silver mane straight back so that it curled above his collar.

"The DA managed to persuade the judge that you're a flight risk."

"Then it's your job to *un*persuade him. I am *not* a flight risk. I'm innocent and that will be proven in court!"

Flight risk . . . the Bronx DA had argued that since the Dormentalist Church was a globe-spanning organization, its leader might find shelter among his devoted followers anywhere in the world. Fineman had spoken of Luther's lack of criminal history, of his obvious ties to the city, even offered to surrender Luther's passport and post a two-million-dollar bond. But the judge had sided with the DA.

Luther was convinced now that someone high up was pulling the strings in this plot against him.

"We'll worry about that later. The first thing I want to do is have you held here pending our appeal."

"What do you mean, 'held here'? I want you to get me *out!*"

"I mean that until I do get you out, I want you here as opposed to Riker's."

Luther's heart quailed. Riker's Island . . . home to some of the city's most violent criminals.

"No . . . they can't."

Fineman shook his head. "If you can't make bail or, as in your case, you're denied bail, that's where they put you."

"You can't let them!"

"I'll do my damnedest to prevent it."

"That's not saying you *will,* that's only saying you'll *try.*"

Fineman leaned forward. "Mr. Brady, I'm going to be frank with you."

A sting of alarm raced through him—this couldn't be good—but he didn't let it show.

"I should hope so."

"They have a good case against you. So good that my contacts in the DA's office tell me there's talk of seeking the death penalty."

Luther squeezed his eyes shut and began again the mantra that had sustained him through the endless night in this concrete-walled sty. This cannot be happening . . . this can*not* be happening!

"But before the DA does that," Fineman added, "you may be offered a deal."

Luther opened his eyes. "Deal?"

"Yes. Let you plea to a lesser charge that—"

"And admit I murdered a man I've never met or even heard of until after he was dead? No, absolutely not. No deals!"

A deal meant prison, probably for most if not all his remaining years. Prison meant that his life's work, Opus Omega, would remain unfinished. Or worse, finished by someone else . . . someone else would claim the glory that Luther deserved.

No. Unthinkable.

"They'll regret this," Luther said, anger seething through his fear. "I'll put thousands—*tens* of thousands—in the streets outside the courthouse and outside this prison. Their voices will shake these walls and—"

Fineman raised a hand. "I'd go easy on the protests. So far the DA hasn't mentioned those photos. If you push him too hard, he might release them. Just for spite."

"No . . . no!"

"Look, Mr. Brady. I've already put someone on the dead man, to dig up anything and everything known about him. I've got to tell you, in just a matter of hours he was able to come up with whispers about blackmail. This plays right into the DA's hands."

"Doesn't it play into our hands too? If the man was a blackmailer, it means he had to have enemies. We can—"

"But your pistol has been identified as the murder weapon, and the victim's prints are on it; probably his blood as well. And the photos found in his home were of you."

Luther could take no more. "I didn't kill him!" he screamed. "Do you hear me? I didn't do it! There must be some way to prove that!"

Fineman didn't seem the least bit ruffled.

"There is. We need someone, *anyone*, who can vouch for your whereabouts at or near the time of the murder."

Luther thought of something. "My E-Z Pass! It will show my tolls to and from the cabin on the night of the murder!"

Fineman shook his head. "That proves that your transponder made the trip, not you. I need a person, a living, breathing person who saw you far from the crime scene that night."

Luther thought of Petrovich. Maybe there was a way to have him vouch for Luther's presence at the cabin that night without incriminating himself.

"There might be someone. His name is Brencis Petrovich. He, um, made a delivery to the cabin Sunday night."

"Do I dare ask what?" Fineman said.

Luther looked away. "I'd rather you didn't."

3

"What's wrong, Jack?" Gia said. "You're not yourself today."

His mood concerned her. He'd come in looking tired and worn-out but hadn't wanted to say much. She hadn't told him yesterday about the near miss by that truck; Vicky had been around and Gia hadn't wanted to frighten her. Considering his mood, maybe this wasn't the right time either.

He sat slumped in an overstuffed armchair before the TV. It was tuned to a cable news channel. He looked up and gave her a wan smile.

"You mean, not my usual life-of-the-party self?"

"You'll never be the life of the party, but you seem like you're a hundred miles away. And I know what that means."

"It's not what you think."

She'd seen him like this before and she did know.

"One of your fix-its isn't going well, right?"

He straightened in the chair and motioned her closer. When she got within reach he took her hand and guided her onto his lap. He slipped his arms around her and nuzzled her throat.

"I have no fix-its in progress."

His breath tickled so she pulled back a few inches and looked at him. "I thought you said you were running two."

" 'Were' is right. They're done. It's just that things didn't turn out so good for one of my customers."

That had such an ominous tone. They had agreed last year that Jack would give her no more than a vague outline of what he was up to. He didn't feel he should name names or give specifics about what people had entrusted to him. And that was fine with Gia. She'd worry if she were privy to the details.

All she knew about these jobs was that one had to do with a blackmailer and the other with finding a missing son for his mother.

"Is he all right?"

"Let's not talk about it. It's over."

If it's really over, she thought, then why are you like this? But she knew better than to ask.

"At least we still have a healthy, thriving baby."

This morning's follow-up ultrasound had shown, in Dr. Eagleton's words, "a perfectly normal twenty-week fetus."

Fetus? She remembered thinking. That's no fetus, that's my baby.

Jack's arms tightened around her. "Wasn't that great to see him moving and sucking his thumb? God, it's amazing."

"*Him?* They still don't know the sex."

"Yeah, but I do. I—"

She felt Jack tense. Without releasing her he reached for the TV remote. As the sound came up she heard something about a woman entombed in concrete.

"*. . . confirmed the remains as those of missing New York reporter Jamie Grant. Sources say early indications are that she was buried alive in the concrete.*"

"Oh, God!" Gia said. "How awful."

Jack made no comment. His gaze remained fixed on the screen. He seemed hypnotized.

"*Symbols molded into the concrete column have been identified as similar to those found throughout the world in temples of the Dormentalist Church, and the mold for the pillar was discovered hidden in a New Jersey concrete company owned by a member of the church's High Council.*

"*Ms. Grant was a respected journalist and a fearless critic of the Dormentalist Church. Her murder has sent shockwaves throughout the world of journalism. We mourn her passing."*

"Wait a minute," Gia said, straightening and looking at Jack. "Wait just a minute. Didn't you say that the son you were looking for was a Dormentalist?"

Jack continued to stare at the screen. "Did I say that?"

"Yes, you did. I remem—"

He tightened his bear hug. "Just a sec. Look who's doing a perp walk."

She turned back in time to see a vaguely familiar-looking man being led from a doorway to a police car.

"In a related story that may or may not be coincidence, Luther Brady, head of the Dormentalist Church, is a suspect in the murder of an ex-cop in the Bronx. He has been denied bail."

Gia swiveled to face Jack. "Did you have anything to do with this?"

It was the first time all morning she'd seen him smile.

"More bad news, I'm afraid," Fineman said.

Luther Brady lifted his head from where he'd been resting it on his arms, which were folded on the table. He was numb.

They'd found Grant's body. How? The news story said the Pennsylvania authorities had acted on a tip. From whom?

It had to be an insider, but that didn't make sense. Everyone high enough up to have known will be under investigation now.

Nothing made sense anymore.

Luther looked at Fineman, dapper as ever. "How could things get worse?"

"Mr. Petrovich is not available, it seems. My investigator learned he drove off in his van and never came back. The van was found abandoned in Lower Manhattan. The police report mentions bloodstains on the front seat. Petrovich appears to have vanished."

Luther lowered his head again. What else could go wrong?

Petrovich had been a long shot anyway. A guy with his record probably didn't want to get within a mile of a police station, let alone walk in to swear to a statement.

"I've had feelers about a plea bargain," Fineman said.

"I will not—"

"Don't reject it out of hand, Mr. Brady. Give it careful consideration. You know what's going on outside. Your church is getting heat from all sides. It looks for all the world like someone in your organization killed that reporter to shut her up. That's not going to help you one bit."

He wanted to grab Fineman's silk tie and tell him that yes, he was part of the Grant bitch's death, a big part, and part of a host of others too, but he had nothing to do with this one. On this count he was innocent.

But he said nothing.

Fineman wasn't through, however. "Plus you've got to realize that if the DA should go public and announce that he's seeking the death penalty, your chance for a deal will be gone. He'll be locked into that position and won't be able to let you plead down without suffering serious political fallout."

Luther didn't see that he had a choice. Making a deal meant losing his freedom but keeping his life. No deal gave him a shot at freedom, but the downside was death. Luther had decided he'd rather be dead than spend the rest of his life behind bars.

"No deals." He raised his head and looked Fineman square in the eyes. "An innocent man doesn't make deals."

At least the photos were still under wraps. He prayed to whatever power had guided him thus far that they'd stay that way.

WEDNESDAY

1

"Gevalt!" Abe said as he studied the hot-off-the-press copy of *The Light*.

Jack had hung around the newsstand down the street, waiting for it to be delivered. He bought a copy as soon as the string on the bale was cut and walked directly to Abe's, reading it along the way.

Four words took up the whole front page.

**SPECIAL
JAMIE
GRANT
ISSUE**

The first five pages were filled with loving tributes to a fallen colleague. But starting on page six, the paper tore into Luther Brady, saying that even if he personally had nothing to do with Jamie Grant's death, he'd fostered the tactic of ruthless retaliation against any and all critics of the Dormentalist Church, creating an atmosphere of disregard for the rights and well-being of anyone considered an enemy of his church.

And then the pièce de résistance: censored photos of an unidentified man—obviously Brady on closer examination—with the two boys. The paper said that it had received these photos the day before, with a note purportedly from the man Brady was accused of killing. The photos and the note had been forwarded to the police.

Abe looked up from the paper. "You're involved in this, aren't you?"

Jack tried for a guileless look. "Who, me?"

"You think I'm going to buy that I'm-so-innocent *punim*? I'm not. You promised me when I found you that Beretta that you—wait a minute. Wait just a minute." He narrowed his eyes and pointed a stubby finger at Jack. "Brady's supposed victim wouldn't happen to have been shot with a nine millimeter, would he?"

"That's what I hear."

"And that nine millimeter wouldn't happen to have come from a Beretta, would it?" Abe turned his palms up as his fingers did a come-here waggle. "So tell me. Tell-me-tell-me-tell-me."

Jack told him, giving him a *Reader's Digest* version of Sunday night and Monday morning.

When Jack was done, Abe sat back on his stool and waved a hand at the spread-out pages of *The Light*. His voice was hushed.

"You did this? By yourself you brought down a global cult?"

"I wouldn't say 'brought down.' It hasn't gone away. I can't see it ever going away completely."

"But you kneecapped it."

"Yeah, but it's still got more than enough members and resources to go on burying their pillars."

All Dormentalism might be reeling and in disarray, but Brady's machinery still existed. Before too long a new insertion site would be chosen, and another Dormentalist High Council fanatic would be preparing another column . . . and setting up another victim.

"A moratorium they'll call. Too many eyes looking at them. And without their guiding light . . ."

"Yeah, he's out of the picture for good, I hope."

"If not, it won't be for lack of trying on your part. But whatever, the Dormentalist Church is—"

"Hang on," Jack said. "Turn up your radio a sec." Jack thought he'd heard Brady's name.

Abe always had a radio going and, natch, always tuned to an all-news station.

Sure enough, the newsreader was saying that the Bronx DA had announced he was seeking the death penalty in the Cordova murder case. She also mentioned that Luther Brady had been denied bond and would be transferred to Riker's Island later this morning.

"Mazel tov," Abe said, beaming. "You should tell your lady friend."

"I'll bet she knows."

But giving Herta a call wasn't such a bad idea. Jack whipped out his cell phone and dialed her number.

No answer.

Probably out shopping . . . but a hint of warning put him into motion.

"I think I'll tell her in person."

He gave Abe a wave and headed for the door. When he hit the sidewalk he broke into a loping run toward Columbus Avenue, looking for a cab.

2

"She's gone!" Esteban looked upset.

Jack tried to keep his cool as unease writhed through him.

"What do you mean, gone? When did she go out?"

"She didn't just go out, she left. Men came and packed up all her things, and she left. Her apartment is empty."

"You sure she left on her own? Could she have been kidnapped or something?"

Esteban shook his head. "Oh, no. She left me a nice note and a very generous gift. I will miss her."

"Then where'd she go?"

A shrug. "She did not say. I know she was not jump-ing her rent because she is paid up until the end of the year."

Had she been frightened off, or was this one of those my-work-here-is-done things?

Jack ground his teeth. He still had so many unanswered questions.

"She was a nice lady," Esteban said.

"Yeah, she was." He clapped him on the arm. "And you were a good friend to her. I know she appreciated it."

Jack left a beaming doorman behind and headed for First Avenue. He needed another taxi to take him to his rental car. He had two more stops to make before he re-turned it.

As Jack walked away from Sister Maggie's flower-smothered grave, he heard someone call his name.

"Jack! Would you be having a moment to spare?"

Jack turned and saw Father Edward Halloran, an aging leprechaun in a cassock and Roman collar, hustling to-ward him across the grass. Father Ed had said the funeral mass, which Jack had skipped, and recited the graveside prayers. Jack had been touched by the hundreds of tear-ful, mourning parishioners who had made the trip from the Lower East Side to pay their respects to a beloved teacher.

"What happened, Jack?" the priest said in a low voice. Tears rimmed his eyes. "May the Lord strike me dead if a finer, sweeter, more God-loving woman ever walked the earth."

Jack looked at the bare trees rimming the fading green of the lawn, the ornate, old-fashioned gravestones filling this Queens graveyard.

"Yeah, she was something."

"But who—?"

"Doesn't matter anymore."

"Of course it does! He must be—" And then his words cut off. He looked up at Jack. "Ah, would you be telling me that he's passed beyond human justice?"

"I'll let you draw your own conclusion."

"Sure and I'll be knowing what happened to a certain fellow I asked you to keep an eye on a while back. Hasn't been seen or heard from since, has he?"

"Not by me, at least."

Father Ed sighed. "I don't want to be after condoning such things, don't you know, but, well, if justice was done, then, I guess justice was done. Still that poor woman . . . what was done to her. We had to keep her coffin closed."

Jack tried not to remember the sight of Maggie inside that body bag.

He took a breath. He'd planned to catch Father Ed later today or tomorrow at the rectory. Wanted to discuss something with him. Might as well do it now.

"On the subject of Sister Maggie, how do I set up an education fund in her name?"

Father Ed's eyes widened. "Why would you be doing that?"

"Something she told me . . . about some girl named Fina who'd have to leave St. Joe's because of money problems."

"Serafina! Yes, Sister Maggie was looking for a way to keep the Martinez children in school. Did you meet them?"

"No . . ."

"Then why would you be wanting to help?"

The leftovers from the twenty-five large Herta had given him plus the cash he'd boosted from Cordova came to a tidy sum. He couldn't very well return it to Herta.

"Let's just say I don't want to see her forgotten. Maybe you can set something up where some money can be invested, use it for the Martinez kids till they move on to high school, then use what's left for other kids who need that kind of help."

"Why, that's wonderful, Jack. The Sister Mary Margaret O'Hara Education Fund . . . it has a nice ring to it, don't you think? I'll get on it right away. When would you be sending the check?"

"Check?"

"Well, I assume you'll be wanting the tax deduction."

"Already have plenty of those. Cash won't be a problem, will it?"

Father Ed's eyes twinkled. "No problem at all."

Luther Brady moved in a daze.

A chain ran between his feet. His wrists were chained to his waist. A cop led him down a hallway of the detention center. Another followed, and one on either side guided him by the elbows. They were moving him quickly toward a rectangle of light—a doorway to the outside. And beyond that, a van to take him to Riker's.

Visions of being gang-raped by a parade of huge laughing black men weakened his knees. There had to be Dormentalists in prison. All he needed were a few . . . for protection . . .

And then he was squinting in the sudden glare of sunlight. After a second or two he realized that it wasn't the sun alone, but camera lights as well. And reporters flanking his path to a police wagon, machine-gunning questions as they shoved microphones at his face.

He blinked, then straightened as he realized that this was his chance to present his case, create sound and video bites that would air again and again.

"I'm innocent!" he shouted, slowing the pace of his walk. "Innocent, I swear it!"

He scanned their faces. Some he knew, some he didn't. Through hundreds of public appearances he'd honed his natural ability to project sincerity and dignity. He called on that ability now, looking them directly in the eyes and showing no fear.

"But what of the evidence, those photos?" someone said.

"Lies and forgeries. This is all a colossal frame-up to discredit me and Dormentalism! You'll see! The truth will out! The truth—!"

The words died in his throat as he recognized a face in the crowd, toward the rear. Not a reporter. No, he'd seen this face in the temple. He was the one who'd pretended to be Jason Amurri, the one Jensen had wanted so badly to find.

As their eyes locked, Luther Brady saw something there, and it ignited an epiphany: This man was behind it all.

No. He couldn't be. That would be saying that one man had exposed Opus Omega, killed Jensen, and framed Luther for murder.

Impossible!

But then the man lifted his right hand, folded it into a gun shape, and pointed it at Luther. He smiled, cocked his head, and snapped down the thumb trigger.

"There!" Luther shouted. "Over there!" He struggled against his chains. If only he could point! "There's the man responsible for all this! There's the real killer! Grab him and ask him! He'll . . ."

People turned to look, but the man was gone.

And all the cameras were still running.

Luther Brady put his head back and screamed out his anger, his frustration, his helplessness, and most of all, his horror.

www.repairmanjack.com